PLAYBOY'S
COLLEGE
FICTION

PLAYBOY'S COLLEGE FICTION

PLAYBOY PRESS

P&P

NEW YORK, NEW YORK /HANOVER, NEW HAMPSHIRE

Playboy's College Fiction
A Collection of 21 Years of Contest Winners

Edited by Alice K. Turner

Foreword by Thom Jones

Playboy Press
New York, New York / Hanover, New Hampshire
Playboy's College Fiction

Copyright © 2007
by Playboy Enterprises International, Inc.
All rights reserved

For information about permission
to reproduce selections from this book, write to

Playboy Press / Steerforth Press
25 Lebanon Street
Hanover, New Hampshire 03755

Library of Congress Cataloging in Publication Data

Playboy's college fiction : a collection of 21 years of contest winners /
edited by Alice K. Turner ; foreword by Thom Jones. — 1st ed.
    p. cm.
  ISBN-13: 978-1-58642-134-2 (alk. paper)
  ISBN-10: 1-58642-134-4 (alk. paper)
  1. Short stories, American. 2. American fiction—21st century. 3.
American prose literature—21st century. I. Turner, Alice K.
  PS648.S5P535 2007
  813'.0108–dc22

                              2007023854

FIRST EDITION

Contents

Foreword

by **THOM JONES**

As a student at the Iowa Writers' Workshop I had the good fortune to study under William Price Fox. Fox actually read student manuscripts. He showed us how to fix them and relaxed us enough at times to make writing something close to fun. One afternoon Bill read the lead sentence from an old student manuscript: "Here's a good one for y'all. Tell me what you think. 'The sun punched through the window like an angry fist.'" A hand flew up with blinding speed and a student said, "I'd like to steal that line."

It was like standing on the beach in a state of befuddlement seconds before a tsunami hit the shore. The room was engulfed with such a roar of laughter that the fifth floor of the English-Philosophy Building shook. A buffalo stampede.

"I'd—ha ha ha—like to steal that line." It was a foot-stomping good time. Writers are very sensitive and can fall into states of catalepsy over a sardonic remark. The slightest perception of ridicule may result in a series of suicide bombings. "Do you think I'm funny? Answer the question. Funny how? You mean funny like I would like to steal that line? Are you accusing me of plagiarism?"

In 1994 I was invited back to Iowa as a visiting professor and to this day, nobody understands why I wasn't furiously indignant that an Iowa MFA applicant plagiarized a few paragraphs from a short story I published in *The New Yorker*. The writer incorporated them into a story of his own (which was pretty darn good, actually) and submitted it with his application. A perspicacious student reader caught on to the ruse and the poor fellow did not get into the Writers' Workshop, but received instead a Frank Conroy "warning from hell." So why wasn't I mad? Why indeed? What does a writer need most? To be read, understood, loved, adored even. Fame and fortune would be lovely, but the approbation of readers, even if it's just one reader, is what keeps a writer addicted. He craves more and more, the embrace of a larger audience, entrée to the sacred world of the sophisticated literati. His addiction carries him above and beyond such trifling necessities as food, drink and air. He reads night and day, the classics, the genres, telephone books, cereal boxes. He walks the streets buried in existential gloom and prays for a miracle to happen.

Miracle scenario: A book in print with unbelievable cover art, blurbs from the heavens and a mighty damn fine author photo as well. Starred reviews in *Kirkus* and *Publishers Weekly*. The blessings of Michiko Kakutani of *The New York Times*. Each and every major literary award, short of the Nobel Prize (that one will come later). Word of mouth does its mainstream magic, which sends the book soaring to the top of the bestseller charts where it attracts unusual attention. Harry Potter marries Lolita!

Hollywood calls. Will it be Fox? MGM? "Call from Martin Scorsese on line six." "For Christ sakes, tell him to get in line! I'm on a conference call with Marlon, Meryl, Sean and Willis. Tell Marty I'll get back to him, and while you're at it, can you get someone to bring me a sandwich?" No wonder this writer is so good—he's got a powerful imagination.

Real world: He sends work to agents and publishers, enters contests that offer twenty-five dollars and two free copies of the sponsoring publication (circulation two hundred). He collects enough rejection slips to paper a three-car garage and just keeps on truckin'. His all-time favorite song is "Please Mr. Postman" by the Marvelettes. He applies to the MFA Writers' Workshop at the University of Iowa, nudging his manuscripts to masterpiece level by plagiarism. Seriously, who in the hell will ever know? Hmmm. Just about everyone. It's rare for a writer to get away with even the smallest stolen line. There are just too many people reading forensic-detective novels, so many in fact they outnumber members of the KGB and CIA many times over.

So I couldn't be too upset with the hapless Iowa applicant. He picked excellent lines to steal.

Winning *Playboy*'s College Fiction Contest guarantees an audience in the millions, and pays real money too. So what must a college writer do to win this enviable prize? Plagiarize from a professional, send home-baked cookies to the editors or simply out-write the one thousand other contestants?

There is, I believe, a common misconception that short stories must be easy to write because "well, because they are short." Au contraire. Writing a great short story is like telling a good joke at a bar. You have to get in and get out with perfect timing. The least hesitation or nuance in the tone of voice can make the whole thing fall flat, especially if the joke sucks in the first place. There is little room for languorous description in a short story. There is no time for lengthy exposition, no place for detailed background information and digression. The characters may be compelling enough to carry a novel, but in the rigors of the story form the protagonist must be involved in only one perfect, complete episode. Writing a short story that's picked as the best in a thousand is a lot harder than it looks.

The 997 who fail to gain first, second or third place must face yet another dose of anguish and self-doubt. You can see them prowling the streets in Goodwill ensembles, hands in pockets, yet another day of Kierkegaardian despair and shame after a long shift as a fry cook at Fat Eddie's diner.

Back to the pestilential hovel to stare at that blank computer screen, feeling cut off from life itself. It has been said that you need to write about one million words, several very long practice novels, before you know what you're doing. This explains why even your own mother vamooses when she sees you bearing down on her with a fresh fifteen-pound manuscript. Writing is harder work than "work." It requires talent, perseverance, faith and knowledge—and a little bit of luck. The winners in this anthology are to be saluted. They have both talent and mettle. Let's hope we will be seeing a lot more of them in the future.

Night Vision

by PHILIP SIMMONS
1986

My first apartment: clothes on the floor, dishes in the sink, I don't hear word one from anybody. I knew from the mailboxes that somebody name of Leonard DuPree had the unit next to mine; my first day, I went over to say hello. I could hear that the baseball game was on, but when I knocked, he killed the volume. I knocked again. Nothing. Dirty linoleum hallway, humming fluorescents, stink of a cigar—I stood there and counted the locks on Leonard DuPree's door: one, two, three, four.

I had made the big move to Boston, left my mother and everything else back in Kansas City: I want to meet people, right? A man wants to know his neighbors. Now, if you don't meet a neighbor right away, it's hard to do it at all. I mean, the man lived right *next* to me. I could hear when he took a shower. In the hall, I smelled what he was eating. Once you get past a few days, maybe a week, it gets embarrassing. What would I say? A few times I heard him working his locks just when I was about to go out, and I'd wait until the hall was quiet. I didn't know what the man looked like.

Of course, I could read his mail. The magazines, at least: They get left out on the steps for anybody to see. I know, for example, that Riggins in 302 gets *Oölogist* magazine. Eggs. I've seen Riggins in the hall a few times, a little guy, fingers like a baby's. I picture him with his folding aluminum ladder (they show these in the ads) sneaking up into a tree to snatch eggs out of a nest.

1

Not that I'm a thief. I put everything back when I'm done reading it. But this is what got me onto DuPree in the first place. Now, I like to look at the rod-and-gun magazines as well as any guy, but this was no *Field & Stream* man. I read articles on "The Home Defense Perimeter" (think of trip-wire flares in your shrubbery), "Consumer's Guide to Assault Rifles," you name it—radiation burns (disgusting, even if the pictures *were* faked). Bombshelter design. Communist guerrillas in Des Moines. He gets a newsletter from a group called Apocalypse Commandos.

Now, I'm not much of a mixer: I don't bowl or play golf; too clumsy for dancing. Like anybody, I was after some guys to go to a ball game with, have a few beers. I have no objection to a new outlook—a man has to have interests, after all. I'm not a man who shuts his eyes. I figured maybe this stuff DuPree was into would be my angle.

Of course, there were people at work. My first real job after I got my B.S. in communications: It's a direct-mail firm. If you have a credit card, you know what I mean: Could be an oil company, a department store, what difference does it make?—they send you whole bundles of fliers advertising stuff they want you to buy on credit. These people hire us to put together the whole package: select the products, write the ad copy, print the fliers, do the mailing, everything. Comprehensive.

There are some attractive girls in the office. Take Yolanda, by the bubbler. I haven't gotten up the nerve to talk to her. She has this strawberry-blonde hair down her back and comes in wearing these tight skirts that make my toes curl. I go over for a drink five or six times a day. Just one or two gulps and then you crush the cup in your palm. Yolanda Hiss. I picture us back at her place after work, on the couch, a samba playing on the stereo and my hands up under one of her fuzzy sweaters, nothing between her skin and cashmere. She lies back so her hair spreads out on the cushions. Her lipstick is smudged on her upper lip, and when she smiles, I see it on her teeth; but would you care? She's just reaching down to pull her sweater over her head when there's a noise at the door, and then, "Hey, Chico," she says, "what's going on?" And then my luck would be to turn around and see some guy in a leather vest and metal-studded wristbands, hear the quick snick as he opens the black-chrome handle of his butterfly knife and moves toward me, making practice slices through the air.

You could see there wasn't much chance of real movement on that front. Which is why I sent off for the starlight night scope. Here's a simple thing I don't understand. I read the entire *Time/Life* World War Two series without paying a cent. Last month, I checked my blood pressure and pulse every day—free. Electronically! I had to send the gizmo back, of course, but I have all the numbers written down. Free-trial offers. Why more people don't take advantage, I don't know.

Now, the upscale end of the Leonard DuPree market, as I like to call it, is in high tech. Your laser rifle sights, biotelemetry equipment, infrared cameras, what have you. The starlight scope, for example, is light enhancement. Takes available light and magnifies it so you can see like it was daytime. Looks like binoculars except bigger and you strap it to your head. This stuff was all there in his magazines: *Fighting Man, Survive!, Shooting Monthly.*

I kept an eye on outgoing mail. People leave letters sitting out for the mailman to pick up. I tried holding them up to the light, like anybody would, but you can never quite make anything out. So I wrote down the addresses and then went through the magazines, matched them to the ads. This was how I knew DuPree had gone for the night-scope offer—an expensive piece of equipment, the best thing to come along in a while. I had my order in the next day.

Of course, I had my eye on incoming mail, too. Peeked through the little air holes on the front of each box. Funny how some people leave their mail in the box two, three days at a time. Don't they know it's dangerous? I had seen a free-trial offer in a hobbyist's catalog for a battery-powered drill, small and lets you drill at right angles in tight places. I saw how the locks worked. I figured I open my box, reach up and put two small holes through the wall between DuPree's box and mine; then I jam my arm up my box, work my tools through the holes to pop his lock and I'm in. It would be easy.

A few days after I sent off for the night scope, I saw him. I had guessed which one was DuPree's truck all along: two-foot clearance under the axles and a gun rack in the cab. In fancy script just above the front grille, it said ONLY THE STRONG SURVIVE. Back home, you might not have noticed a truck like this. One day after work, it was parked right in front, with the doors open and no one in it. There was a kayak lashed to the top; in the bed were a cooler, a backpack and a pair of boots. I was starting up the walk when he came out—plain white T-shirt and camouflage pants. Couldn't have been more than twenty-five. In one hand, he held a hunting bow—wicked curves and counter-weights on stalks. He walked kind of funny, a long stride with a hitch in the middle, a little bounce up onto his toes. Going off to kill animals. There was a strap across his chest; when I passed him, I saw the brass arrowheads poke out of the quiver. His head seemed too small for his body, patchy hair like mold. He kept his eyes turned away. I couldn't think of anything to say.

3

When I got inside my door, my heart was racing. I pictured him stopping me on the walk, blocking my way. He would do some karate thing, make his hand like a knife and tap me with his fingertips on my breastbone.

"I seen you," he says.

"What's that?"

DuPree smiles without showing his teeth.

"Your hand up the mailbox like you was checkin' a cow's ass." He says everything real slow. "One pretty clever fellow."

"No," I say. "Not really." I look down at my shoes, thinking about running, but he's faster.

DuPree raises my chin with his forefinger. His eyes are like smoked glass. He shows me the fingers of his right hand, held together like a wide blade. I see muscles flex between the knuckles. His breath is sweet with mint.

"Touch my mail," he says, "I wave your lungs like flags."

But this was not the way it went, and I stayed out of the mailboxes, and it was two weeks before I saw him again. I had come home from work and gone into my usual routine: put on the TV, took out the frozen broccoli, made a hamburger, tried to relax. I live simply: one pot, one pan. My mattress is on the floor. I turned to the educational channel to look at one of the animal programs. Zebras. Why not? I like the outdoors as much as the next individual. Later, I got undressed and went to bed but couldn't sleep. I was thinking about DuPree. I imagined maybe going along with him one time, up to Maine or wherever, out in the woods doing hot dogs over a fire, and maybe I take along a bottle of schnapps. The fire lights up his face, makes his eyes look bugged out of that round head of his; there are night sounds all around us.

"You shoot?" he asks me.

"No, my father——" I was going to tell him I never got much of a chance because my father died before he could show me.

"Tomorrow, you're gonna shoot," he says.

"Bear," I say.

"You bet," says DuPree. Bear season is why we're up there, and DuPree's brought along a rifle for me to use.

But what if I don't get the chance, because that night, zipped into a mummy bag in the tent, I hear pawing and snuffling outside and barely have time to curse my luck before the claws slice through the wall of the tent like razors? I've heard of this happening.

Across the street from my window is a parking lot; I heard someone running out there. I listened to sneakers on the pavement, echoing off the buildings all around, a soft, firm patting sound. I listened for a while before I got up on my knees on the bed. I raised the shade a foot and looked out. It was DuPree, all by himself, running laps around the parking lot just inside the chain-link fence like he was in his own private compound. Just the one man out there under the streetlights on the asphalt. He wore a sweat suit that could have been gray or white. He ran for a while more and then picked up a jump rope. He went for ten minutes straight, the rope ticking the pavement and up on his toes, pumping. After that, he started on the wind sprints. He got down in a lineman's crouch, then lunged forward. Down low for the first few strides, then his chest up and out, arms making tight uppercuts as he busted it diagonally across the lot. When he finished with that, he ran twice more around, then jumped the fence and walked away down the street.

I lay back down on the bed and shut my eyes. I followed DuPree. In my mind, I went with him down the street and around the corner, past the broken benches at the bus stop and east, across the city, walking those long strides with the hitch, the bounce up on the toes, down the long streets, to another building across town, up the stairs, hand on the banister, clutch and slide, one flight, two flights, three, and I'm there. I open the door to Yolanda's apartment. I don't need to turn on a light. Walk softly to her bedroom, and inside, there's a streak of light that's gotten in under the shade, fallen across her bed. She's asleep on her side, turned away from me, knees drawn up, and I slide in under the covers to nestle against her, feel her warmth, my legs behind hers, shins against her calves, my belly against her soft rear, chest against her back. I reach one arm around and without waking, she takes my hand between her warm palms and holds it against her chest. I lie still, feel her slow rise and fall, let her breaths become my breaths, and that way I get to sleep.

When I got home from work the next day, there was a package on the steps. I got it inside on my eating table and slit the packing tape with a jackknife. Styrofoam pellets all over the place, but it was there. The starlight night scope, heavier than I expected—three or four pounds, easy.

I took it into the bedroom closet, got down on the floor with my back against the wall. I slipped it on over my head, fit my eyes against the rubber sockets and tightened the straps. I pulled the door shut. Nothing. Not a goddamn thing. Then I remembered it was light enhancement; you had to have a little light to begin with. So I opened the closet door a tiny crack and, sure enough, I could see my shirts. I could see a ways up inside the sleeves. A twelve-hundred-dollar piece of equipment. I picked up a shoe and looked down inside the toe.

There was only one person to show this to. I figured I was ready.

There was a sound like tearing strips of cloth. I banged on his door. The sound stopped and I banged again. Nothing. I waited a minute, then hit the door harder.

"DuPree!" I yelled. I hadn't meant to yell so loud. "Open up," I said.

I waited, and then there was the snick and clack of the four locks.

The door opened a crack, and Leonard DuPree looked at me above a length of chain. He had gray eyes. He kept his mouth shut.

"I'm the guy from next door," I said.

I held up my night scope, and his eyes narrowed.

"You been readin' my magazines," he said.

"No," I said.

"I seen you," he said.

The door shut, then opened all the way. Somehow, when his hand came toward me—you see something in the movies so many times—I thought he was going to take a fistful of my shirt at the throat and hoist me up so that my toes danced on the floor. I was moving back when his hand stopped, fingers pointed at my stomach.

"Lenny DuPree," he said.

"I live next door." We shook.

DuPree was broad-shouldered but lean. Had a two-day beard and that butch cut, thin fuzz all over his head. A round face, but the skin was tight; muscles moved when he talked.

"Some stunt, reading people's private mail." He smiled without showing his teeth.

I shifted my weight to my other foot. "Not really."

"Oughta get your own subscription sometime." His smile got bigger. "Come on in," he said, and stepped back.

I wasn't sure what to do.

"Aw, come on," DuPree said, waving me in. "I don't give a shit about that."

It was dark in DuPree's apartment, but I knew the layout, same as mine. I walked past the kitchenette—smell of hamburger and onions—into the one big room, DuPree behind me. The shades were drawn and the baseball game was on the TV.

"I didn't read anything personal," I said.

DuPree opened his mouth and laughed without moving his head.

"But you would have, right?"

I didn't say anything to that.

"That's all right, good buddy. I don't give one shit. Fact is, I knew you was gettin' that scope, 'cause I checked *your* mail." DuPree made a wheezing sound, took me a second to know it was another kind of laugh. "Bet you didn't figure on counterintelligence, huh?"

DuPree seemed relaxed; his arms swung loose as he walked to the other end of the room to switch off the television. I couldn't let my hands hang, put them in my pockets.

He had picked up a roll of duct tape.

"I was just doing a little experiment," he said. "Oughta be up your line."

DuPree made the ripping sound, peeled a strip of tape off the roll. He went to a window and taped the shade shut around the edges, so that no light got in. I saw that most of the windows were already done.

"Here you go," he said, and tossed me another roll of tape.

I turned it around in my hands.

"You got your scope already?" I asked him.

"You bet," he said.

I went to work with the duct tape, and we did the rest of the windows without talking, the room getting darker. My heart was beating fast when he stuck on the last piece of tape. The apartment was as dark as it could be, a little light leaking in under the door to the hallway. I could just make out the outline of my hand in front of my face and, across the room, DuPree, moving.

I picked up my night scope, slipped into the headband, tightened the straps.

"How about that," DuPree said.

I could see plain as day. DuPree had nothing on his feet, camouflage pants, white T-shirt, hands on his hips. The scope covered half his face, the lenses like huge eyes. The main feature of the room was the king-size water bed with vinyl-clad padded frame and digital heat control. Never seen a girl around his place, but I guess he was prepared. On a dolly near the bed, he had the nineteen-inch color console rigged up with a VCR. Above the bed, he had a framed poster advertising bird shot, the grouse flushed and rising, the rifle aimed. On another wall was a poster where you looked through a rifle sight, cross hairs in the form of a peace sign trained on an advancing soldier: PEACE THROUGH SUPERIOR FIREPOWER. One corner of the room had a mat on the floor for his weights: He had a bench-press set complete with leg lifts, grip squeezers, a rack of dumbbells and, next to it, an exercise bike with digital mileage and heart-rate readouts. On the wall above the bike was a piece of paper that said, WORK HARD OR DIE. Over his sofa was a pretty nice picture of a waterfall and some mountains on black velvet, and there were other things on the wall: old swords and helmets and more sheets of paper stuck on with tape. Words in black marker: The one nearest to me said, GOOD POSTURE SAVES LIVES.

Below the scope, I saw DuPree's mouth crack into a smile. "A little tired of bein' stuck in this shithole building, am I right?"

I was smiling, too. "You got ideas?" I asked.

"Hoo! A dude who's after *ideas*." DuPree shook his head and took two loping steps over to his dresser, picked up some kind of short curved sword, might have been Turkish.

"Sure, I got *ideas*" he sneered, slicing an X in the air. "My big idea is how about we go kick some ass?"

A little later, we were in DuPree's truck, headed for the South End. DuPree had provided the paraphernalia. We both wore black turtle-necks covered with lightweight black jackets that hid the shoulder hol-sters. As we drove, I practiced reaching under my left arm and pulling out the expanding steel whip: Press a button and the thing zips out to a flexible eighteen-inch baton with a heavy knob on the end. I slipped my hand through the wrist strap, gripped the handle and tapped the knob against the dashboard.

"I like this," I said. "Only twenty bucks?"

"You bust somebody's skull, you're not careful," DuPree said.

DuPree's holster held a Browning nine-millimeter automatic. "Now, I'm not gonna use this," he had said. "This is just a friendly fight." In his boot was a trench knife with knuckle-duster handle and black Teflon-coated blade, good for the night work.

"This is a nonlethal exercise," DuPree said.

The jackets had shoulder patches, insignia of the Apocalypse Commandos: the letters A.C. with a lightning bolt through them and a skull and crossbones beneath. Apparently, a member name of Stick had been put in the hospital by some people in the South End. "Dominicans," said DuPree. "Baseball fans." We were going to pick up Stick's brother and the three of us go pay a visit.

"Don't worry," DuPree said. "We're just gonna put a little scare into some people."

"I'm not worried," I said.

The truck was set up high on stiff shocks that took the potholes hard. Cars got out of our way. I had the window down and my arm hanging out to feel the night air. It was cool, late August.

"Nice truck," I said. Turned out DuPree was from Iowa, so there was a whole lot that didn't need to be said about trucks and driving with your arm hanging out, looking for something to do. "Good to get out," I said.

"Get out, have some fun," said DuPree.

"Nothing wrong with that."

We pulled alongside the plaza of the Christian Science Mother Church, where there's a reflecting pool couple of football fields long and half a one wide. That's where we saw him: a big black guy up on the rim of the pool, gliding along on roller skates.

"Dumbass gonna get hisself wet, he slips off," said DuPree. He whistled out the window and the guy hopped down off the rim and skated over. He was a good skater, did a couple of spins on the way. He had the jacket and the night scope on a strap over his shoulder, same as us.

"Meatlux," the man said. I was looking for some kind of fancy handshake, but he gave it to me straight. I figure Meatlux was 6'8", not counting the skates. Built like a Buick.

"Call me Meat." His hands were the size of dictionaries. "Pleasure to make your acquaintance," he said.

"Nice skates," I said.

He didn't take his eyes off me. "They serve."

We drove Mass. Ave. toward the South End. I was in the middle, my leg pressed against Meatlux's, like sitting next to a warm rock. You could see muscles through his clothes like potatoes through a sack. Meatlux had to bend his head forward in the cab, and there was a bead of sweat running down from his temple to his jaw.

"Are the police in on this?" I asked. "I mean, are they looking for the guys who got your brother?"

Meatlux snorted and looked away out the window.

"Ain't exactly police kind of work," said DuPree.

"Allow me to edify my man here concerning some of the rules of justice," Meatlux said. "By which this great society of ours operates."

"Don't get huffed up," DuPree said.

"Rule number one: Do unto others as they do unto you."

"Be cool," DuPree said.

"Rule number two: Terrify the mothafuckers in the process."

"Always gotta open his mouth before a fight," DuPree said.

"Don't know why we have to have a new man with us," Meatlux announced loudly to the windshield. "Just another body for yours truly to watch out for."

"You just watch out for yourself," I said.

"Ooh, I like that," Meatlux said. "Bad man."

"Dude's all right," DuPree said. "He's got resources."

"Bad little dude with resources, is that right?"

"They serve," I said.

Meatlux shook the seat with his laugh. "Ooh, I like that."

"Dude just got thrown over by his old lady," DuPree said.

I had told DuPree about Yolanda, at work, and he had made more out of it than I intended.

"I hear *that*," Meatlux said. "Need to swing out a little, am I right? Stir up the holy hormones a little bit. You're talking to a man who *knows*."

We crossed a bridge over the train tracks and right away, whole blocks of old brownstones are burned out, windows gone, air-raid territory. DuPree decided to leave the truck out of harm's way, so we parked and headed on foot down Columbus Avenue. There was glass all over the street, but Meatlux skated right down the middle, anyway, doing fancy spins and little hops. There were some guys hanging out on the stoops, but they all stopped to watch Meatlux skate.

"Damn showboat," DuPree said to me. "Stay away from the doorways."

We kept off the sidewalk, walking near the curb, the street getting darker as we went, with most of the lights busted. Metal grates were pulled down over the shop fronts; signs in Spanish: NO TOCAR, AQUI SE COME BIEN. Meatlux was making a spectacle, flapping his arms like a bird and screeching so it echoed down the street.

"Way he's trained," DuPree said. "Black belt. You terrify the enemy."

There were little boys running ahead of us on either sidewalk. They ducked in and out of buildings quick as goats. There were girls, too, their braids flapping.

"Kids should be home this time of night," DuPree said.

When we passed open doorways, you could hear people running up and down stairs. I heard ringing telephones and women's voices through upstairs windows. They seemed to be saying urgent things, but of course I don't understand Spanish. There were men looking serious in the doorways, arms folded, dark shirts with the collars wide open, a little gleam of gold at the neck. I almost wished I could say something they'd understand. I had one quarter of high school Spanish, but the only words I could remember were for fork and airplane. *"Tenedor,"* I said to myself. *"Avion."* That was about the extent of it.

"Yankee, go home," I heard somebody say, and there was raw laughter in one of the doorways.

DuPree walked with that stride of his, up on his toes. He wasn't even looking at the people on the sidewalk.

"My opinion is surprise," he was saying. "Way I see it, you give 'em terror *and* surprise the same time. But this is his show. We're just support on this one."

"Is he armed?"

"Shit," said DuPree. "I seen him break guys in half almost by acci-dent." DuPree whistled and Meatlux rolled up beside us, smiling.

"Show him those things you got," DuPree said.

I had seen the eight-pointed Ninja throwing stars in DuPree's maga-zines. Meatlux held one out, shiny in his big palm. I was starting to feel a little queasy. "You said nonlethal."

"Fear thee not, my man. I'm just going to sit some people down, is all."

"We just show the flag a little," DuPree said. "Nothin' serious."

"Sweet, sweet is revenge," said Meatlux.

My stomach was tight as a nut when we finally reached the place. Steps led down from the sidewalk to a basement door. Back home, steps like these are covered up with a bulkhead and used to store old gar-den tools. But here were the words EL CLUB SPORT painted on a wooden board above the door. No windows on the place at all.

"I'm trusting you guys," I said.

"Be cool," DuPree said.

Meatlux had his eyes on the door like he was seeing through it. He spoke softly. "Be cool and terrible."

"You got the fuse box," DuPree said.

Meatlux nodded. "Mine."

"I got the door," DuPree said.

"Me?" I asked.

"Keep thee by my right hand, my man, and witness my wrath." Meatlux crouched down and locked the wheels on his skates. All three of us put on our night scopes.

"Ready," said DuPree.

"Check."

We went through the first door and were in something like an alcove, facing another door. Meatlux moved to his left and opened the fuse box on the wall. "Lights out," he said. DuPree kicked open the inner door and we went in.

"Greetings, sports fans!"

The Dominicans were all talking at once, I figure about twenty of them, in a place no bigger than my basement back home. They sat around small wooden tables, smoking, the air hot and foul with smoke and booze. The concrete floor had manhole-size craters chipped out of it; there was a big crack running down one wall, leaking brown ooze. The bar was some planks set on oil drums, the guy behind it so small he must have been standing on a box, white sleeves rolled up on his scrawny arms. The wall behind him was mostly covered with baseball pennants and photos of Latin ballplayers. There was a jukebox against the far wall, dead, and a television set on the end of the bar, ditto. They all must have been watching the game when we hit the power, because their chairs were all pointed that way. Now they scraped around.

The thing was, everybody was in suit and tie. I mean it: charcoal gray, blue pin stripe, Pierre Cardin, you name it. Gold cuff links, shiny shoes—these guys outclassed the bankers downtown. Only exceptions were some of the younger guys, not much more than kids; they wore V-neck sweaters and buttondown shirts. Everybody was still talking like we weren't there.

"Okay, you Zambo mothafuckers," Meatlux yelled, getting their attention. "Allow me the pleasure of some polite conversation."

At the table nearest us, a guy struck a match. The night scope made his face shine like the moon. He was done up in a white suit, black silk tie, the knot pushed out by a gold collar bar. His face was pocked like he slept on golf cleats.

"Iss a private club," he said.

"We just joined," Meatlux said.

"*Hijo de la gran puta*" came from the back of the room.

"He refer to your mother's profession," said the man in the white suit.

Meatlux took in the room with a sweep of his hand. "Witness, my man, the pleasures of good society."

Each table had one bottle on it. "Check it out," I said. "Chivas Regal."

Several of the men looked pleased about this. "*Aqui lo tomamos suave*," said an older guy, fingering the lavender handkerchief that poked from the pocket of his gray suit.

"Here we drink cool," the guy in the white suit said.

"Eat shit," said DuPree.

"The joys of repartee," Meatlux said.

There was a fat man at the table working his jaw, trying to say something: "The electric, please, for watching *los* Yankees bankrupt *los* Indians of Cleveland."

"*Chinga tu madre*," Meatlux said.

Everyone started talking again, and a few more people struck matches. One big guy got up and felt his way to the bar, whispered something to the bartender.

Then the guy in the white suit stood up, smiling. Now he held a cigarette lighter with a flame half a foot high, painful to look at. "My friends," he said, "you are wearing your welcome."

12

"I like that," Meatlux said. The bartender began to hand baseball bats across the bar. These were passed around to several men, who then stood up.

"Looks like we got a ball game," DuPree said.

"Now, gentlemen," Meatlux said, "before we take our leave, there is the matter of the inhospitable treatment afforded my younger sibling."

At this point, something happened that we hadn't figured on. The bartender slapped two big flashlights down onto the bar and there was a white flash like screwdrivers being driven into my eyes. I pulled off the night scope and couldn't see a thing but the two lights. I was aware of a chair flying past my head and a lot of howling. Somebody grabbed my arm; DuPree said something I couldn't make out and pulled me toward the door. I saw Meatlux kick somebody, then something heavy whomped my left arm and I sat down hard, with wood breaking near my head and Meatlux yelling something that sounded Chinese. When I got to my feet, my arm was numb. It looked like Meatlux had knocked a couple of guys down—they were rolling on the floor—and everybody else was yelling without going near him. My left arm wouldn't move, so the best thing I could figure was to go for the steel whip with my right hand. I got it out okay, but before I was ready to hit anything with it, all the noise stopped.

DuPree had pulled his knife. He stood in a half crouch in the doorway, his back toward the street.

"Whenever you're finished, Meat. I got the door."

The Dominicans kept their distance, everyone waiting for someone else to make the next move. The two on the floor made low groans. Then men began to move, slowly, shifting in the beams that cut like headlights through the room. The light was in my eyes and it was hard to see. The crowd of bats was raised like a thicket.

Over by the bar, an older man was brushing his suit with a whisk broom.

A muscular kid in a V-neck sweater stepped toward me, smiling, the bat resting on his shoulder like he was on deck. He was a lefty. The others inched closer behind him and I could begin to make out the faces. Everybody with some manner of smile, some tight-lipped, some showing teeth. The guy in the white suit was choked up on the bat for the short swing; the fat man had his hands apart as if to bunt; most of the younger guys gripped to hit the long ball.

I wagged my steel whip in front of me, but then it slipped out of my hand, clattered on the floor. I had forgotten to use the wrist strap. A few of the men laughed, and I found myself raising my arms over my head. My left arm wouldn't move, so all I could do was stick my right in the air.

"Friends," I said.

I heard a few sniggers, and then there was one word that came to me. *"Amigos."*

The V-neck kid made a sudden move to his right and swung at Meatlux. Meatlux took the bat away from him and knocked him down with some fancy legwork, the kid on the floor holding his knee and yelling something horrible. The guy in the white suit jabbed me in the chest with the end of his bat, knocked me back against the wall.

"Closing time," DuPree said, and Meatlux moved past me to follow him out the door.

"Exeunt, stage rear," Meatlux said. "Farewell, citizens."

I turned to follow, but somebody on the floor grabbed my foot and I stumbled. I had a hand on the doorframe and pulled myself up, then made it up the stairs to the street.

They were already half a block away, DuPree running, Meatlux skating, faster than I could imagine, whooping as they went. I tried to start after them, but there were hands on me. Little hands. Kids. They could have been asking for money, little spic kids with moist hands and those big brown eyes, grabbing my arms. Boys and girls both, their hair cut in bangs and dirt smeared on their faces like in some food-relief poster.

"Mister," they said. "Hey, mister."

I pushed through them and ran. DuPree and Meatlux were a block ahead, getting hard to see in the dim light. My left arm still wouldn't move and I used my right hand to hold it to my side. There was pain in my chest and I had trouble breathing, but I was running just the same. The night scope was still there, bouncing against my chest, the strap cutting into my neck.

When I checked back over my shoulder, I saw there was no one following. Just the group of kids on the sidewalk staring after me. I put my head down and tried to make my feet move faster. When I looked up, DuPree and Meatlux were gone. The truck was only two blocks away, maybe three, I didn't remember. The street was empty ahead. They'd have to come for me. They'd come and get me. I hurt, and it hurt to run, but that would be conditioning, I figured. It was my first time. It was just a matter of getting into shape.

In Love with Rachel

by **STEVEN PLOETZ**
1987

Taylor orders a vodka martini. Made with Finlandia vodka, he speci-
fies. He is late, but Rachel, as he has known she would be, is later.
He watches the barman mix his drink and admires the skills—the quick,
sure movements, handling the bottles with ease, putting them back
without looking, the spill-less pour. The making of a vodka martini is a
comforting routine, something Taylor knows he can depend on. There
is a story that goes with the bar. Taylor knows this from talking to the
present owner. He told him the man who originally opened it did so in
1912. He sold it in 1918, though, after his son was gassed and died in
the third wave over the top at Ypres. Mustard gas, Taylor remembers.

Hanging on the wall opposite a picture of Cole Porter in a tux and
slicked-back hair is a gas mask. It is old—its leather peeling, hoses
cracked, eyepieces thick and cloudy like the glasses of someone with
very bad vision. Taylor doesn't know if he believes the story about the
bar. Probably, it has been there long enough, though. He doesn't know
where Ypres is or what mustard gas does to you.

The barman puts a napkin down and then puts the drink in its frosted
glass on the napkin. Taylor's money, including a dollar tip, is already on
the bar. Taylor takes his drink to an overstuffed red-leather booth at the
back of the room, where he can see the entrance. His feet rise off the
floor as he sinks into the sagging springs. He touches the breast pocket
of his blue blazer for the envelope, then pulls it out to be sure. After

drinks, Taylor has planned dinner and a play for himself and Rachel. He has made the dinner reservation for seven fifteen at a new restaurant he has heard is very good. He checks the tickets' date and the time and seat numbers. The play is also new and it received a very good review in the *Times*, though Taylor, not trusting the reviewer, called an actor friend, who assured him it should not be missed. Taylor puts the tickets away and takes a sip of his drink, holding it on his tongue. It is well made, the proper mix of vodka and vermouth, chilled just right.

It is four fifteen when Rachel walks in, searching the room for him, while Taylor watches her from behind. Other men in the bar look at her, too. They turn away from their talk and drinks and look. Taylor understands. She is beautiful—tall and thin, with a girlish figure and thick, curly light-brown hair she tries to keep tied back with a slim black ribbon. No make-up. Dressed in a simple but expensive white-cotton dress, her legs stockingless, long and slightly tanned, her shoes open-toed and red.

Those shoes. Taylor has seen those shoes before, those ugly shoes. He was with Rachel when she bought them. They were walking and the shoes in a store window caught her eye. Immediately, Rachel ran into the store. Later, she explained that she had felt sorry for the shoes. They were so ugly no one else would have bought them. And if she didn't, little children in Ecuador would starve. Starting at the age of four, they are forced to leave their homes in the barrio and go out into the jungle and trap anteaters for the leather. They leave their mothers and fathers, everyone they care for, and travel alone. They don't want to, they are frightened in the jungle, it is dark and scary, but they have no choice. It is what they have always done. The anteaters are big, with bristly fur, sharp claws and long, rough tongues that feel like sandpaper on the skin. They live in holes dug deep into the earth. Sometimes the children have to crawl down into these to catch them. Sometimes the children meet another child already in the hole and they hunt together, clinging to each other. Either way, alone or in pairs, it is very dangerous work. Fire red, two straps hugging the instep, heels too sharp—Taylor hates those shoes.

Rachel turns around and searches the back of the barroom. Taylor admires the way she moves—light, graceful, her dress flaring out at the hem like a dancer's. And she did used to be a dancer, when she was younger. She dreamed of being a great ballerina, of traveling all over the world. But then one day she was warming up, just moving slowly across the floor, and she fell. She never danced again. It was her medial collateral, a very important connection, she told him. The one that holds everything else together. Taylor has seen the small scar on her right knee. The orthopedist brought in a plastic surgeon to close the incision. He knew she was a young girl with pretty legs and did good work. It barely shows.

Rachel catches sight of Taylor, waves a big wave, as if she has just come back from a long trip, and walks toward him. He does not wave back. "I'm sorry I'm late," Rachel says, standing before him at the edge of the booth.

She captures his hand in mid-air and slides into the opposite side of the booth. The bartender comes over and she orders a drink, like Taylor's, and smiles again, soft pink lips sliding over hard white teeth.

The drink arrives and Rachel takes a sip. "Do you want to know why I'm late?" she asks. Taylor clears his throat to answer and Rachel pulls his hand across the shiny black table toward her, wrapping it up tightly with her other hand. "Well, I had trouble with a cab. At first I couldn't find one and when I finally did, it had the most peculiar driver. Do you want to hear about him?"

With his free hand, Taylor fidgets with his drink, drawing a careful grid in the condensation clinging to the cold glass. "Okay," he says. "Tell me about this cabdriver."

Relaxing her grip on his hand, Rachel leans back into the heavy red upholstery. "To begin with," she says, "he was foreign. But they all are nowadays, aren't they? I don't know exactly where he was from. From the East, definitely, but not Arab or Chinese. From somewhere in between—one of those little mountain countries where it snows all the time and the men all carry rifles on their backs because there are bandits everywhere. His English was good, though; very practiced, I guess you could call it. But not schoolish. More like he had learned it from watching old movies and speaking along with a dialogue."

"He sounded like Cary Grant?" Taylor asks.

"No," Rachel answers, "but he did have an accent. Not like Cary Grant's but one that was very thick and rich, like cream. That's not what you notice most about him, though."

"No?"

"The shaved head, that's probably what really gets your attention. Smooth and shiny. That and the mustache. The mustache was definitely hard to ignore."

"A mustache that can't be ignored?"

"Well, it was so big, how could you?" Rachel says. "Anyway, I flagged him down in the Village and told him I had to go uptown. I told him I was late. Traffic was heavy, but he drove very fast, with great skill, weaving in and out, making pedestrians jump back onto the curb. We hadn't gone very far, though, when he suddenly pulled over. I gave him the address again, thinking that maybe he had forgotten it and was lost. But he just shook his head. 'Is there something wrong with the cab?' I asked, but he didn't answer. I sat there for the longest time, not knowing what to do. It was very strange."

"How long?" Taylor asks, concerned.

"I don't know," Rachel says with a small shrug of her narrow shoulders. "A long time. And when I finally reached for the door handle, he turned around quickly and grabbed my hand. 'Don't worry,' I told him, 'I'll pay what's on the meter.' It was then I noticed he was crying. Heavy tears rolled down his face and collected in his mustache.

"'No,' he said, shaking his hairless head but letting go of my hand. 'Do not worry about money. All I want from you is for you to listen. I have a story to tell, a very sad story. I must tell someone. I cannot ride around all day with people close enough to me to touch and not tell them. It is too hard to keep it inside me. Please, would you listen?' Really, Taylor, I didn't know what to do. It was scary, so I told him I would listen. What else could I do?"

"You could have got out of the cab and hailed another one," Taylor says. He glances over at the bar quickly. It is crowded, not a seat open, and people are beginning to drink with their sleeves rolled up.

Rachel's thick hair is coming free from its ribbon and falling down over her shoulders. Taylor notices how even in the dim light of the bar, the loose ends shine.

"He was a hard worker," she continues. "Days, nights, holidays—no shift was too long. He even started to sleep in the garage so he could take over for any of the other drivers who were sick or just too tired to go on. And he was really close to getting what he wanted when something happened and ruined everything."

"Someone checked his immigration status."

"You see, one night, after he had been out driving for hours," Rachel says, "he went back into the garage to get some rest before going out for the morning rush hour. This was during the very same week that everything he had worked for was to come true. That's important to know. He was going to get his own medallion and he was going to be reunited with his wife. He had already sent her the airline ticket.

"Anyway, he was so excited he couldn't sleep. So, to pass the time, he started playing backgammon with some of the other drivers. He really loved backgammon, used to play it all the time back in his native country; but after he came to America and started working, he never allowed himself to play. He didn't want to waste the time. This night was an exception, though. He felt he could relax.

"He started to play with a new driver and the games were very difficult and close. The new man played recklessly, relying more on luck than anything else. My driver knew he was a better player, but he still kept on losing. He lost game after game."

Resting her slim, tanned arms on the table, Rachel leans toward Taylor. "It was not so much that he lost that bothered him but the *way* he lost. All his clever gambits and patient plans were swept aside by his opponent's impulsive gambles and lucky throws of the dice. He became very angry. When the other driver suggested they bet on the games, he accepted."

"Even though he kept on losing?" Taylor asks.

"That's right," Rachel says. "The thing is, the other driver kept on winning. His luck never ran out. This only made my driver even angrier and he kept on increasing their wagers."

"That was a very foolish thing to do."

"Maybe, but he couldn't quit."

"Why not?"

"Because he had already started to play, and once you start, you can't quit," Rachel says. "But listen, things got even worse. Gradually, he realized he was being tricked. The new driver wasn't just lucky. He had seen it before with other very good backgammon players. They pretend to be lucky fools, but all the time they are really playing a very subtle and sophisticated game. Now it was he who felt like a fool, but he couldn't back down. It was too late. As the stakes grew, the dispatcher called in the other drivers from the road and the garage became filled with men straining to see the action on the board, the movement of the dice."

"Why didn't one of them stop him?" Taylor asks.

"Because . . ."

"Because why? Weren't they his friends? It doesn't make sense."

"Because they couldn't, that's all," Rachel says. "He wouldn't have let them. The game went on and in time, everything he had worked so hard for was lost. This man whom he barely knew had won the good life that was going to be his and his wife's.

"Then, still sitting over the board, he took out his wallet, Taylor, and pulled out a picture of his wife. An old black-and-white picture showing her standing next to a fountain in a garden in a country thousands of miles away. He showed it to the other driver, who was impressed by her beauty, and suggested that they play one more game. If he lost, he would give him his wife."

"They started to play for this guy's wife?" Taylor asks. "What kind of thing is that to do?"

"He had to keep on playing. He didn't even really know why. Part of it was that he had lost and wanted to get even. He wanted to show he was the better player, that he was in control. But there was something else, too. He just couldn't seem to quit, even though he knew he should. They started another game, but he couldn't concentrate. The dice felt so heavy he could barely lift them, the black and white pieces blurred together and he couldn't tell them apart. Of course, he lost.

"As you can imagine, he was destroyed. He left the garage and was certain he would have to kill himself. Back where he came from, he would have put the rifle that had belonged to his father—and *his* father before him—in his mouth and pulled back the trigger with his toe. Or he would have thrown himself into some snowy mountain gorge. Obviously, he couldn't do those things in New York, but there are plenty of bridges and tall buildings and subway platforms to jump off of. It is easy to kill oneself in New York. But then he realized that would not be good enough. He owed his wife even more.

"So, for the longest time, he walked the streets. He was in a daze. It had been cold but had turned warm suddenly and he was covered with sweat. All the people on the street were in good spirits, their faces bright and happy, and the cabdriver looked at them and couldn't understand how they could be that way when he was so miserable. Late in the day, after wandering around for hours, he found himself in front of a tattoo parlor in the Bowery, on a street filled with boarded-up hotels, dark storefronts, alleys blocked with razor wire."

Rachel stops telling the cabdriver's story to take a sip of her drink, holding the cold liquor in her mouth. She pushes some of her stubborn curly hair behind her ears, smooths her dress in her lap and smiles. "Do you know what happened at the tattoo parlor?" she asks. Taylor shakes his head, looking at her lips wet from the martini. Slowly, he raises his hand and glances down at his Rolex.

"I thought we'd go to dinner," he says. "There's this new restaurant. I was told it's very good. The *Times* gave it two stars."

"The Cajun one?" Rachel asks. "The one where the chef went to Harvard but then dropped out to study cooking with some old woman in a swamp? He lost an arm hunting alligators?"

"I don't know," Taylor says. "Maybe it's a different one. I made reservations for seven fifteen." He looks up at Rachel, catching her bright green eyes.

"Do you want to know what happened in the tattoo parlor?" she asks again, and this time Taylor nods slowly. "Good," she says.

"You see, all the time the cabdriver was telling me his story, he kept on wiping away the tears on his cheeks with the back of his hand. It was strange. Some of the tears wouldn't go away, no matter how hard he seemed to rub.

"'You have noticed!' he said to me, very excited. 'These tears on my face that will not be wiped away. Yes, they are tattoos!' Those are what he had done that first night in the tattoo parlor. He called them reminders of his pain, tears that will last forever. But they were only the beginning. Since then, he has gone back to the tattoo parlor every day."

"He was probably in prison," Taylor says. "I saw something about that on TV, tattoos of tears. The reporter said it was some kind of initiation rite. They do it with ballpoint pens."

"I saw that, too. The reporter got his wife to claim he had raped her so he'd be sent to Attica and could see what it was really like. She was supposed to recant her story in a few months but started to have an affair and decided she didn't want him back. So she kept silent. He tried everything to get out—wrote letters to newspapers, his Congressman, the President, even went on a hunger strike. . . ."

"Anyway," Taylor says, "you should really be more careful. Are you sure you didn't get his name or number?"

"No, Taylor," Rachel says. "You aren't paying attention. Listen. The cabdriver undid a bright blue scarf that he had wrapped tightly around his neck and unbuttoned the collar of his shirt. What I saw were slim, delicate fingers—a woman's fingers—curling around his neck. They were the most amazing color: pale gold, as if lighted by the sun, with nails of flaming red. On one finger, there was a wedding band that was a sick, tarnished green. Farther down his neck, I could see the hands that these fingers belonged to, hands that rose up out of his shirt. And on his chest, I could see the top of a head—thick, wavy black hair, wild and unkempt, the beginning curve of a forehead. It was exactly as if a woman were on top of him, resting her head on his chest, making love to him or struggling to hold him down and choke out his life."

"He had a whole woman tattooed on him?" Taylor asks.

"That's right."

"Everything? I mean . . . in color?"

"In the tattoo parlor, he gave the artist a picture of his wife and told him that he wanted it done life-size, just as if she were on top of him."

"All done with those needles?" Taylor asks. "Like they do hearts on sailors' biceps? One prick at a time. That would be——"

"Excruciating," Rachel says. "And slow, too. The artist warned him about that. He also told him it would be very expensive. He did not work cheap. But the driver said that was not a problem. He welcomed the pain and no longer had anything else to work for. Now he drives his cab and takes whatever he earns down to the tattoo parlor. The artist stays open for him and they work through the night. The cabdriver is his greatest creation. The picture of his wife is almost finished: When it is, the cabdriver said there will be no escape. His wife went with the other driver, just as he said she would. He has not seen either of them since. He heard they moved to Florida. When he stands before a mirror, she stands in front of him. When he makes love to another woman, she lies between them. He can always feel her fingers on his throat."

Rachel is finished. She smiles at Taylor. It is a small smile, but it grows. "So, that's why I'm late," she says. "What do you think?"

Taylor looks at her. He doesn't know what to think. He never knows. The story about the cabdriver may or may not be true. That hardly matters. It is the story that matters, and that's all. A story is a story and it is the duty of the teller to make it as interesting as possible. Those are the rules Rachel plays by.

● ● ●

The bartender brings over a second round of drinks without being asked. Taylor takes a quick sip and then looks at his watch again. "We can still go to the theater," he says. "There's still time. It's supposed to be a fine play."

"I heard about that play," Rachel says. "The playwright is from South America somewhere and he was imprisoned for years by the ruling junta. They tortured him, beat his feet with rubber hoses, worked him over with a cattle prod."

"A cattle prod? The electric kind?" Taylor asks. He takes a gulp of his drink.

Rachel picks up her glass, holds it up to her mouth and then bites gently down on the rim with her front teeth. She sticks the tip of her tongue down into the glass until it just touches the surface of the liquor. "Hmmm . . ." she says, setting the glass down. "No, I don't think I want to go to the play." She reaches across the table and touches his arm. "Now it's your turn, Taylor," she says, playing with the cuff of his shirt. "Tell me a story."

Rachel knows she is a good storyteller. It is something she has worked very hard for. She also knows that Taylor is not. Despite this, Rachel is not willing to give up. She cares too much for Taylor and feels that, with her help, there may be some hope for him. In the pursuit of a story, she is both uncompromising and relentless. Taylor has known this about

Rachel since the time they met. He had been taken to an art opening by a friend and noticed Rachel standing at the edge of the crowd. She looked out of place and a little silly to him, dressed in a black silk dress and rubber beach sandals. She was very beautiful, though, and on his way out, he asked if she would like to share a taxi with him. It was snowing, not the best weather for beach sandals. Rachel said she would and during the ride uptown, she told him about herself. She worked at another gallery, so went to lots of openings. She didn't care for her job, though, and made no secret of it. She supposed they might get around to firing her, but that didn't bother her. She lost jobs all the time, it seemed. It was her tenth job since leaving college. What she really wanted to do was to be a painter herself.

Obviously, she was very confused. Taylor had seen women like her before—at college, at parties, walking down the street. They always seemed to work in galleries, sell flowers from street carts with bright umbrellas, go to Europe to study and have affairs with married Frenchmen or German anarchists from wealthy families. He understands women like her and usually they don't interest him. But there was something else about Rachel. In the cab, he listened to her talk, slid closer to her on the hard seat. And when, right before the cab reached his building, Rachel asked him to tell her a story, he told the driver to keep driving. That first cab ride ended up costing him $72.40.

Once, Taylor recalls, after he and Rachel had been going out a few months, she grabbed hold of him and wouldn't let him get out of bed and go to the bathroom until he told her a story. He had tried and tried. Finally, in desperation, he dredged up what he knew was a rather lame anecdote about Rusty, a calico cat he had had when he was seven.

Almost in disgust, Rachel had let him get up. While he was in the bathroom, though, standing over the bowl, she stood outside the door and told him another story of her own. She was just a little girl, no more than five or six. Standing in the back of her big sister's closet, enjoying the dark, the lingering smell of perfume on the clothes, the delicious danger of being in a place that was forbidden to her, Rachel was surprised by the sound of footsteps coming up the stairs. The door to the room opened and she heard the voices of her sister and her boyfriend. Boys were forbidden in the bedroom. Rachel would have loved to tell on her, but their parents were out and she was trapped, afraid to move.

The two of them giggling, the sound of the window being pushed open. She could smell cigarette smoke, another thing her sister was forbidden to do. Then Rachel heard the sound of zippers being pulled and snaps being undone, her sister's vague protests, which soon gave way to laughter, and the bedsprings' squeak. Suddenly, Rachel had to go—*really had to go*—to the bathroom. There was no escape. She waited and waited, but they were still out there—the bed rocking up and down, a few soft, whispered words, the Beatles' album *Rubber Soul* playing over and over again on her sister's small phonograph. Rachel began to cry. She wiggled and cried. The dark closet frightened her now. She was afraid of what would happen when she was found out. Her parents would punish her. Her sister would hate her. And what was her sister doing, anyway? Was she okay?

As the first drops began to trickle down her legs, Rachel crawled into the very back of the closet. There she found an old can of mothballs. She had always loved the smell of mothballs. In the dark, tugging down her panties, she squatted, held the can between her legs and peed.

The smell filled the closet, clung to the clothes. It made Rachel's skin feel electric and prickly, made her eyes water. She had never smelled anything quite like it before, anything so strong and intoxicating. It was strange, though. She suddenly felt faint and began to cough. She tried not to—her sister would hear—but she couldn't help herself. Something was wrong. Her throat burned and she collapsed on the floor. There were loud voices in the room, her sister's and her boyfriend's; they had heard. Then there was a long, long scream.

She awoke in the hospital. Her mother was there and her father, standing around the bed. Her sister was there, too, sitting in tears in a chair near the door. A thin sheet of plastic separated Rachel from all three of them. Later, Rachel learned there had been a chemical reaction between the mothballs and her urine. Some sort of gas had been created that had made her pass out. It spread into the bedroom and made her sister's boyfriend pass out, too, when he was still on top of her sister. She had thought he died and screamed so loud that the neighbors called the police. That was how the police found them when they burst through the door.

After hearing this story, Taylor came out of the bathroom and was unable to sleep. He sat up that night in a chair, watching Rachel sleep peacefully. Whenever he felt himself drift off, he slapped himself hard across the face.

Also, since that night, Taylor has become convinced he has exhausted his life's resource of stories. Every sadistic football coach, lecherous baby sitter, outrageous roommate and senile relative he has ever encountered has been put to use.

Recently, Taylor has even tried to recycle stories he has already told Rachel. He has shifted them around, changed some names, switched locations. But Rachel sees right through their flimsy fabric. She takes his deceit rather badly, too. It is almost as if he has betrayed her. Taylor knows he could make something up, something completely fictitious and outrageous, and Rachel would be pleased. That is what she is after.

Each evening, he looked back on his day, saw it stretched out behind him and shook his head. What happened was what he had expected to happen. It did not beg comment, let alone retelling. Taylor began to feel for the first time at a loss, strangely helpless. Maybe it would be possible for him to borrow some stories from his friends and co-workers. David, who worked in Research, two floors below Taylor's, had been in Vietnam. He had flown in B-52s, a navigator, so he knew the country only from a long distance away, looking through a tiny window. But he still knew many things that he would talk about when asked. He knew the sound the bombs made when they exploded: thunder, as if somewhere it were going to rain. Actually, he had never really heard that sound. They dropped the bombs and were already on their way back home to Thailand by the time they hit the ground. But once, while sitting in a restaurant in Bangkok, David talked to a Marine who had heard the bombs. He told him what it was like. Taylor was too young to have been in Vietnam, and Rachel knew it. Still, he thought he might be able to use some of David's stories. He would change the specific details, but maybe the principle would still apply.

Taylor looks at Rachel, who sits waiting patiently. He sighs deeply. "How would you like to go to a movie?" he asks.

Someone has left behind a newspaper in the booth, the *Post*. Taylor picks it up and looks for the movie listings. Before he finds them, he passes articles about how coffee causes cancer, certain vegetables prevent cancer and a woman in New Jersey whose husband has been locked up in a Russian prison since 1918. "Here," he says. "Around the corner, there is one about pirates who get sent into the future and teenagers who get sent into the past. Down the block, there is one about a woman who kills her child in a concentration camp."

Rachel shakes her head. "No, Taylor," she says. "It's your turn."

She waits. Taylor clears his throat. He begins one story and stops. Then another.

Rachel waits, carefully shredding her napkin and then trying to fit all the pieces back together again. As he struggles, she absent-mindedly runs her index finger along the rim of her glass. There is an unseen chip and on the third pass, the finger is cut. A drop of blood appears. Rachel holds the finger over the glass. The drop grows heavier and heavier and then falls into the drink. The cool, clear liquor is infused with streaks of bright red. A new drop appears on the finger replacing the old. Rachel holds it up to her face and looks at it casually. She sticks it into her mouth and gently sucks.

Taylor watches Rachel's glass. The tiny drop of blood spreads easily throughout the drink. It does not float to the surface or sink. No part is safe from it.

"Do you remember that story I told you?" Rachel asks.

"I remember," Taylor says, still staring at the drink, his voice loud enough for people at the other tables to hear. He does remember: the summer she turned sixteen, out all night on the beach with her boyfriend, huddled under a blanket, kissing and drinking strawberry wine, the fight with her father when she got home that ended up with his calling her a slut. Twenty-nine stitches in her left hand. That was how Rachel had replied to her father's accusation. Ever since she told him, when they hold hands, Taylor catches himself carefully examining her palm. He looks for the long, thin white line.

Rachel's finger starts to bleed again. She sticks it into her mouth for a second and then holds it out on the table in front of Taylor. It is the index finger of her left hand.

"See," she says. "There's no great damage."

Taylor takes Rachel's hand. "This place should be more careful," he says. "Someone could be seriously hurt. They could sue. You should really be more careful, too." He dabs at the tiny cut with his napkin, looks at the spot of blood on the white paper and then presses down on the finger until its tip turns purple.

Rachel tells another story. It takes place in the not-too-distant past, a story about her going up to Boston for what was to be a guiltless abortion. She never told Taylor she was pregnant. Her trip to Boston was to visit friends, that was what she did tell him. Everything was going to be taken care of.

The clinic was very clean, the staff friendly. In the waiting room, all the plants had somehow been made to bloom at the same time. The doctor introduced himself and shook her hand. He told her to call him Bob. In the "procedure room," as Bob called it, there were problems. She already had the gown on, had already been put on the table, her feet were in the stirrups, but they had to wait. There were problems with the machine. Bob said there wasn't enough suction. He would have it taken care of, would see to it personally.

She was led into a small adjacent room to wait. Marge, the nurse, told her that was where she would recover, after it was over. The door to the procedure room was partially open and it was not long before she could see Bob and a man wearing blue chinos and a blue shirt with MURRAY written above the left pocket enter the room. Murray was carrying a big toolbox and Bob told him there was definitely a suction problem. Murray assured him that it would be no problem, it happened all the time, and he would take care of it. He pulled out a big wrench.

Back on the table again, legs apart, Rachel counted her breaths, one to ten, one to ten. Now it would be over. Bob apologized for the delay and Marge took her blood pressure and pulse. Not records but close. This would make her feel better, Bob said, taking a syringe from Marge and putting it in her vein, and he was telling the truth. Immediately, she felt better. She felt great, warm and relaxed. She felt just like she was coming, right there on the table, and that struck her as being funny. She even began to laugh. Something had to be reversed, mixed up and confused.

Later, on her way back from the clinic, she stopped at a toy store in Cambridge. It was having a sale, things left over from Christmas. She bought a big German Teddy bear that cost so much she had to use her American Express card. Spring had not arrived yet. The wind was blowing hard and cold. Bob had given her three little white pills "for the pain, one now, two later." He had told her to go right home and lie down, but she took a long walk instead, her collar turned up against the wind, the bear held tightly to her breast.

She walked for hours. Night came and she still walked. She felt that she wanted to cry, or at least that she *should* cry, but she couldn't. The big German bear was supposed to help; it had big soft ears and sad brown eyes. Standing alongside the Charles, she said goodbye to the bear. It had failed her and she was going to throw it into the dark, icy river.

There was something wrong. She began to shiver. Her coat was heavy and warm, but she felt so cold. And she hurt. All three of Bob's pills were gone and she still hurt. She began to walk again, trailing the Teddy bear behind her. It began to snow, a soft, late-season snow. The flakes hung in the air, caught in the light from street lamps. The snow muffled every sound, cars glided by, moving silently, like sleds on invisible runners. She couldn't even hear her own footsteps. She knew that if she called out for help or screamed, there would be nothing. Not a single sound. Stopping for a moment, she looked down at the snow beneath her feet and saw spots. Deep red, they clung to the top crust of snow and then slowly began to spread out at the edges, soaking in.

On Mass. Avenue, she found a cab, slowly disappearing under the snow, and got in. Blood was everywhere. She didn't want the cabdriver to see, though, didn't want his cab to be covered with her blood. She took the German bear that cost $117 and wedged it tightly between her legs. She was sure it could absorb every drop of blood she had in her. It was a big bear.

In the emergency room, they took the bloody bear away from her. She held tight, but it slipped away. A little boy who was waiting with a bag of ice held over one eye saw the bear and began to cry. It was given to a black orderly wearing a white T-shirt with yellow stains. She watched as he shoved it through a little door in the hall marked INCIN-ERATOR. She began to cry.

• • •

Rachel and Taylor slide out of the booth and meet at the end of the table. Rachel smiles at him, touching his shoulder. "It's okay," she says. "You can give me one later." Rachel fusses with her hair, trying to keep it back, but gives up. Taylor sets down a $20 bill for the bartender.

It is late. They have been in the bar for a long time. It is too late for dinner and the theater. Too late for movies. Outside it is warm, though. Spring. Several cabs pass by with their lights on, but neither Taylor nor Rachel raises a hand. They decide to walk back to Taylor's apartment. It is a long distance, but they decide to walk, anyway. They have each other for company.

Across the street, a new building is being constructed. It is just a skeleton of cement and steel, but already it is very tall. At the four corners, there are very bright lights and on every floor, workmen are busy. They walk back and forth across the thin girders, in constant motion. The building grows higher and higher. Taylor didn't even notice it when he walked into the bar.

"Was this here before?" he asks.

"What?" Rachel asks, taking Taylor's arm and guiding him down the street.

"This building. I've never seen it. Was it here before? I want to know."

"Oh, that," Rachel says, still walking. "Haven't you heard? About the Brazilian industrialist. And his wife who disappeared in the jungle while collecting butterflies. It was thought she had gone to live with this tribe of cannibals. Anyway, he swore that if she ever came back——"

"Never mind," Taylor says, looking back over his shoulder and counting the floors.

• • •

Rachel and Taylor make love. Rachel sits on top of him, rocking her hips. With his eyes closed, Taylor thinks of being on a ship far out at sea. With the index finger of each hand, Rachel traces the outline of Taylor's body on the bed. She starts at the top of his head and pulls the fingers down slowly, until they are past his knees. Then she pulls them up until they meet at the beginning. Later, Taylor and Rachel lie in each other's arms. Rachel falls asleep, but Taylor cannot. He reaches over to the nightstand and grabs the remote control for the TV. He turns on the VCR but keeps the sound off. A movie he does not recognize fills the twenty-five-inch screen. Such colors. They are so bright he has to squint. A woman dances with a Dixieland band in the streets of Las Vegas, but her husband is far away. He stands out in the desert and watches a young girl walk a tightrope under a million bright stars.

Taylor turns off the VCR and turns on the TV. He goes through the many channels. They flash before his eyes. Wars are being fought, loves falling apart, drains unplugged right there in front of him. He wonders which one he should watch but can't decide.

Taylor places the remote-control unit under his pillow and lies back down on it. The pressure from his head keeps the channel-changer button depressed and the channels whirl by, a continuous electronic scroll. He watches the pictures. The constant flash and flicker begin to make him dizzy.

Watching the TV, Taylor becomes confused. He tries to concentrate, but there, before his eyes, wars are being unstuck, drains heroically conquered, stubborn loves dissolved and washed away. He reaches under the pillow to find the remote control. He wants to turn the TV off, but it's not there. It must have slipped down between the mattress and the headboard, he decides. Taylor wedges his hand into the narrow space but can't reach it. The button is still depressed and the channels continue to whirl.

Taylor turns over onto his stomach and sticks his hand farther down in search of the remote control. He sticks it in up to the elbow and then, getting up on his knees, jams it in all the way up to his shoulder. He still can't find it. His finger tips crawl slowly, methodically over every inch of the dark space. Taylor sits up. Below him, he can see part of the outline of his body that Rachel traced. Most of it has been wiped out, but the heavy cotton sheet still holds parts—a broad shoulder, a bony hip, a left elbow. Pushing hard, feet kicking, Taylor tries to force his arm down ever farther into the narrow space, but his legs become tangled up with the blanket. Falling forward, he hits his head on the smooth oak headboard with a crack.

Lying on his back again, Taylor tries to fit back into the outline. It is almost completely gone now, but he tries, thinks he can make out some faint lines—the thigh here, the hand there—thinks he can remember how it all was. He stares at the TV, bright colors and patterns twisting back on one another as in a kaleidoscope. He breathes hard. Outside the window, Taylor hears a siren, fast and shrill, go by, and then another. He tries to concentrate again, not on the TV but on other things. He counts heartbeats, then the drawers in the dresser, the bricks in the wall.

The only thing to do, Taylor knows, is to get up and turn off the TV by hand. He feels too dizzy, sick. Desperate, he slowly lowers an exploratory foot to the floor, but he can't find it. It's not there. Suddenly, the floor, the walls, everything that used to make up the room is gone, replaced by flashing, flickering, whirling blue light.

He turns onto his side and faces away from the TV. Rachel is still asleep beside him. Taylor is so sick he doesn't know what to do. He's adrift in an angry ball of blue light and there's no escape, no other place to go. Taylor and Rachel are so close, the tips of their noses touch. He touches Rachel gently on the shoulder and she opens her eyes slowly, by fractions.

"Rachel," Taylor whispers. His throat is dry, he can barely speak. He swallows hard, but it does not help. "I have a story to tell you." Rachel smiles and Taylor sees between her lips not teeth but a thin, hard band of blue light.

"I'm listening," she says.

"I am not of your world," he continues. "My people came to earth thousands of years ago and assumed human form. We have waited. We are patient as a race. But one day a message, too faint to be heard by any ears except our own, will come from our ruler and our plans will be put into effect. Some of your people will be enslaved, some sent back to our galaxy as food; most will simply be destroyed. This was a secret, but I just thought you should know."

Rachel's smile broadens. She throws a leg over Taylor, pinning him to the mattress with a warm, soft thigh. "Oh, Taylor," she says. Her mouth is filled with blue light, her breath so hot it burns his face. "I'm so glad you told me. Because, you see, I'm not from this planet, either. It is an alien and strange place. My people came here a very long time ago. We've been at war with your race since the beginning of time." Rachel puts an arm around Taylor and holds him in a tight embrace. "And you see, Taylor, I've been waiting right here for you. I've been waiting for a million years."

The Hotel-Motel Bar & Grill

by VALERIE VOGRIN
1988

PROPRIETOR: Izard McAdoo, high school English teacher, divorced, weekend father, albino, heir to modest fruit-spread fortune. Chief patrons: Elizabeth, twelve, Ellen, ten, Ted, thirty-three.

The spirit of the Hotel-Motel Bar & Grill was derived from Iz's life-long affection for the strangeness of hotels and motels. The quilted bed-spreads, the shag carpets, the garbage cans with plastic liners and the television sets bolted onto fiberboard dressers. The foreign smells of transience and disinfection. In those odors, and in the Yellow Pages of an unfamiliar town, the clanging of wire hangers and the hollow knock of empty bureau drawers, he always caught the nuance of possibility. What had started out as a lark, playing "tavern" with his daughters on Sunday afternoons (which consisted mostly of charging them Monopoly money for colas and treats), ended up as a full-scale project that transformed his luxurious, if somewhat sterile, Southern Cal hacienda-style condo. He had chosen to upgrade the ambience of a tourist-trap family-inn sort of place, yet the basic attractiveness of the Hotel-Motel Bar & Grill lay in its lack of normalcy. It was his home but not his home.

Ellen and Liz both shared their mother Amy's ever-present tan and gray eyes. Ellen's features still appeared pliable and innocent, framed in little-girl pigtails or braids. Liz's nose and cheekbones were already sculpted into model beauty, and she came to visit with at least three varieties of gels and fixatives for her salon-coiffed hair.

"What's the difference between a motel and a hotel?" Ellen asked.

"A motel's a hotel with a parking lot," Liz answered in a patronizing tone.

"Don't hotels have parking lots, too?"

"Daddy!"

"Relax, Elizabeth." Iz leafed through the dictionary. "A hotel is 'a public house that provides housing and usually meals and various services,'" he read.

"What kind of services?" Liz asked, precisely raising one eyebrow in a way he had thought only her mother could, cocking it a full half inch and holding it for several seconds, and Iz realized she was trying to embarrass him. He refused to falter.

"You know—shoes shined, clothes pressed, room service, wake-up calls."

Liz smiled a small smile, barely revealing teeth, but said no more. "Just like here," Ellen said. "Damn straight," Iz replied, leaning over to tickle them both.

• • •

After considerable thought and purchase, Iz had managed to cover just about every imaginable amenity. Cleanliness was important: daily change of sheets and towels for guests and sparkling-clean water glasses and wrapped perfumed soaps on the bathroom countertops. To have the water pressure perfectly adjusted, the vodka chilled, the limes fresh, the ashtrays spotless, the plants lush and the air fragrant and gently circulated by ceiling fans—that attention to detail made Izard's adrenaline rush.

Liz and Ellen took notice of everything, from additions such as the big-screen TV and the onyx backgammon table to the more subtle touches. On cool nights, they liked to sleep with the windows wide open, but then complained about cold feet. His solution was to buy hot-water bottles, which he ceremoniously placed at the ends of their beds when he tucked them in. He loved the moment when the warmth sank in, when their faces registered twin expressions of contentment; he sometimes thought this endeavor was charmed. Liz and Ellen loved the exclusivity of the arrangement, though Hotel-Motel etiquette required proffering hospitality to other guests, too.

Amy would shit, simply shit, if she ever came in; to her, the apartment would represent two of his most irritating qualities: the ability to enjoy himself and his inherited money. Not that much about him seemed to please her now; in the two years since their divorce, most of her sentences began with the phrase "The problem with you is . . ." and ended with "Grow up." He never instructed the girls not to tell Amy anything that went on, but he trusted them to know it wasn't the smoothest move. He savored their present ages, when those issues did not have to be discussed, though it felt like borrowed time, as if he had the pleasure of those two wonderful girls for just a short time before they grew up and into Amys, lovely Amys.

PETER PAN LAND

What Ted Maupin, fellow English teacher, running partner, former roommate, cynic and meddler, called the Bar & Grill. Ted had a stock set of ready lectures. He was 6'3" with linebacker girth, and he seemed particularly fond of backing Iz up against his car in the high school parking lot, standing almost close enough to brush him with his immense black beard.

"Izard, my friend, when you moved into a place of your own, the idea was that you were a single grown man who wanted to fuck single grown women in the privacy of your own home."

"I take women home."

"For the moment, I'll even overlook the paltriness of your conquests in order to stick to my point, which is the following." Ted took a deep breath. "Instead of a love nest, you've set up a fantasyland for pre-adolescents. You make little sandwiches and kiddie cocktails when you should be out making time with voluptuous lovelies."

"Jesus, Ted, I just happen to think my kids are a little more important than my libido."

"I suppose worrying more about whether a bed is properly made than whether there's a woman in it in the morning is normal for a thirty-four-year-old man?"

"And you think with your dick—hardly a qualified judge of normal human behavior," Iz replied.

"This is old, Iz. Let's bury the hatchet." So saying, he turned and walked toward his car.

"Besides, what could be more romantic and/or sexy than the comforts of a luxurious hotel? Beats car sex or meeting roommates in the hall."

"Yeah, yeah, yeah. You're right, I'm wrong, silly old dickbrained Ted. Why don't you just invite me to come over on Sunday and shut up?" He got into his car and slammed the door.

Iz waved. "See you Sunday."

• • •

On the inside of the master-bedroom door hung the only physical reminder of his marriage to Amy, a sign they had stolen on their honeymoon. At two or three in the afternoon of their second day in Acapulco, he insisted that they needed to take at least one walk on the beach. He felt queasy and jittery, not unlike the way he'd felt as a child after eating a dozen candy bars or an entire bag of candy corn. He wanted to be vertical, to stretch, to breathe deeply, expelling lust and fatigue into the fresh beach air. Through tickling and teasing, he carefully cajoled Amy into getting dressed and was just finishing up himself when he heard her laugh. He found her doubled over and pointing at a sign. It contained the standard instructions for what to do in case of fire, yet the designers of the warning had, for some reason, decided to emphasize one phrase in red block letters: IF YOU CANNOT LEAVE THIS ROOM, PLEASE CALL THE FRONT DESK.

Amy fell to her knees and crawled toward the night stand. She picked up the phone. "Help us, help us, please," she said, giggling. He crawled over to her and pushed her back onto the bed. He laughed with her, tears in his eyes. She laughed harder, and at the end of each phrase of her laughter, he heard a grace note of hysteria. She clung to him then, and tiny strings pulled at his skin until he was as tight as she, and he kissed her mouth shut and moved with her. They tugged at their clothes and each other until everything was tangled and damp, and they didn't leave the room for two more days.

Izard ached for the feeling, the dizzy feeling of wanting someone that much.

DECORATOR TIPS FOR ALBINOS

Iz did not spend a lot of time in front of mirrors, because when he did, he often found himself engaged in monologues with refrains of "I do not look like a bunny rabbit, a tall, scared, undernourished bunny rabbit. I am an eccentrically and distinctively virile man."

Thus, personal vanity figured into planning the decor of the Bar & Grill. Wine colors were a must, for at certain times of the day, his irises glowed an odd Burgundylike shade, and he enjoyed accentuating the disquieting effect that had. He contrasted the paper smoothness of his skin with elaborately brocaded upholstery on couches and love seats and the chaise in his bedroom, and with deeply ribbed corduroys on the easy chairs and ottomans. He had the painters drop infinitesimal amounts of red into the white paint for the walls, calculated to highlight the faint flush that so often rose to his cheeks. To offset that narcissism, he purchased towels and sheets in blues and browns so deep and rich that his pallor appeared comic. For all his efforts, almost everyone was too polite to mention his mien. Only Ted, broad, dark, sarcastic and Sicilian, found the subject worth noting.

Iz scrubbed and polished and fretted. If there was one thing he counted on in the women he did bring home, it was a pleased reaction to the carefully wrought luxuries: the extensive collection of compact discs, hidden stereo speakers in each room, track lighting, heat lamps in the bathrooms, inches-deep plush carpet. But his last would-be conquest, Nora, had refused to take The Tour, his spiel concerning ceiling heights, the techniques used on the silk-screen prints in the hallways, the miraculous abilities of the kitchen appliances and the pedigree of the audio-visual equipment that usually helped get him through the initial consternating stages of seduction. After a few moments of going-nowhere banter in the foyer, Nora had put her hand on the doorknob and shot him what he took to be a defiant look.

"You know, Iz," she said, "not everyone wants to be a guest."

He scrubbed between the pale-green tiles of the bathroom shower stall, remembering how he had felt shamed, confused. He saw that he was basically different from women he met. When he was in their homes, it wasn't as a true guest. They assumed so much. "Use my towels, my toothbrush; help yourself in the refrigerator, liquor cabinet." And they believed that to be a complimentary attitude. But a guest felt cared for. Couldn't they see that presenting clean linens, a fresh toothbrush and even scouring mildew were real acts of affection? A woman he loved, or might love sometime in the future, should not have to look at gunk stuck in the grout; the tiles should feel smooth and slick beneath her wet feet.

FORAYS INTO THE GOURMET WORLD

The Bar & Grill wasn't official until Iz bought the grill. Liz and Ellen assured him that they would like nothing more than to live solely on grilled-cheese sandwiches for the rest of their lives, at least the rest of their lives that fell on the weekends they spent with him. They were flexible to a point—after some debate, they decided to allow him to experiment with cheeses other than American. After three months, he sensed that he might be able to sneak other foods onto the menu. He purchased an encyclopedia of creative cookery and found what he was looking for in the A's—appetizers galore!

Liz raised the eyebrow and Ellen's lip curled when he brought out the first plate of his concoctions.

"What are those?" Ellen nearly whined.

"Stuffed-olive canapés," he answered.

"What's a canopy?" Ellen asked.

"*Canapé* is the French word for couch," Liz replied.

"Doesn't look like a couch to me," Ellen said, and both girls looked at him.

"*Canapé* does mean couch, but also appetizer," Iz replied. "It's sort of a little seat for whatever you decide to put on top." They didn't say anything for a moment. Then Ellen laughed.

"A sofa for olives. I like that."

It turned out that there was very little resistance, though each new presentation had to be officially approved. He placed the offering directly between them on the bar. When Liz gave a nod, they reached their hands out simultaneously. Liz had adopted Amy's taste-testing technique, and he watched her closely with some dismay, knowing that Ellen was mirroring every move. Liz held up the meat-stuffed grape leaf to just beyond the tip of her nose. She closed one eye and regarded it with the other—the one sure eye of a jeweler peering through his loupe. Then Liz nodded again and each girl popped the entire appetizer into her mouth. If she liked it, Liz's expression always indicated some surprise that Iz had managed to pull it off again, and he had to remind himself that she wasn't Amy, that she was only twelve. When Ellen liked something, she immediately gobbled five or six, until Liz stopped her by reaching over to wipe her mouth with a cocktail napkin.

One weekend, he got carried away, serving fried-cheese *profiteroles*, egg-and-anchovy mousse, antipasto, *pâté maison* and clam-macadamia puffs. They especially liked the hors d'oeuvres with silly names: pigs in blankets, seafood pretties, angels on horseback, crab dabs, henhouse nomads and quark snacks. Soon they demanded participatory rights; they took to renaming the selections and insisted that Iz type up a menu including the new names. Thus, guacamole became purée de green and barbecued chicken wings were known as hot quackers. The menu had one caveat, printed at the bottom in bold letters: CAVIAR WILL NOT BE SERVED TO NO ONE FOR NO REASON.

• • •

Iz clutched the phone and struggled to fully open his sleep-stuck eyes.

"What's the matter, Amy?"

"For starters, Ellen's ophthalmologist says that besides being perilously nearsighted, she's also got astigmatism."

Izard propped himself up on an elbow. "I thought the school nurse or somebody was supposed to catch stuff like that in the first grade."

"Seems Ellen knew something was wrong, so she stood behind the kids with glasses and memorized what they said."

"She cheated on a vision test?" he said, chortling. "That's rich."

"I'm glad you think it's funny that your youngest daughter could have been flattened in traffic . . ." she trailed off. "Anyway, what it really is is one more unexpected expensive expense."

"I'll take care of it, Amy."

"Oh, that's right, Mr. Wizard comes to the rescue—he leaps tall buildings with checkbook in hand."

Izard pulled the covers over his head and braced himself.

"Goddamn you." Three solid raps echoed in Iz's head as she emphasized each syllable by beating the receiver against something hard. He guessed a headboard.

"Are you still there?" Amy asked, her voice sounding drained.

"Yes, Amy, I'm still here."

"It's my *job*, too. My boss is a total ass, besides the fact that he refuses to pay me what I'm worth."

So that was the real problem. But what did she want from him? He wanted to make it better, but how? Every neuron in his brain shrieked, Don't say it, don't say it, don't—— "Listen, Amy, if you hate the job that much, why don't you quit? I'd be happy to help you out financially until——"

"You think everything is that easy? You know what you are, Izard? A goddamned child. In the real world, people *earn* their living—you can't just walk away from your lemonade stand when it stops being fun." She sighed. "When are you going to——" Her voice broke, and then it came, a crash and a muffled metallic ring.

"Please send me the bill," Izard said to the dead line.

Izard dialed Ted's number and began uttering apologies before Ted had a chance to speak.

"Never mind, dearest pal, *I* don't need my beauty sleep. However, I assume there's a reason for this call?"

"Amy," Izard answered. "Amy called."

"Let me think; what brand of fatherly malfeasance is it this month?

Scuffed patent-leather shoes? More overly extravagant gifts? She's not still mad about the fighting kites, is she?"

"No. This call was a report of financial fiasco." He paused. "I think she's really distraught, though."

"Iz, when you've got an apocalyptic mentality, a dollar bill lost in a change machine is a disaster. Don't let it get to you."

Izard laughed.

"Can we go back to sleep now?" Ted asked.

UNCLE AWFUL BEARING GIFTS

A typical Ted-style surprise visit: He arrived at the door holding a carton. Liz forgot herself for a moment and joined Ellen in hollering "Uncle Awful, Uncle Awful" and trying to snatch the carton away from him.

Ted retained his hold on the box.

"This is for your father, the fair-haired innkeeper." He handed the box to Iz. "In this box, you will find a marvel of modern technology, an appliance that will revolutionize the way you do business."

After cutting through layer after layer of packing tape with a steak knife, accompanied by a chorus of "Hurry, Daddy, hurry," Iz finally got the box open. He saw only a glint of stainless steel before Ted snatched the box from his hands.

"Let me show." Ted removed the contraption and flung the box aside. "This, my friends, is *the* absolute finest automatic ice crusher. Not only is it fast as a whip but you get three choices of how fine to crush the ice."

An hour later, after every cube in the house was crushed, Ellen finally broke down.

"Didn't you bring *us* anything?"

"You still owe me five dollars from pool last time," Liz said.

"All in due time. I can't believe either of you could think for one moment that I'd forget about you." Ted pulled two small boxes from his jacket pocket. "Not that either of you greedy Guses deserves these."

Liz and Ellen grabbed the boxes, which were quickly found to contain very special plastic swizzle sticks—pink elephants on Liz's set and orange giraffes on Ellen's.

"We need to have mar-teenies so we can use them," Ellen announced.

"I haven't forgotten the five dollars," Liz told Ted.

"Double or nothing?"

Liz did the eyebrow thing. "It's your money."

Ted snorted and Iz winced. He played bartender, mixing doubles for himself and Ted, Squirt and lime juice for the girls.

"Don't forget the olives," Ellen reminded him. He grimaced but dropped three olives into each glass. Then they all migrated, drinks in hand, to the Billiard Room.

"Tracy Jacobs has a Bumper Pool table in her basement, but it's tiny and it's got cat fur all over it," Ellen said as she dragged a step stool over to the table to make her shot. Iz choked back a laugh. Her next play was without benefit of the stool. Although her accuracy on long shots was erratic, Iz guessed glasses would take care of that problem. He guessed that with her steady aim and nice smooth stroke, she would grow into a dependable player—no flash—but rarely missing routine shots. On her shot, Liz stalked to the table, abruptly leaning over to attempt a difficult carom. He watched the cue ball hit the three into the four ball, which sank soundly in the center of a side pocket. When Liz was hot, like today, she beat Ted for real; when she was cold, Iz had seen Ted purposely miss in an attempt to head off a snit.

Liz banked the eight ball into a corner. "You lose, Uncle Awful. Put down your drink and rack 'em up."

"I need a refill," Ellen announced.

"Me, too," said Ted and Liz. Iz obliged and went to fetch a second round. When he returned, Liz looked up from her shot.

"You're the best daddy in the whole wide world," she announced.

"You're the best daddy in the whole wide world," Ellen echoed.

When Ted repeated it for the third time, Iz felt like crying.

When Ted was $40 down, he announced that there was a television special on bears he couldn't miss.

"Didn't we just see a show on bears?" Ellen complained.

"That was polar bears—this one's on black bears," Ted said.

"Let's watch MTV in the other room," Liz suggested to Ellen. As they headed down the hall to the Game Room, Iz heard Liz musing over how to spend her winnings.

Iz switched on the set and stirred a pitcher of martinis.

"C'mon, friend, lighten up," Ted said.

Iz smiled. "I'm trying."

"You know, the only thing better than a good bear story is a good woman," said Ted.

"Smooth transition, guy." Iz heard fake heartiness in his voice.

"I thought so. Anyway, I've sort of been seeing someone."

"That's a bit vague. . . . Are we talking a new squeeze or a potential Aunt Evil for my daughters?"

"I think I'd say the latter."

"Oh." Iz took a big gulp of martini.

"Don't go sad on me again, all right? Besides, she's got this great friend."

Iz laughed. "I *knew* there had to be a punch line."

"I'm serious. She's a zookeeper, Iz. A perfect match for a strange white beast like you."

"Ho, ho, ho. I've never let you set me up before and I'm not——"

"Not even if she lets you wear the duck mask?"

Iz laughed again. "Absolutely not."

NEON AND MARTINIS AND THE CONSCIENCE
OF THE SINGLE FATHER

When Iz woke up, he immediately knew he would look like a rabbit in every mirror in the place, and even from his bed, the Hotel-Motel felt desolate. That usually heralded the onset of a weekend alone, but sometimes it happened on days like today, when Liz and Ellen were fast asleep in the thick, curtained dark of the guest rooms, floating far away in little-girl dreams.

At that point, it was important not to look at a clock. He kept his eyes to the front and headed directly to the bar, so there was no reason to suspect that it was not a proper hour to begin drinking. He switched the coffee maker on and pulled a beer from the refrigerator. For not the first time, he wondered what Ellen and Liz would think of him when they grew up to realize how much booze three double martinis really was. Maybe he would have gotten his act together by then, or at least changed his act, so it wouldn't matter. They could all have a laugh at that old guy—the silly, half-drunk, dandy divorcee who collected neon beer signs. Yet that seemed unfair to the Hotel-Motel Bar & Grill, a betrayal of his vision. He wanted his daughters to know what genuine fun was, so that no matter what forces pulled at them in years to come, there would be a solid, happy memory of their threesome.

The entire project could also be seen as at least marginally educational. Not just drink making, either. They knew how to tip, how to give change, how to be polite, how to roll egg rolls and bake pretzels. They knew something of style and a lot about bears and whales and lions and rain forests and football. They would never be hustled at pool or cards, though they might be tempted to do the hustling, and they were probably hopelessly spoiled forever. Nothing wrong with that; Iz wanted them to have high expectations.

God, he'd been over this a hundred times with Ted. They had both lost patience with the part of him that wouldn't shut up about it.

"Christ," said Ted, "you'd think it was a federal crime to want to be loved."

THE WIFE AND THE BARFLY

When the doorbell rang on Sunday afternoon, Iz was expecting Ted, so he was surprised when he opened the door to a small woman with big flaming-red hair. She stuck out her hand.

"I'm Irene, the zookeeper. Ted told me to meet him here."

"I'm Izard. Come on in," he stammered. "Did Ted say he'd be here?"

"He's not here?"

"No, not yet, but I am expecting him. I mean, Ted's a lot of things, but dependable, I mean undependable, isn't one of them."

Irene laughed, but Izard saw her shrink up in front of him, and he responded with a sudden impulse to protect this woman that superseded his desire to strangle Ted. He took her arm.

"Let me show you around."

She followed his lead silently through the first part of The Tour but took her arm back in the Billiard Room.

"Let me look for a minute." She circumnavigated the room, ran her fingers over the green felt of the table and rolled the seven ball into the eight ball so it made a nice smack.

"Darts is my game, really. I've always thought I needed to be three or four inches taller to play pool really well."

Iz pointed toward the dartboard. "Would you like to give it a try?"

When she took the darts in her hand, he noticed that her fingernails were painted an orange-red that matched her hair. She threw a dart, but it wavered, missing the board and landing in the cork beneath it.

"I'm nervous," she said, and she wrapped her arms around her shoulders and squeezed. Iz restrained a shiver. "I've got to pull myself together," she added. Her second dart hit the heart of the bull's-eye. "Better," she said, taking his arm. "Can I see the rest?"

When they reached the TV Room, she turned to him and smiled.

"This really *is* PeterPanLand, isn't it?"

Iz nodded. PeterPanLand—he wanted her to repeat it again and again, running the words together as she just had. For a moment, he imagined her petite body softly enveloped between his bed sheets, her hair fanned out brilliantly on a navy-blue pillowcase.

"Daddy?"

Iz turned to the doorway, where Liz and Ellen stood watching them. Oh, that's just wonderful, he thought. Caught acting like some demented pubescent, thinking wild thoughts about the skin of a total stranger. Four gray eyes remained trained on his face.

"Sorry, Liz, Ellen. This is Irene. She's a friend of Uncle Awful's."

Their eyes softened slightly at the mention of Ted.

"Only Uncle Awful isn't here yet, so we have to entertain Irene for a while. Okay?" His voice sounded ridiculously smarmy. "Make yourself comfortable. Can we get you anything to drink? You name it, we've got it." Shut up, shut up, you're making it worse, he thought.

Irene looked directly at Liz and Ellen. "Does anybody around here know how to make a mai tai?"

Iz watched them nod in unison and head behind the bar. Iz felt himself about to panic; he grabbed some quarters from the tip jar and headed for the jukebox. "Any requests?" he asked.

"Bon Jovi," Liz said.

"The fast one," Ellen added.

Iz looked at Irene. "Something festive," she said.

Right, he thought, that's definitely what's needed. "Ellen, would you fix me a martini while you're at it?"

He was afraid to look at Irene, even with the martini. He tried to concentrate on what she was saying about the zoo, but whenever he focused on her face, he stared, and his brain took stock without permission—white skin, almost as pale as his, but flecked with gold-dust freckles, and the hair a mesmerizing red, more hair than could possibly be on one head, yet there it was, soft and bouncing slightly as she spoke. He found it difficult to speak; his lips felt swollen and he pressed the cold rim of his glass against them. He strained to reenter the conversation. Something about the gestation period of elephants.

"The door was wide open." Ted was standing in the room. A woman with short black hair and a long white skirt leaned against his arm. Her shoes were in her hand, along with an unlit cigarette, and her feet and the bottom of her skirt were splashed with mud.

"Hello, Liz, Iz, Ellen, Irene." He paused to wink at Iz. "This is Aunt Evil, but I'm afraid she's not at her best today. We've just finished up the Invisible Man Run."

"I thought you liked this woman, Ted," Iz said.

"What's the Invisible Man Run?" Irene asked.

Ted grinned boozily. "What it is is getting into a cab and heading for the sleaziest bar we know of in Southern California—The Lone Eagle—and having a drink, traditionally a straight shot of tequila. Then you go from tavern to tavern, guzzling a drink at each establishment as you methodically and drunkenly work your way home. What's our record, Iz?"

"I don't remember," he answered too quickly.

"C'mon, Daddy. We know you know," Liz said.

"Something like three hours and forty-five minutes," Iz answered reluctantly.

"Yikes. How many bars are we talking about?" Irene asked.

"Twenty-three. Am I invisible yet?" This was the first and last thing Aunt Evil said. Ted led her to a chair and gave her a light.

"Yikes," Irene repeated, "I think I'll wait to sign up until I see if she survives."

"I think we need some food," Ellen said, and Iz felt incredibly happy as she and Liz ran off to the kitchen. Perfect hostesses in the face of this nonsense. Once they were gone, Ted and Irene watched Iz. Ted grinned madly and Irene's clear green gaze made his lips tingle again, so he distracted himself with a demonstration of the new ice crusher. Half the cubes in the freezer were pulverized before Liz and Ellen returned with pizza rolls and clam dip.

"We weren't expecting a party," Liz said apologetically, though she looked pleased, gray eyes sparkling.

"Neither was I," Iz said in Ted's direction.

"But it certainly is festive," Irene said and smiled.

"Festive," Ted repeated, and everyone laughed.

"The door was wide open, so I didn't ring."

Iz's shoulders tensed; he knew without looking that the voice belonged to Amy. Who invited her? He wanted to giggle—no—he had to deal with this situation thoughtfully, if not entirely soberly.

"Amy, what are you doing here?" He decided to stall. Amy didn't look good, sort of crushed. Her spiky short hair drooped, waiflike, and her lips were taut, as though she hadn't laughed in a long time. She even slouched. But her gray eyes were clear and stern as she snapped her gaze almost audibly from her daughters to Ted to the disheveled Aunt Evil to Iz and back to Liz and Ellen.

"Amy must've heard we were having a party," Ted said jovially.

"Amy." Izard shot a warning shot to Ted. "You're certainly welcome here."

"May I speak with you privately?" Amy's voice was low. Iz wobbled to his feet and followed her to the kitchen.

"I didn't plan on barging in," she began.

"Well, I must say your unprecedented appearance *is* along rather unexpected lines."

"Are you drunk?" Her voice raised half an octave.

"You were about to explain your barge, were you not?"

"As if *I* should do the explaining." She looked over her shoulder at the door to the living room. "Shit, Iz, this is just too much. This isn't a home, this is a playpen."

"You haven't even seen it."

"It's gross." Now her volume increased. "I don't need to see any more."

He set his glass down on the countertop and reached his hands toward her shoulders. "But, Amy, it's all in fun."

She shrugged his hands away. "Oh, sure, booze and food and games and a bunch of goddamned drunks." Her voice was loud enough to be heard in the other room.

"Be reasonable. Please."

"What I just walked in on is reasonable? Besides, I don't feel reasonable—I got laid off."

"Maybe it's for the best. I mean, you were miserable——"

"Oh, shut up."

Iz was afraid to say anything more. He knew he wasn't thinking clearly about anything except wanting Amy to relax, wanting to be back with the others. Amy was silent for a moment as her eyes flicked over the gleaming appliances, the hand-painted countertop tiles, the monolithic side-by-side refrigerator-freezer.

She sighed. "I just don't think I have the strength to look for a job right now."

"Why don't you take a little time off first?" Izard hurried to the sink and rummaged in a drawer beside it.

"You want me to take a vacation? I lose my job and I'm supposed to go lallygag on a beach somewhere?" Her voice rose again.

Izard pulled his checkbook from the drawer with a flourish.

"Why don't you at least think about it? I'll write you a check and——"

"No!"

His hand froze.

"What does it take to——" She took a step forward and grabbed his martini from the countertop and hurled it toward the sink. Beside him, the heavy glass exploded against the stainless steel; Iz watched a lone olive bounce off the edge and land on the floor.

"Amy, I'm sorry. We'll work it out later, okay? Please?"

"No. It's not okay. Not okay at all." She started to cry.

Izard fled, flinging himself out the swinging door in time to see Irene flee toward the master-bedroom suite. Liz and Ellen and Ted panned right as he pursued. The bathroom door clicked shut. He approached it, taking a deep breath. As he knocked, he heard the sound of china against brick coming from the kitchen.

"Are you okay?" he asked.

"I'm sorry," Irene said. "I'll come out in a while."

He heard two more splintering crashes. Too loud to be anything but dinner plates. He tried to organize his thoughts. "Is there anything I can do?"

"Not really. I guess it's just nerves. Surly lions I do fine with, but——"

"Situations like this?"

She laughed. "I'm not sure I knew situations like this really existed. I mean——" This time the crashing was sustained, and Iz pictured the slivered remains of a dozen champagne goblets scattered across the kitchen floor.

"Hey, stay in there as long as you want," Iz said.

"Thank you. I'll be fine. Go ahead and check on——"

"I should, thanks, but I'll be back. You hang on." He turned away.

"Izard?"

"Yes?"

"Great bathroom."

When Izard stepped into the living room, six gray eyes pounced on him, waiting for him to do something. Ted seemed absorbed in fiddling with the jukebox. Izard noted with relief that Amy's hands were empty, resting lightly on the back of a chair. Standing there with her shoulders sagging slightly, she would have again appeared helpless if her eyes had relented.

Suddenly, Supertramp burst from the speakers. "Even in the quietest moments . . ."

"Very funny, Ted."

"I thought so."

"You would," Amy said.

Izard hoped sarcasm was a good sign; perhaps she was sapped of her anger.

"Down, girl," Ted replied as he bent over Aunt Evil.

"What's funny?" Ellen asked. Iz saw Ted tenderly grasp her hand. He thought of Irene lighting up his pale-yellow bathroom. He wondered if she was sitting on the toilet seat, if her head was bowed. He imagined her hair brushing the checkerboard tiles.

"Maybe we should go, Mom," Liz said. Iz noted with satisfaction that her eyebrow was cocked, but in Amy's direction, not his.

"I think not. Like your Uncle Ted said, this is some party," Amy said.

"Now can we play spades?" Ellen asked.

Aunt Evil moaned.

"Maybe *we* should be leaving," Ted said. "He who fights and runs away, etc."

"No," Iz said quickly, "I think playing cards is a dandy idea. Why don't Liz and I get everybody a drink? Yes?"

This time everyone's gaze turned to Amy. Her eyes gleamed for a second.

"Mom?" said Liz. Amy looked down. Did her eyes soften? Still, she didn't speak.

"We're having a special on frozen margaritas due to a surplus of crushed ice," Ted offered.

Amy looked up. "Thank you, Ted. I think I will have one. Strawberry."

Ted moved Aunt Evil to the couch and Liz got a blanket to cover her. After some debate, Ellen conceded to playing rummy rather than spades if she got to keep score, and even Amy finally agreed to play if she didn't have to sit on the floor.

Between turns, Amy swirled her drink dangerously close to the rim of her glass and she snapped down her discards, but she kept getting good cards and Iz saw that she was pleased. Ted hummed. Izard prayed to the card gods and thought he felt Liz and Ellen praying, too.

"I win," announced Amy. Liz grabbed Amy's almost-empty glass without asking and headed for the bar.

"I demand a rematch," Ted said.

"Deal me out of this one," Iz said. He got up from the table and took four beers from the refrigerator and a bottle opener from the drawer.

"Where are you——" Liz cut her sister off with the whirl of the blender. Iz headed toward his room. Amy shot him a malevolent glance, then turned to Ted.

"Why is it that men think it's attractive to wear their shirts unbuttoned to the middle of their chests?" she asked as Ellen began dealing. Iz didn't hear Ted's response.

He tried to walk steadily, tried to reassure himself. So they would have their first date through a bathroom door. So what? He sat down next to the door and tapped it lightly with a bottle. "Do you want a beer?"

Her voice came from just the other side of the door. "Is it safe to open the door?"

"Relatively. Definitely safe to crack it." He snapped the top off one beer and lined the other bottles up against the wall. From the living room, he heard a murmur suggesting relative peace. He smiled.

"Are we talking cold beer?" she asked.

"Cold. Very cold." Iz watched the knob turn slowly. "So, tell me, Irene, what made you decide to become a zookeeper?"

The Madison Heights Syndrome

by A.M. WELLMAN
1989

There's this tape I have that I watch from the eleven-o'clock news, Bernie Smilovitz doing the sports, talking about the Tigers down at the stadium tonight taking on the White Sox. "We have highlights," he begins, and there's Cliff Spab standing on the pitcher's mound, about to toss out the first ball to Mike Heath, standing by the backstop. "Now watch this," Bernie says as all of a sudden Spab takes off for center field, the camera catching him from behind as he runs with that ball, focusing on the SPAB 15 on his back, a real jersey the Tigers made for him, and when he gets out in center field, he rears back and flings that ball, just pegs that motherfucker into the upper-deck bleachers. The crowd goes nuts.

I remember walking back to the infield, across the greenest grass in the tricounty area, and it felt good. Watching it makes me feel good.

• • •

But I'm not in Tiger Stadium now, I'm in Colwood, Michigan, living in the R Street Theater. It's a pretty cool building. They don't show movies here anymore, though the place is intact. The seats are still all here, facing a big blank white screen.

My room is on the second floor, above the lobby, across the hall from the projection booth. The owner, Streeter, promises to show me how to run the projector someday. He thinks he has some old stag movies, smokers, sitting around somewhere.

The window in my room overlooks the theater marquee. At night, I turn on the blank sign from a nearby switch and lie down and watch the lights move across the ceiling.

I don't leave the building. Streeter brings me food. The other day, he brought me a newspaper. The *Detroit Free Press*. Headline, page 1A: "CLIFF SPAB STILL MISSING." I barely glance at it before going to the sports. As I do, I look up at the old man and he's grinning at me. "What the fuck," I mutter. "I ain't missing, I'm right here."

• • •

I don't know what's going on anymore. There's nothing wrong with that. That was cool once, back when my life was simple. Working at the Oakland Mall Burger King, I spent my days waking up, punching in, slopping up, punching out. I didn't give a shit, and on a job like that, that's the only way to go.

Then came the weekend and me and my buddy Joe Dice would go out cruising the northeast suburbs of Detroit in my green '73 El Camino. We'd be out there, driving around, picking up chicks, cranking up the radio, laughing our asses off.

Working and cruising. Like I said, things were simple.

And that's what we were doing, Joe and I, the night of the now-famous hostage crisis in Madison Heights, Michigan. Friday night, the two of us punched out at the Home of the Whopper and hit the streets. Two A.M. or so, we figured on getting some beer and heading home, so we stopped in that 7-Eleven on John R between 13 and 14 Mile.

Inside, they got us. Stuck guns to our heads, handcuffed us. It would be thirty-six days before I left that goddamn store.

• • •

I know Streeter's daughter, that's how I know Streeter. Stacy Streeter. Nice chick, good-looking, she's got a decent apartment, makes some decent money; she's a few years older than me, no big deal.

Let's just say we met at a party.

Stacy, having seen the whole thing on TV, knows more about the Madison Heights hostage crisis than I do, but I can't get her to believe that. I haven't seen her since I got out, but I've talked to her on the phone.

"What happened in there?" she asks me.

"Nothin'," I say.

"Bullshit," she tells me.

Well, what the fuck am I supposed to tell her? That I drank a lot of beer, ate a lot of burritos? "What happened in there?" she asks. I think I went nuts in there, that's what I think happened, but I'm not sure.

• • •

Now Streeter's bringing me a copy of *Time* magazine with my picture on the cover. Again. Not a photo this time—but a goddamn *painting*. "WHERE IS CLIFF SPAB?" the cover reads.

I read the article about America's newest folk hero and his cult following; I read their analysis of the Spab phenomenon. They say I'm "indicative of the growing dark side of the Pepsi Generation." Gee, I can't wait to show this to my grandkids.

I'm watching TV with Streeter now and a commercial for *Time* comes on. When they flash an 800 number, I dial it.

"Yo," I say. "Cliff Spab here. Tell your bosses they can have an exclusive interview for one million dollars cash."

The operator hangs up. Streeter snickers at me as I stare at the receiver. I sort of shrug, hang up, get myself another beer.

• • •

In the 7-Eleven, they had a video camera, these guys with the panty hose on their heads. Every day or so (though none of us knew what day it was or even if it was day or night), they'd come in with that camera and we'd sit there and say something. I don't know how, but the cops would get the tape and then they'd show it on the news.

Eventually, Joe and I and Wendy Pfister, this Hazel Park chick stuck in there with us, started cutting loose for the camera. Joe would reel off a couple of dirty jokes. Wendy might talk about how wonderful this whole experience was, how she was finally at peace with herself. I did lots of weird shit, but the tape that caught everyone's fancy was when I dared the panty-hose guys to blow my head off.

I don't know why I did it, I just did. Look at that tape. There I am in that now-famous black Doors T-shirt, my left wrist handcuffed to the metal folding funeral-home chair I'm sitting in, screaming into the camera, "What's the matter, you chickenshit or something? Come on, ya fuckin' pussy, kill me, I fuckin' dare ya. Blow my fuckin' brains out, come on. You chickenshit or something?"

That made the evening news, of course, and when one of the panty-hose guys hit me, hard, in the mouth and I'm spitting blood all over the place, it didn't hurt my standing in the public eye.

Streeter tells me those black Doors T-shirts are selling out all around the country.

• • •

At the beginning, there were five hostages, including myself. I got to know them all pretty good, I guess, which isn't to say I liked all of them. Kim Martin was a bitch. Not just a bitch, either, but a whiny bitch. She was the one working at the store the night the panty-hose guys showed up. Oh, Christ, she drove everyone nuts; she just didn't know how to shut up. She didn't like the guns or the cigarette smoke or the language or the beer or the handcuffs, and she didn't deserve to be in here, because she was a woman and she had a husband and a kid and on and on . . .

We must've been in there a week when a couple of the panty-hose guys came into the little office where the five of us were sitting in a circle and announced that they were going to let a hostage go. We got to pick who it was, we were going to vote on it; we just couldn't vote for ourselves.

Kim Martin received four votes, I got one.

So one of the panty-hose guys all of a sudden whips out his gun and blows Kim Martin's brains out. Shot her three times in the left ear. Just like that.

They brought the video camera in then and took some pictures of her body, then they stuck her in the freezer.

• • •

Another guy, this rich old white guy named Milton Morris, lasted about another week. Oh, he was cool enough, for an old guy. Smoked three free packs of Vantage 100s a day and drank his fair share of beer.

Then, one day, Morris is just sitting there with us, just hanging out, and he drops dead. Natural causes, a heart attack, probably. The panty-hose guys went nuts, whining about how it wasn't their fault, and finally they figured, Fuck it, and shot him like they did Kim Martin, three bullets in his now-dead brain. Dragged in the video camera, took some pictures, then stuck him in the freezer.

That left three of us.

• • •

Stacy calls me, seeing if I'm doing okay, telling me she's coming up to Colwood next weekend. Asking me when I plan to return to the public eye.

I'm happy where I am, I tell her. Someday, sure, I'll put the black T-shirt back on and do the Cliff Spab bit for everybody, but not now.

When?

Never?

I tell Stacy about how when I went home after I got out, when the cops were through with me, they drove me to my house and everybody on the fucking block is there and all the trees got these fucking yellow ribbons all over the fucking place. And at my house, the mayor of Madison Heights is standing there on the front porch, waiting to give me the key to the city or some bullshit. I say to him, "Who the fuck are you?" and then blow him off, go into the house. Go into my room, put on a Stones album I've been craving for the past month, lie down on my bed, and then my old man comes storming into my room and he's pissed.

He's going on about what the hell am I doing in here, don't you know that's the goddamn mayor standing out there, get your ass out there and hold a press conference, now.

I'm, like, Hey, guy, fuck you. I don't need this shit. If I don't go out there, what're ya gonna do? Send me to my room without dessert? Why the fuck don'tcha just stick a gun to my head, handcuff me to a chair? That'll accomplish a hell of a lot.

The motherfucker hit me. In the mouth, same as those panty-hose guys did. I started spitting blood like I did that time.

My old man just left the room after that, just left me alone.

The neighbors went home, but those fucking reporters stayed in the street, waiting for me to come out.

• • •

I saw Wendy Pfister being interviewed by Barbara Walters last night. Now, Wendy Pfister is, like, *the* all-American girl, an extremely courageous young woman, role model for teenagers everywhere. It also helps that she's willing to talk to the media, unlike some ex-hostages I could name.

Oh, Jesus, yeah, it's the scam of the century, Wendy sitting there looking good, really good, sitting across from Barbara Walters in a comfortable chair, legs crossed, hair fluffed, smiling behind a $1,000 make-up job or whatever, talking about God, country; telling kids to "Just say no," with a perfectly straight face. Acting so fucking wholesome you just wanted to puke.

Streeter's watching this with me, wondering why I'm laughing. "Look at her," I'm saying, "look at her. Do you realize this chick listens to Zeppelin albums, that she put away two packs of menthols a day, drank at least as much as I did?"

"No," Streeter says.

"Do you know what she had in her purse when she walked into that store? Huh? I'll tell ya what she had; she had two ounces of marijuana in her purse. Two fucking ounces. I'm talking teenager on drugs and she's probably gonna get a medal next week from Nancy fucking Reagan or something."

"What's the point?" Streeter asks.

"I'm sayin' I heard America's new sweetheart use the F word, that's what I'm sayin'."

"I know what you're saying, Spab. I'm asking you what's the point?"

"Who gives a shit what the point is?" I say.

• • •

So I stayed in my house for a week or so, my parents pissed at me, all those reporters outside, and then I went to that ball game. My brother took me. Scott Spab. He set the whole thing up with the Tigers, got them to make me that jersey.

He was cool about keeping me away from the reporters. Hustling my ass out the stadium before the game started, before anybody could catch us. The reporters really pissed him off when I was in that store, the way they kept on sticking cameras in his face, expecting him to cry for them or something.

After that game, I stayed in his apartment for a few days. He lives in Center Line Gardens, in Warren, which is cool because the whole complex is private property and the cops would keep the reporters at the gate if they ever found out I was there. Which they did—my parents told them.

But eventually, I got sick of it, so one night, I got into the trunk of my brother's car and he took me out to the Somerset Mall parking lot in Troy, where Stacy had left a car for me. The keys were in the ignition and I shagged ass getting to the R Street Theater, driving up to Colwood.

My brother went back to his apartment, found I wasn't there and called the cops.

• • •

Stacy's with me now, here in Colwood for the weekend, and we're watching *Nightline*, a special show on Cliff Spab. First up was FBI special agent Shawn Parsley, the Fed who took my statement at the Madison Heights police station after I got out of captivity "We are treating Cliff Spab's disappearance with the utmost seriousness," he said. "Mr. Spab is a disturbed young man in desperate need of help."

The prick.

Then my parents came on and I'm thinking, What is this, *This Is Your Life* or something? They gonna have on my second-grade teacher or some shit? So my folks are saying how much they miss me, mentioned as how they thought I needed help and how all is forgiven, as if this is anybody's business to show on network TV and all.

Then they brought on some shrink who talked about the Stockholm syndrome, how I was probably fucked up because I missed my old panty-hose buddies from the store. Then he started on about stress. And then he explained the Spab phenomenon, how kids look up to me because I got to live out my fantasies of youth and I represent something to this country and whatever. Huh?

And then, oh, Jesus, Wendy Pfister came on. Oh, God, she was looking good. Every time I see her, I think. Goddamn, she's looking good. Smiling at the fucking camera, oh, God, she looked good.

"Spab, if you're watching this," she says, and I blink, surprised—I've been watching her, not listening to her—"call me. Your brother has my number. Call me, we'll talk and I won't tell anybody we did."

Oh, God, oh, God, oh, God, and at that point, Stacy and I go down to my room and I turn on the lights of the marquee and when we finish, I fall asleep watching those lights move across the ceiling.

• • •

Do I trust her? I know Wendy Pfister, I was in that store with her for thirty-six days and I see her on TV now and think, that's not Wendy

Pfister, that's just a character on TV, just like Archie Bunker or Lucy Ricardo or Hawkeye Pierce. But then, what about this enigmatic, larger-than-life guy from Madison Heights who made those wacky videos in captivity, tossed a baseball into the bleachers? Now I worry; What if that asshole really is the real me?

I'm starting to feel like I'm in over my head. Suppose I did come out of hiding. Would I be able to keep the scam working? Could I act like the mythical figure I've become? Do I want to?

Stacy knows me. She says the Cliff Spab they know is the real me. So does Streeter. He reminds me about the time I called *Time* magazine, how that's just the sort of thing Cliff Spab would do.

Stacy talks about the FREE CLIFF SPAB NOW T-shirts and the SPAB RULES bumper stickers, shows me a copy of my first *Time* cover, me in that black Doors T-shirt daring a panty-hose guy to blow my head off.

"Enjoy it while it lasts," she tells me, "and, for Christ's sake, at least make a few bucks out of it.

"I can't support you forever," Stacy says, "even if I can afford it."

I'm nuts, Stacy. I can't take this shit. Oh, God, anonymity would be so sweet right about now.

• • •

But now Stacy's pissed at me. There's a story in the *National Enquirer*, a chick saying she fucked me in the ladies' room at the Ram's Horn in Warren, on Dequindre between 12 and 13 Mile. This story is, fortunately or unfortunately—take your pick—true. After Tiger Stadium, my brother and I stopped by the Ram's Horn because it didn't look too busy. It wasn't; the waitresses, three of them, were standing around doing nothing. They recognized me, went nuts, asked for autographs, and then I took one of them back to the ladies' room and she yanked up her brown polyester skirt and we had two and a half minutes of decent sex. Something like that, I was pretty drunk. What the fuck do I know?

So now this chick's made more money off my name than I have.

Stacy's left Colwood, told me to fuck off. Streeter's being cool, but I think he's pissed at me, too, fucking around on his daughter like that. So I guess I can't stay in Colwood much longer. I don't want to, either. I need to find a new hiding space.

• • •

Joe's the one guy I need to hang out with for a few hours. The two of us need to go out cruising all night. Need to cruise the northeast side until the Camino's out of gas, need to find a chick or two and feed lines of bullshit out into the world in general.

That's the way it was, back when things were simple. We owned that goddamn city, Joe and I. Three A.M., all alone cruising Dequindre or Van Dyke or some shit, passing beneath those yellow streetlights, we owned, *owned* that fucking town. It was ours for the taking.

Those nights were the best. Madison Heights was the greatest city in the world to me. I could feel it in the night, that charge in the air. Cruising was the only thing I ever wanted to do, cruising all night long.

I say that and I turn to Joe, sitting in the passenger seat of the Camino, and he gives me that goofy Joe Dice grin and says, "Hey, guy, fuckin' you know it."

• • •

I call Wendy late one night, waking her up. I'm drunk, again, and as it turns out, so is she. Her mother went to bed early, leaving Wendy to scarf her vodka.

"You're fulla shit," I tell her.

"Yeah, right," she says. "Look who's talking. Mr. I Am God, Fuck All of You."

"That shit wasn't my idea."

"Yeah, right. You think this was my brainstorm, this Miss Apple Pie bullshit? Christ, my mother's the one behind the whole thing, running my life, picking out my clothes, telling people I'll be on their sorry-ass TV show."

"That's too bad. How much they pay you for that Pepsi ad? Or was it Coke?"

Wendy sighed. "Two hundred and thirty-six thousand dollars, plus some change every time they show it."

"Sounds cool. Come on up and visit me. You can buy the beer."

"I'd like to."

"Of course, I'll need a note from your mother."

"No problem. I got my own car now. I'll do what the fuck I want. I think you got the right idea, Spab, disappearing like that. Don't these people realize I just want to forget the whole thing, the whole fucking thing?"

I say nothing. Jesus Christ, I think, she's hit it right on the head.

"Spab?"

"Sorry, Wendy."

"No problem."

"I've finally figured it out," I say, "you know? I mean, Jesus, Wendy, why didn't I think of it before? All I want to do more than anything else is forget the whole thing. It all goes back to being in that goddamn store. I keep dwelling on it; I'm sitting here whining about everything else and, Jesus, Wendy, it's driving me nuts . . ."

"You remember that shrink on TV the other night?" she asks.

"On *Nightline*?"

"Yeah," she sighs. "Spab, he got it all wrong when he started going on about the Stockholm syndrome. That's bullshit. What we're talking about here is something new, a disease only two people in the world have, and do you know what it's called?"

"What?"

"It's called the Madison Heights syndrome. The only people who caught it were the people in that store. That means you and me, Spab."

"Oh, Christ, Wendy."

"And that asshole shrink, he'll never know what the Madison Heights syndrome is, because he wasn't in that store with us, and if you weren't in that store——"

"You can shut the fuck up," I say.

"Right," Wendy says.

Nobody says anything. "I want to see you, Wendy," I say finally. "I gotta see you."

"If I come see you, they'll follow me and find you, wherever you are."

"Let 'em," I say, and I realize that the scam, the fame, the hiding, none of it matters.

I tell her how to get to R Street, say good night, hang up, open another beer. Put on my black Doors T-shirt and cue up that videotape of me at Tiger Stadium. It feels good. Oh, Jesus.

• • •

On the thirty-sixth day, the beer ran out.

Joe, Wendy and I, when we were in that store, if we weren't drunk, we were stoned, and often we were both. And then the beer ran out and we had to come up with a plan.

On the thirty-fifth day, Wendy had asked one of the panty-hose guys one more time when we were going to get out of there, and he said, again, "When there is total nuclear disarmament in the world."

So we weren't the only lunatics in that store.

So the three of us came up with a plan. And it worked. Sort of.

They came in with that video camera on the thirty-sixth day. Wendy's sitting there across from me and she's talking to the camera and all of a sudden, I stand up, dragging my chair from my wrist, I turn around and pull down my pants. Just yanked 'em down. Yeah, guy, there they are, motherfuckers, both cheeks of the famous, hairy Spab ass. In your face. Kiss 'em, why don'tcha?

The panty-hose guys go nuts, Wendy's talking, my ass is hanging out, the camera guy doesn't know where to point the camera, all this out-of-control shit going on, and nobody's paying attention to Joe, and then Joe picks up his chair, chained to his wrist, picks it up and brings it down on the head of one of the panty-hose guys. The panty-hose guy goes down, Joe Dice grabs his gun. The panty-hose guy starts bleeding, blood seeping through the nylon covering his head.

Now the other panty-hose guy, the one with the video camera, is reaching for his gun, can't get to it; he doesn't want to drop the camera, and Joe shoots him in the head, kills him, just like that. Oh, Christ.

Joe's going to the door of the office now, the office he hadn't left in thirty-six days, stopping to kill the guy that he hit with the chair, shoot him in the brain. Wendy and I are freaking and Joe's at the door, firing shots into the store, and I grab the cameraman's gun and Joe sees me with it. "Give it to me!" he screams, and I'm about to hand it to him when—bam!—he doubles over, falls back, shots coming from inside the store and Joe's bleeding on the floor now, on his back, and like a fucking idiot, I'm still trying to hand him the gun, but he just looks at me, grins and shakes his head no. Just gives me that goofy Joe Dice grin and shakes his head no.

He's fucking *smiling* at me. Oh, God. Oh, shit.

I get a good look at his stomach then as it begins to leak all over the floor, Joe Dice's intestines, and then I look at Wendy standing over Joe and the two dead panty-hose guys and then the police knocked on the door, asking if everything was all right.

And then Joe Dice died.

• • •

Things change when the reasons for doing them change. That's what happened when we were in that store for thirty-six days; the rules of the game were tossed out the window; survival no longer depended on working, learning, morals, values, none of that. Survival depended on eating, drinking, sleeping, shitting, pissing. Thinking.

That's what I learned in the 7-Eleven. That's what you gotta understand. The rest of my life, I'll play that life game I learned in school, also from my folks; I'll be lying, just bullshitting.

Sure, I wish things could be the way they were. Like I said, waking up, punching in, slopping up shit, punching out. Cruising. Simple shit like that.

Sometimes, after cruising all night, Joe and I would walk over to this schoolyard and hit rocks with a baseball bat as the sun came up. I'd swing and really connect with one of them stones and I'd imagine that I just cranked one over the 365-foot mark in left center field down at Tiger Stadium.

But now I've been to Tiger Stadium, I could have really done that, cranked one over the 365 mark. I could be doing that today, hitting a home run to win the world series or whatever, but even if I did, as I did it, I'd be imagining, just wishing I was back in that Madison Heights playground, knocking a pebble into the rising sun.

The Night My Brother Worked the Header

by **DANIEL MUELLER**
1990

Last day of the salmon season, Old Windell gave a knife to Larry Olseth and put him on the butcher line next to me. "Be nice to him, Agnes," Windell said. The salmon dropped every three and a half seconds from the stainless-steel header and crowded through the open gate as if still alive. They plopped onto the belt headless, one to a slot. We kept up pretty well. Uma-san and Saka-san, the Japanese butchers, slit the bellies, throats and bloodlines. I separated the egg sacs from the guts and dropped them down the metal chute to the egg house. The sacs toppled into the flow like lopped-off pairs of orange fingers and disappeared around the first bend in the rickety converted rain gutter. Windell winked at me.

"Okay, Agnes?" he said.

"Okay," I answered.

"*Aa-o!*" sang Paolo, the big Filipino slimer at the end of the belt.

"*Aa-o!*" sang Dung-Dong, the old Vietnamese scraper two positions down.

On the butcher line, that's how we talked, a sung language. But as soon as Larry Olseth started butchering fish, the singing stopped. He stood on the line between Uma-san and me, as tall and awkward as an ostrich. His thin wrists stuck out from his sleeves like bare bones. His blond, feathery-haired head stuck up a foot above everybody else's, on a neck as thin and gristly as boat line. He was cute enough, but he'd never butchered salmon before. Uma-san let him try every sixth fish, and believe me, it wasn't pretty. He gouged stomachs open and ripped into meat. He wrecked egg sacs without blinking an eye. When he told me he loved me, I nearly took his knife and slit his throat.

We were processing grade-A sockeye salmon, the only fish that came to our cannery and freezing plant that were anywhere near good enough to vacuum-pack in cellophane and sell to the Japanese. Most of the fish we got were soft, smelly chum salmon, silver salmon bloated with gas, humpy salmon falling off the bone and covered with growths. Sometimes we got king salmon as large as men; they smelled worse by far than any other fish, on account of the extra meat. But the salmon on the belt that morning were fine, marvelous fish that shimmered under the overhead lights. Were it not for the blood that drained from their necks and bellies, they might've passed for fish brooches inlaid with turquoise and quartz, like those worn by women east of here, in places like Wrangell and Ketchikan.

So we handled them with care. No one wanted to bruise a freezer fish. Old Windell had told us at breakfast he would be counting the number of fish Ido-san, the Japanese grader, tossed into the plastic tote marked CANNERY. We had to be careful, he said, if we wanted our jobs back next season. Every fish that went to the cannery troughs, through the washers, fin shredders and rotary mincers, every fish that got stuffed into a can, sent down the chinks over the weights and scales, down the long greased rail into the five-hundred-gallon pressurized steam cooker, meant a loss for the company. Add it up, he told us. Weigh it against the cost of labor. Anybody here think he's inexpendable?

"I said I love you, Agnes." Larry Olseth had blue eyes that could turn a person to stone.

"I heard you," I said.

There was a window on the butcher line. It was huge and without glass. During the winter, you could look through it to the sea, but in salmon season, it was blocked by two stainless-steel crab cookers, one stacked on top of the other. The morning Larry Olseth started butchering, a beam passed over the top of them and made a rectangle of light on the belt between him and me. The salmon moved into it and became flames I wanted to touch, not through gloves with cotton liners but with bare hands. But I'd handled enough fish to know how cold and wet they were. Fingering the rough skin would only have wrecked the illusion. To me, the salmon looked foil-wrapped, as beautiful as the chocolate Christmas fish the outpost store in Ahkiok received each year in time for Lent.

"Leave with me tomorrow on the plane," Larry Olseth said. I knew, without having to look up, that he was making himself look more pitiful than any dog in our village.

I was glad Carl was out of earshot. I didn't want my brother, the butcher-line foreman, thinking anything funny was going on. Five feet above the rest of us, on a platform made out of pine boards and reinforced metal, he operated the salmon header, a circular saw for taking the heads off fish. From where I stood on the line, I could see him out of the corner of my eye, in yellow rain pants and brown plaid shirt, his braid coiled snakelike in the hair net outside his collar, his thumbs hooked in the gills of a sockeye salmon. His job was to clamp the fish into the six spring-loaded adjustable collars on the crown of the header and make sure none of them fell off before hitting the sixteen-inch circular blade. Loaded with salmon, the header looked like one of those merry-go-rounds at the fair, the kind with swings, only when the fish got three quarters of the way around, they dropped like sausage links onto a tray table and their heads tumbled down a wooden slide into a four-by-four plastic tote.

"We'll live with my friends Eric and Fran," Larry Olseth said. "They're spray-paint artists. They've got a studio next to the electrical plant in Union Way. Wait till you see it, Agnes. Graffiti poems on the walls and ceiling. Paintings of shrunken heads and bicycle handle bars. Eric's got one of a fire hydrant and all around it are these yellow cats. Not dogs but cats. It's terrific. He's got it displayed in their bedroom, under the basketball hoop."

"Someone's missing throats!" Dung-Dong said, and he didn't mean Uma-san or Saka-san.

"Throat, throat, throat," his brother Hwen-Mao said. "Three throats!"

Larry Olseth hummed a song when he told me we'd hike the Tibetan plain. "I've got this friend, Arun. He owns a restaurant in Mussoorie, India. We'll leave from his place. Think of it, *masala dosa* for lunch, *tandoori* chicken for dinner. In the evenings, we'll bathe in the headwaters of the Ganges, pray to the sacred Siva, sleep under the Hindu heaven. Imagine, Agnes, riding a one-humped camel, meals served to us on banana leaves, sipping arrack and reading Upanishads to each other until dawn."

The crew was quickly becoming annoyed. No one liked the looks of Larry Olseth's fish. We kept looking down the belt to see how Ido-san was grading them. If too many fish went into the wrong tote, we might have to find new jobs. Windell wouldn't fire a college boy, we knew that, even if he sent five thousand fish to the cannery. Larry Olseth butchered in jerks, like he was gutting a deer. He shoved in the knife the way you would bust open a sternum, and he carved mouths in the gullets, complete with curling lips. After a while, I had to stop watching him.

"Cut the throats!" Dung-Dong said.

"The bloodlines!" Hwen-Mao said. "Cut the bloodlines!"

"This is what we'll do," Larry Olseth said. "We'll stock a cupboard with sex tools. Vibrators, dildos, fruit-flavored jellies. We'll only use condoms with little nubbins on them, and we'll videotape our sexcapades. In Korea, Agnes, men and women pull strings of pearls out of each other. We can order through the mail. I'll get two, one for each of us."

"Look," I said and held up a fish. Eggs poured out its open neck like bath-oil beads. "I'm behind because of you."

Dung-Dong was losing his patience. "Goddamn," he said, and shook his head. "Goddamn."

Paolo's voice boomed from the end of the line. "Too much blood in the fish!"

"Goddamn." Dung-Dong couldn't scrape the blood if the bloodlines weren't cut.

The fish with guts in them were two slots from Hwen-Mao's scraping spoon. Between them and me were no fewer than six fish. Larry Olseth turned his eyes on me. They were as blue as a pair of marbles. "What's eating you, Agnes?" he asked. Just then, I backed into the steel toe of Hwen-Mao's rubber boot and I landed flat on my back on the carpet of guts. Spleens and intestines covered my face. Larry Olseth offered me his hand.

"Stop the belt!" Hwen-Mao said when he opened a fish and saw its guts and eggs intact.

Carl turned off the belt and came around the far end of the header. "What's going on?" he asked, picking up an end wrench from the box of tools and slapping it in his palm a few times. No one wanted to annoy Carl. He was strong enough to throw a wrench five times the length of the one in his hand, sure-sighted enough to hit an empty beer can from twelve yards. When Carl was only fifteen, Windell had caught him with his daughter up on Alitak Mountain, fucking on the flat slab of rock next to the fallen-down radio tower. Windell marched him down the side of the mountain back to the cannery, a rifle barrel pointed at his head. Then he handcuffed Carl to the flagpole for the night, and in the morning, Carl watched the helicopter lift off with the girl in the cockpit. The next summer, Windell made Carl foreman. At nineteen, he was a better foreman than men twice his age.

"The new guy," Dung-Dong said.

"What new guy?" Carl asked. He knew who Dung-Dong was talking about, but playing stupid was part of the game. Most of the people on the butcher line couldn't have explained a situation in English to save their lives, which was why we made an effort to get along.

"The new guy," Dung-Dong said, and motioned with his head.

Carl looked at Larry Olseth, but his back was turned, helping me pick gonads and bladders off my jacket. Anger flashed in my brother's eyes, but Larry Olseth was as oblivious to it as a fish on the belt. "I'd like to take you right here, Agnes. Right here in the guts," Larry Olseth whispered. Carl lowered himself off the platform, came up to me on the other side of the belt and slid two slick fingers underneath my chin.

"You all right, Agnes?" he asked.

"Yes, Carl," I said, and pushed Larry Olseth away.

"You fall by accident, or somebody push you?"

"Nobody pushed me, Carl," I said.

He looked at me. "You need to be meaner," he said. One of the ways he had tried to make me meaner was by putting the barrel of a deer rifle to my temple. "Look out the window and make up a story," he would say, punching out the safety on the magazine. And looking into the winter fog, which rose up out of the sea as thick as grass, I would begin a story about the Japanese glass float, the plastic doll's leg or the teacup handle of Chinese porcelain—all bits of exotic jetsam I'd discovered while digging for steamer clams. But before I could get past the setting, he would make the hammer click-click-click in the hollow chamber. "You're boring me, Agnes," he would say. He believed that to live year round in Ahkiok, Alaska, a person had to be mean. I believe a person mustn't get bored. He withdrew his fingers, which left my throat wet. I watched him grab the rail of the platform and pull himself back up. When Carl was halfway back, Dung-Dong said, "Aren't you going to say something to the new guy?"

Carl spun around. He thought a moment. "I might tell Windell Dung-Dong's getting too old to work."

"I'm not too old!" Dung-Dong shrieked. Some refugees worked until they were one hundred.

Carl started up the header. "Life's short, Agnes," Larry Olseth said. The fish came one to a slot, packed in as tight as the links on a watch band. Larry Olseth said, "All right, Agnes. I'll do the job right."

"You couldn't if you tried," I said.

"Oh, yeah?"

"Yeah," I said.

But he did. He bowed to Uma-san and asked him to teach him the Japanese way of salmon butchering. Uma-san raised his eyebrows so they looked like little V-shaped temples on his forehead. "Japanese way?" he asked.

"Yes," Larry Olseth said.

I was amazed. Larry Olseth's fish improved as soon as Uma-san showed him how to hold the knife and glide the blade. He slit the throats, bellies and bloodlines perfectly, so that the egg sacs slid out as smoothly as Popsicles. We were happy. Hwen-Mao and Dung-Dong scraped the snakes of blood off the spinal columns and flung them at Chung-Soo when he came to collect the tote of fish heads. "Good job, Larry," Uma-san said. Paolo's voice boomed in song.

For a while, total harmony united us, from the slimers and the scrapers on down the line to me, the egg puller. I asked Larry Olseth, "Why'd Windell put you on the butcher line? You've never even butchered before."

"Because I asked him to," Larry Olseth said.

"And he just did it?"

"Sure. I told him I was in love with you, Agnes. I said, 'Listen, Windell, if you don't let me butcher fish next to Agnes Agnug, it'll be your fault if I leave tomorrow and never see her again.'

"He said, 'You're absolutely right, Larry. If I did that to you, I'd be unable to sleep nights, I'd be so disgusted with myself. I'll put you on the butcher line first thing after ten-o'clock mug-up.'"

I shook my head.

"Seriously, Agnes. I asked him to put me here and he did."

That didn't surprise me. The college boys wore caps advertising the names of their fathers' firms: National Can Company, American Clip Manufacturers, Mermaid Ocean Delicacies. Larry Olseth's cap said CRYOVAC, the company that made the bags we froze the fish in. Still, it angered me.

Larry Olseth said, "Leave with me tomorrow and you'll never be poor."

"But I don't love you," I said.

"You don't?"

"No," I said.

"But you told me you did."

• • •

True. Three nights earlier, I had told Larry Olseth I loved him. How it happened was, I was sitting on his bed when he handed me a mirror with two big lines of cocaine on it. "Use this," he said, and handed me a rolled-up hundred-dollar bill. We took turns snorting, and when we were through, he set up two more lines and told me I could have them both. I did, and when they were gone, I thought I'd never seen a handsomer boy.

I said, "Let's go for a walk on the pier." He slipped a pint of Johnnie Walker into his jacket and held the door for me. Outside the dorm, a big full moon had risen over the ocean. I said. "The killer whales will be feeding tonight."

We sipped whiskey as we passed the machine shop. Through the cracked window, the drill presses and band saws looked like people hunched over in the darkness, but I wasn't afraid. I'd walked to the end of the pier plenty of nights—sometimes alone. In front of the freezer, I bit Larry Olseth's ear and told him, "Put your arms around me, Larry." He did, and I asked him if he wanted to go to a place only I knew about, a secret place under the dock.

"Yes," he said, and I led him by the hand to the slippery wooden ladder at the end of the pier.

The rungs were wet and cold. When I came within three feet of the glistening water, I called up to him, "Come on, Larry." As I reached with my foot for the slick plank, I could see him start down the ladder, one foot at a time, the soles of his sneakers flitting between the rungs like ghosts. I gripped the rope railing and balanced across the narrow beam, crunching barnacles under my boots, to the bed made out of old two-by-fours. "Come on," I said. A good two feet above the high-water mark, the bed was the perfect place to keep blankets and cigarettes. I reached for Larry Olseth and he handed me the bottle and climbed in next to me. Above us, moonlight filtered through planks in the pier, making bars across our faces. Below us, we heard the swish in water, killer whales drawn to the shimmering schools of Dolly Vardens underneath the dock. I said, "Kiss me, Larry." He unzipped my pants. I said, "Yes, finger me, Larry." And while he did, I said I loved him.

● ● ●

At the end of the line, Paolo sang a love song with French words in it. Larry Olseth butchered only every fifth fish, but they were turning out as good as either Uma-san's or Saka-san's, so Uma-san asked him to try every fourth fish. "Okay," Larry Olseth said.

"You're the little girl that I adore," Paolo sang.

"Love needs time to evolve," Larry Olseth said. "It doesn't happen overnight. Like a seed, it needs to be nurtured, watered, given sunlight."

"I could never love you," I said.

"Then forget about love," Larry Olseth said. "Think of the drugs."

• • •

I did. Underneath the pier, I told Larry Olseth about the deaths, about kids I knew killing themselves for no reason. Most of them did it in the winter, when the horizontal rains slashed against the aluminum siding of the houses for months at a time and no one had any hope of cocaine coming around until May. A boy told his family he was going out to kill a deer. A girl said she was going for a walk and her father hung the rifle on her shoulder for protection against bears. They'd place the end of the barrel against the roof of their mouths and push the trigger with their thumbs. I told Larry Olseth to imagine ripping planks for coffin wood from the floors of the abandoned seiners south of the cannery. That's what little kids in the village did. I told Larry Olseth about the suicides of E.J., Myra and T. Pontiac, and before that of Rhoda, Ewell and Buster, kids who had climbed up the mountain out of the world. Then I told him what I had told many people, that the way to end all the discontent and needless destruction of our youth was to maintain a steady flow of drugs into our community year round.

• • •

"I love you, I love you, I lo-o-ove you," Paolo sang. Things were going fine. Only diseased fish went to the cannery. Ido-san sent the rest to the freezer.

"We send the coke third-class parcel post," Larry Olseth said. "It's cheap. Nobody checks it. It gets here."

Uma-san said, "Real good, Larry. Real good." He was referring to Larry Olseth's fish, which were good, mostly. A couple of times, I noticed a throat or a bloodline that wasn't cut all the way, but I wasn't going to say anything about a couple of salmon. For never having butchered before, he was doing a very good job. Then Uma-san raised his eyebrows. "You try every third fish, Larry?"

"Sure," Larry Olseth said, and Uma-san made a joke in Japanese that I didn't understand.

Larry Olseth had to work his knife fast now, and some of his cuts were a little sloppy. "Your dream, Agnes. You said it was a sign."

• • •

Yes. Underneath the pier, I told Larry Olseth about the night last March when T. Pontiac came to my house all drunk, asking me whether I had anything to smoke. Just cigarettes, I whispered. He wanted sheesh, he said. But he stood in the kitchen, anyway, eying me as if I were the drugs themselves. I pushed him toward the door. From inside his jacket, he pulled out a pack of Viceroys. They were drenched through. He said he was going to smoke them one after another until they were gone, and then he was going up the mountain to blow off his head.

I said, Not now, Pontiac, you'll wake people. We both laughed hard—but quietly—so that we *wouldn't* wake people. So many kids had killed themselves, mentioning it was almost a joke between us. Pontiac kissed me on the mouth and left through the side door into the rain.

I crawled back into bed with my sister's baby. Carol had won a scholarship to pharmacology school in Anchorage, so every night after she left, I put her little girl, Sarah, between my breasts and went to sleep listening to the little puffs of air, in and out. When the gun went off, I dreamed I'd been shot through the heart. I felt the penetration of bullets and the flip of my body onto the pebbles. I looked up and seven hunters in mukluks formed a circle around me. A boy with feathery blond hair knelt beside me. Move her from the spot and she'll die, said one of the men. No, she won't, said the boy. He stood me up on the stones to show them. Thank you, I said, thank you very much. When I awoke in the morning, no one had to tell me that Pontiac was now dead, for I knew it as if I had had a vision.

• • •

"Remember, Agnes," Larry Olseth said. "Underneath the pier. You told me I was the blond-haired boy of your dream. You can't deny it. You said it was a sign."

"A sign of what?" I asked.

"How should I know?" said Larry Olseth. He missed some more throats and bloodlines. He cut them, just not deeply enough, so the egg sacs came apart in my glove. Still, I said nothing. He was trying to do a good job.

"Very fast learner, Larry." Uma-san could say that because he didn't have to pull the egg sacs or scrape the blood from fish that were only half finished. Then he said, "I leave now. Bye-bye, Larry," and set down his knife. "You butcher with Saka-san. Every other fish. Japanese." Taking off his apron, he made another joke that nobody except Saka-san understood, then removed his gloves and hung them on the wall behind him. He was done for the summer. Even though it wasn't quite noon, he was going to Japan House to pack his things for the flight to Tokyo in the morning. As he walked through the fork gate behind the header, the fish rolled upon Larry Olseth like waves, pushing him like a raft at sea, until he was butchering fish right next to me, jamming me in the ribs with his elbow.

"Throat!" Dung-Dong said.

"Bloodline!" Hwen-Mao said.

"Agnes," said Larry Olseth. None of the throats and bloodlines were cut now. Sac upon sac ripped in my glove. "Leave with me. It's written in the cosmos. It's meant to be."

Two more sacs ripped in my glove. "I'll leave with you, Larry"—these were my exact words—"when all the throats are cut!"

My brother Carl looked at me from the header. All he had heard me say was that I'd leave with Larry.

• • •

Around three in the afternoon, we finished butchering the last tote of salmon. Carl told us that before we could leave, we had to sweep all the guts into the drains, hose down the header, belt and tray tables and sponge-mop all the fish scales off the butcher-line wall. I beat Dung-Dong to the broom, which meant that the old Vietnamese had to wipe down the header, which was an okay job if Paolo kept the fire hose down. Carl started up the crown lift, forked the tote of fish heads and drove off to dump it from the end of the pier. While the rest of us worked, Larry Olseth leaned against a runner of the garage door, smoked cigarettes and stared at me with his blue eyes. He had kept up all afternoon, the same as Saka-san. Once he'd adjusted to the pace, nobody could complain about his work, not me, not Dung-Dong, not Hwen-Mao.

I kept my eyes on my broom. The purple livers, floppy white gonads and pink strings of tissue swirled like sunset clouds in the whirlpools above the drains. Larry Olseth was going to leave tomorrow on the plane. I had that thought as I swept out fish heads from underneath the belt and sent them coasting off the end of my broom like shuffleboard pucks. I aimed them at the drains, where they plopped through to the ocean below. Maybe we could be pen pals for a year or two or until we forgot the looks of each other's faces.

"Goddamn."

I looked up. Mario, the quiet slimer, was talking to Paolo about orange picking in Stockton, California, where the Filipinos spent the nine months they didn't spend here. This sort of thing happened every day. Paolo got interested and forgot he was holding the fire hose. My face had been blasted plenty of times. This time, though, it was Dung-Dong. The water came straight up and exploded off Dung-Dong's face like fireworks.

Of the twenty or so people who had seen Dung-Dong carried off the line on a stretcher two seasons earlier with a collapsed aorta, not one stepped in to do anything. Larry Olseth, of all people, pushed the fire hose down, and when he did, Paolo said, "Keep your hands off me, you white fucker." His stomach was as big around as a backyard cooker.

The old Vietnamese climbed down off the platform, his hair as wet and bristly as a newly hatched bird. "Where's Carl?" he asked. "He'll take that goddamn thing out of your hands."

Paolo called the old man a cocksucker and held the nozzle level with the crotch of his rain pants. Dung-Dong made a beeline for the garage door, his wrinkled face trembling like fish wrap in the breeze. Larry Olseth followed him out the door and leaned against a stack of pallets. It made me sick to think he was above having to help us with cleanup.

I climbed the header platform to finish wiping off the scales and blood from the collars, crown and blade. I loosened the bolt on the blade and took it off so that I could pick out the globs of guts that were wrapped around the rotisserie like rubber bands. Dung-Dong returned as I was tightening the blade down. "I thought you went to get Carl," Paolo said as he wheeled around.

"Carl went to the village," Dung-Dong said. "I saw him driving the skiff."

Ahkiok was four miles away by water, which meant Carl had left for the day.

"No," Paolo said, beaming.

"Go ahead, call me a liar," Dung-Dong said.

The fire hose twisted on the floor like a snake. "Another day, another dollar," Paolo said as he turned off the water. I climbed off the platform, though I hadn't finished cleaning it, walked past the fish house, the egg house, the freezer plant, but I found only Carl's crown lift, plugged into a socket in the side of the warehouse, and the hosed-out tote drying in the sun. In the slip where Carl tied up the skiff each morning hung the bowline. Its frayed end wafted back and forth in the current like hair, entangling the legs of starfish stuck to the piling. Normally, he wound and tied the rope and set it neatly under the seat.

"Agnes." I felt Larry Olseth's cool hands soft as a down-filled hood over my ears. "I'm gone from here."

"What do you mean?" I asked, trying to size him. He had dark plates under his eyes that made him look pitiful and charming at the same time.

"This place is not reality," he said. "I'm here, yes. But really, I'm not." He put a wad of Red Man as big as a jawbreaker under his lip. "I've lost my mind, Agnes. It's aeons from here. Off the coast of Egypt where Odysseus's men ate lotus leaves and dreamed of mountains and waterfalls so real they wanted to stay there." He cleared his throat and drooled a string of saliva a foot long off the end of the pier.

"So I'm saving that old Vietnamese man's life back there—what's-his-name, Ding-Bat. But what I'm thinking about is this thing I read about how botanists identified a certain hallucinogenic fern they believed to be the actual lotus eaten by the mariners. You saw that Filipino giant. He wanted to rend me limb from limb, but what I'm thinking about, Agnes, is picking the little ferns and stuffing them in my bag."

"Come on," I said. "Let's get out of here."

"All right," he said. We took off our rain gear and boots, hung our pants and jackets on nails in the cloakroom, clipped our gloves to the clothesline. I asked Larry Olseth whether he had any coke.

"Of course," he said, so we walked side by side in broad daylight past the open door of the machine shop, past the high-pitched whir of the power grinder, past the flying sparks of old Dan the machinist. We walked through the center of the mess hall, past Tiny, the head cook, singing, *"Doo-doo-doo-didlee-doo-didlee-doo-doo!"* He would be gone tomorrow. At the top of the stairs, we walked past work boots, deck boots, tennis shoes, past coveralls hanging from hooks and spotted with grease. No girls or women were allowed in the men's dorm. That was Windell's law. Larry Olseth opened the door to room six.

"We should be quiet," I said. Larry Olseth locked the door. His underwear, socks, shampoo, washcloths lay on his bed, ready to be packed. I moved a couple of his shirts and made a place for myself on the bedspread. He opened the drawer of the bureau, removed a blue bag with a black drawstring. Inside it were the mirror and the canister of coke. "Tomorrow, Agnes, I'll be back in Seattle." He dumped some of the chunky white powder onto the mirror and began to chop it with a razor blade. We spoke through our noses because a misdirected breath could send the particles flying. "The first place I'm going," Larry Olseth said, "is Umberto's Italian Ice. For some raspberry." With the edge of the blade he made four thick lines. "You ever wanted something so bad you could taste it?" he asked.

"It wasn't raspberry," I said.

"Coke whore," Larry Olseth said. He handed me the mirror and the rolled-up bill. I snorted my lines a third at a time, each one a burst of coolness like a breeze in my head, like the mist that curls off the breakers at high tide. I asked whether there was more.

"More what?"

"You know," I said.

"What's left on the mirror. Go ahead, lick it off." I did, and felt the tingle on my gums and tongue as I reached for the fly of Larry Olseth's jeans.

● ● ●

At three A.M., we woke to Carl's pounding. He wanted us to let him in or he'd blow down the door.

"What do you want?" Larry Olseth asked. My hand rested on his bare chest. My lips were at his ear.

"I'm going to hide in the closet," I said. "If he finds me here, he'll cut me into strips and stuff me into a crab pot."

Larry Olseth looked at me. "I'm serious," I said.

"Let me in," Carl said. As quietly as I could, I slipped off the bed, put on my clothes, picked my shoes and socks up off the floor. I didn't do the zipper because I thought it would make too much of a sound.

"Can't we ignore him?" Larry Olseth said from the bed. "Won't he just go away?" Carl pounded the door. "Give me a minute." Larry Olseth rose from the bed and covered himself with a white bathrobe. As I moved into the closet, my head nudged a bunch of loose hangers. "Dang," I said, trying to steady about thirty of them with my hand, but they clanged anyway like chimes inside a clock. I pulled the closet door shut from the inside, slowly, to keep the hinges from snapping.

"Now," Carl said, "or I'll blow down the door."

"I'm coming," Larry Olseth said. I heard the lock on the door click and my brother step into the room. The overhead light came on, making shafts inside the closet at my feet, above my head and through the cracks in the panels. I moved to the far end of the closet and pressed myself against the wall.

"Where's Agnes?" Carl asked. He was scanning the room, taking in the stuff on Larry Olseth's bed and the indentations left by our bodies. I knew he was looking for things of mine in the mess the way he looked for deer droppings on the side of the mountain. "She's been here," he said. "Her scent is here."

"She left hours ago," Larry Olseth said. "She said she was going back to the village."

"I've been to the village," Carl said.

"Yeah?" said Larry Olseth.

"She wasn't there."

He paused. "You two fuck like rabbits, or what?" he asked.

Larry Olseth shook his head. "This is crazy, Carl."

"So you two think you're leaving tomorrow on the plane?"

It was funny. Larry Olseth was in the bedroom and I was in the closet, but in that instant—the instant when we knew why Carl had come—our heads were as linked to each other as boats in tow. Larry Olseth laughed, not because anything was humorous. "We were kidding around, Carl. She never said she'd go."

"I heard what she said."

"I've got a *girlfriend,* Carl," said Larry Olseth. "Allison's her name. Allison Wheeler. We've set the date."

"What were you doing with a fifteen-year-old, then?" Carl asked. I heard the click of the safety and knew then that Carl had brought the deer rifle along with him. But I wasn't worried about Larry Olseth. The gun never had any bullets in it. Besides, it was me Carl wanted, not him.

"So what did you promise her?" Carl asked. "The world?"

"I didn't promise her anything."

"We'll wait for her and see," Carl said. "In the meantime, I want you to tell me a story."

"Okay," Larry Olseth said. "Ever hear the one about the sailor?"

"The sailor and the midget?" Carl asked.

"That's a different one," Larry Olseth said. "In this one, he's sitting at supper with his wife and kid."

"Tell it," Carl said.

"The guy's spent his whole life collecting things," Larry Olseth said. "He's done pretty well for himself. Even on the junky items. One day, a dervish passes his house and sees the marble pillars and onion domes and thinks to himself, 'Why should he get to bask in Allah's favor, eat pecans, drink tea, when I'm lucky to get a slice of goat cheese?' The more he thinks about it, the more pissed off he gets. 'I work at least as hard as him. Yet I go hungry while he dines on the brains of monkeys.'"

"Get up," Carl said. I heard the rustle of bedding, the sigh of the mattress, as Larry Olseth stood up. "We're going for a walk," Carl said, and I heard Larry Olseth's feet on the carpet. "Keep talking," Carl said. "You're getting me interested." The hinges creaked as Larry Olseth opened the door. Through the wall of the closet, I heard them in the hall. I opened the closet door and crept across the room. I peeked around the molding as the two boys moved past rooms 11 and 13.

"So the sailor invites the guy in," Larry Olseth said, "puts him at the head of the table, says, 'Eat.' So the guy eats. The sailor says, 'Perhaps when you've heard my story, you'll think twice before you envy me again.'" Larry Olseth opened the door of the second-floor landing.

"Out," Carl said, and pushed the barrel into the back of his head.

They were moving down the steps. I crept down the hall after them and opened the door at the end of the hall and slipped into the night. Their footsteps creaked on the stairs like boats against the pier. "'On my first voyage,' says the sailor, 'the captain mistook the back of a sea monster for a small island.'" Larry Olseth stepped onto the sidewalk, a ghost in his white bathrobe. The rifle barrel linked them like a horse and rider. "'Some of us disembarked. Soon the ocean quaked. The island sank beneath our feet. We watched our ship depart without us.'" I followed them past the nurse's office, the laundry room, the main desk. The moon was as full as the underbelly of a whale. There were no clouds, no colors, only shades of white and black. "'Some were devoured by the monster. Others by the sea. But by the mercy of the waves, a few of us were thrown ashore on the island of Cassel, once the waiting grounds for grooms of the benevolent maharaja but now the home of the giant, man-eating Cyclops.'"

I stayed in the shadows next to the carpentry shed, crouching behind the concrete blocks stacked next to it. They disappeared behind the corner of the machine shop. When I came to the corner, I made myself as long and narrow as a drain spout and poked my head into the walkway.

"She's out there," Carl said. "She's listening." He pushed Larry Olseth past the cannery, the paint-supply closet, the scale room, luring me along with the sound of Larry Olseth's sweet voice.

"'He scooped us up in his hands the second we arrived and locked us in his cave.'" They came to a halt in front of the entrance to the butcher line. I followed in the darkness, darting between the stacks of pallets.

Carl dropped the key to the garage door on the concrete apron. "Open it," he said. As Larry Olseth picked up the key, I realized he was telling this story to save my life. He thought the longer he kept Carl interested, the more time I would have to go get help. And the truth was, I'd have banged on the door of Windell's cottage, screamed bloody murder to the stars had I truly believed Larry Olseth was in danger.

The garage door rattled on its runners. "'He looked at each of us. He picked me up by the neck. Then he set me down. I wasn't savory enough for him. He had his eye on our captain.'" I moved along the outside of the corrugated shed. Lights came on above the butcher line. A thousand tiny rays shot out holes in the metal sheeting. On the other side were the belt, tray tables and header.

"She's out there," Carl said. "I smell her." I was beside the entrance, next to the block of light, my back pressed against the runner.

"'The Cyclops ran a spit through the head of our captain, then hung him over the fire to cook.'" From the butcher line came the clank of bolts being loosened. Larry Olseth saw what I had been trying to tell him all along—that there was nothing Carl wouldn't try if he thought it had the power to frighten.

"Louder!" Carl said.

"'That night, I dreamed of a plan! When the Cyclops asked my name, I told him it was *Noman!*'"

Carl started up the motor on the header. "She's out there! Tell the story louder!"

The belt started to roll with Larry Olseth collared to it. "'When the Cyclops was fast asleep, I took a spit out of the fire! I climbed his hair! I stood before the huge closed eye!'"

"Agnes!" Carl screamed.

"'I lifted the orange tip!'"

"Agnes!" he screamed again.

"'I drove it into the yellow yolk——'"

I stepped into the light as Carl shifted the rotisserie into gear. Behind it, in a convergence of steel orbits, the blade spun at hundreds of revolutions per second. I walked through the puddles behind the belt. "Go ahead," I said.

"Agnes," Carl said, and shouldered the rifle.

"Agnes!" screamed Larry Olseth, legs flailing as he came round the other side of the machine, arms struggling with the spring-loaded collar.

Carl fixed my forehead in the sight. I saw his eye, brown and luminous, on the lens of the scope. As I climbed onto the header platform, I heard the click-click-click of the hammer in the chamber.

"Carl," I said. I put up my hand and knocked the barrel of the rifle aside. He stumbled against the gear shift, knocking it into neutral. Before he could recover, I turned off the switch. I reached for the rifle and threw it down the wooden slide for fish heads.

"You're a whore," Carl said.

"I'm a whore. Right, Carl," I said.

I unlocked the collar from around Larry Olseth's neck. Under his jaw was a red welt that would turn blue on the plane.

"Larry Olseth," I said. My boots were inches deep in the slime we hadn't cleaned up, and I picked a length of intestine off his white robe. "Here," I said, and handed it to him. "To practice on." My eyes met his as the slimy piece slipped from his hand onto the floor.

"Don't forget," I said to them both, and I made a little bow, the way Larry Olseth had done to Uma-san, and I left. Someone else could clean up.

Crew Cut

1991

I got my hair cut today in honor of this trip to visit my mother. I had the guy cut it so short in the back that when I rub my hand against it, it feels prickly, so rough and razor sharp that it makes my hand tingle.

The guy says to me, "A pretty girl like you shouldn't have such short hair—yours is so nice and thick—you sure you want to do this?" I just nod and watch him clip away until all my curls drift to the floor. It's weird seeing it on the ground, a shaggy carpet that a few minutes before was attached to my head. It almost looks lonely.

I doubt that my family will make a big deal about my hair. It's always so loud and crowded in my house, with the five of us, plus my dad, and other people passing through. Whether it's the radio, the TV or the humming of the dishwasher, there's always some sort of noise beneath the chatter. I imagine our house as a winter coat that's too small for the fat man wearing it; one false move and the whole thing will rip apart, bursting at the seams.

When I walk into the house, Janie, my thirteen-year-old sister, glances up from the kitchen table, where she's doing her homework. "Sammy, what did you do?"

I just shrug my shoulders. "I couldn't deal with it anymore; it was always getting in the way."

The twins pay no attention, sitting zombielike, their mouths agape as one of the Ninja Turtles—Michelangelo, I think—gets beaten over the head. A couple of minutes later, Kevin barrels down the stairs, sticking his tongue out at Janie. "What's for dinner?" he asks me sweetly.

"I don't know. It's not my turn."

"Yeah, uh-huh, it is. I called Daddy at work and he said," Kevin whines.

"I have to pack," I say, rolling my eyes. "Well, fine. If I'm in charge, we're having pizza," I announce, picking up the phone and dialing.

Janie, my dad and I take turns with dinner. After my mom left three years ago, when I was twelve, Dad drew up a schedule, neatly charted and drawn with a ruler. "You guys have to pull your own weight around here," he told us. "I can't do everything."

Janie and I do the shopping. Dad gives us a check at the beginning of the week, $50, and we all go to the market together, the little ones in tow. Kevin and the twins shuffle their feet, grabbing and pleading for candy they've seen advertised during Saturday-morning cartoons. We all have weak spots; I'm a sucker for exotic fruits, anything that I've never tasted before—passion fruit, cactus apples, kiwis and kumquats. But we can't indulge often. Doing the shopping ourselves makes us hyperaware of prices. We're probably the only kids in school who watch eagle-eyed for specials on bacon, who know that $1.89 is a great price for a carton of orange juice.

Dad never asks us what we get, never questions our decisions, except for the time we got twenty-three Hungry-Man dinners for the week. He's not home much and when he is, he sinks into the easy chair and tells us to keep it down. "I listen to people complaining all day long," he tells us when the twins ask him to settle a dispute or when Kevin pleads for a new skateboard. "Can't you guys give me a little peace and quiet?"

He's not a tyrant or an ogre or anything. He's just tired, permanently tired, I'd say, and has been for as long as I can remember. He's a sales rep for a light-fixture company. Sometimes, when we're all eating dinner and making a fuss—Kevin telling knock-knock jokes and the twins stuffing unwanted food into their napkins—Dad will sit there, silent, his eyes wandering around the room, like he's pulled a layer of film over them. He's wondering how he ever ended up in this situation. It's as if he took a wrong turn somewhere and can't get back on track.

• • •

We haven't seen our mother in more than a year. The last time was for dinner. She called the house about a week before and told us she would be passing through and wanted to take us out. "A *real* dinner," she said. "I want to take you kids someplace nice. Sergio's is still there, isn't it?"

The sky's the limit with Mom.

Janie spent hours helping the twins get ready, dressing them in the ruffles and bows my mother adores. About ten minutes before we were supposed to leave, I slid into a black-leather miniskirt, applied a streak of crimson to my lips and piled my tangled curls on top of my head, remembering full well that my mother likes me to wear my hair down. Janie shook her head disapprovingly. "Why can't you at least try?"

I just smirked and grabbed a twin with each hand. "Come on, we don't want to keep Mommy waiting."

When we got to the restaurant, she looked exactly the way I remembered her. Platinum hair sprayed into place, lipstick that precisely matched her nail polish, birdlike bejeweled hands. As the little ones ran up and hugged her, almost knocking her to the ground, I stood back. "Where's Samantha? Where's my first-born?" she said, looking around till she spotted me.

We sat in the elegant dining room, the little ones' faces hidden behind enormous menus, and she asked us about school, friends, sports. "Janie, are you still taking ballet?"

"We're getting toe shoes next week."

"That's wonderful. This may sound old fashioned, but there's nothing like ballet to give a girl grace and poise. What about your ballet, Samantha?"

"I quit."

"Oh," she said, and gave me a puzzled look. "Honey," she said, leaning over, smoothing my hair, "you need some new clothes. I'll give you the money. You're such a pretty young lady, you should take advantage of your looks."

I said nothing. Her eyes got glittery, and she turned to the other kids. She raised a glass of champagne. "It's so good to see all of you. I wish I could come more often, but it's hard to get away. If only I could show you kids some of the things I've seen."

"Take us somewhere. Take us somewhere really good," Kevin said, jumping up and down on his chair.

"Where do you want to go? Las Vegas, Tahiti? How about Disneyland?"

"The moon, Mommy! I want to go to the moon!"

"You've got it!" she said, toasting him. "Next summer vacation, the moon it is!"

A month after our dinner, extravagant presents arrived: an Erector

Set for Kevin, a Barbie ice-cream shoppe for the twins that they already had and matching Laura Ashley dresses for Janie and me. That night, Kevin mumbled to me when I put him to bed, "When is Mommy coming back to take me to the moon?"

• • •

About a month ago, she called me. "Samantha, honey, I have a big surprise for you, a belated fifteenth-birthday present."

"Yeah?" I said, suspicious.

"I have to go to Miami—to this medical convention I booked speakers for—and I want to take you with me. Not any of the other kids, just the two of us. I don't have that much work, just a couple of meetings, and you're big enough to take care of yourself. It would be more of a vacation than anything else. Just an excuse for us two girls to play together for a couple of days in the sun. What do you say?" she said, suddenly aware that I hadn't spoken.

"I don't know. I'm not sure if it's such a good idea." I wrapped the twisty phone cord around my wrist until red marks appeared.

"Why not? It'll be so much fun. Samantha, you'll go back home golden brown and everyone will be so jealous of your tan. We'll have a great time, I promise."

"I'll have to ask Dad," I said, knowing he wouldn't care one way or another. "How would I get there?"

"I'll send you a plane ticket. You can take the train to Philadelphia and fly from there."

"Wait, Mom. Could I take the train all the way?"

"Samantha, it's more than a thousand miles to Miami. The train would take forever, and besides, trains today are awful——"

"I'll only come if I can take the train," I interrupted. "I know you don't understand, but I don't want to fly."

"Oh, honey!" she exclaimed. "Oh, honey, you're not afraid to fly? Samantha, it's really perfectly safe."

"Mom, I'll come if I can take the train."

That settled it. After a flurry of I'm-so-exciteds and I-can't-wait-to-see-yous, she hung up. It didn't bother me that she thought I was scared. Whatever she wanted to believe was fine with me. The longer the train ride took, the better. It would be one of the first times I would be alone for more than a couple of hours in my life. No brother and sisters to look after, no parents breathing down my neck. It was a good-enough trade in my eyes to make up for three days or so of dealing with my mom.

● ● ●

Janie watches me pack, sitting cross-legged on the floor of the room we share as I stuff clothes into a bag.

"I'm so jealous of you. You're going to eat in great restaurants, go shopping, swim in the ocean, all while I sit here freezing in New Jersey. I hope Mom takes me somewhere when I'm fifteen."

"Don't bet on it. You can't depend on her. It's going to be fun, but she'll watch me like a hawk. 'Don't sit like that, Samantha, it's not lady-like.' 'Let's go out and buy you some *real* clothes, Samantha; you don't need to wear hand-me-downs.'" I imitate her high voice and clucking noises of disapproval.

Over the past year, I've started shopping in dusty, dimly lit secondhand stores, rummaging through boxes of jumbled clothing. I wear faded and sometimes ripped men's jeans several sizes too big for me, so large that I swim in them. I cinch them tightly around my waist with my favorite find, a belt with a brass buckle in the shape of Texas, the words DON'T MESS WITH TEXAS embossed on it. I wear men's work shirts, broadcloth pinstripes with buttondown collars and a previous owner's initials stitched into the breast pocket. I've been wearing hats. A five-gallon hat and a bowler are my favorites, but I think I'll retire them for a while, to show off my newly shorn head. The only part of my outfits my mother will approve of are the camisoles: They're mostly white, lacy and look like they should smell of moth balls. But I don't hide them; I wear the shirts unbuttoned so the lace of the camisoles peeks through. I can just hear what my mother will say.

She would throw a fit if I told her about the sex. How sometimes after school, I go out behind the soccer field and into the woods near the boys' school. Even though they come in pairs or clusters of three, we go one at a time, while the others kick up dirt or throw stones waiting for their turns. They're well-behaved, polite boys. Sometimes, while I'm pulling down their pants—I love the charged sound of the zipper slowly unzipping—they'll ask me, their voices breathless, "How about if you meet me in town on Saturday night? I'll take you out in my car." I shake my head no, diving down. I enjoy it and so do they—why make it more complicated?

Sometimes I feel like telling my mother when she calls and asks, "How's school, Samantha?"

I want to answer, "It's okay. I had a math test today that was pretty hard, but I gave this guy a blow job after school and that cheered me up."

I don't think she'd take it all that well.

• • •

Janie mumbles something and rolls back over when the alarm goes off. When I steal out of the dark room, all I can make out of her is a lumpy figure under the covers and masses of curls covering her pillow. I walk to the corner and wait until the bus lumbers up, its headlights still beaming.

The brightly lit train station is worlds apart from the stillness of the early morning. It's bustling, brimming with men and women in business suits, hurrying to buy the paper and a cup of coffee, or making one last phone call before the train arrives. They're all probably taking the train into Philadelphia or maybe New York. I doubt that anyone here will be going to Florida with me.

I sit down on one of the straight-backed wooden benches, hugging my bag close. I don't want anyone to get the idea that just because I'm young and traveling alone, I'm an easy target. There's a family sitting across from me. Two little kids climb all over their mother as if she were a jungle gym; her hands are everywhere, wiping the snotty nose of one, grabbing a half-eaten lollipop from the other. They bombard her with questions: "When are we going?" "How long till we get there?" I'm glad I'm leaving home for a while.

The board lights up with the track number for my train and swells of people crowd the stairway to get downstairs to the platform. I climb on the train and find myself a seat.

"Tickets! Tickets, please!" the conductor bellows as he slides open the door to my car.

"All the way to Miami, huh?"

"Yeah."

"Well, young lady," he says, smiling at me, "you've got a nice long ride ahead of you. We should be arriving in Miami in a little more than twenty-four hours—around nine A.M. tomorrow."

As he moves on to the woman in a business suit sitting across the aisle from me, I settle back into my seat and fall asleep to the rhythmic clanking of the wheels.

I wake up several hours later to the sun shining so brightly in my eyes I can't even focus. My whole body is stiff from sleeping in a cramped position for so long. As I stretch out, I see that the businesswoman is gone. Now sitting across the aisle from me is a woman with gray hair pinned into a disheveled bun, playing cards with herself.

Noticing that I'm awake, she smiles at me and says, "Lord, child, I didn't think anything would bring you back to the land of the living."

I just nod.

"I'm going to visit my son and new grandchild—my first granddaughter, mind you; there are already three boys ahead of her. They live in Raleigh," she says, nodding back at me.

"Where are we?" I ask, looking out the window at empty fields and a ribbon of highway that looks like it's chasing the train tracks.

"Oh, about twenty minutes, half an hour outside of D.C. How far are you going?"

"Miami."

"My God, honey, you've got a long ways to go. Want me to get you something from the club car? I'm going."

"Well, okay, if you could," I say. "Orange juice or apple, whatever they have." I reach into my pocket, but she shakes her head.

"My treat," she says, and wobbles down the aisle, clutching the tops of seats so she won't fall. I settle back into my seat and put on my headphones. As Sinéad croons to me about another lost love, I think about my mother.

• • •

I was eight when my mother first left, or at least that's the first time I remember. She taped a note to the refrigerator, between the macaroni collages and the finger paintings. It said something like, "(1) Mike—lunches for girls are inside. (2) Don't forget to pick up the laundry Friday. (3) I've gone away for a while. Be back soon. Love, Carole. P.S. Samantha and Janie, be good to Daddy. XXXXOOO, Mommy."

She left for good about a year after the twins were born. She told us she was going away for a couple of weeks to Aunt Carrie's in Arizona. "Even mommies need vacations," she said, smiling, as she brushed her lips against our foreheads—but I knew she wasn't coming back.

Dad didn't like us to talk about her. He never forbade it, but he didn't like it. After a while, we just stopped bringing up her name. By the time she called to tell us about her new job booking speakers for conventions all over the country, we had already fashioned a routine without her.

• • •

The woman across the aisle gives me a tiny bottle of orange juice and begins to collect her baggage.

"Raleigh! All passengers for Raleigh, North Carolina, next stop!"

"Enjoy your granddaughter," I say as she hurries down the aisle. "Thanks for the orange juice."

Our car begins to lurch and I feel the brakes pleading the train to a complete stop. New people board, elbowing their way through the crowded aisle.

Except for the juice, I haven't had anything to eat all day, and my stomach has started to grumble and groan. I leave my jacket so people will know the seat is taken—and make my way to the club car.

• • •

I come back loaded down: barbecue potato chips, chocolate-covered peanut-butter cups and a Coke. Someone is in the seat next to mine and I'm annoyed, but I have no right to be. Luckily, my window seat is still free. If he's a pest, all I have to do is lean against the window and pretend I'm asleep.

"Excuse me."

He looks up at me, startled, as if I've interrupted him or something. "Yeah?"

"That's my seat," I say, gesturing to the window with my chin.

"Oh, sorry." He gets up and moves out of the way so I can get in. He has a long face with perfectly straight dirty-blond hair that hangs in his eyes. He's wearing a faded orange T-shirt with GO CLIMB A ROCK printed on it and when he stands up, I notice how loose his jeans are; they sit low on his hips and look as if there's very little keeping them up.

I squeeze past him into my seat and pick up the copy of *Rolling Stone* that I bought in the train station.

"Nice day for a train ride," he announces.

"Hmmm."

"How far you going?"

"Miami," I answer, looking him straight in the face. He looks away.

"I'm going there, too," he tells me. Then there's just silence.

I turn to look out the window. I had thought there would be some interesting scenery, that when we entered the South, I would see a difference, or at least feel a difference. But I don't. It looks like the same flat land I left behind in New Jersey.

"You always had such short hair?"

"What?"

Embarrassed, maybe realizing it wasn't the most polite thing to ask, he repeats it.

"No. Why?" Why the hell does he care?

"I don't know." Mr. Go Climb a Rock shrugs his shoulders. "I like it. I just wondered."

I pull my headphones out of my bag. De La Soul pounds loudly in my ears, a steel curtain of sound isolating me from the rest of the world. While Mr. Go Climb a Rock stares ahead, fixating on something that I can't make out, I study his face. He looks older than I first thought. His skin is pitted and he has tiny wrinkles that radiate like sun rays from the corners of his eyes. He turns to look at me, but when he does, I twist around and curl up against the window, pretending I'm asleep.

• • •

I wonder if my mother is dating anyone now. I can just imagine what she's like around guys—men other than my father, I mean. I just hope that if she has a hot date, I don't have to watch. It honestly makes me sick.

"Excuse me," I say to Mr. Go Climb a Rock. He gets up as I grab my small bag and move into the aisle.

In the cramped bathroom, I sit on the toilet breathing heavily. I hold my face in my hands. I don't know why I agreed to this in the first place. Every time I see her or think about seeing her, my stomach gets so knotted up I can't breathe. She doesn't have a hold on you anymore, I tell myself. I stand up, throw cold water on my face and give myself a good, long stare in the mirror. My features seem odd to me, naked and out of place: my blue eyes puffy and too far apart, my lips too pale and cracked.

I reach into my bag and pull out a heavy black eyeliner and carefully outline my eyes. It doesn't look right, so I extend the lines to my temples. My eyes still look strange, but in a good way. I put on scarlet lipstick until my lips look stained with blood. My cheeks are pale; I pat on powder until they become even whiter. I unlock the door and open it, only to find Mr. Go Climb a Rock standing there.

"Sorry," he says, cheeks turning red. "I didn't know——"

"That's okay." I start to squeeze past him, to make my way out of the bathroom, but he's standing in the way and staring at me and all of a sudden, I realize that I don't want to go back to my seat at all.

I grab his hand and pull him in after me. He doesn't protest, doesn't say anything. He just smiles and lets me lead the way. The bathroom stinks of stale cigarette smoke and urine. I slide the lock on the door closed and sit on the toilet. While he's pressed up against the door, I slide my hands down to his hips, ease off his jeans and start to go down on him. He stops me, grabbing my hands.

"C'mere," he drawls, saying it as one word. He pulls me up, smiling slowly, but I hold back.

"No, you come here."

"Have it your way," he says, and comes to me.

He sits down and I pull off my jeans and straddle him. He doesn't say anything, doesn't try to woo me, and I'm glad for that. He just tightens his grip, his arms weaving through my underarms, his hands grasping the back of my neck, holding on.

"Spartanburg," I hear the conductor yell. "Next stop, Spartanburg. Five minutes."

As the train lurches and staggers, I can feel that Mr. Go Climb a Rock is about to come. I push off his thighs and climb off him before he does. I pull on my jeans, put on more lipstick, staring into the dirty mirror. He hasn't moved, but I can see him watching me in the mirror's reflection.

"Do you want me to go out first, or do you want to?" he asks me.

I don't turn around. "What are you talking about?" I'm still studying myself in the mirror, the palm of my hand grazing the back of my head, running against the grain of my hair.

"If we walk out at the same time, people will wonder."

"So?"

"I just thought you might care."

"No."

"All right," he says, standing up and pulling up his pants. "Let's go."

I open the door and step outside into the aisle. Nobody turns around to stare, and nobody seems to notice two people coming out of the bathroom instead of just one. I walk back to my seat and Mr. Go Climb a Rock follows, sliding in next to me.

I stare out the window. I know Spartanburg can't be that interesting, but I have the urge to jump off the train and stay, not showing up in Miami at all.

"What are you looking at?"

"Not much," I answer, turning around to face him.

He nods and keeps nodding for a while, as if it were conversation in itself.

"I'm going to try and get some sleep," I say, rolling my sweater into a ball and leaning it up against the window.

He nods again but doesn't answer.

"Good night," I say, even though it's still light outside.

I spend the rest of the train ride in a daze or a doze, sleeping in snatches. At one point, about three in the morning, I wake up hungry.

I walk to the club car, but it's closed. Instead of going right back to my seat, I stand at the front of the car, watching people sleep. It seems so peaceful being in a room filled with strangers, not knowing or feeling responsible for any of their problems. The sway of the train and the steady rhythmic clanking of the wheels seem luxurious somehow. It's like a long soak in a steaming hot bath to be speeding along in the middle of the night toward Miami.

• • •

When I wake up again, it's morning and so bright that for a moment, I'm scared that I've missed the stop. But the conductor comes around and, after seeing my worried face, informs me that it's still forty-five minutes to Miami.

Mr. Go Climb a Rock is still asleep, curled up in his seat, his mouth opening and closing as if he is chewing on something. I start gathering my stuff, putting away my Walkman and magazines, taking out my make-up kit and toothbrush.

In the bathroom, I spend a long time lingering over every detail. During the night, I almost forgot what I was doing on this train, but now that we're nearly there, it's becoming real, almost too real for me to deal with. What am I going to say to her?

Back at the seat, Mr. Go Climb a Rock is awake and is contorting his body in the strangest way. He sees me watching him, but he doesn't stop.

"I need to crack my joints when I wake up in the morning. I'm just addicted to it," he explains.

Shrugging my shoulders, I squeeze past him to my seat.

"So, you never told me what you'll be doing in Miami," he says.

"Visiting my mother."

He nods. "Maybe we could see each other while you're there."

"I don't think so."

"All right," he says, humoring me.

We turn from each other; I start looking out the window and he turns toward the aisle. We don't say anything to each other the rest of the way to Miami.

When I step off the train into the crowd of waiting people, she's the first person I see. Arms outstretched, a smile fixed on her face, she must have spotted me before I saw her, because she's gesturing wildly for me to hurry over. She's wearing lilac shorts with a matching striped shirt, twirling her sunglasses in one hand. I feel rumpled just looking at her.

"My baby, my baby girl," she murmurs as she wraps her arms around me. "Let me take a look at you."

I stand back stiffly for inspection.

"My God, Samantha, what in the world did you do to your hair?"

I don't answer.

"Okay. Okay. It doesn't really matter. I'm just so excited to see you. Come on, let's get out of here. Is this all you brought with you?" She grabs my small bag and starts pulling me toward the stairs. Just ahead of us, I spot Mr. Go Climb a Rock, looking lost.

"Hold on, Mom," I say as I break free of her hold. "I want you to meet somebody." I reach for his hand. "Umm, Chris," I say, looking him in the eyes, "I want you to meet my mother. Mom, this is Chris, Christopher . . . uh . . . Marks. Chris, this is my mother."

"It's nice to meet you, ma'am," he says politely. "Your daughter, well, she's something."

Her head is cocked to one side and she looks at him distrustfully. "Yes, my daughter is something. Excuse me, Mr. Marks," she says, nodding faintly, "we have to be leaving now. It was very nice to meet you."

"Maybe I can see you at some point over the next few days?" Mr. Go Climb a Rock asks me.

Before I can say anything, my mother answers for me. "I'm so sorry, Samantha and I have a lot planned for our vacation. I don't think we'll have the time. Come on, Samantha."

As she pulls me toward the exit, I turn to wave to Mr. Go Climb a Rock. He's just standing there, looking sort of confused, the only person standing still in a sea of rushing, harried people.

Outside, the hot air hits me full blast, sticky and stifling, like I've walked into an enormous hair drier. I already feel out of place; a pale, sallow creature trying to blend into a smiling, tanned crowd.

In the car on the way to the hotel, my mom plays tour guide: "Samantha, look down that street—there's the beach! Aren't the palm trees wonderful?" She keeps up the chatter. "Isn't it amazing to be able to wear shorts in January? You know, Samantha, we're traveling in style. The hotel is gorgeous, it's got everything you could possibly want."

After a careful pause, she continues, "Maybe the beauty parlor can do something with your hair. What did you do, Samantha?"

"I cut it, Mom."

There's another pause. She pats my leg, smiles and says, "Did I tell you the hotel is right on the water? I really love it down here—sunshine three hundred sixty-five days a year. What more could you want?"

• • •

The hotel is pink and turquoise, heavily mirrored, a glittery structure that's shaped more like a boat than a building. Inside, the air is frigid and everything's blown out of shape, yanked from its context. The walls are stark, blinding white; steel sculptures in geometric shapes, like giant Tinkertoys, sit on pedestals flanking the entrance hall. On the other side of the lobby, water cascades from a rock garden, then snakes through the lobby, emptying into a pond filled with Japanese goldfish.

"It's a great place for a convention," my mother says, surveying the scene with satisfaction. "Our room is on the fifth floor, overlooking the pool. You're going to love it."

The room is standard decor compared with the lobby. We unpack, my mother carefully unfolding and hanging her blouses and suits, while I yank my clothes out and stuff them into drawers. I catch her glancing at me in dismay. "Honey, you've gotten so tall in the last couple of years, I bet we're almost the same size. Try this on," she says, holding a delicate mauve silk blouse under my chin. "This would look gorgeous on you."

"I don't think so." I flop down on the nearest bed. "It's not my style."

She sighs and hangs it up. "Well, honey, okay. Maybe we can check out the shops in the mall later. But right now, I'm going to have to meet some people from the convention for an hour or two. I wish I didn't, but I do."

She takes a pink suit into the bathroom to change, but her voice goes on relentlessly, "Why don't you check out the pool while I'm gone? It's enormous! Or, no, you must be hungry after that long trip. You can go to any of the restaurants and put the bill on your room key. Or order from room service if you're tired. There's a list of all the movies they have and the cable stations right on top of the TV. And there are Cokes and stuff in the minibar. Just leave me a note if you go to the mall or the pool. And we'll go out for a terrific dinner tonight."

"Mom?" I call. "Why wouldn't you let me see that guy?"

"What guy?"

"From the train."

"Samantha." Her head appears in the doorway. "We don't have that much time, and I want to spend it with you, not some stranger from a train. Besides, I bet that man was twice your age."

"If that's the way you want it, fine," I say. "Just fine."

She reappears, pink and perfect. "Samantha, I just want you to know how happy it makes me to have you here. I'm so glad we can be friends."

She ducks out, waving, not waiting for my response, and the door slams behind her.

"'Bye," I say.

• • •

The pool really is enormous and brilliant blue in the hot sunlight. No one is swimming, but people are sitting under striped umbrellas or lying in lounge chairs working on their tans, and waiters are taking them drinks and sandwiches. I think of going back up for my bathing suit, but maybe I won't stay long. Instead, I take off my shoes and roll my jeans above the knee. I sit at the shallow end, with my feet on the second step, cooling them in the water. New Jersey seems a long way away.

When the waiter comes by, I hold up my hand with the room key in it. "Can I get a drink?"

He's about twenty-two, wiry and dark, maybe Mexican or Cuban. "What can I get you?" He doesn't have an accent when he answers.

"A blue Hawaiian?"

He gives me a sharp look and laughs. "In three years, maybe." He keeps walking, delivering drinks to the next table. On his way back, he says, "Want a Coke? Or something?"

"Rum and Coke?"

He crouches down and grins at me. "What do you need a drink for? How old are you, anyway?"

"Believe me, I have serious reasons for needing a drink. Besides, I'm almost eighteen."

I can tell he doesn't buy it, but he's playing along. "You know what they say about almost."

"Yeah, horseshoes and hand grenades, right?" I say. "But who would know?"

"Listen, I can't," he says, and looks at my room key. "But if you're desperate, what's wrong with the minibar?"

"What?" I say, not knowing what he means, but then I realize that the thing my mother said had the Cokes in it must have liquor in it, too. "Oh, sure," I say, "but who wants to drink alone?"

"I'm off at three," he says. He stands up and raises his eyebrows.

"Room 503," I say, raising mine.

He definitely looks surprised, starts to say something but moves on. He turns around and looks back at me, then gives me a thumbs up.

• • •

It's nearly four thirty when the door opens abruptly, casting harsh light through the room. I see my mother's silhouette in the door frame.

"I'm going out to wait by the elevator for exactly ten seconds," she says, her voice straining for composure. "Mister, you'll be gone when I get back. Samantha, you wait for me here."

The waiter apologizes quickly as he hurries out the door. I am left with two gin and tonics and my mother to face.

She returns and stands at the door, hands on her hips. "Was this *really* necessary, Samantha?"

"Yeah, actually, it was necessary," I say, my head down, eyes on the carpet. For some reason, I feel calm, though my heart is racing.

My mother is livid, pacing back and forth like she's in a cage. "Just what is it that's troubling you? Why do you insist on spoiling this for both of us? Why ruin it, Samantha?"

"What makes you think you haven't ruined it already?"

"And what is that supposed to mean? You are a fifteen-year-old *child* and you are acting like a——"

"How would you know what I am?" I interrupt, raising my head. "You've seen me maybe three hours in the past three years. How much chance to be a *child* do you think I get cooking dinner, doing the laundry, buying the *fucking* groceries?"

She drops her hands from her hips and looks toward the ceiling, exasperated. She doesn't reply. How can she?

I've made my point. I grab my bag and push past her to the door.

"What are you doing?" she demands shrilly.

"Leaving."

"You can't."

"Yeah, I can. You should know about *that*."

I close the door behind me and duck into the stairwell so she can't catch me by the elevator. I hurry down one flight of stairs, then slow down for the remaining flights. The door at the bottom of the stairwell opens onto the pool area.

Instead of going back to try to find the lobby, I walk over to the pool. The area is almost deserted, with empty lounge chairs and steam rising off the pool in the late-afternoon sunlight. I take my shoes off again and roll up my jeans. I sit down at the shallow end, where I sat before, and think about Kevin and Janie, how much they'd love this pool. The bright blue water invites me to slide right in. But I don't. I just sit there, really quiet, moving my hand back and forth, gently skimming the surface of the water.

My mind wanders and I think of my train ride. I wonder what Mr. Go Climb a Rock is doing. Not in an abstract sense but what he's actually doing this moment. I wonder what he thinks I'm all about. And what about the others? Then again, they probably don't care.

In some ways, I long to be back on the train, not with anyone else but myself, speeding toward some exotic place: Los Angeles, New Orleans, San Francisco. But it really wouldn't matter where. I draw my knees to my chest, hugging them tight, and despite the warm kiss of the sun, I shiver.

I remember that the room I've just left overlooks the pool. I look around, counting up five floors. She's there, behind the glass of the sliding door, looking down at me. It's too far for me to be able to see her expression. For a long time, we stay like that, like statues, neither of us moving, and then my hand raises first to the rough stubble on the back of my head and then upward to give a small, almost imperceptible wave.

The Greyhound

by **DANIEL LYONS**
1992

What we stole was a greyhound. Her name was Coco and she belonged to Rocco Giaccalone, president of the local chapter of the women's garment union. Giaccalone was a dime-store mafioso, a fat old man who wore sweaty suits and sharp-toed shoes and who supposedly once snipped off the thumbs of a driver who'd stolen a few cartons of cigarettes from one of his trucks.

That story about the thumbs was the first thing my roommate, Evan, and I learned when we moved to the North End of Boston. The second thing we learned was that everyone hated us. We couldn't leave because we'd signed a one-year lease ("Old World charm," the ad said), and so there we were, two pallid young college grads trapped in the land of the swarthy people.

Giaccalone's racing dog was as skinny as a runway model, with a face like Sophia Loren's and eyes like big saucers of milk, and when she walked down Hanover Street, I swear those foolish guineas would stand aside and start to whisper. Coco had been a big champion at Seabrook and Wonderland. I won ninety dollars on her once, before Giaccalone took her in payment of a gambling debt and made her sit by his table in his Caffè Tripoli like a slave begging bits of pastry.

"It's fucking disgusting," I said, watching Coco snap a piece of chocolate-covered *pizzelli* from Giaccalone's hand, which glittered with gold rings the size of walnuts. "A dog like that, a racing dog—you can't keep it as a pet."

"What," Evan said, "they should build it a shrine?" Evan is a software programmer, like me, and like me he is not a geek. He reads Freud and Campbell and cyberpunk novels, and once, at a party, I saw him drive an earnest, hairy-legged Cambridge girl to tears by insisting that he no longer believed in anything. The next morning I walked into the living room and found her sitting on the couch, wearing Evan's *Star Trek* T-shirt and drinking a cup of coffee.

"I won ninety dollars on that dog once," I told Evan.

"You thought I forgot since the last time you told me?"

I called for our bill and, sure enough, the fucker tried to cheat us; he'd charged us four dollars instead of three.

"Amigo," I said.

"That's Spanish," Evan said.

"Whatever. Hey. Waiter."

He pretended he didn't speak English and insisted we pay four bucks. I tried to make myself clear: "No fucking way," I said.

Meanwhile, Giaccalone had turned in his chair and was taking an interest. The waiter ran back and whispered to him, and then the fat bastard started calling us faggots and had his nephew Tony throw us out.

We went to the water and got wasted on fog cutters. When we got back, every parking space in the North End was taken, so I moved the barrels out of the space reserved for Giaccalone's Fleetwood and put my Toyota there.

"Fuck him," I said. "I live here, too."

"I love it when you get all drunk and Catholic and indignant," Evan said.

We staggered up the four flights to our apartment and crashed. In the morning, when I stepped outside to get the newspaper, I found the Corolla slumped on the pavement with all its tires slashed.

● ● ●

Giaccalone, being the fat prick that he was, said he didn't know anything about any tires on any faggot's car. The waiters stood behind the counter washing dishes. The old guineas in back looked up from their game of dominoes, then kept playing.

"So nobody here saw anyone near my car," I said.

"Nobody here saw nothing," Giaccalone said.

• • •

The desk cop at the police station—whose name was Incorpora, which is, of course, Italian—gave me a report to fill out and said there was nothing they could do. I asked why they couldn't look around a little, maybe pressure an informer. "What do you think this is," he said, "*Starsky and Hutch*?"

That afternoon, when a crew from the garage came to replace the tires, a crowd gathered on the sidewalk, and Mrs. Ronsavelli, our neighbor from across the hall, clucked her tongue and shook her head and whispered to the other old ladies in Sicilian.

"What could you possibly have been thinking?" said Maria Colon, the Puerto Rican girl who worked in the laundry on the first floor of our building.

I wanted to tell her that in any other city, in any other place, this would not have happened. Nowhere else in America, I wanted to say, would a greasy, shit-filled *crespelli* like Rocco Giaccalone be allowed to tyrannize a neighborhood. But it was a hot day, I was still woozy from the fog cutters and there was no use making speeches.

"It was late," I told her. "I was tired."

"And drunk, too, probably." She smiled and pulled her curly brown hair away from her face. "You Irish, you shouldn't drink."

Maria was wearing a pair of cutoffs. The puny white crescents of her ass were peeking out beneath the fringe. I thought again about asking her out. She worked for the guy who owned our building, and every once in a while she'd sneak up to our place for a cup of tea. One time, I'd made plans to have dinner with her, but then I found out she had a daughter, so I canceled. Told her I had the flu. But now, with my car up on jacks and my luck running off in a dozen crazy directions, I saw in Maria the promise of a sane life. I saw Sunday dinners and afternoon screwing, a little bedroom with floral wallpaper and a crucifix hanging over the door. I pulled Evan over beside the tow truck and asked him if he thought she'd give me another chance. "Give me some advice," I said.

Evan adjusted his glasses and eyed the crowd. "Move your car," he said.

• • •

For days I paced back and forth between the kitchen and living room, cooking up schemes for revenge. The good plans, like smashing the windows in Giaccalone's Fleetwood, were too dangerous. The safe ones, like waking him with phone calls in the middle of the night, were so silly that to carry them out would only humiliate me further.

And then, on Friday night, while we were out on the fire escape with a bottle of White Label, we saw a dog wandering down Hanover Street, poking her nose into the trash bags on the sidewalk.

"Is that Coco?" I said.

"No," Evan said, "it's the world's tallest rat."

"Fucking Giaccalone. The guy should be shot. A dog like that, out eating garbage."

"Someone should give her a good home," Evan said. I smiled at him and he smiled at me, and before we knew it, we'd staggered downstairs and opened the door. Then Coco was in our apartment, wolfing a piece of New York strip that we diced up and placed in a bowl for her. She darted around the apartment, sniffing at the furniture. Then, without so much as a whimper, she curled up in an armchair and fell asleep.

I balanced myself on the arm of the chair and stroked her neck. "The great Coco," I said.

Evan lay on the couch. "The great Coco," he muttered.

"Did I tell you I once won ninety dollars on this dog?"

He began to snore.

I lay on my bed in my shorts. "Ninety dollars."

• • •

Next morning, as ever, the white cups gleamed in their racks behind the counter at Caffè Tripoli, the pastries lay in rows in the cases and the air had that wonderful, bitter taste of espresso.

But anyone could see that something terrible had happened to Giaccalone. There were dark circles around his eyes. His hair had not been combed. He was chain-smoking. He ignored his sweet roll and coffee. He picked up the paper and put it down, then sat wringing his hands and looking out the window like a zombie.

Tony ran in and whispered into his uncle's ear. The old man said something. Tony shook his head. The old man cuffed him and said, "Then try again," and Tony ran out.

I held the *Globe* up in front of my face. "This is better than sex," I said.

"I can't remember what sex feels like," Evan said.

"Like your hand, only warmer. You think he suspects us?"

"This guy?" Evan stirred sugar into his cappuccino. "This guy couldn't suspect his way out of a broom closet."

We took a cannoli home for Coco. She met us at the door, wagging her stumpy tail. "Look, she actually likes this fucking dump," Evan said.

She had finished the bacon and eggs that I'd put out for her, and there was a fresh loaf of dog crap on the newspaper under the kitchen table. I rolled up the paper, tossed it into the trash and set out a new sheet.

Evan bent over. "Wait a minute—my mother's soup bowl? A dog is eating out of my mother's china?"

"Relax. A dog's mouth is way cleaner than a human's. Everybody knows that."

"I don't know that." He picked up the bowl and put it into the sink.

There was a knock at the door. I looked out the peephole. Mrs. Ronsavelli was in the hallway, craning her neck up at me. "Christ," I said, "it's the Bride of Frankenstein again."

"Has she got Gus with her?"

"No," I said.

Gus, the neighborhood plumber, visited the Bride two or three times a week. He carried his toolbox as if he had come to fix something, and in a way, I guess he had, because he always came out after an hour or so with his hair messed up and a spring in his step.

"What the fuck does she want?" Evan said.

"What, I'm a mind reader? Get the dog out of here."

She knocked again.

I said, "Just a minute."

"It's Mrs. Ronsavelli. I need to talk to you."

"Okay," I said. "Just a minute."

Evan took Coco into his room. "Ask her if she's wearing any underwear," he said.

The Bride spidered into the room. "You boys were playing that music again last night. I asked you not to play that music."

"That's a nice dress, Mrs. Ronsavelli."

She clicked her tongue against her teeth, then spied the newspaper on the floor. "You have a pet?"

"Our pipes leak. Maybe you could send Gus over next time he's here."

She scowled. "There are no pets here. They bring fleas."

"We don't have a pet."

"You've heard about Mr. Giaccalone's dog?"

I shook my head. "You mean Coco?"

"Gone." The old lady nodded.

"The people from the race track took her?"

She peered up at me through her thick glasses, which magnified her eyes and made her look like a creature from outer space. "Where is your roommate?"

"Doing errands. I was just running out myself."

I opened the door. She began to step out, then stopped and wagged her finger. "Pets bring fleas," she said.

• • •

The original plan was to hold Coco hostage for the weekend, just long enough to put old Giaccalone into the cardiac unit at Mass General. But on Sunday morning I opened the *Globe* and found he'd placed an ad offering a five-thousand-dollar reward for the return of his dog.

"Well, folks," I said, "it's a whole new ball game."

Evan, of course, had to pretend that he had morals. It's a Jewish thing, King Solomon and all that crap. Catholics, we just swing away, like Wade Boggs with a three-and-two count, and when the sinning's done, we go to confession and have our souls wiped clean.

"I don't know," he said. "I mean, it's one thing to pull a hack, but this—this would be stealing."

I reminded him that I had gone along with his idea to put the Jerusalem B virus in the sales department's computers and that I'd shared the blame with him when he couldn't clear it from the server. "You owe me," I said. "Besides, the fucker ruined my car. He owes me for those tires."

"What if they catch us? They'll cut off our fucking thumbs. How do you type without thumbs?"

"You tap the space bar with your stump."

In the end he came around, as I knew he would. He wanted to do it as much as I did. Who wouldn't? The clincher was when I reminded him that his $3,200 Visa balance was going to cost him $576 in interest alone this year. "You pay it off, you can start all over again," I said.

"Okay, okay, I'm in," he said. Now that we were partners he was all excited. "The neighborhood's talking about it," he said. "They've got posters up everywhere and they've got all the little kids out hunting around. It's fucking crazy. By the way, I saw Maria."

"Did she say anything about me?"

"She said you're a fag and you wear your pants too high."

"Blow me."

"I'm off baby food."

• • •

We rented post-office boxes in Andover, Newburyport and Boston, all under false names, and arranged to have the mail to the Boston box forwarded to Andover, and the mail to Andover forwarded to Newburyport. This was my plan. "Clean, simple, elegant," I said.

Evan smirked. "Childish, low-tech, thoroughly unworkable."

"Hey," I said, "we're not dealing with rocket scientists here."

But when we called Giaccalone's reward hotline and Evan said, in his Squeaky the Clown falsetto, that we wanted the money mailed to us, the guy laughed. "It's those fucking kids again," he said. "Hey, mail *this,* motherfucker." Then he hung up.

"Look," Evan said, "why don't we just take the dog down there, tell them we found her and collect the money?"

"Golly, Evan, why don't we jump in front of trucks on I-93? Why don't we wander around Roxbury at night? They won't pay us—they'll fucking kill us."

He lay down on the couch and adjusted his glasses, which he'd repaired with black electrical tape so that they made him look like someone who'd escaped from an asylum. This was appropriate, since outside our little hostage den the city was going crazy.

On Salem, on Prince Street, on the door of St. Anthony's Social Club—the whole North End was papered with Coco posters, and up on Bunker Hill, little packs of children spent their evenings running through the backyards calling for Coco. Reward posters filled the grocery store windows; the ushers at St. Stephen's handed them out at Mass, stapled to the parish bulletin. At night, Gus snuck down the alley behind our building, calling to the dog, then ran up the back stairs and gave the Bride the high hard one.

• • •

On Wednesday Giaccalone raised the reward to $10,000, and the *Herald* ran a story on the front page with a picture of the old crook looking distraught and holding a framed photograph of Coco. The headline read, LOST DOG BRINGS $10,000 REWARD; "SHE'S LIKE MY CHILD," CAFÉ OWNER SAYS.

"*'Café owner?'* That's like calling Charles Manson a youth-club director," I said.

"I didn't know he owned the café," Evan said.

"Christ only knows what he owns." I tossed the paper onto the coffee table. "Anyway, ten thousand bucks. I feel like goddamn Julius Rosenberg."

"What?"

"You know, with the Lindbergh baby. Julius and Ethel Rosenberg."

"The Rosenbergs didn't steal the Lindbergh baby."

"Well, that's what you say. But from what I've read, there was proof."

"The Rosenbergs were convicted of spying."

"What?"

"It was a different case. The Lindbergh baby was taken by someone else."

"Well, whatever." I picked up the paper. "That's what I feel like."

"You're going to feel like Jimmy Hoffa if we wait much longer."

● ● ●

Coco was not just a dog, she was the *über*-pet, and I hated the fact that we had to keep her cooped up, because she had way too much dignity for that. Take the TV remote. She knew that when I watched TV, I didn't play with her, so she used to hide the remote. Only after I'd played with her for a while would she lead me to it. I had nine credits toward a master's degree and this dog was teaching me tricks. And then, as if to insult me, right in the middle of playing she'd drop into an armchair and fall asleep, and I'd be standing there with a chew toy in my hand, feeling like a fool.

She'd been spoiled. When we brought her bones from the butcher or toys from the pet store at the mall, or when we covered her armchair with a comforter or gave her one of my sneakers to chew—never, not once, did she show any appreciation. She used our gifts and played our fetch game and let us pet her, but she kept us at a distance. I was never sure whether she loved us or despised us.

"She reminds me of a girl I went out with in college," Evan said. "Beth Heidelman from Shaker Heights. Total JAP"

"Be serious," I said. "You went out with a girl in college?"

Like fools, we competed for Coco's affection. We fed her steak at night, bacon and eggs in the morning, and at lunch we took turns driving home to feed her hamburger and give her fresh water. I mean, it was sick. A lot of times I'd stop on the way and pick up a cannoli, just so I could stand there, enraptured, and watch as she snapped up the chunks of ricotta cheese with her long, muscled tongue.

At night, when we got home, she met us at the door. We started calling her the Wife. She watched movies on the VCR with us, she hid behind the armchair and peeked out, and if she slept in Evan's room, I felt—well, I felt jealous.

• • •

We worked at a place called Ionic Software, developing (I use the term loosely) a groupware program called Nectar. The project was two years past deadline, the fake-tan assholes in marketing were screaming for code and we were nowhere near done. The thing was crawling with bugs; every time we fixed one, we created two. It was insane. We'd long ago decided that Nectar would never actually work and that we were simply biding time until marketing caught on and fired us. "Who gives a shit about groupware, anyway?" Evan used to say. "I mean, why do these people want to work in groups in the first place?"

Now, with a dog held hostage in our apartment and the Mob ready to drill us new assholes, neither of us could concentrate long enough to even look for bugs in Nectar, let alone fix them. Evan spent his days going for coffee and hovering around the girls in the sales department. I played video games, and in the evening I found excuses to visit Maria at the laundry.

"We've got a pool going," she said. "Pick the day that Coco comes back and you win the money."

"What if she doesn't come back?"

"We give the money to the church. We're selling Coco T-shirts, too." She held up a shirt with a picture of Coco and the words HAVE YOU SEEN ME? silk-screened on the front. "Blue or white. Ten dollars. You want one?"

I bought two—white, extra large—and took them upstairs and showed them to Evan. "This whole fucking neighborhood is out of its mind," I said.

He was in his bedroom at his computer, trading e-mail on one of the X-rated bulletin boards. Coco was asleep on his bed, muzzled and leashed to the bedpost.

"Look at this shit," he said.

I leaned over and read the semicoherent ravings of some fool talking about his hard-on to a woman named Gloria and following her orders to put an ice cube up his ass.

"Who are these sick fucks?" I asked.

"The guy is an account executive in New York."

"What about Gloria?"

"*C'est moi.*"

"What?"

A line appeared on the screen: WHAT SHOULD I DO NEXT?, it read.

Evan typed: TAKE A PAPER CLIP AND CLIP IT TO YOUR RIGHT NIPPLE. THEN DO THE LEFT.

A line appeared: YOU'RE VICIOUS, GLORIA.

Evan typed: THAT'S MISTRESS GLORIA TO YOU, SCUM.

"This is disgusting," I said. "Even for you."

"Last week I made him singe the hair off his balls with a lighter."

A line appeared: I'M BLEEDING.

I flipped off the computer, grabbed Evan by the shoulder and reminded him that we might be bleeding ourselves, and bleeding profusely at that, if we did not come up with a way to ransom back the dog.

"Fuck off," he said. "You're the mastermind here."

• • •

We went to Caffè Tripoli. "We can't stop going," I had said. "If we do, we'll look like suspects."

"Good thinking, Raskolnikov," Evan had said.

No sooner had we ordered coffee than Tony appeared at our table. "Hello, ladies," he said. "How're those new tires?"

"Great," I said. "How's the missing dog?"

He snickered. "Why, you got her? You fucking her in the ass? You're sick of doing it to each other, is that it?"

"You sound jealous," I said.

"Fuck you. You know what I think?"

"I didn't know you did think."

"I think you wouldn't know what to do with that dog because it's a girl."

"Tony," Evan said, "what *is* that perfume you're wearing?"

• • •

We were in the lab at work, reading other people's e-mail messages off the server, when the solution came to me.

"Evan," I said, as we closed another of the pathetic love letters that our boss, McTwigan, had been sending to one of the sales assistants, "can you hack into a bank?"

"Depends. If it's a 3090, like at Mass First, sure."

"You can get in and get out?"

"Reilly," he said, "on a 3090 I'm Jesus Christ. I can walk on fucking water, okay?"

I switched on his modem. "Then start dialing," I said. "I'll make coffee."

After three hours of fucking up, we tapped into the Mass First host system. We created a new account, using the name Gloria Domina; we gave her a balance of $250.

•   •   •

The next day I went to the branch office on Hanover Street. "I'd like to make a deposit into my wife's account," I said. "I don't have her passbook."

"No problem," the teller said.

She called up the Gloria Domina account, took my $100 and handed me a receipt that showed a $350 balance. "Have a nice day," I said, and after I walked out, Evan walked in and opened an account in his name.

•   •   •

That night we called Giaccalone's hotline. I listened on the extension; Evan did the talking. "Don't hang up," he squeaked. "We're serious."

"All right, Tinkerbell," the guy said. "Give me the numbers on the dog's ID tag."

"Two-seven-five-five."

"Shit." He rustled a piece of paper. "Okay, what's different about the dog's left front paw pad?"

Evan looked at me. I lifted the paw; it was white. I mouthed the words *It's white.*

"It's white," Evan said.

"Okay, pal. You bring us the dog, we pay you the money. It's as simple as that."

"It's not that simple. Get out a pencil and paper and I'm going to give you a name and a bank account number where I want you to deposit the money."

"Oh, fuck. You're not going to pull this shit again, are you?"

Evan gave me his little-kid-lost-in-the-mall look; I couldn't take it anymore.

"Look, jerky," I said, "the dog hasn't eaten in three fucking days. You make us wait another day and we're going to turn her into hamburger."

"Who the fuck was that?"

"Nobody," Evan squeaked. He waved at me to shut up. "But . . . but we'll do what he said. We'll do it, believe me."

"Hold a minute." The man went off the line; when the line opened again, Giaccalone was speaking.

"I want to hear her bark," he said.

"You what?"

"Bark, dick breath. How do I know she's still alive? Make her bark."

I took off Coco's muzzle, wrapped my arm around her and pinched her, hard, on the neck. She yelped.

"All right, you sick fucks. Give me the account number. And if we don't see that dog by tomorrow night, we go to the bank and freeze the account. And then we come looking for you."

"It's Mass First," Evan said. "The name is Gloria Domina. D-O-M-I-N-A. The account number is one-one-two-one-three-seven-five."

"Domina?" he said. "Isn't that the broad who goes out with Angiulo? Hey, who is this? Is this fucking Angiulo?"

"Just make the deposit."

"Hamburger?" Evan said. "We're going to turn her into hamburger?"

"I had to get his attention."

"You're a deviant, Reilly. A complete and utter deviant."

● ● ●

At ten thirty the next morning we tapped into the Mass First system. Gloria's balance was $10,350.

"I could cry," I said.

Evan transferred the money to his account and we drove to the Mass First branch at the mall and withdrew the money. We went back to work looking as if nothing had happened, which is not an easy thing to do when you're carrying $10,350 in cash in your backpack. We tapped into the Mass First system again. We vaporized Gloria Domina and closed Evan's account.

"No fingerprints," I said. "No paper trail."

"So how do we get rid of the dog?"

"Piece of cake."

"Really? How?"

"Don't worry."

"Don't worry? Don't fucking worry? What, you don't have a plan?"

"I have a plan," I said. "It's in the gestation phase."

The problem, of course, was the Bride. She ran to her peephole whenever anyone so much as moved in the hallway. There was no way to get the dog past her.

"We could wait until the middle of the night," Evan said.

"Too risky. She might be up soaking her hemorrhoids."

We went home and sat in the apartment and tried to come up with something. Meanwhile, down on Hanover Street, a couple of Giaccalone's thugs were standing on the sidewalk in leather jackets and driving gloves, scanning the street like Secret Service men.

"By now they've been to the bank," I said. "They know the money's gone."

Evan let the curtain fall back across the window. "I can't believe I let you talk me into this." Coco pressed her face against his cheek and tried to lick him through her muzzle, but he pushed her away. "Fuck off," he said, then went to his room.

• • •

I sat down; I stood up. I lay on the couch. But for the life of me, I couldn't think of a way to get that dog out of the building. But then Gus came poking along after dark, calling to Coco in the alley behind our building.

"Out looking for Coco again?" I asked as he skipped up onto our landing with a flashlight in his hand.

"For ten thousand bucks? You bet. And, well, Mrs. Ronsavelli's been having some trouble with her kitchen sink, so since I was going by . . ."

The Bride opened her door and glared at him. "Mr. Reilly has been having trouble with leaks in his apartment," she said. "Maybe you should have a look over there, too."

"Ours seems to have taken care of itself," I said.

"Good, then." She yanked the poor sap into her kitchen.

I ran to Evan's room. "T minus ten minutes and counting," I said. "Get your big raincoat, put it over the dog and wait here."

I ran downstairs to the laundry. Maria was getting ready to close up for the night.

"Maria, this is an emergency," I said. "Do you still have the passkey for the apartments?"

"No—it grew legs and ran away." She reached up and took the key from a nail on the wall behind her. "What's the matter? You lock yourself out again?"

"It's Mrs. Ronsavelli. We heard a crash, and then she was making, like, this moaning sound, and then there wasn't any sound at all."

"Jesus Christ," she said, then blessed herself and ran up the stairs behind me.

We stood outside the Bride's door. "Hear anything?" I whispered.

"I hear a noise." She leaned closer. "There it is again."

"You go in," I said. "I'm going to call an ambulance."

Evan and I were down the stairs and opening the back door for Coco when the shouting began. The Bride was screaming in Italian, Maria was screaming back in Spanish—God knows what they were saying—and by the time Gus came flying down the back stairs with only his T-shirt on and his pants unbuttoned, Coco had raced down the alley and out of sight.

"How're those pipes, Gus?" I said.

"Go fuck yourself," he said, then ran off down the alley.

For a moment Evan and I stood looking at each other and not talking; it was one of those fine, clear times when your heart seems to open up and everything good about life rushes in.

"Okay, then," Evan said. "Let's get wasted."

We drank champagne, we ate lobster and we put caviar on crackers, which, after I tasted one, I threw into the sink. Evan did his impersonation of Tony. We threw the money around like confetti. We drank a bottle of Madeira and a bottle of Armagnac, and I got so loaded that at one point I was going to light a Macanudo with a $100 bill, but Evan stopped me.

"A toast," I said, lifting a glass of port. "Good guys one, guineas nothing."

Then I passed out. When I woke, it was morning and I was lying beneath a blanket of bills, like a kid in a leaf pile. The room was strewn with ashtrays and bottles and empty boxes, and there was a smell of smoke and food gone bad. My mouth tasted like I'd spent the night going down on a menstruating monkey. Outside, a truck groaned in the alley. The sun laid a pale line along the tops of the buildings across the street; the light was still too thin to warm the air. The room seemed dead, like a beach the day after a storm.

"Evan," I said.

He turned but didn't answer. He lay on the couch with a newspaper over his face, which was just as well, I thought, because what I wanted to say might be embarrassing. I lay on the floor, unable to sit up. To move was to feel my brain slosh across my head and collide with the side of my skull.

"You know, I was thinking I might take my money and open a little restaurant. You know? Like a breakfast place."

"Reilly," he said, "fuck off."

I tried to sit up, but the room tilted and spun like a carnival ride and I had to lie back down. "Also," I said, "I'm going to ask Maria out. I'm going to make a life for myself."

"I'm going to puke," Evan said, then dragged himself off to the bathroom.

I listened to him retch, then drifted back toward sleep. Outside, a man was singing while he unloaded a truck and a boy was calling his friends out to play. Birds sang on the phone wires.

I woke to the sound of a dog barking outside. The barking was close. I opened my eyes. Evan was standing at the window, looking down at the street. He seemed as if he might get sick again.

There was pounding on the door. "Open up," Mrs. Ronsavelli said. "Somebody wants to see you."

My head felt as if it might split open. "Say it ain't so," I said.

But Coco kept howling and throwing herself at our door, Mrs. Ronsavelli continued to knock and I, flat on my back, felt weightless and empty. Evan fell onto the couch, face down. From the street came the sound of slapping footsteps and men swearing in Italian.

I reached for the phone and managed to knock the earpiece out of its cradle. I dialed zero; there was nothing. I clicked, then clicked again. The line was dead.

Equilibrium

by **ROLAND N. KELTS**
1993

I am living with a woman as strong as a nightclub bouncer. She lifts her weights and does her dances with hell-bent intensity. She takes her morning coffee coal black and chases it with a juice mix: light on the mango, heavy on the lime, straight from the blender. She is up by six A.M. at the latest, donning her tight black jogging bra with the turquoise straps, contorting herself into various positions to stretch out. She leaves me behind—or, rather, leaves me her behind, just a flash of it, shiny spandex, a convex tease of muscle and flesh disappearing through the bedroom door. Her keys jangle down the hallway. The front-door locks snap open, the door slams shut. Her running shoes bounce lightly down three flights of stairs and onto the empty street.

We met as seniors at the state university and called it dating. The summer after graduation, we began living together in this one-bedroom apartment here in Portsmouth, New Hampshire, just behind the bakeries on Market Square. When I met Mary she had soft curves and long, reddish-brown locks. She was girlish. Vulnerable, I suppose, but irresistible in a baggy denim jacket adorned with pins that said LOVER-GIRL and I STOP IN THE NAME OF LOVE. She also giggled a lot, loudly, at nearly everything I said and did.

In the year and a half since graduation she has transformed herself. She met a weight trainer-dancer named Stevie down at the bar where she works, and she metamorphosed in the gym. Now, at twenty-four, she has a body that issues demands just moving across the kitchen tile. She walks with a self-assurance that practically glows. Her thighs are fibrous walls of tissue, rigidly toned and taut, impervious. Her biceps seem permanently flexed, her breasts raised and poised. Mary is firm everywhere, as though her curves have been chiseled down. She could easily strangle me now, I am quite certain.

• • •

When Mary returns from her jog I am still in bed, sprawled across the futon, embarrassed to find my hand between my legs, squeezing gently. She is in the shower before I can pull my hand away, wipe the sleep debris from my eyes and begin an intermittent succession of smelly yawns. I hear her hums and moans through the sizzle of steam and spray: She is satisfying herself in the shower, no doubt. It happens. I lean forward. The voice is rich, self-obsessed, reciting a low, incantatory chant that gets louder fast. The sound is sensual, urging on the voluptuous hot, the rushing wet, the steady, driving pulse of the nozzle itself to . . . well, yes: to justify her love.

"Madonna's a blonde," I shout dryly when the shower ceases.

The curtain draws back with a vibrant scrape. The door is yanked open. Mary stands naked, shoulder-length hair crinkled and dampened black. She wraps a crimson towel firmly around her waist and brushes her hands lightly across her behind.

"She's a brunette, really," Mary says.

She looks down, stretches back, admires her sleek, pinkish torso. "In heart, soul and spirit, a natural-born brunette. Get with it, babe. She's dyed for effect."

• • •

Mary seems to dance all day, aerobics and jazz, though the latter has little to do with Miles or Coltrane. She takes dance classes downtown at the Portsmouth recreation center. On weekends she dances to her workout tape in the living room, wearing a loose-fitting halter top that hangs above her navel and skintight leotards. Late afternoons she changes into jeans with frayed cuffs and a torn white T-shirt (JESUS SWEETS printed across the chest) and heavy Doc Martens. Her bartending job down by the harbor starts at six, and at five-thirty Mary throws a metal cross around her neck and is gone. She eats at work.

She is home before I return from the radio station. I am a DJ, strictly local. The studio is within walking distance, blocks away. I do a jazz show between midnight and two A.M. called *Joey's Swingshift*. It is not a good job and it's getting worse. WZSZ is under new management as of a month ago—some investors from Boston—and they're trying to phase out what they call in their staff memos "eclectic" programming. I've been told by reputable inside sources that *Joey's Swingshift* is near the top of their list. Even now, with my coterie of listeners and live, in-studio interviews, I am not attracting new sponsors and I am not paying my share of the rent.

• • •

While Mary pulls on her leotards and sweatpants over by the closet, preparing for her morning classes, I contemplate having a cigarette. To her credit, Mary does not pressure me to quit. She half jokingly considers self-destruction a sign of masculine intelligence. I am trying to quit on my own, but at times like this—mornings especially, when Mary is getting dressed less than fifteen feet away—a good dose of nicotine might help. I can't stand these feelings of need.

"Joey, baby," Mary says slyly, slowly, not turning around. I grunt, feigning indifference. Then I yawn. "I might be going to New York this weekend," she says. She looks at herself in the full-length mirror. "That MTV audition. I already told you. Last week." She spreads her feet apart and begins to stretch, left to right, bending at the middle. "Do you remember?"

I try to retrace the week's conversations in my mind: Monday, Tuesday, Wednesday, Thursday, Friday. No, Friday is today. I run my fingers through my hair and squint, feeling grumpy and ugly and looking worse, I'm sure. Ever since college the days of the week have seemed to spill into one another like dominoes. I have to check the digital calendar in the studio at work just to remind myself which day's weather I'll be reading from the wire. Without classes, who can keep track?

"Ah, yeah. That's right," I say, though in fact I cannot remember a New York conversation. I reach for a tissue and blow my nose noisily, emitting the hissing-honking sound I used to associate with older men. "That's right," I repeat. "But I thought you thought it wouldn't happen."

"I still don't know," she says. She straightens up and leans toward the mirror to rub at the corner of her eye with her pinkie finger. "Stevie'll let me know tonight. But if we go, we're leaving tomorrow morning. Early."

Stevie: a huge man, a silent man, high cheekbones and a deep, dark, almost mahogany complexion. He trains with Mary at Body Pain Plus and she sleeps in his apartment on occasion, though Mary denies there is any sex between them. According to Mary, the issue is beyond discussion. I do not talk to Stevie, he does not talk to me. I do not want to know the details of their relationship. What could I do anyway?

Mary turns and faces me, stands solid, stiff-backed, arms akimbo. "Go back to sleep, Joey," she says. "You look miserable."

• • •

We are still lovers, but it is not easy. We have lost the equilibrium of love, I think. She is too strong now, too fast. The balance has been tipped.

In my view, Mary and I have sex a lot. I am beginning to think that lovemaking is something you do in the early stages of a relationship, before the need for ritual sex takes hold, before a standard is set and must be maintained. There is no reason for Mary to want lovemaking anymore. With her body and drive, she makes conventional love seem inefficient, too passive.

When I go home from the station, Mary is hiding. I climb three flights of stairs, turn the key in the lock, open the door to a dark apartment. One of Mary's sex cassettes is playing low—ninety minutes of pure Madonna. Our apartment is barely furnished; there aren't that many places to hide. She is behind the sofa, the shower curtain or inside the closet. I close the door gently, slip my glasses into my satchel and ease it to the shag carpet. I proceed cautiously, quietly forward, arms extended in defense and a kind of titillating fear. This lasts for about a minute, two at the most, with me creeping forth in the black, losing my bearings, expectant and deeply aroused. Mary is upon me then, naked, leaping out of nowhere to wrestle me down, sometimes slamming me hard against the floor. She struggles with my shirt (she has ripped through several), tears at my belt buckle and zipper, throws my shoes back at the wall. My cries of resistance—some half genuine, others wholly staged—spur her on, make her crazier, hungrier. She applies a series of paralyzing holds: half nelsons, leg scissors, full nelsons, headlocks. The pain is momentary and oddly erotic; Mary keeps moving, never in one position very long. She grips me until it hurts, then lets go. She pinches, tugs playfully at my hair, flips me over and lands on my back. Everywhere we touch, her body is solid and slippery, surfaces of brawn and bone and breast.

When she grows bored with this stage, tired of toying, she leads me by the arm (or drags me by the legs) into the bedroom and onto the futon. She is on top, looming above in a pale blur, stroking fast, swatting me to attention. Finally, I am allowed to enter. The penetration is sudden, a pair of hands at my pelvis, fingers pressing flesh, seeming to push me from below out of the futon's hot fabric. She forces herself down and I strain in, violently, again and again. She shoves me away when I come, stands up and places one foot on my stomach. She licks her finger and begins touching herself, groaning softly. I fall asleep, exhausted. I will awaken the next morning, sore and dazed, as Mary dashes out in skin-shaped spandex and jogs.

• • •

Mary is late returning from her afternoon training session with Stevie, so I sit on the living-room couch to eat a bologna sandwich and the remains of a pasta salad. Because Mary rarely eats here, I do the shopping, and because I have very little money, these are the things I buy. The bologna has the vaguely nauseating smell of what it is: processed meat. But it tastes okay.

The playlist I've drawn up for tonight's show is packed with saxophone giants: Coltrane, Parker, Carter, Webster, even some Stan Kenton big band from the Fifties. My interview guest is a young player from Boston—older than I am, of course, but young for his sudden success. Bobby Gladstone is already a name in New York, or so I've read in his promo clippings.

I finish the sandwich and plunk the nearest video into Mary's VCR. It is a compilation labeled MADONNA SHOTS on a piece of masking tape attached to the side. The screen blinks, quavers, then clears and brightens. Madonna appears in black and white wearing dark lingerie and shoving a muscular black man into a bed with huge, bright pillows. I turn the volume down and watch as she slowly mounts the man without addressing the camera, without even bothering to lip-sync. The camera pans across the room and there are more men, arms crossed over husky chests, positioned around the bed in a semicircle, eyes fixed on Madonna and her partner. The men approach the bed and appear to join in, and soon there is a mass of bodies on-screen, clamoring, touching, licking and kissing in slow motion.

The image flickers and twists and is gone, replaced by Madonna onstage arching her back while two male dancers—shirtless, in black suspenders—squat beside each of her legs and paw at her thighs. This Madonna's hair is drawn up high in a long, platinum ponytail pulled back tight and erect. A portable microphone device is wrapped around her head, extending a small, black orb in front of and just below her mouth like a morsel of bait. Her breasts are covered by two white cone-like cups with spiky points. Her face tenses suddenly as she reaches down between her legs and grabs at her crotch. She closes her eyes.

I switch off the television and VCR and stand up to stretch. My body still aches from two nights ago, the last time Mary and I had sex. The VCR flashes 12:00, but my watch reads just past four and Mary is still not home.

Back when she was just beginning to hold her workouts with Stevie, I asked Mary about Madonna's appeal.

"Control," she said. She hovered over the blender, gazing at the swishing mess of mango and lime. "That's what Madonna's all about. The power to be who you want, when you want."

"Looks like simple exploitation to me," I said, leaning against the kitchen wall. "Sexploitation, to be exact. Part of a long tradition of por-nography."

"You're wrong, Joey," she said. The blender has stopped. "Madonna's is *self*-exploitation. It's totally different. Everyone's exploited anyway. But Madonna's got it on her own terms. She turns the tables. That's power."

They didn't sound like Mary's words then, not the Mary I thought I'd known. I couldn't think of a good comeback. I wondered if Stevie was teaching her those things, but I kept my mouth shut. It was risky.

She lifted the cover off the blender and stuck her finger inside, then brought it dripping to her mouth.

"Yuk," she said, licking her upper lip. "Not enough lime."

● ● ●

The old Mary had a diary—a slim, private journal bound in pink cloth. She kept it on a bedside table in her tiny dormitory single, conspicu-ously accessible, tucked beneath her clock radio. I searched through the pages for my name while Mary showered in the stalls a few doors down. I found it as a heading, JOEY, underlined and written above the question "Am I a priority in his life?"

I stared at it. I imagined Mary's voice—slightly plaintive, direct, ear-nest—speaking the words: "Am I?"

I thought I heard Mary's slippers shuffling down the hall, so I closed the book and slipped it back under the radio. But the question stayed with me. It was troubling. "Priority" seemed like such a heavy word. I was busy back then. I managed the campus radio station, played rhythm guitar in a blues band, drank beer with the artist types downtown. I was a communications major, a budding media star, with my measured delivery and silken on-air voice. Everyone listened to my show.

And Mary was an English major who liked pink. I didn't want to be with her too much. I kissed Mary in her room. I slept with her. But I didn't want to be identified as hers: the boyfriend of a simple girl.

Alone with me Mary would talk of missing Peterborough, the small town where she grew up. She talked about her friends there as if they were still in high school; she reminisced about climbing Mount Monadnock, about ice-skating after midnight, about slumber parties and long walks around her snowy neighborhood. She laughed easily and sometimes started crying in the same breath, sniffing quietly, reaching around for an embrace. She had a little Gund teddy bear on her bureau. She joked that I was her big teddy, her big bear. I never knew what to say.

• • •

The phone from the kitchen frightens me, ringing in sharp, loud bursts. I am supposed to be reviewing my Bobby Gladstone questions, but instead, I have spent the past half hour sifting through clothes in Mary's closet, trying to find a diary, a notebook, anything in her hand-writing. Mary doesn't talk about her past anymore. Apparently, she doesn't keep track of the present, either.

The answering machine clicks on and Mary's voice filters through the speaker. She starts to say something about Stevie as I pick up the phone.

"Oh. Hi," she says. "I didn't think you were there."

"I'm always here," I say.

"Aw, Joey. Lighten up. Listen. I'll be home soon, but I'm eating dinner at Stevie's tonight, so I won't be around long."

"What about New York?" I ask.

"That's why we're eating together. We still have to work things out."

"Don't you have to bartend tonight?"

"I called in sick." She pauses, says something to someone away from the receiver. "Joey? I'll be home in a few minutes. I just called to let you know. I didn't want you to be worried."

"I am," I say.

"Well, don't be."

• • •

When Mary enters the apartment she heads directly for the bedroom and closes the door to change—no time for a hello. Usually she leaves the door open at least enough for us to talk. I am listening to a Bobby Gladstone demo tape on her stereo in the living room. I turn the music down and knock.

"Can I come in?" I say.

"I'm changing," she says. "Come in if you want."

I push open the door as Mary is zipping up her jeans. She looks up, brushes the hair back from her face.

"Whatsa matter, Joey?" She pouts her lips in mock pity. "You look so sad."

"I don't want you to go to New York."

It doesn't have much of an impact. She folds her arms across her breasts and tips her head back, smiling. "Well," she says. "That's nice to hear, but you're a little late."

I would like a cigarette now. I lean against the wall, pressing my hands to the smooth plaster behind me.

Mary picks up her shoes and walks by me quickly. I follow.

"I don't have time for this," she says, flopping down heavily on the couch, making the springs squeak. The corner of my playlist sticks out from beneath her thigh. Mary tugs at it and it rips. Then she lifts her legs and pushes the paper to the floor.

I sit down next to her, watching as she ties her shoes. "I thought we could do something this weekend," I begin. "Together. Maybe go dancing on the harbor cruise, have dinner, see a movie. Whatever."

"Bad timing," she says. "Besides, since when do you dance?"

I think of putting my arm around her while she is hunched over, drawing her close to me. But her shoulders jut out sharply, looking reproachful as she works at her laces. I reach toward her, eyeing her pumping back muscles, then rest my hand on the cushion.

"I'm not happy with things," I say.

Mary leans back and sighs. "That's not my fault," she says. Her voice is toned down, painfully reasonable. "I've told you before you could get another job on the side. And there are other radio——"

"I'm not happy about us," I say. "You and me, I mean."

She turns to me, her brown eyes dark and stubborn. "Joey, let's not argue now," she says. She reaches behind my neck and pulls me to her lips, kissing me roughly. She winks. "We can fight later."

"I'm serious," I say. As she makes to rise from the couch I reach out to grab her arm. It is a sudden movement, and I am surprised by how thin her wrist feels in my grip. I am more surprised when she sits down again, closer to me.

I let go of her wrist. My eye muscles tingle. I take off my glasses.

"Could you just spare me a couple minutes?"

Mary is silent. I press my fingers to the inner corners of my eyes. Without my glasses, everything near me is blurry.

"I miss the old Mary," I say.

"There is no old Mary," she says. "There is just me. I may have changed a little, but I'm the same person, Joey. You know that."

"Then I miss what we used to do. Or what you used to do, what you used to say to me. You used to keep a diary."

"You read that, didn't you?"

"Not the whole thing," I say. "I took a few peeks."

"You shouldn't have," she says.

"Why?"

My neck feels hot. I put on my glasses and turn toward her. Mary leans back, places her hands behind her head. She stares at the ceiling.

"Because it was my private life, Joey. That's why. It's none of your business."

"But it is my business," I say. "It's my business to know what you think of me. Isn't it?"

Mary regards me distantly, her eyes direct, focused, motionless. She tilts her head to one side, squinting darkly. "If it was so important," she says, "why didn't you just ask me?"

I hadn't actually anticipated Mary's response, a question easily superior to mine. The advantage shifts in an instant. Just holding her gaze becomes a struggle.

I take a shallow breath that is meant to be deep. My left eyelid starts to twitch. "All right then," I say. "Why do you stay with me?"

"Joey."

"I mean it. I don't have much to offer you now. I'm no muscleman, my career is going nowhere, and even sex——"

"Don't talk like that," Mary says. She puts her hand to her forehead. "My God. You are so blind sometimes. You get fixated on one thing, and then you define the rest of the world that way."

"What do you mean?"

"Listen to yourself, will you? You're trying to fit me into some stereotype just because I work out. What makes you think I want a muscleman?" She shakes her head. "Jesus. I'm not that simple, you know. If you'd been paying any attention to me, instead of snooping around in my diary, you would know that by now."

I look away. Mary's portable TV stares back at me from the corner, distorting our reflections on its curved screen.

Her hand closes around mine and I tense.

"I don't know what it is you want anymore."

"Stop saying that," she says, her voice close to my ear. "It's so self-defeating, not to mention boring. This isn't a business. I don't want some kind of product from you. You're supposed to surprise me, remember?"

I feel her entwining our fingers together, clasping tightly.

"You're not who you've come to think you are, Joey. Give me credit for knowing at least that much about you. And give yourself a chance. Stop pretending that the past is romantic just because it's gone."

I am frightened by how patiently Mary can say these things. When she gets serious like this, she makes me feel naked, skinless even, as if she is shining a bright light over everything.

"What about Stevie?" I ask.

She leans forward and kisses me on the cheek, resting her lips there momentarily, leaving a fine, moist sensation behind. "Now, *he*'s just a muscleman," she says. I glance down, half relieved to see her smile. "I've told you many times that Stevie is a friend, but just for you I'll repeat it. He's given me a lot of confidence. And," she draws away slowly, releasing my hand, "he just might get me a dancing gig so I can quit that ratty bar."

She stands abruptly, pushing her hair back behind her shoulders. "But I'm late now, Joeykins. I have to go." She pivots and heads for the front door, grabbing her keys from the hook on the wall. I watch as she stalls, placing one hand on the doorknob, adjusting the cross around her neck with the other.

"Maybe I'll tune in tonight," she says, looking down. "So play something for me, will you?"

• • •

In the elevator on the way up to the studio I scan over my interview notes one last time. My Gladstone angle is going to be jazz and the younger audience. Most of Bobby's listeners are older than he is, middle-aged or beyond, and they often ask him to play tunes that were popular forty or fifty years ago. The music can't survive on nostalgia. Neither, it appears, can a DJ.

I am greeted by a yellow Post-it note attached to the glass of the studio door. "See me," it says. It is signed by Ernie, the new station manager. Inside the booth, Boommaster Billy is playing his funk-and-rap show, bobbing up and down to his throbbing headphones as he smokes a tiny hand-rolled cigarette.

Ernie is not usually here when I come in. No one is, in fact, except Billy. But there is light in the office across the hall, so I go over and tap on the door with my pen.

"Joe?"

"Uh-huh."

"Step inside."

Ernie is sitting behind a computer and a calculator and a mass of papers scattered over the top of his desk. He is a heavyset man in his early fifties and he is almost entirely bald. Tonight he is wearing a stiff white dress shirt with a dark bow tie. His sleeves are unbuttoned, rolled back above his wrists.

"Sit down," he says, still gazing into the computer screen and motioning to a chair filled with account books and assorted paraphernalia. He glances at the chair. "Ah, forget it. You've got your show coming up anyway, right?"

I nod. "Jazz."

"Right, right. Jazz." Ernie switches off the computer and swivels to his side to face me directly. He places his elbows on the desk and folds his hands. "Look," he says. "I am in the unfortunate and unenviable and highly unpleasant position of having to officially cancel your show." He spreads his palms out briefly, looking stern and apologetic at the same time. "Now, I want to put this to you straight: It is not a position I like, believe me. I'm a tired man. And I know you fellows work damn hard. Just today, in fact, I've been in here since six this———"

"I saw the memos," I say. "I don't mean to interrupt, but I was aware of the situation. I understand. At least I've got my regulars. I'll do the last show for them." I manage a pinched smile.

"Regulars, regulars," Ernie says, picking up his pen and pointing it at me. "You see, right there's your problem. Regulars aren't enough in a town this size." He drops the pen, scratches his brow and sighs. "It ain't Boston, you know. There aren't enough regulars to go around. Your show's for purists. You're a bit of a purist yourself, Joe. And what happens is, you get a tiny audience for this show, a tiny audience for that, but no definitive mass, no real numbers. And then," he gestures toward me with his index finger, "you're not getting any newcomers. No new listeners. That's the problem."

I smile again, wanting badly to leave. The studio door opens in the hall behind me. "Hey, anybody seen the swing guy?" Billy asks.

"He's right here," Ernie calls back.

"Tell him he's got fifteen minutes."

Ernie rises, reaches across his desk and shakes my hand. "You better get in there," he says. "I'll tell you what. Come in on Monday. We'll talk, see if we can give you some office work till you find something new. How's that?"

I continue grinning and nodding as I turn toward the door.

"Oh, and by the way," Ernie says, "the Gladson guy won't be here. He, uh, got stuck down in New York. Other obligations. You know how these musicians are."

"Glad*stone*," I say.

"Right, right. The jazz guy."

• • •

I play the opening theme music—Miles Davis's *Kind of Blue*—and listen to my prerecorded voice-over introducing "two hours of hip and happening tunes." Mary once said I sound like I'd been smoking pot when I made the recording. Tonight the voice sounds exactly the way I feel: weary and distant, struggling in tape hiss.

"Welcome to *Joey's Swingshift*," I say, fading the introduction with one hand and presetting a commercial with the other. "We will be doing an all-request show tonight, so I want all you swingin' night owls and werewolves to get to the nearest telephone and give me a call. 555-9079 is the number. Show some life and let me know what it is you really need to hear." I flick on the commercial tape and fine-tune the output frequency. If no one calls, I'll put on the Bobby Gladstone CD and crank it up here in the booth. What the hell.

While a woman's voice rambles on about the importance of environmental action, someone raps on the studio door. It is Ernie, dressed in a beige trench coat and smoking a pipe. He shrugs his shoulders at me, then breaks into a big, goofy smile that seems to say *"C'est la vie."*

I shrug and smile back. "Goodnight, Er-nee," I sing out, approximating the tune of "Goodnight, Irene," the old Leadbelly classic. I wave my right hand in a broad, exaggerated way.

Ernie's smile evaporates. He gazes at me numbly for a moment, then turns and heads off down the corridor. Either he didn't think the joke was funny, or he didn't get it.

The McDonald's spot is the last in the series, and I am about to cue up Coltrane's "Giant Steps" when the red light on the studio phone begins to flash. I turn down the mike input and grab the receiver.

"ZSZ," I say.

There is silence on the other end,

"Hello?" I say.

"Uh, yes. Is this Mr. Swingshift?" The voice is slow and wobbly. An elderly man.

"That's actually the name of the show," I say. "I'm Joey."

"Oh."

"But that's okay," I add quickly. "What can I do for you?"

"Well, I was wondering if you would play a favorite song of mine. An old chestnut. Goes way back." He chuckles.

"What is it?"

"It's a song called 'Chelsea Bridge,' I believe. Has a nice saxophone melody and, I think . . . now, let's see if I can remember this right. Ah, I think it's Ben Webster who wrote it."

"Chelsea Bridge." I reach for the Gladstone CD case and read through the track list. Number six. It's a beautiful rendition.

"Yes. Of course. I'll put it on. But it was written by Billy Strayhorn. Webster used to play it a lot and he recorded it. In fact, a lot of musicians have recorded it since, but Strayhorn wrote the tune."

"Oh, that's right," he says, and I imagine him glancing away, squinting, looking into himself, into the past. "Billy Strayhorn wrote that, didn't he? That's right."

"I'll play the song," I say. "But who is it for?"

"Beg your pardon?"

"Do you want to dedicate the song to somebody?"

"Well, no," he says, as if I'd just asked him something mildly embarrassing. He chuckles again. "No, this one's just for me, I guess."

Suddenly I realize I forgot to start the Coltrane record. The VU meters are motionless, stuck on zero. Nothing's playing. "I have to go," I say. "I . . . I'll play it." I hang up.

I fumble for the mixing board and hit the turntable with my elbow. The needle draws across the vinyl with a sickening scrape. I lift the stylus from the record, trying to steady my hand, and set it down on the opening grooves. Then I hit PLAY. The album spins, the music starts.

I lean back in the tattered studio chair and sigh. Three minutes of dead air, at least three. I let the airwaves go silent—no commercials, no DJ, no music. Nothing but hiss. If Ernie heard it he is fuming right now. Dead air is a no-no on any show, even after midnight.

I push off with my foot and wheel the chair over to the jazz library— two shelves of compact discs, one of vinyl. Ben Webster is nestled in the W's, right where he should be. I pull the record from its sleeve and dust it off. The label reads NEWPORT JAZZ FESTIVAL, 1958.

I decide to play both versions—Webster's first, then Gladstone's. As I place the vinyl over the turntable, then slip the CD into the player, I think about the man who called. What is a man of his age doing awake so late at night? He probably lives alone. Most of my listeners are like that, I'm sure: loners who use the music for companionship. Maybe his kids are grown, his wife is dead. Maybe she's away. Perhaps she left him.

But then, what can I ever really know about my listeners? I hear their voices, they hear mine. I sit inside this dark booth and imagine their lives.

Maybe the man who called is not at all who I think he is.

The Coltrane slows, his solo descends and fades. I adjust my headphones and lean over the mike. "We have a dual dedication tonight," I announce, lowering my voice to convey wee-hour intimacy. I have never dedicated a song to anyone before—it's against station policy for DJs to use the airwaves that way. But in less than two hours I won't be a DJ, at least not an employed one. "The first is for the swinging gentleman who requested the song, and the second——"

I set the turntable into motion with my free hand, raising the volume carefully. "The second is for the *Swingshift*'s most loyal listener, our A-number-one groove sister. This being the last night we all spend together, dear listeners, it's about time I sent one out to the sweetest soul ever to savor these smooth sounds: my Mary."

It is a winning dedication, I think. My delivery was impeccable.

I turn up the studio monitors, and Webster's full-bodied tenor breathes to life. The applause from years ago trickles away in the background. You can hear the air through his reed, and the sound aches.

● ● ●

Outside the apartment door I pause while fitting the key. There is no good reason for doing this. Mary's probably spending the night at Stevie's place, planning for their early departure together, planning for New York.

I turn the key and press the door open. The dark of the apartment recedes from the hallway light. Out of habit I creep in slowly, quietly, but there is no Madonna music playing and, I am quite sure, no Mary lying in wait. I keep my glasses on.

"Mary," I whisper. Nothing.

I straighten up and let my satchel drop to the floor. It lands on the carpet with a dull thud. This whole thing is absurd. There's no one here.

"Mary, Mary, come and scare me," I say aloud. My voice sounds sing-songy, comical in this little apartment. "Come and scare me if you can, come and scare your only man." I'm beginning to feel light-headed. Giddy. It doesn't matter what I say now. I'm off the air for good.

I close the front door (the neighbors might think I'm nuts) and flick on the overhead light. Next to Mary's TV against the far wall is her big black boombox, surrounded by stacks of cassettes. I kneel down beside them and slip the top one into the deck, not bothering to see who it is. Surprise me. I press the power switch, I turn it up a little, I hit play. I feel like dancing.

The music starts in the middle of something I don't yet recognize. The beat is strong but bouncy. If it's not Madonna, it's close enough.

I rise to my feet and start doing a kind of wiggling thing, trying to get my body to move fluidly, down and dirty. I grind my hips, raise my arms above my head. My back arches as far as it will go. I'm a bit stiff and I'm sure I look like an idiot. But I close my eyes and refuse to think about it. I'm not doing all that badly.

"Shake your body," the singer says.

Suddenly, someone's hip slams into my own and I am knocked off balance. I steady myself.

"Use your knees, boy!" Mary commands over the music. "You're swaying like a tree."

A smile flashes across her face, then contracts into a grimace. She is dancing in her boxer shorts and an oversized T-shirt. Her eyes flutter shut. Her hair flops around unevenly, lank and matted on one side.

"You're here," I say dumbly, standing motionless while she gyrates only a few feet away. "It's you."

"Move, Joey, move!"

I hesitate, watching her as she whirls around and works her backside into the air. Mary has a way of inhabiting her dancing, of living inside the moves. It's mesmerizing. I have questions to ask, but the rhythm seems to insist, so I start to dance again, using my knees as much as they will allow me to. "Shake your body," the voice sings over and over.

When the song finally finishes I reach down and click off the tape deck. Mary reaches for my free hand. "Come on," she says, pulling me toward the dark bedroom.

"Wait a minute," I say. "Hold on. What the hell are you doing here?"

"I live here," she snaps. She curls her arm round my waist and draws me to her side. She raises her chin provocatively. "Got a problem with that?"

"You were in the bedroom?"

"Bingo! That's where I was. Sleeping—or at least trying to. I thought you'd come in and crash. I didn't expect to be entertained."

"Are you still going to New York tomorrow? With Stevie?"

"Today. In a few hours, in fact. Six A.M. sharp. Stevie's picking us up. Got that? We have to catch an eight o'clock flight out of Boston, so I've already packed your duffel for the weekend: three pairs of underwear, three pairs of socks, four shirts and two pairs of pants, one casual, one formal. Oh, and also your blazer." She runs the tip of her index finger along my collarbone and stops at the base of my neck. "Unless, of course, you'd rather stay here and learn how to dance alone."

I search for the right response, a quick comeback, but I am totally unprepared. What I say emerges without prompting: "They fired me tonight, Mary. They let me go."

She presses her lips to my chest. "I know," she says. "I heard your announcement on Stevie's radio. I said, 'Isn't that great? Joey has no good reason to stay home this weekend. No more reasons to say no.'"

I encircle Mary with my arms and press my hands against her upper back. Her muscles relax, softening beneath my grip.

I whisper into her ear. "Did you hear the song? My dedication?"

She nods. "Mmm-hmm. At Stevie's. I heard the show."

"Did you like it?"

"Loved it, babe. *Loved* it."

I hold her to my chest with all my strength. Her body is solid, steady, warm. In a few hours the sun will rise. And I feel wide awake.

Buckeye the Elder

by **BRADY UDALL**
1994

Things I learned about Buckeye a few minutes before he broke my collarbone: He is twenty-five years old, a native of Wisconsin and therefore a Badger. "Not really a Buckeye at all," he explained, sitting in my father's recliner and paging through a book about UFOs and other unsolved mysteries. "But I keep the name for respect of the man who gave it to me, my father and the most loyal alumnus Ohio State ever produced."

Buckeye had stopped by to visit my sister, Simone, whom he has been seeing over the past week or so. Though Simone has been yammering about him at the dinner table, it was the first time I'd actually met him. When he arrived, Simone wasn't back from her class at the beauty college, and I was the only one in the house. Buckeye came inside for a few minutes and talked to me like I was someone he'd known since childhood. He showed me old black-and-white photos of his parents, a gold tooth he'd found on the floor of a bar in Detroit, a ticket stub autographed by Marty Robbins. Among other things, we talked about his passion for rugby and he invited me out to the front yard for a few lessons on rules and technique. He positioned himself in front of me and instructed me to try to get around him while he demonstrated the proper way to wrap up a player and drag him down. I did what I was told and ended up with two-hundred-plus pounds worth of Buckeye driving my shoulder into the hard dirt. We both heard the snap, clear as you please.

"Was that you?" Buckeye said, already picking me up and setting me on my feet. My left shoulder sagged and I couldn't move my arm, but there wasn't an alarming amount of pain. Buckeye helped me to the porch and brought out the phone so I could call my mother to pick me up and take me to the hospital.

● ● ●

I'm sitting in one of the porch rocking chairs and Buckeye is standing next to me, nervously shifting his feet. He is the picture of guilt and worry. He puts his face in his hands, paces up and down the steps, comes back over to inspect my shoulder for the dozenth time. The fractured bone pushes up against the skin, making a considerable lump.

"Snapped in two, not a doubt in this world," says a grim-faced Buckeye.

He puts his face right into mine as if he's trying to see something behind my eyes. "You aren't in shock, are you?" he asks. "You don't want an ambulance?"

"I'm okay," I say. Other than being a little light-headed, I feel pretty good. There is something gratifying about having a serious injury and no serious pain to go with it. More than my shoulder, I'm worried about Buckeye, who acts like he's just committed murder. He asks me if I wouldn't just let him swing me over his own shoulders and run me over to the hospital himself.

"Where is my self-control?" he questions the rain gutter. "Why can't I get a hold of my situations?" He turns to me and says, "There's no excuses, none, but I'm used to tackling guys three times your size, God forgive me. I didn't think you'd go down that easy."

Buckeye has a point. I am almost as tall as he is, though at least sixty pounds lighter. I'm embarrassed for going down so easy. I tell him it was nobody's fault, that my parents are generally reasonable people and that my sister will probably like him all that much more for it.

Buckeye doesn't look at all comforted. He keeps up his pacing. He berates himself with his chin in his chest, mumbling into the collar of his shirt as if there is someone down there listening. He rubs his head with his big knobby hands and gives himself a good tongue-lashing. There is an ungainly energy in the way he moves. He is thick in some places, thin in others, with joints like those on a backhoe. He's barrel-chested, has elongated, piano player's fingers and is missing a good portion of his right ear, which, he told me earlier, had been ground off by the cleat of a stampeding Polynesian at the Midwest Rugby Invitationals.

I can't explain this, but I'm feeling quite pleased that Buckeye has broken my shoulder.

When my mother pulls up in her new Lincoln, Buckeye picks up me and the chair I'm in. With long, smooth strides he delivers me to the car, all the time saying some sort of prayer, asking the Lord to bless me, heal me and help me forgive him.

• • •

One of the more important things that Buckeye didn't tell me about himself that first day was that he is a newly baptized Mormon. I've found out this is the only reason my parents ever let him within rock-throwing distance of my sister. As far as my parents are concerned, solid Baptists that they are, either you're with Jesus or you're against him. I guess they figure Buckeye, close as he might be to the dividing line, is on the right side.

In the week that has passed since the accident, Buckeye has turned our house into a carnival. The night we came home from the hospital, me straight-backed and awkward in my brace and Buckeye still asking forgiveness, we had a celebration—in honor of who or what I still can't be sure. We ordered pizza, and my folks, who almost never drink, made banana daiquiris while Simone held hands with Buckeye and sipped ginger ale. Later, my daiquiri-inspired father, once a 163-pound district champion in high school, coaxed Buckeye into a wrestling match in the front room. While my sister squealed and my mother screeched about hospital bills and further injury, Buckeye wore a big easy grin and let my father pin him solidly on our mint-green carpet.

I suppose there were two things going on: We were officially sanctioning Buckeye's relationship with Simone and at the same time commemorating my fractured clavicle, my first manly injury. Despite and possibly because of the aspirations of my sports-mad father, I am the type of son who gets straight A's and likes to sit in his room and make models of spaceships. My father dreams that I will play point guard for the Celtics one day. My own chief aspiration is to write a best-selling fantasy novel.

My sister goes to beauty school, a huge disappointment to my pediatrician mother. Simone can't bear to tell people that my father distills sewer water for a living. Though I love them, I sincerely believe my parents to be narrow-minded religious fanatics, and as for Simone, I think beauty school might be an intellectual stretch. Our family seems to be no more than a bunch of people living in the same house who are disappointed in one another.

But we all love Buckeye. He's the only thing we agree on. The fact that Simone and my parents would go for someone like him is surprising when you consider the coarse look he has about him, the kind of look you see on people in bus stations and in the backs of fruit trucks. Maybe it's his fine set of teeth that keeps him from looking like an out-and-out redneck.

• • •

Tonight Buckeye is taking me on a drive. Since we met, Buckeye has spent more time with me than he has with Simone. My parents think this is a good idea; I don't have many friends and they think he will have a positive effect on their agnostic, asocial son. We are in his rust-cratered vehicle, which might have been an Oldsmobile at one time. Buckeye has just finished a day's work as a pantyhose salesman and smells like the perfume of the women he talks to on porches and doorsteps. He sells revolutionary no-run stockings that carry a lifetime guarantee. He has stacks of them on the backseat. At $18 a pair, he assures these women, they are certainly a bargain. He is happy and loose and driving all over the road. He has just brought me up to date on his teenage years, his father's death, the thirteen states he's lived in and the twenty-two jobs he's held.

"Got it all up here," he says, tapping his forehead. "Don't let a day slide by without detailed documentation." Over the past few days I've noticed Buckeye has a way of speaking that makes people pause. One minute he sounds like a west Texas oil grunt, the next like a semieducated Midwesterner. Buckeye is a constant surprise.

"Why move around so much?" I wonder. "And why come to Texas?"

He says, "I just move, no reason that I can think of. For one thing, I'm here looking for my older brother, Bud. He loves the Cowboys and fine women. He could very well be in the vicinity."

"How'd your father die?" I say.

"His heart attacked him. Then his liver committed suicide and the rest of his organs just gave up after that. Too much drinking. That's when I left Wisconsin for good."

We pass smelters and gas stations and trailers that sit back off the road. This is a part of Tyler I've never seen before. Buckeye pulls the old car into the parking lot of a huge wooden structure with a sign that says THE RANCH in big matchstick letters. The sun is just going down, but the place is lit up like Las Vegas. A fleet of dirty pickups overruns the parking lot.

We find a space in the back and Buckeye leads me through a loading dock and into the kitchen, where a trio of Hispanic ladies is doing dishes. He stops and chatters at them in a mixture of bad Spanish and hand gestures. "Come on," he says to me. "I'm going to show you the man I once was."

We go out to the main part, which is as big as a ballroom. There are two round bars in the middle of it and a few raised platforms where half-dressed women are dancing. Chairs and tables are scattered all along the edges. The music is so loud I can feel it bouncing off my chest. Buckeye nods and wags his finger and smiles at everybody we pass, and they respond like old friends. Buckeye, who's been in Tyler less than a month, does this everywhere we go. If you didn't know better you'd think he was acquainted with every citizen in town.

We find an empty table against the wall right next to one of the dancers. She has on lacy black panties and a cut-off T-shirt that is barely sufficient to hold in her equipment. Buckeye politely says hello, but she doesn't even look our way.

This is the first bar I've ever been in and I like the feel of it. Buckeye orders Cokes and buffalo wings for us both and surveys the place, occasionally raising a hand to acknowledge someone he sees. Even though I've lived in Texas since I was born, I've never seen so many oversize belt buckles in one place.

"This is the first time I've been back here since my baptism," Buckeye says. "I used to spend most of my nonworking hours in bars like this."

While he has told me about a lot of things, he's never said anything about his conversion. The only reason I know about it is that I overheard my parents discussing Buckeye's worthiness to date my sister.

"Why did you get baptized?" I ask.

Buckeye squints through the smoke and his voice takes on an unusual amount of gravity. "This used to be me, sitting right here and drinking till my teeth fell out. I was one of these people, not good, not bad, sincerely trying to make things as easy as possible. A place like this draws you in, pulls at you."

Watching the girl in the panties gyrating above us, I think I can see what he's getting at.

He continues: "But this ain't all there is. Simply is not. There's more to it than this. You've got to figure out what's right and what's wrong and then you've got to take a stand. Most people don't want to put out the effort. I'm telling you, I know it's not easy. Goodness has a call that's hard to hear."

I nod, not to indicate that I understand what he's saying but as a signal for him to keep going. Even though I've had my fair share of experience with them, I've never understood religious people.

"Do you know what life's about? The *why* of the whole thing?" Buckeye says.

"No more than anybody else," I say.

"Do you think you'll ever know?"

"Maybe someday."

Buckeye holds up a half-eaten chicken wing for emphasis. "Exactly," he says through a full mouth. "I could scratch my balls forever if I had the time." He finishes off the rest of his chicken and shrugs. "To know, you have to do. You get out there and take action, put your beliefs to the test. Sitting around on your duff won't get you anything better than a case of hemorrhoids."

"If you're such a believer, why don't you go around like my parents do, spouting Scripture and all that?" I reason that if I just keep asking questions I will eventually get Buckeye figured out.

"For one thing," Buckeye says flatly, "and you don't need to go telling this to anybody else, I'm not much of a reader."

I raise my eyebrows.

"Look here," he says, taking the menu from between the ketchup bottle and the sugar bowl. He points at something on it and says, "This is an A, this is a T and here's a G. This says *hamburger*—I know that one. Oh, and this is *beer*. I learned that early on." He looks up at me. "Nope, I can't read, not really. I never stayed put long enough to get an education. But I'm smart enough to fool anybody."

If this were a movie and not real life I would feel terrible for Buckeye—maybe I would vow to teach him to read, give him self-worth, help him become a complete human being. For the climax, he would win the national spelling bee or something. But this is reality and as I look across the table at Buckeye, I can see that his illiteracy doesn't bother him a bit. In fact, he looks rather pleased with himself.

"Like I've been telling you, it's not the reading, it's not the saying. It's only the doing I'm interested in. Do it, do it, do it," Buckeye says, hammering each "do it" into the table with his Coke bottle. He leans into his chair, a wide grin overtaking his face. "But sometimes it certainly is nice to kick back and listen to the music."

We sit there quietly, me doing my best not to stare at the dancer and Buckeye with his head back and eyes closed, sniffing the air with the deep concentration of a wine taster. A pretty woman in jeans and a flannel shirt comes up behind Buckeye and asks him to dance. There are only a few couples out on the floor. Most everybody else is sitting at their tables, drinking and yelling at one another over the music.

"Thanks, but no thanks," Buckeye says.

The woman looks over at me. "What about you?" she says.

My face gets hot and I begin to fidget. "No, no," I say. "No, thank you."

The woman seems amused by us and our Cokes. She takes a long look at both of us, with her hands on the back of an empty chair.

"Go ahead," Buckeye says. "I'll hold down the fort."

I shake my head and look down into my lap. "That's quite all right," I say. I don't know how to dance and the brace I'm wearing makes me walk like I have an advanced case of arthritis.

Buckeye sighs, smiles, gets up and leads the woman out onto the floor. She puts her head on his chest and I watch them drift away, swaying to the beat of a song about good love gone bad, until they are obscured by the smoke.

When the song is over Buckeye comes back with a flushed face and a look of exasperation. He says, "You see what I mean? That girl wanted things and for me to do them to her. She wanted these things done as soon as possible. She asked me if I didn't want to load her bases." He plops down in his chair and drains his Coke with one huge swallow. It doesn't even make him blink.

• • •

On our way home he pulls into the deserted front lot of a drive-in movie theater and floors the accelerator, yanking the steering wheel all the way to the left and holding it there. He yells, "Carnival ride!" and the car goes round and round, pinning me to the passenger door, spitting up geysers of dust and creaking and groaning as if it might fly into pieces at any second. When he finally throws on the brakes, we sit there, a great cloud of dust settling on the car, making ticking noises on the roof. The world continues to hurtle around me and I can feel my stomach throbbing like a heart.

Buckeye looks over at me, his head swaying back and forth a little, and says, "Now doesn't that make you feel like you've just had too much to drink?"

• • •

Simone and I are on the roof. It's somewhere around midnight and there are bats zooming over our heads. We can hear the *swish* as they pass. I have on only a pair of shorts, and Simone is wearing an oversize T-shirt. The warm, grainy tar paper holds us against the steep incline of the roof. Old pipes have forced us out here. Right now those pipes, the ones that run through the north walls of our turn-of-the-century house, are engaged in their semiannual vibrational moaning. According to the plumber, this condition has to do with drastic changes in temperature. We could either pay thousands of dollars to have the pipes replaced or we could put up with a little annoying moaning once in a while.

With my sister's windows closed it sounds like someone is crying in the hallway at the top of the stairs. My parents, with extra years of practice under their belts, have learned to sleep through it.

Simone and I are actually engaged in something that resembles conversation. Naturally, we are talking about Buckeye. If Buckeye has done nothing else, he has given us something to talk about.

For the first time in her life, Simone seems to be seriously in love. She's had boyfriends before, but Simone is the type of girl who'll break up with a guy because she doesn't like the way his clothes match. She's known Buckeye for all of three weeks and is already talking about names for their children. All this without anything close to sexual contact.

"Do you really think he likes me?"

This is a question I've been asked before. "Difficult to say," I tell her. In my young life I've learned the advantages of ambivalence.

Actually, I've asked Buckeye directly how he feels for my sister, and this is the response I got: "I have feelings for her, feelings that could make an Eskimo sweat, but as far as feelings go, these simply aren't the right kind. There's a control problem I'm worried about."

"He truly loves the Lord," Simone says into the night. My sister, who wouldn't know a Bible from the menu at Denny's, thinks this is beautiful.

Over the past couple of weeks I've begun to see the struggle going on within Buckeye, a struggle in which the Lord is surely involved. Buckeye never says anything about it, never lets on, but it's there. It's a battle that pits Buckeye the Badger against Buckeye the Mormon. Buckeye told me that in his old life as the Badger he never stole anything, never lied without first making sure he didn't have a choice, got drunk once in a while, fought some, cussed quite a bit and had only the women who wanted him. Now, as a Mormon, there is a whole list of things he has to avoid, including coffee, tea, sex, tobacco, swearing and, as Buckeye puts it, "anything else unbecoming that smacks of the natural man."

To increase his strength and defenses, Buckeye has taken to denying himself, testing his willpower in various ways. He goes without food for two full days. While he watches TV he holds his breath for as long as he can, doesn't use the bathroom until he's within seconds of making a mess. As part of his rugby training, he has filled an old tractor tire with rocks and made a rope harness for it. Every morning he drags it through the streets from his boarding house to our house, which is at least three miles. When he comes inside he is covered with sweat but will not accept liquid of any kind. Before taking a shower he goes out to the driveway and does a hundred pushups on his knuckles.

Since they've met, Buckeye has not so much as touched my sister, she tells me, except for some innocent hand-holding. Considering that he practically lives at our house and already seems like a brother-in-law, I find this a little weird. Buckeye's noncontact love is making Simone deranged, and I must say I'm enjoying that.

I sit back and listen to the pipes moaning like mating animals behind the walls. Hummingbird Lane, the street I've lived on my entire life, stretches off both ways into darkness. The clouds are low and the lights of the city reflect off them, giving everything a green, murky glow. Next to me my sister chats with herself, talking about the intrigues of beauty school, some inane deeds of my parents, her feelings and plans for Buckeye.

"Should I get baptized?" she says. "Do you think he would want me to?"

I snort.

"What?" she says. "Just because you're an atheist or something."

"I'm not an atheist," I tell her. "I'm just not looking for any more burdens than I already have."

• • •

In the morning, on Sunday, Buckeye comes to our house a newly ordained elder. I come upstairs just in time to hear him explain to Simone and my parents that he has been endowed with the power to baptize, to preach the Gospel, to administer the laying on of hands, to heal. It's the first time I've seen him in his Sunday clothes: striped shirt, blaring polyester tie and shoes that glitter so brightly you would think they'd been shined by a Marine. He's wearing some kind of potent cologne that makes my eyes tear if I get too close. Damn me if the phrase doesn't apply: Buckeye looks born again. As if he had just been pulled from the womb and scrubbed a glowing pink.

"Gosh dang," Buckeye says, "do I feel nice."

I can handle Buckeye the Badger and Buckeye the Mormon, but Buckeye the Elder? When I think of elders I imagine bent, bearded men who are old enough to have the right to speak mysterious nonsense.

I have to admit, however, that he looks almost holy. He's on a high, he's ready to raise the dead. He puts up his dukes and performs some intricate Muhammad Ali footwork—something he does when he's feeling particularly successful. We all watch him in wonder. My parents, just back from prayer meeting themselves, look particularly awed.

After lunch, once Buckeye has left, we settle down for our "Sabbath family conversation." Usually it's not so much a conversation as it is an excuse for us to yell at one another in a constructive format. As always, my father calls the meeting to order. Then, my mother, who is a diabetic, begins by sighing and apologizing for the mess the house has been in for the past few weeks; her insulin intake has been adjusted and she hasn't been feeling well. This is just her way of blaming us for not helping out more. Simone breaks in and tries to defend herself by reminding everyone she's done the dishes twice this week. My father snaps at her for not letting my mother finish, and things take their natural course from there. Simone whines, my mother rubs her temples, my father asks the Lord why we can't be a happy Christian family and I smirk and finish off my pistachio ice cream. Whenever Buckeye is not around, it seems, we go right back to normal.

Not only does Buckeye keep our household happy and lighthearted with his presence, but he has also avoided any religious confrontation with my folks. Buckeye is not naturally religious like my parents, and he doesn't say much at all, just goes about his business, quietly believing what the folks at the Mormon church teach him. This doesn't keep Mom and Dad from loving him more than anybody. Buckeye goes fishing with my father and is currently educating my mother on how to grow a successful vegetable garden. My parents are biding their time until Buckeye comes to his spiritual senses. Then they will dazzle him with the special brand of truth found only in the Holton Hills Reformed Baptist Church, the church where they were not only saved but also met and eventually got married. Until now, though, I would have to say that Buckeye has done most of the dazzling.

● ● ●

One of the big attractions of the Mormon church for Buckeye is that it doesn't have any outright prohibitions against shooting things. Buckeye owns two rifles and a handgun he keeps under the front seat of his Oldsmobile. Today, I've got a .22 (something larger might aggravate my shoulder) while Buckeye is toting some kind of high-caliber hunting rifle that he says could take the head off a rhino. My parents have taken

Simone to a fashion show in Dallas, so it's just me and Buckeye out for a little manly fun in a swamp, looking for something to shoot. The afternoon is sticky and full of bugs, and the chirping of birds tumbles down out of old moss-laden trees. A few squirrels whiz by and a thick black snake crosses our path, but Buckeye doesn't even notice. I guess if something worthwhile comes along, we'll shoot it.

Buckeye and I share secrets. I suppose this is something women do all the time, but I've never tried it with any of the few friends I have. I tell Buckeye that even though I've never been with a girl and have no business fretting about such a thing, one of my biggest worries is that I will be sterile. I started worrying about it after reading an article on the tragedy sterility can cause in people's lives. When I get through the entire explanation, Buckeye looks at me twice and laughs.

"You've never popped your cork with a girl?" he says. The expression on his face would lead me to believe that he finds this idea pretty incredible. I am really embarrassed now. I walk faster, tripping through the underbrush so Buckeye can't see the blood rushing to my face. Buckeye picks up his pace and stays right with me. He says, "Being sterile would have been a blessing for me at your age. I used to lay pipe all over the place, and while nobody can be sure, there's a good chance I'm somebody's papa."

I stop and look at him. With Buckeye, it's more and more secrets all the time. A couple of days ago he told me that on a few nights of the year he can see the ghost of his mother.

"What do you mean, 'nobody can be sure'?" I say.

"With the kinds of girls I used to do things with, nothing was certain. The only way you could get even a vague idea was to wait and see what color the kid came out to be."

There's a good chance Buckeye's the father of children he doesn't even know, and I've got baseless worries about being sterile. Buckeye points his gun at a crow passing overhead. He follows it across the sky and says, "Don't get upset about that, anyway. This is the modern world. You could have the most worthless sperm on record and there'd be a way to get around it. They've got drugs and lasers that can do just about anything. Like I say, a guy your age should only have worries about getting his cork popped. Your problem is you read too much."

I must have a confused look on my face because Buckeye stops to explain himself. With a blunt finger he diagrams the path of his argument on my chest. "Now, there's having fun when you're young and aren't supposed to know better, and then there's the time when you have to come to terms with things, line your ducks up in a row. You have to have sin before there's repentance. I should know about that. Get it all out of you now. You're holding back for no good reason I can see. Some people hold it in until they're middle-aged and then explode. And frankly, I believe there's nothing quite as ugly as that."

We clamber through the brush, me trying to reason through what I've just heard and Buckeye whistling bluegrass tunes and aiming at trees. I haven't seen him this relaxed in a long time. We come into a clearing where an old car sits on its axles in a patch of undergrowth. Remarkably, all its windows are still intact and we simply can't resist the temptation to fill the thing full of holes. We're blazing away at that sorry car, filled with the macho euphoria that comes with making loud noises and destroying things, when a Ford pickup barrels into the clearing on a dirt road just to the south of us. A skinny old geezer with a grease-caked hat pulled over his eyes jumps out.

To get where we are, we've crawled through a number of barbed-wire fences, and there is not a lot of doubt we're on somebody's land. The way the old man is walking toward us, holding his rifle out in front of him, would suggest that he is that somebody, and he's not happy that we're on his property. "You sons of bitches," he growls once he's within earshot.

"How do you do?" Buckeye says back.

The man stops about twenty feet away from us, puts the gun up to his shoulder and points it first at Buckeye, then at me. I have never been on the business end of a firearm before and the experience is definitely edifying. You get weak in the knees and take account of all the deeds in your life.

"This is it," the man says. He's so mad he's shaking. My attention never wavers from the end of that gun.

"Is there some problem we don't know about?" Buckeye says, still holding his gun in the crook of his arm. I have dropped my weapon and am debating whether or not to put my hands up.

"You damn shits!" the man nearly screeches. It's obvious he doesn't like the tone of Buckeye's voice. I wish Buckeye would notice this also.

"You come in here and wreck my property and shoot up my things and then give me this polite talk. I'm either going to take you to jail right now or shoot you where you stand and throw you in the river. I'm trying to decide."

This man appears absolutely serious. He is weathered and bent and has a face full of scars; he looks capable of a list of things worse than murder.

Buckeye sighs and points his rifle at the old man. "This is a perfect example of what my uncle, Lester Lewis, retired lieutenant colonel, likes to call 'mutually assured destruction.'" Buckeye loves the idea. "We can both stay or we can both go. As for myself, this is as good a time as any. I'm in the process of putting things right with my maker. What about you?"

I watch the fire go out of the old man's eyes and his face get slack and pasty. He keeps his gun up but doesn't answer.

"Shall we put down our guns or stand here all day?" Buckeye says happily.

The man slowly backs up, keeping his gun trained on Buckeye. By the time he makes it back to his pickup, Buckeye has already lowered his gun. "I'm calling the police right now!" the man yells, his voice cracking into a range of octaves. "They're going to put you shits away for good!"

Buckeye swings his gun up and shoots once over the man's head. As the pickup scrambles away over the gravel and clumps of weeds, Buckeye shoots three times into the dirt behind it, sending up small puffs of dust. We watch the truck disappear into the trees and I work on getting my lungs functional again. Buckeye retrieves my gun and hands it to me. "We better get," he says.

We thrash through the trees and underbrush until we find the car. Buckeye drives the thing like he's playing a video game, flipping the gearshift and spinning the steering wheel. He works the gas and brake pedals with both feet and shouts at the narrow dirt road when it doesn't curve the way he expects. We skid off the road once in a while, ending the life of a young tree, maybe, or putting a wheel into a ditch. But Buckeye never lets up. By the time we make it back to the highway we hear sirens.

"I guess that old cooter wasn't pulling our short and curlies," Buckeye says. He is clearly enjoying all this—his eyes are bright and a little frenzied. I hang my head out the window in case I vomit.

• • •

Once we get back to civilization Buckeye slows down and we meander along like we're out to buy a carton of milk at the grocery store. The sirens have faded and I don't even have a theory as to where we might be until Buckeye takes a shortcut between two warehouses and we end up in the parking lot of the Ranch. The place is deserted except for a rusty VW Beetle.

"Never been here this early in the day, but it's got to be open," Buckeye says, still panting. I shrug, not yet feeling capable of forming words. It's three in the afternoon.

"When's the last time you had a nice cold beer?" Buckeye says a little wistfully.

"Never, really," I admit after a few seconds. What I don't admit to is that I've never tasted any form of liquor in all my life. My parents have banned Simone and me from drinking alcohol until we reach the legal drinking age. Then, they say, we can decide for ourselves. Unlike Simone, I have never felt the need to defy my parents on this account. When I get together with my few friends we eat pizza and play Dungeons and Dragons. No one has ever even suggested beer. Since I've known Buckeye, I've discovered what a sorry excuse for a teenager I am.

Buckeye shakes his head and whistles in disbelief. I guess we surprise each other. "Then let's go get you a beer," he says. "You're thirsty, aren't you? I'll settle for a Coke."

The front doors, big wooden affairs that swing both ways, are locked with a padlock and chain. Buckeye smiles at me and knocks on one of the doors. "There's got to be somebody in there. I know some of the people who work here. They'll get us set up."

Buckeye knocks again but doesn't get any results. He peers through a window, goes back to the doors and pounds on them with both fists, producing a hollow booming noise that sounds like cannons in the distance. He kicks at the door and punches it a few times, leaving bright red circle-shaped scrapes on the tops of his knuckles.

"What is this?" he yells. "What is this? Hey!"

He throws his shoulder into the place where the doors meet. The doors buckle inward, making a metallic crunching noise, but the chain doesn't give. I try to tell Buckeye that I'm really not that thirsty, but he doesn't hear me. He hurls his body into the doors again, then stalks around and picks up a three-foot-high wooden cowboy next to the cement path that leads to the entrance. This squat, goofy-looking guy has been carved out of a single block of wood and holds up a sign that says COME ON IN! Buckeye emits a tearing groan and pitches it underhand against the door, succeeding only in breaking the cowboy's handlebar mustache.

Buckeye has a kind of possessed look on his face, his eyes vacant, the cords in his neck taut like ropes. He picks up the cowboy again, readies himself for another throw, then drops it at his feet. He stares at me for a few seconds, his features falling into a vaguely pained expression, and sits down on the top step. He sets the cowboy upright and his hands tremble as he fiddles with the mustache, trying to make the broken part stay. He is red all over and sweating.

"I guess I'll have to owe you that beer," he says.

• • •

Simone, my father and I are sitting around the dinner table and staring at the food on our plates. We're all distraught. We poke at our enchiladas and don't look at one another. The past forty-eight hours have been rough on us: My mother has had a diabetic episode and Buckeye has disappeared.

My mother is upstairs, resting. The doctors have told her not to get out of bed for a week. Since yesterday morning, old ladies from the church have been bringing food, flowers and get-well cards in waves. In the kitchen, casseroles are stacked into pyramids.

And nobody has seen Buckeye in two days. He hasn't called or answered his phone. My father has just returned from the boarding house where Buckeye rents a room. The owner told him that she hadn't seen Buckeye either, but it was against her policy to let strangers look in the rooms.

"One more day and we'll have to call the police," my father says. He's made this exact statement at least three times now. Simone, distressed as she is, cannot get any food in her mouth. She looks down at the food on her plate as if it's something she can't fully comprehend. She gets a good forkful of enchilada halfway to her mouth before she loses incentive and drops the fork back onto her plate. I think it's the first time in her twenty-one years that she's had to deal with real-life problems more serious than the loss of a contact lens.

• • •

Three days ago, one day after the incident with the guns, I spent the entire morning nursing an irrational fear that somehow the police were tracking us down and a patrol car would be pulling up outside the house any minute. I was the only one home except for my mother, who had taken the day off sick from work and was sleeping upstairs.

I holed up in my basement bedroom to watch TV and read. About four o'clock I heard a knock at the front door and nearly passed out from fright. I had read about what happens in prisons to young, clean people like me. Trespassing and destruction of property, not to mention shooting in the general direction of the property's owner, might get Buckeye and me some serious time in the pen.

The knocking came again and then the front door creaked open. I pictured a police officer coming into our house with his pistol drawn.

I turned off the light in my room, hid myself in the closet and listened to the footsteps upstairs. It took me only a few seconds to recognize the heavy shuffling gait of Buckeye.

Feeling relieved and a little ridiculous, I ran upstairs to find Buckeye going down the hall toward my parents' room.

"Hey, Bubba," he said when he saw me. "Nobody answered the door so I let myself in. Simone told me your mother's sick. I have something for her." He held up a mason jar that was filled with a dark green substance.

"She's just tired," I said. "What is that?"

"It's got vitamins and minerals," he said. "Best thing in the world for sick and tired people. My grandpop taught me how to make it. All natural, no artificial flavors or colors, though it could probably use some. It smells like what you might find in a baby's diaper and doesn't taste much better."

"Mom's asleep," I said. "She told me not to wake her unless there was an emergency."

"How long's she been asleep?" Buckeye asked.

"Pretty much the whole day," I told him.

Buckeye looked at his watch. "That's not good. She needs to have something to eat. Nutrients and things."

I shrugged and Buckeye shrugged back. He looked a little run-down himself. His hair flopped aimlessly around on his head. He rubbed the jar in his hands like it was a magic lamp.

"You can leave it and I'll give it to her. Or you can wait until she wakes up. Simone will be home pretty soon."

Buckeye looked at me and weighed his options. Then he turned on his heels, walked right up to my parents' bedroom door and rapped on it firmly. I deserted the hallway for the kitchen, not wanting to be implicated in this in any way. I was there only a few seconds when Buckeye appeared, short of breath.

"Something's wrong," he said. "Your mother."

My mother was lying still on the bed, her eyes open, unblinking, staring at nothing. Her skin was pale and glossy and her swollen tongue was hanging out of her mouth and covered with white splotches. I stood in the doorway while Buckeye telephoned an ambulance. "Mama?" I called from where I was standing. For some reason I couldn't make myself go any closer.

I walked out to the front yard and nearly fell on my face. Everything went black for a moment. I thought I'd gone blind. When my sight came back the world looked so sharp and real it hurt. I picked up a rock from the flower planter and chucked it at the Conleys' big bay window across the street. I missed, and the rock made a hollow thump on the siding. If I had played Little League like my father had wanted me to, that window would have been history.

I reeled around in the front yard until the ambulance and my father showed up. I hung out in the corner of the yard and swung danger-ously back and forth in the lilac bushes. I watched the ambulance pull up and the paramedics run into my house, followed a few minutes later by my father. Neighbors began to appear, bald and liver-spotted heads poking out of windows and from behind screen doors.

When my father came out, he found me sitting in the gardenias. He told me that my mother was not dead but that she'd had a severe dia-betic reaction. "Too much insulin, not enough food," he said, wiping his eyes. "Why doesn't she take care of herself?"

I'd seen my mother have minor reactions, when she would get numb all over and forget what her name was and we'd have to make her eat candy or drink soda until she became better. But nothing like this. My father put his hand on my back and guided me inside, where the para-medics were strapping her onto a stretcher and trying to pour orange juice down her throat. She didn't look any better than before.

"She's not dead," I said. I was honestly having trouble believing my father. I thought he might be trying to pull a fast one on me, saving me from immediate grief and shock. To me, my mother looked as dead as anything I'd ever seen, as dead as my aunt Sally in her coffin a few years ago, dense and filmy, like a figure carved from wax.

My father looked at me, his eyes moist and drawn, and shook his head. "She's serious, Lord help her, but she'll make it," he said. "I'm going to the hospital with her. I'll call you when I get there. Go and pray for her. That's what she needs from you."

I watched them load the stretcher into the ambulance and then went upstairs to pray. I had never truly prayed in all my life, though I'd mouthed the words in Sunday school. But my father had said that was what my mother needed, and as helpless and lost as I felt, I couldn't come up with anything better to do.

I found Buckeye in my sister's room kneeling at the side of the bed. My first irrational thought was that he might be doing something ques-tionable in there, but then he started speaking and there was no doubt that I was listening to a prayer. He had his face pushed into his hands, but his voice came at me as if he were talking through a pipe. I can't remember a word he said, only that he pleaded for my mother's life and health in a way that made it impossible for me to move away from the door and leave him to his privacy. I forgot myself completely and stood dumbly above the stairs, my hand resting on the doorknob. Buckeye rocked on his knees and talked to the Lord. If it is possible to be humble and demanding at the same time, Buckeye was pulling it off: He dug the heels of his hands into his forehead and called on the Almighty in a near shout. He asked questions and seemed to get answers. He pleaded for mercy. He chattered on for minutes, lost in something that seemed to range from elation to despair. I had never heard anything like it before. Light shot up and down my spine and hit the backs of my eyes. I don't think it's stretching it to say that for a few moments I was genuinely certain that God, who or whatever he may be, was in that room. Despite myself, I peeked around the door to make sure there was really nobody in there except Buckeye. He finished and I went down the hall to my parents' room. I sat down on their bed and mumbled to no one in particular that I backed up everything Buckeye was saying, 100 percent.

We went to the hospital, and after an eternity of reading women's magazines and listening to Simone's sobbing, a doctor came out and told us that it looked like my mother would be fine, though we were lucky we found her when we did because if we had let her sleep another half hour she certainly wouldn't have made it. Simone began to sob even louder and I looked at Buckeye, but he didn't react to what the doctor said. He slumped in his chair and looked terribly tired. Relief sucked everything out of me and left me so weak that I couldn't help but let loose a few stray tears myself.

While my father filled out insurance forms, Buckeye muttered something about needing to get some sleep. He gave Simone a kiss on the forehead and patted my father and me on the back and wandered away into the dark halls of the hospital. That was the last we saw of him.

● ● ●

My mother's nearly buying the farm and the disappearance of Buckeye, the family hero, has thrown us all into a state. I poke at a mound of Jell-O with my fork and say, "I bet he's just had a good run of luck selling pantyhose. By now he's probably selling them to squaws in Oklahoma." I don't know why I say things like this. I guess it's because I'm the baby of the family.

My father shakes his head in resigned paternal disappointment and Simone bares her teeth and throws me a look of such hate that I'm unable to make another comment. My father asks me why I don't go to my room and do something worthwhile. I decide to take his advice. Simone looks like she's meditating violence. I thump down the stairs, turn up my stereo as loud as it will go, lie on my bed and stare at the ceiling. Before I go to sleep I imagine sending words to heaven, clouds opening up before me to reveal a light so brilliant I can't make out what's inside.

I'm awakened by a loud grating sound like a manhole cover being slid from its place. It's dark in my room, the music is off and someone has put a blanket over me. There is a scrape and a thud and I twist around to see Buckeye stuffed into the small window well on the other side of the room, looking at me through the glass.

He has pushed away the wrought-iron grate that covers the well and is squatting in the dead leaves and spiderwebs that cover the bottom of it. Buckeye is just a big jumble of shadow and moonlight, but I can still make out his smile. I get up and slide open the window.

"Good evening," Buckeye whispers, polite as ever. He presses his palms against the screen. "I didn't want to wake you, but I brought you something. Do you want to come out here?"

I run upstairs, go out the front door and find Buckeye trying to lift himself out of the window well onto the grass. I help him up and say, "Where have you been?"

When Buckeye straightens up and faces me, I get a strong whiff of alcohol and old sweat. He acts like he didn't hear my question. He holds up a finger, indicating for me to wait a moment, and goes to his car, leaning to the right just a little. He comes back with a case of beer and bestows it on me as if it were a red pillow with the crown jewels on top. "This is that beer I owe you," he says, his voice gritty and raw with drink. "I wanted to get you a keg of the good-tasting stuff, but I couldn't find one this late."

We stand in the wet grass and look at each other. His lower lip is split and swollen, his half-ear is a molded purple and he's got what looks like lipstick smudged on his chin. His boots are muddy and he's wearing the same clothes he had on three days ago.

"Your mother okay?" he says.

"She's fine. They want her to stay in bed a week or so."

"Simone?"

"She's been crying a lot."

For a long time he just stands there, his face gone slack, and looks past me to the dark house. "Everybody asleep in there?"

I look at my watch. It's almost three thirty in the morning. "I guess so," I say.

Buckeye says, "Hey, let's take a load off. Looks like you're about to drop that beer." We walk over to the porch and sit down on the steps. I keep the case in my lap, not really knowing what to do with it. Buckeye pulls out two cans, pops them open, hands one to me.

I have the first beer of my life sitting on our front porch with Buckeye. It's warm and sour but not too bad. I feel strange, like I haven't completely come out of sleep. I have so many questions looping through my brain that I can't concentrate on one long enough to ask it. Buckeye takes a big breath and looks down into his hands. "What can I say?" he whispers. "I thought I was getting along fine and the next thing I know I'm facedown in the dirt. I lost my strength for just a minute and that's all it takes." He gets up, walks out to the willow tree, touches its leaves with his fingers and comes back to sit down. "I think I got ahead of myself. This time I have to take things slower."

"Are you going somewhere?" I ask. It seems to be the only question that means anything right now.

"I don't know. I'll keep looking for Bud. He's the only brother I've got. I've just got to get away, start things over again."

Not having anything to say, I nod. We quietly drink a couple more beers together and stare into the distance. I want to tell Buckeye about hearing him pray for my mother, thinking it might change something, but I can't coax out the words. Finally, Buckeye stands up and whacks some imaginary dust out of his pants. "I'd leave a note for Simone and your folks . . ." he says.

"I'll tell them," I say.

"Lord," Buckeye says. "Damn."

He sticks his big hand out for a shake, a habit he picked up from the Mormons, and gives me a knuckle-popping squeeze. As he walks away on the cement path toward his car, the inside of my chest feels as big as a room and I have an overpowering desire to tackle him, take his legs out, pay him back for my collarbone, hold him down and tell him what a goddamn bastard I think he is. This feeling stays with me for all of five seconds, then bottoms out and leaves me as I was before, the owner of a long list of emotions: sorry that it had to turn out this way for everybody, relieved that Buckeye is back to his natural self, pleased that he came to see me before he left, afraid of what life will be like without him around.

Buckeye starts up his battle wagon and instead of just driving slowly away into the distance, which would probably be the appropriate thing to do, he gets the car going in a tight circle, four, five times around in the middle of the quiet street, muffler rattling, tires squealing and bumping the curb, horn blowing, a hubcap flying into somebody's yard—all for my benefit.

BUCKEYE THE ELDER

I go into the house before I hear the last rumbles of Buckeye's car die away. I pick up the case of beer to hide under my bed, already planning a hell-raising beer party for my friends. I figure it's about time we did something like that. On the way down the stairs, I wobble a little and bump into things, feeling like the whole house is pitching beneath my feet. All at once it hits me that I'm officially roasted. Gratified, I go back upstairs and into my father's den, where he keeps the typewriter I've never seen him use.

I feed some paper into the dusty old machine and begin typing. I've decided not to tell anyone about Buckeye's last visit; it will be the final secret between us. Instead, I go to work composing the letter Buckeye would have left had he only learned to write. I address it to Simone and just let things flow. I don't really try to imitate Buckeye's voice, but somehow I can feel it coming out in a crusty kind of eloquence. Even though I've always been someone who's been highly aware of grammar and punctuation, I let sentence after sentence go by without employing so much as a comma. I tell Simone everything Buckeye could have felt and then some. I tell her how much she means to me and always will. I tell her what a peach she is. I'm shameless, really. I include my parents and thank them for everything, inform them that as far as I'm concerned, no two more Christian people ever walked the earth. I philosophize about goodness and badness and the sweet sorrow of parting. As I type, I imagine my family reading this at the breakfast table and the heartache compressing their faces, emotion rising in them so fully that they are choked into speechlessness. This image spurs me on and I clack away on the keys like a single-minded idiot. When I'm finished, I have two and a half pages and nothing left to say.

I take the letter out on the front porch and tack it to our front door, feeling ridiculously like Martin Luther, charged with conviction and fear. I go back inside and try to go to sleep, but I'm restless—the blood inside me is hammering against my ribs and the ends of my fingers, the house is too dark and cramped. Instead of going up the stairs, I push out my window screen, climb out through the well and begin to run around the house, the sun a little higher in the sky every time I come around into the front yard. I feel light-headed and weightless and I run until my lungs are raw, trying to get the alcohol out of my veins before my parents wake up.

What Can I Tell You About My Brother?

by **RYAN HARTY**

1995

O n his third night home from boot camp my brother killed Rob
Dawson's black Labrador retriever with a Phillips-head screwdriver.
He'd gone mad, is how he explained it to me later, and his madness had
to do with Bethany Anne Armstrong, a beautiful brown-haired junior
at Edgewood High School. Before my brother had joined the Marine
Corps, Bethany Anne had been his girlfriend. They'd been crazy in
love for a year and a half. Then, during his sixth week of training, my
brother received a letter that told him Beth now went out with Rob
Dawson, the senior quarterback of my football team at Edgewood High.
Victor killed the dog in the backyard of the Dawson home, a three-story
mansion in Hillside Heights that overlooked our whole sleeping town.
He left the body in the lighted blue swimming pool, disappeared under
the hedges and didn't come home until the next afternoon.

• • •

Late that night I heard the chirp of tires through my open window,
the idling of a smooth, unfamiliar engine. A car door slammed. I heard
footsteps, and then Rob Dawson was screaming at my father through
the screen door, banging his hand against the jamb. My father's voice
was thick with sleep or drink. I lay in my dark room, ten feet away,
underneath my open window.

"You let me talk to Victor!" Rob said, his voice high-pitched and loud. His sneakers scraped on the wooden porch.

"Victor's not home," my father told him. "What the hell is this now?"

"He fucking killed my dog!" Rob threw a fist at the screen so hard it rattled my window. I was sure he'd bust into the house.

"Just settle down!" my father pleaded. "You're wrong here. No. Victor didn't do that."

"Bullshit, man. It was him. I know he's back in town."

Kneeling on my bed then, I peeked out the window. It was dark, but my room looked out on the porch, and I could just make out Rob's face and his blond hair catching yellow light from the porch lamp, shoulders rigid and neck bent forward. I didn't know him well. A sophomore at Edgewood, I was two years younger and had spoken with him only a few times. "Just tell me where the bastard is!" he yelled.

"He's gone," my father said. "Not here."

"I swear I'll kill the son of a bitch!"

Something else was said that I wasn't able to make out, and then Rob stopped shouting, just suddenly. His mouth came open and he stared at my father through the screen.

I realized that my father was crying. "Oh, Lord," he cried. "Oh, my boys."

For a moment, standing in the light, Rob appeared to be unable to move. Then he swung around and ran back to the street, where he got into his Jeep and laid a strip of rubber down the blacktop.

I heard sobbing from the doorway still, a muted noise almost like laughter. Then the screen creaked open and I watched my father step out onto the lawn, where he stood in his bare feet looking slowly up and down our street. After a moment he turned back to the house. There was a time, I knew, when he would have waited for Victor to come home to beat the hell out of him. But he was old now; his heart was bad. There wasn't much he could do.

• • •

The next day after practice I showered and changed, then went back to the field to look for a lens that had popped out of my glasses during drills. I crawled on hands and knees around the blocking sleds, worried because my father could get ugly about buying new glasses every fucking second if his mood was bad. It was a day of cloudy light that made you squint, October but still warm, and as I searched I couldn't keep from thinking about my brother. I imagined him standing in the dim light up in Hillside Heights, his hair shaved off for the Corps, fists clenched and darkened with blood.

I was still looking when Rob Dawson came out of the locker room, shirtless, a duffel bag slung over his shoulder. I'd seen him in practice earlier and had been afraid of what he might do, but our eyes had not met then. I'd gotten the feeling he wanted to avoid a confrontation. Now he came down the asphalt strip that led to the practice field, right toward me. He stopped a few yards off, stared at me, then looked away at the high clouds scattered to the west, picking at a scab on his elbow. "What are you doing?" he asked. My voice cracked as I explained.

Rob nodded. He started to search for the lens, not on all fours but bent over just slightly, his hair still wet and combed back in rows.

"It's no big deal," I said. "I can find it." I wanted him to leave.

Rob bent down and parted the grass with his fingers. The lens winked in the sun as he held it up.

"Oh, man," I said. "Thanks, I guess."

Rob tossed me the lens, then sat down on the grass beside me. He didn't smile. On his face was his usual expression—a faint smirk, almost nothing at all.

It would have been awkward to leave at that point, though it was definitely what I wanted to do. The day had gone on too long. All day people who had heard about what happened had stared at me as if I'd killed Rob's dog myself.

Rob plucked grass with his fingers, seeming to find interest in something behind me. After a while I turned to see what was there—only the goalposts and a line of oleanders—and when I turned back Rob's eyes had gone narrow and were fixed on me. "So, what can you tell me about your brother?" he asked.

"What do you mean?"

Rob tossed a pinch of grass to the wind. "So far I've only heard he's an asshole," he said. "And I've got every reason in the world to believe it." He frowned and looked away for a moment, then looked back, his eyes surprisingly calm. "What I want to know is if there's anything good about him. Most of the time there's something—some good thing— about everyone."

I nodded, turning the lens in my fingers. Rob kept his eyes on me, serious, waiting. There were good things, I knew that, but there were bad things too. My brother had beaten me up and embarrassed me, had done things that would have made me hate him if he were anyone else. But he had also protected me. He was my brother, and what I felt was complicated. I had no idea how to explain it, especially to a guy whose dog he had killed.

"He's an asshole," I said finally, just wanting to leave.

Rob nodded. Then he stood up and brushed dead grass from his Levi's. "That's too bad," he said. "Come on. I'll give you a ride home."

"All right," I said.

But as soon as I said it I wished that I hadn't.

• • •

When I was twelve, and my brother fifteen, I knocked the iron off the ironing board and burned a hole in the carpet, and my father completely lost his head. Holding me down, he touched the iron to the back of my neck, blistering the skin. I ran out into the empty street, screaming, and saw curtains part in the houses all around. After a moment my brother came out the front door, leaving it wide open, his arms full of bottles as he walked with determination across the lawn. "Okay, now," he said to me. "Okay." As he set the bottles on the sidewalk one of them broke and he said, "That's my point. Right there's my point." He grinned, his eyes small and strange. Then he picked up a bottle and threw it end over end so it shattered against the side of our brick house.

He handed one to me. "Do it, bro," he said, nodding with his long dark hair in his face. I threw the bottle. When it exploded against the carport, Victor laughed crazily. My father came into the doorway in his work clothes, navy blue Dickies and steel-toed boots, looking suddenly old and frail. He nodded, then went back inside. Victor kept handing me bottles. I couldn't stop laughing, though I was crying still. Wiping a forearm across his face, Victor said, "Yeah, bro! Do it! Do it!"

This might have been the kind of thing that Rob wanted to hear—a good thing about my brother. But I didn't think he would understand it. I kept it to myself as we walked across the parking lot.

• • •

The inside of Rob's Jeep looked as if it had never been spilled on. Leather smell came from the upholstery and the dash was shiny black. I wondered if Rob would ask for directions, and hoped he would, hoped we could pretend he had not been to my house the night before. But he drove east down Benlow Drive, toward the poorer section of town, without speaking. Rob lived exactly the other way. If you looked you could see his house in a cluster on the wooded hill behind us—Hillside Heights, brown and white squares between the oak trees.

"I watched you in practice today," Rob said. "You run a quick pattern. You should get some playing time."

"No," I said, "I don't think so." I was one of the fastest players on the team, it was true, but I was only a sophomore, and small, a second-string flanker brought up from JV.

We came to a red light and Rob looked at me. Behind him were the wrecking yards—rusting cars stacked in rows. "How would you like to get in the game against Galt on Friday night?" he asked.

"How?"

"Don't worry about that." The light changed and he accelerated through the intersection.

"I don't know," I said. I hadn't expected anything like this. Galt was our biggest game of the season, both teams coming in undefeated. I didn't want Rob to do me any favors. Still, I wanted to play, I knew that much. "I'd like that, I guess."

"I bet," Rob said, adjusting himself in the seat.

I looked out the window at the empty lots where Indians sold painted pottery and statues. Then we came into the rows of flat houses. We passed the street where Bethany Anne lived with her mother and her stepfather, who worked at the paper mill where my father had been a lineman before his heart attack. Rob looked down the street as we passed. A police car was angled in front of one of the houses.

"Did you wonder why I didn't call the cops?" Rob asked.

"I didn't know you didn't."

"That's not how I do things," he said. He gave me an even, arrogant look. But then his face went soft and he glanced away, holding tight to the steering wheel. He seemed less confident now, and that made me nervous for some reason. I got the idea he was thinking about his dog.

"I'm sorry it happened," I said.

"Hey," Rob said. "This is not your problem, all right?"

I nodded, though I couldn't help thinking it was my problem, that I had to share the blame in some way, though I didn't know how or why. We were turning onto my street and I looked out the window again, at yards with cars on concrete blocks, toddlers in their underwear playing on the sidewalks.

And that's when I saw my brother. Victor lay on a towel on our yellow front lawn, bare-chested and wearing cutoffs. Rob saw him too, and cocked his head up like a startled animal.

"All right," Rob said, and pulled the car to the curb. "Here we go now."

When he had come to a stop he looked at me, a strange expression on his face. He was almost smiling, but there was tension at the corners of his eyes. "If you think I know what to do here, you're wrong," he said, and pulled the brake handle back. "I haven't decided anything." He got out of the Jeep slowly, walked around the front and paused there for a moment. He banged his palm once on the metal hood, staring at my brother. "Okay, fucker, let's go," he said. And then he bolted into the yard. I got out of the car and froze with my hand still on the handle.

My brother was not quite standing when Rob hit him the first time, on the temple. He ducked away and lifted his hands to his head like horse blinders and Rob popped him again. Victor, still hunched over, tried to swing his back around, but Rob was moving quickly, staying in front. He shuffled with his legs spread, rotating his chest to swing with both hands, and I heard the sound of the punches—dull thuds at the back of my brother's neck and shoulders. I was about ten yards away. My brother was bigger than Rob and had been in a lot of fights, but he wasn't even trying. He slumped around, and his head jerked down each time Rob connected.

"Fight me!" Rob said. He tried to lift my brother, his fingers going into Victor's face. "Fight me, you lame fucker!"

Victor pulled away and stood up straight, taking a step backward. He sucked in air, his hands held up as if surrendering. Then he shot me a nervous glance and turned back to Rob. "Fuck it," he said, "hit me." A line of blood came down from his eyebrow and his eyes shifted quickly. With his hair shaved off, he looked ridiculous somehow. His head was too small and his nose too long. And then he started coughing and couldn't stop. He bent over with his fist at his mouth. It was depressing.

Rob stared at him for a moment, then backed away, panting. He leaned over, hands on his knees. "You're an asshole," he said. "Everyone's told me that, even your brother here."

I turned my head as Victor looked at me. A few houses down a lady in a yellow sundress peered at us, holding a hose over her dead lawn.

"You're pathetic," Rob said. He looked at Victor closely, as if to make sure he'd heard what he said. "Do you have anything to say for yourself? Huh?"

"I don't," my brother said.

"Is something just the matter with you?" Rob said. "Are you completely fucked-up?"

My brother closed his eyes and opened them again.

Rob made a noise then—"Hah!"—just a small laugh that got out of him. He looked at me, shaking his head. Then he turned and walked across the lawn. He got into his Jeep, which was still running, and drove off looking straight ahead. I watched him disappear around the corner.

"Jesus, Tommy," Victor said, almost whining. "I really needed that." I was afraid he might start to cry.

"I didn't think you'd be here," I said.

"You brought him home," he said. "You brought him right to our house." And, letting himself fall onto the towel, he buried his face in his hands. He coughed again, just once. We were both quiet for a while. I looked up and saw a jet pulling a line of white across the sky.

Then, holding his arms out and attempting to smile, Victor said, "Check out this tan." His arms, face and neck were brown, while the rest of him was bone white. Blood was drying on his collarbone. "It's embarrassing."

I didn't say anything.

Victor said, "Tiny O'Smallessey here."

This was an inside joke between us, from when we were kids. To be Tiny O'Smallessey was to be as low as you could be. Victor looked at me and the weak smile dropped from his face. "You probably think I'm crazy," he said.

"I think you're stupid."

"Fair enough," he said, nodding. "I'll catch shit for it, though. More shit."

"He didn't call the cops," I said. When Victor looked at me I said, "He told me that."

He nodded again, looking unrelieved. "He should have." Then he narrowed his eyes and said, "Do you think it's something I don't feel bad about?"

"You probably do," I said.

"Would you believe it was like something I couldn't control?"

"I don't know what I'd believe."

"That's how I'd describe it," he said, "something I couldn't control. Though it seems like bullshit, even to me."

It seemed it to me, but I didn't say so. I sat down beside him.

In the west the clouds had come together and stood there like a dark gray mountain. The air was wet and getting colder. My brother told me what had happened, that he had gone to Rob's house with a screwdriver and a bucket of sand to sabotage the pool pump. But when he got there the idea suddenly seemed pointless. The houses on the hill were so big, the people in them had so much money, that they could just have the pump fixed and be swimming the next day if they wanted. You would have to do something serious to get to them, is what he thought. In boot camp he'd heard about North Vietnamese soldiers leaving the bodies of babies outside fortified U.S. camps, to break our soldiers down mentally. "I don't know," he said. "I saw the dog, you know? He was barking and making a lot of noise. Something clicked in me. At some point I realized what I was doing, but by then he was already dead. I was just crazy. I was crazy, Tommy, the whole time, I swear. When I put the dog in the pool I felt almost like me, but I still wasn't quite me." He looked up. "Do you have any idea what I'm talking about?"

"I wish I did," I said. "But then again I'm glad I don't."

"Yeah, right," he said. "Bingo."

• • •

At practice on Thursday coach Harding worked me in with the first-string offense in scrimmage, but I was nervous and hobbled passes. Everyone had a reason to be mad at me. If it wasn't because I was a sophomore taking playing time from a senior, it was because of what my brother had done. The defense knew which plays we would run before we ran them, and was supposed to compensate by not going full-out. But on four straight slants I got my clock cleaned. After knocking the wind out of me, Tim Zucher pointed at Rob and said, "That one was for you, buddy."

Rob pretended not to hear him.

In the locker room Rob avoided me, but he caught up to me in the parking lot. "Don't worry about today," he said. "You'll be fine tomorrow night."

"I got killed," I said.

"Don't worry about that," Rob said. "You can take it."

I touched a rib that felt broken. "Oh, fuck you, man," I said.

• • •

Victor wasn't around when I got home that night. My father was watching a hockey game in his bedroom, and I sat on the couch in the living room, going over my playbook. My father and I never talked much anymore, which was the way both of us sort of wanted things. We had fallen into that routine after his heart attack.

As I studied I worried about Victor—thinking of him out somewhere with his stupid haircut, schizo, doing God knows what. It made it hard to concentrate. After a while a pizza man came to the door and my father went out and paid him, then took the pizza into his bedroom. Twenty minutes later he came back and dropped half of it on the coffee table.

"Where's Victor?" I asked.

"How the hell do I know? Isn't he gone back already?"

"Not till tomorrow."

He shrugged. Then he looked down at me, arching his eyebrows. "Listen," he said, "is he in some kind of trouble now? There was a kid came by the other night looking for him, looked like he meant to give Victor a hard time."

"I'm not sure," I said.

"This kid was nuts," my father said shaking his head. "I told him to get the hell out or I'd bust him a new hole."

"I don't know," I said. "I haven't heard anything about that."

My father stared down at me, knowing I was lying, probably. "All right," he said. "You hear anything, though, you let me know. All right?"

"All right." I went to the kitchen for some paper towels and he followed me with his eyes. "Hey, I'm watching the Kings," he said, jerking a thumb behind him, "if you're interested. They look good this year. They're beating the crap out of San Jose."

"I've got to study my plays," I said. "I'm going to get into the game on Friday." As soon as I said it I wished hadn't.

My father smiled, suddenly awkward. "That right?" he said. "Hey, that's great." He looked like he meant to say something else, rubbing his palms on his robe. Then he turned and went back to his bedroom and closed the door, and I heard the noises of the hockey game.

• • •

Victor came home the next afternoon when I was there to pick up my playbook. His clothes were a mess and there were bags under his eyes. There was a dark line over his eyebrow where he had been cut in the fight with Rob.

"Where have you been?"

"Out," he said. "But I've got to get to the bus station now."

My father was asleep in his bedroom. Victor hurried to his room to change into his uniform, and when he came back I found my father's keys and we walked out to the truck.

It was a crisp day, the sun cool and white. We drove through town and out Willowpass Road, which led to Downy and the bus station there.

"So where did you go last night, anyway?" I asked him.

Victor laughed, more relaxed now in the truck. "Nowhere," he said. "Well, actually, right up this road here. I hitchhiked. I got a ride half-way to Downy and then changed my mind."

"You walked back?"

"This morning," he said. "Last night I slept in a field. It was funny in a way. Hey, do you remember when we went out and looked for that boy who was lost?" He glanced at me.

Before Victor left for the Marines, he, Bethany Anne and I had joined a search party to help find a Cub Scout who had wandered away from his pack in some nearby woods. We spent a couple of days searching around Turlock Lake, finding nothing but pieces of bleached driftwood that looked like bones. Eventually, after Victor had left, the boy's body was found washed up on the shore of a river.

"Did you ever hear what happened to that kid?" my brother asked.

"He was all right," I said. "They found him." I was surprised to hear myself say that.

"They did," Victor said, and nodded. "Okay, good. I never knew."

We went past rolling hills dotted with oak trees. Up ahead was something on the side of the road, and seeing it my brother leaned forward. "What's that?" he asked.

"No idea."

But when we got closer I saw what it was: a formation of river rocks, set back in a field—a perfectly symmetrical pyramid shape, standing about as high as a man. "Look at that, Tommy, will you?" Victor said. He seemed excited, happy, looking at the rocks, which were all gray and about the size of grapefruit. "Somebody built that, you know?" He glanced at me wondrously. "Imagine doing something like that. That's a job I think I could handle."

We passed it and I watched it get smaller in the rearview mirror.

"You haven't told me much about the Marines," I said.

And Victor didn't look happy anymore, just that quickly. He stared out the window, where the trees had broken to a stretch of green river. "There are some tough motherfuckers. Real tough."

"Do you like it, though?"

"You just deal with it, you know?" He glanced at me. "I don't like it, though, no. I fucking hate it." He tugged at his bottom lip. It seemed he was trying to figure something out, something complicated. "They've got this thing that messes with your head," he said, "where they'll punish everyone in the unit every time you fuck up. You know me, right? I'm a fuckup, I admit it. But I'll pull some bullshit thing, mouthing off or slacking or just doing something wrong by accident, and then suddenly everyone's doing squat-jumps on my behalf. I don't have many friends there, to tell the truth. I'm not a very good Marine." He looked at me seriously. "Though I wish I was. I'd like to be."

We were coming into Downy, past streets of white houses with leaves in the yards, then into the downtown area. I felt like I should say something else, something reassuring, but nothing came to mind. We didn't speak again until we pulled up beside the bus station.

"Well," I said, "good luck, I guess. What is it—Christmas? You'll be back at Christmas?"

He nodded, opening the door. But then he let it close again. "Hey," he said, "how has Dad been lately?"

"All right, I guess."

He looked at me seriously, almost as if he were angry. "How has he been, though, I mean. With you."

"All right," I said. "No big problems."

"Okay, good." Then, opening the door again, he set his duffel bag on the sidewalk. He got out, shut the door behind him and leaned in the window, grinning. "I used to always ask you to show me your muscle, remember? To flex? And now it's actually pretty big." He shook his head. "I never thought it would be, for some reason."

"It's not that big."

"It's not bad," he said. "Man, I wish I could watch you play tonight."

"Me too. I'm starting."

"I didn't know that," he said. But he was distracted, looking around the inside of the truck, at the metal dash and the overflowing ashtray, the beer cans scattered on the floorboards. He turned and glanced behind him, his elbows still on the door—there was an old man eating an apple in the bus station doorway, a woman tugging a child along. Then he looked right at me, and his eyes struck me in a way that was strange. He had come back to a place where his girlfriend was no longer his girlfriend, and had completely lost his head. But now he didn't want to leave. I thought he might get back in the truck and make me drive him home. But he turned and slouched away, his duffel bag slung over his shoulder. And as he disappeared into the station I watched him, his head so unfamiliar with the new haircut that he could have been someone else entirely.

• • •

At the postgame party at Missy Gumble's all the people who had been mad at me were suddenly my friends. We had beaten Galt by fourteen points and I'd had six receptions, one of which I'd turned into a touchdown. I drank beer standing by a wall, and people came up and talked to me. Missy lived in Hillside Heights, four houses from Rob Dawson, and mostly there were seniors at the party, thirty or so, almost all Hillside people.

Rob stumbled across the shiny wooden floor with a cup of beer in his hand. He was with Bethany Anne, who wore his blue-and-white letter jacket draped over her shoulders. At first, Beth seemed frightened to see me—she glanced away at a group of people standing in the kitchen. But when she turned again I smiled and she smiled back. "Hi, Tommy," she said.

"Beth," I said. "Hi. How have you been?"

She bit her upper lip and nodded. "Okay," she said. She folded her thin arms under Rob's jacket. "Not bad."

Rob leaned into me. "I was right about you," he said, and wagged his head. "How does it feel to be a starter?" He was drunk and had asked me that already on the ride over.

"All right," I said.

"That's right," he said. "Stick with me, Pendcrest. You'll go places." Grinning, he draped an arm around Bethany Anne's shoulders and said, "Look at Beth here. Where do you think she would be if she hadn't met me?"

"What do you mean?" I asked, though I knew what he meant. He meant she would still be going out with my brother. It gave me an idea about how Rob liked to think of himself—as someone who helped people less fortunate than he was. But I didn't like to think of him helping me in that way, and I don't think Bethany Anne did either. She pulled away from him and he followed her, saying, "What? What?"

"Where's Tommy Pendcrest?" Tim Zucher said behind me. He stood by a glass table with a group of other seniors. Looking right at me he said it again, winking, then glanced around as if he couldn't find me. He held a bottle and a shot glass. I walked over and Tim filled the glass, spilling a lot on his hands and the table. "All right, you tough little fucker," he said, handing it to me. I had to turn my head and close my eyes after I'd drunk it.

I wandered away, feeling heat in my face and sweat breaking out at my hairline. There was a crowd waiting for the bathroom by the kitchen, so I found another one on the second floor. The window by the toilet looked out on the backyard, and as I peed I stared out at the lighted pool. Groups of people milled around it, floodlights lighting up a patch of lawn. As I looked I imagined a dead black dog, a dark thing on the glowing blue water.

Below me, people were talking. Rob and Bethany Anne and a few others had gone outside and were standing beside the pool underneath the window. I saw the tops of their heads, all of them holding beer cups, the pool light casting wavy lines across their faces. Carl Mathers came out of the house with a jug of wine and joined the group. "So, Rob," he said, "that fucker go back to the Army?"

"Today," Rob said.

"Man," Carl said, and shook his head, "I'd have fucked him up big time. Somebody messes with my dog . . ."

"I fucked him up a little," Rob said. "But I don't know." He held his cup close to his chest and looked like he was concerned about something. "I can't waste my time with that shit. The guy's a psycho."

"Got that right," Carl said. "Fucking nutcase." Then he looked at Bethany Anne, smiled and said, "Oh, sorry, Beth."

People laughed.

Bethany Anne made embarrassed glances, and tried to laugh, smoothing down the front of her sundress. "God," she said. "Would it be possible to talk about something else now? Anything?"

I leaned back from the window, my face going hot as if someone had seen me. I had a strange feeling go through me then. It felt something like homesickness, though I didn't want to go home. I just wanted to leave. I opened the bathroom door and walked downstairs, where I stole a brass lighter from a coffee table and went out the front door.

• • •

Outside, to the side of the driveway, an ivy-covered hill led up ten yards to a line of bushes, and I climbed up and stood at the top, looking down at our town and working the lighter. It was cool out and you could see everything from the hill—downtown and Edgewood High, the paper mill and the park several blocks to the west. I saw the houses of Concord Flats and tried to pick mine out. A full moon shined through clouds, lighting the oak-covered hills.

After a while I started down Hillside Drive toward home. In the house next to Missy's a man stared at me through a second-story window and I stared back, walking, until he went away.

Rob Dawson's house was coming up on the right, all the windows dark, his Jeep parked in the circular drive. Around the side of the house I saw someone in the shadows peeing on a tree, and I knew immediately it was my brother. He tried to duck behind the tree, but when he saw who I was he stepped into the light. He was still wearing his uniform, but it was wrinkled around the crotch and knees. "I just ended up here," he said. "It's not like I have a plan or anything."

"What about the Marines?"

"Well, I'm AWOL," he said, and shrugged. "Probably be in deep shit when I go back. I saw you play tonight, though." He gave me an uneasy smile. "I went to the game and you were great. I was, you know, impressed."

"Thanks," I said.

He cocked his head in the direction I'd come from. "Were you just at that party?"

I didn't say anything.

He nodded. I waited for him to ask if Bethany Anne was there, but he didn't. "I don't know what I'm going to do," he said. "Seems like I should do something, you know? I keep having this crazy feeling that I'm forgetting something."

"It's not crazy," I said.

He laughed and shook his head. "I don't know, man," he said.

We went to the curb in front of Rob's house and sat down with our feet in the gutter. It made me nervous to be there. Victor jerked around suddenly, looking up at Rob's house as if he'd heard a noise from there—the house big and dark, brown bricks and a green metal roof that curled around the edges. "Did you used to think she was in love with me?" he asked, turning back around. "Back when we were together?"

"I thought so," I said, "yes."

"Yeah," he said. Scraping his boots on the blacktop, he pulled his knees in close to his chest. "Like, I think about when Dad was in the hospital and she would go with me to visit him every day. I probably thought more about her than Dad then, which sounds terrible. But I thought about the way things would be with her and it seemed like we would be together, you know, for the rest of our lives. It didn't seem crazy to think that."

"It wasn't crazy," I said.

"I know it's not true, though, now," he said. "I can realize that." He turned away, toward the houses on the other side of the street. "I do want to do something," he said. "I feel like there must be one thing that if I could just think of it, you know?"

"There's nothing," I said. "Doing things is what gets you in trouble."

"True," he said, nodding. "I know. You're right."

We sat quietly for a few minutes. The air had gone thick and dusty in a way that let me know it would rain soon. A car drove by slowly, sweeping us with its headlights. I heard a noise and looked up the hill, where a couple was walking down the sidewalk toward us. I realized with a surge of panic that it could be Rob and Bethany Anne, coming back to Rob's place, though the light was too dim to see well. I stood. "Let's go," I said. "Let's get out of here."

"Right," Victor said. He nodded but stayed where he was. Then he glanced beyond me, narrowing his eyes up the sidewalk. "Jesus, that's them, isn't it?"

"I think so," I said. "Let's just go."

"Jesus, Tommy."

The couple came under the glow of a streetlight, and I saw that it was them. Rob noticed us and stopped. Bethany Anne took two more steps, then looked down at the sidewalk and off to the side, down the hill at where the lights of our town spread out in the valley. She looked frightened.

My brother stood up.

"What the hell's going on here?" Rob asked. He was far enough away that he had to speak loudly, though I could see him well. He stood with his legs apart, holding a plastic cup in his hand.

"Nothing," I said.

Victor leaned in close to me so that I felt his breath on my neck. He whispered, "I've got to talk to Beth."

"You can't," I said.

"Yes, Tommy," he said, "yes."

"What are you two saying?" Rob asked. "What's going on there?"

"Nothing," I said. I glanced at my brother. "He wants to talk to Bethany Anne."

"Oh, Jesus," Rob said. He glared at Victor. "Look, I don't even know what you're doing here. I can't believe I'm seeing you now. You think I'm going to let you talk to Beth? That's bullshit."

"Let me?" Victor said, and took a step forward. "Hey, Beth, can I talk to you, please?" His voice was high-pitched and strained. "I mean it, Beth."

Bethany Anne gave him a pained look, then let her eyes fall down to the sidewalk.

"She doesn't want to," Rob said. "You can see that, right?"

"She does too," Victor said. "Yes. She does." He glanced at me. He looked panicked and that made me afraid. At that moment I would have done anything to make him stop talking, to make him turn around and walk home with me. It seemed almost like he was waiting for me to do that.

"Victor," I said.

But he surprised me. Taking another step toward Bethany Anne he smiled in a natural way that put me at ease. "Hey, Beth," he said. "Come on now. Don't treat me like I'm Tiny O'Smallessey, okay?" He laughed.

I didn't think Beth would know what Victor was talking about, but when I saw recognition flash across her face I realized he must have told her about it. She gave Rob a questioning look and said, "I should talk to him."

Rob blew out an ugly laugh. He was angry in a way I'd never seen him before. "Talk to him then," he said. He took a sip of beer, stepped onto the lawn and walked down toward me.

Victor jogged up to Bethany Anne. I heard him say something quiet, laugh and then say, "Okay, I'll make it simple." He stood with his back to me in front of Bethany Anne, so we couldn't hear what he was saying.

Rob was beside me now. "What's the story, Pendcrest?" he asked.

I shrugged.

"Fine," he said, and turned away. "I'll tell you this, though. You better get your priorities straight, my friend."

I suddenly felt a little sorry for him. He had helped me out by getting me some playing time, and now he felt like I had betrayed him, which wasn't true, really. But I knew that if it ever came down to a choice between my brother and someone else, I would always choose my brother, because doing otherwise would be like not choosing myself. I didn't think Rob could understand that, and it seemed like he could be hurt by not understanding it.

Above us Bethany Anne said, "Oh, no, Victor," and Rob and I glanced up at her. She was smiling, looking down at my brother's hands, which he held in front of him where Rob and I couldn't see them. It seemed as if he were holding something there, but I couldn't be sure. The two of them laughed.

"What a joke," Rob said. "This is idiotic." Throwing his cup of beer on the lawn, he said, "Beth, I'm going inside," and started toward the door.

Then Victor was finished talking and was coming down the sidewalk, grinning, and Bethany Anne was walking across the grass to catch up with Rob. She said good-bye to me and I turned and waved. Rob opened the front door and she followed him inside.

• • •

"What happened?" I asked after the door had closed.

"It went well," Victor said. He nodded thoughtfully and we walked down Hillside Drive. "It went pretty good."

"What did you say?"

"Well, I told her I was sorry about what I did to that dog," he said. "Jesus, Tommy, that wasn't easy. For a minute I thought she was going to cry." Victor shook his head. "But she didn't. She knows me pretty well. She said she thought I must have just been crazy at the time, which is exactly how I told you it happened. Then I asked if it was all right to keep writing her when I got back to the Marines, and she said she didn't mind, though she thought it wasn't a hot idea to think about her too much."

"Probably it's not," I said.

"Not that I can help it," he said, and smiled. "I don't think she likes Rob all that much."

"Why not?"

"I don't know," he said.

We walked until we came to the point on Hillside where it curved around and heads down to town, and then Victor stopped. There were no houses along the street here, just scrub brush and a few oak trees. It was dark. Victor dug into his pants pocket and pulled something out, something small and silver, and held it in his hands. It was a little snub-nosed revolver with a pearl handle. "Then I asked her if she wanted this back," he said.

"Jesus, Victor," I said. "Where did you get it?"

"Beth gave it to me." He smiled, holding the gun on his flat, open palm. "She stole it from her stepdad's dresser before I went to the Corps." He laughed. "Don't look so surprised."

I took the gun and held it, heavy and warm, in my own hand, then gave it back to Victor. I wondered what Rob would think about this, about Bethany Anne stealing a gun from her stepfather.

Victor had walked a few paces off the street into the scrub brush. "Here," he said, waving me over, "I want to show you something else." He dug into his pocket and came out with a bullet, which he loaded into the pistol. "This is something Beth and I used to do out at Turlock Lake," he said, and looked at me. Then he turned his back, brought his arm out full extension and aimed at the moon. "Shoot the moon," I heard him say softly. He pulled the trigger. The gun put out a burst of fire and made a huge crack that rang through the valley.

"Jesus, Victor."

Victor turned and gave me a look that was deadly serious. "She heard that," he said. "She'll know what I did here." Then he looked up the street, grinned and said, "We better blaze."

"Oh, man," I said. We took off. Lights came on in houses all around us, making my heart pound, but soon we were so far away that I didn't worry about getting caught anymore. A light mist had started, wetting my face and hair and brightening in cones under the streetlights. I heard my brother laugh and it made me feel good. I felt close to him in a way I hadn't felt for a very long time. I felt I understood something about him, or at least about why the things Rob tried to do for Bethany Anne and me could never have the same effect as what my brother had just done. But that would have been hard to explain. I couldn't explain it to Rob, I knew that. I had nothing against Rob—he tried to help people, which was right—but there seemed to be a lot he could never understand.

I didn't think he'd understand, for example, why I would laugh, running down a hill in the rain, after my brother had done something as dangerous and stupid as shooting a gun at the moon. But I did laugh. I laughed so hard my side ached. Both of us did. I felt so good, in fact, getting wet and closer to home, that I had to remind myself—and it was like a shock, like getting bad news—that I didn't even want to go there.

Gerald's Monkey

by MICHAEL KNIGHT
1996

G erald wanted a monkey and Wishbone said he could get it for him. Wishbone had a man on the inside. The three of us were burning out badly rusted floor sections of a tuna rig called *Kaga* and welding new pieces in their place, patchwork repairs, like making a quilt of metal. A lot of Japanese fisheries were having ships built in the States; labor was cheaper. This hold was essentially a mass grave for marine life, and it stunk like the dead. The smell never comes out, Gerald told me, even if you sandblast the paint off the walls. The door to the next room had been sealed, so there was only one way in, an eight-foot-by-ten-foot square in the ceiling, and it was almost too hot to draw breath. They seemed connected, the heat and that awful smell, two parts of the same swampy thing.

"Will it be a spider monkey?" Gerald said.

Wishbone shut down his burner and looked at Gerald.

"I don't know. My Jap gets all the good shit. It'll eat bananas," Wishbone said. "It'll scratch its ass. Shit. *Will it be a spider monkey?*"

"Spider monkeys make the best pets," Gerald said.

"Gerald, what the hell do you want with a monkey?" I said.

Gerald started to answer, paused in his burning, white sparks settling around his gloved hands, but Wishbone cut him off. He said to me, "Do not speak until you are spoken to, little man." His voice was muffled and deepened by his welding mask. "A monkey Gerald wants, a monkey Gerald gets. Now run and fetch me some cigarettes."

He stood and stretched his legs. Wishbone was one large black man. With his welding mask and black leather smock and gloves and long, thick legs running down into his steel-toed work boots, he looked like a badass Darth Vader.

"Wishbone, can you read?" I asked him.

He snapped his mask up. His face was running with sweat and his eyes were bloodshot and angry. He was high on something. Wishbone was always high.

"Did you speak, little man? I hope not."

I didn't say anything else, just pointed at the sign behind him: DO NOT SMOKE, painted in red block letters on plywood. The torches burn on a combination of pure oxygen and acetylene, and sometimes tiny holes wear in the lines from use. The welding flames themselves generally burn off all the leaking oxygen and gas. But shut down the torches and give the gas a little time to collect in the air, then add a spark, and the world is made of fire. A spark is rarely enough, but why test the percentages? There was a story around the yard about a guy who'd been breathing the fumes for hours with his torch unlit. When he went to fire it up, he inhaled a spark and the air in his lungs ignited. Afterward, he looked okay on the surface, but his insides were charcoal, hollowed out by fire.

Wishbone glanced over his shoulder at the sign, looked back at me and shrugged. He reached under his smock and came out with a rumpled pack of Winstons. He put a bent cigarette between his lips, struck a match and held it just away from the tip.

"This is my last cigarette," he said. "You have till I am finished to get your ass up from the floor and out to the wagon for a new pack. Let me be clear. If you are not back before I put my boot on this thing, I'm gonna beat you like a rented mule." He spoke real slow, like my English wasn't so good. "Do you understand?"

I got to my feet reluctantly. I said, "Gerald, you need anything?" Gerald shook his head and gave me a wave.

I sidled to the ladder and climbed it slow and easy, no hurry, but once topside, I was gone, the fastest white boy on earth, dumping equipment as I ran, a jackrabbit, skirting welders and shipfitters on the deck, clanging down the gangplank, then up over the Cyclone fence, headed for the supply wagon. It was ninety-five degrees, wet July heat in lower Alabama, but after the hold, it felt good, almost cool. Goose bumps rose lightly on my skin.

Wishbone got off on razzing me. White kid, sixteen, owner's nephew, gone with the summer anyhow. I was his wet dream. We had worked together for a week during the previous summer, my first time on a welding crew, and even then he had no patience for me. He ignored me for the whole week, just looked away whenever I spoke, concentrated on the skittering sparks and pretended I wasn't there. The cigarette runs were new, but I didn't mind so much. Probably he wouldn't have roughed me up if I had refused to play along. He could have been fired, maybe jailed, and he knew it. But I wasn't taking any chances.

Summers at the shipyard were a family tradition. Learn the value of a dollar by working hard for it, that sort of thing. I'd drag myself home in the evenings caked with filth, feeling drained empty, like I'd spent the day donating blood, and there my sister would be, fresh and blonde and lovely, stretched languorously on the couch in front of the television. She'd have on white tennis shorts and maybe still be wearing her bikini top. She spent her summer days reading by the pool, her nights out with one boy or another. She had tattooed a rose just below her belly button by applying a decal and letting the sun darken the skin around it.

"Give me the fucking remote," I would say.

"Blow me."

She was eighteen, off to the university in the fall. By the time I got home, the last of the daylight would be slanting in through the banks of long windows, making everything look dreamy and slow. My sister would yawn and change the channel just to show me she could. "I'm gonna sit down now, Virginia, and take off my boots and socks," I'd say. "You have until I am barefoot to hand it over or I will beat you like a rented mule."

She would smile, adjust her position so she was facing me, draw her smooth knees up to her belly, get comfortable. She'd yell, "Mo-om," stretching the words into two hair-raising syllables. "Mom, Ford's acting tough again."

• • •

Gerald brought a monkey book to the shipyard, smuggled it in under his coveralls, and the two of us sat around on a break flipping through it. He was an older man, nearing fifty, his dark skin drawn tight over his features, worn to a blunt fineness. He had been working for my uncle almost twenty years. Wishbone lay on his back with his fingers linked on his chest, washed in the rectangle of light that fell through to us. He owned the traces of breeze that drifted down through the hatch. I had the book open across my knees, a droplight in one hand, my back against the bluish-white wall. Gerald was kneeling in front of me, watching for my reaction.

"See there?" he said. "Where it says about how spider monkeys make the best pets?"

He reached over the book and tapped a page, leaving a sweaty fingerprint. I flipped pages, looking for the passage he wanted, past capuchins and guerezas with their skunk coloring, past howler monkeys and macaques, until I came to the section on spider monkeys. I said, "Okay, I got it."

"Read it to me," he said.

I cleared my throat. "Spider monkey, genus *Ateles*, characterized by slenderness and agility. They frequent, in small bands, the tallest forest trees, moving swiftly by astonishing leaps, sprawling out like spiders and catching themselves by their perfectly prehensile tails. Their faces are shaded by projecting hairs, blah, blah, blah, four species between Brazil and central Mexico." I skimmed along the page with the droplight. "Okay, here we go. They are mild, intelligent and make interesting pets. There it is, Gerald."

I tried to hand him the book, but he pushed it back to me.

"Look at the pitcher," he said. "Look at those sad faces."

In the middle of the page was a close-up photograph of two baby spider monkeys. They did look sad and maybe a little frightened, their wide eyes full of unvoiced expression, like human children, their hair mussed as if from sleep, their mouths turned down slightly in stubborn monkey frowns.

"Don't nobody got a monkey," Gerald said.

"Michael fucking Jackson got a monkey," Wishbone said.

We turned to look at him. He hadn't moved, was still stretched in the light, legs straight as a corpse. I had thought he was asleep. Gerald said, "Michael Jackson's nobody I know."

"Michael Jackson has a chimpanzee," I said. "There's a difference."

Wishbone sat up slowly, drew in one knee and slung his arm over it. He looked handsome, almost beautiful, in the harsh sunlight, his eyes narrow, his smile easy, perspiration beaded on his dark face. He looked so mysterious, just then. I thought that if I could catch him in the right light, strike a match at an exact moment, I would see diamonds beneath the surface of his skin.

He got to his feet, walked over and squatted in front of me. He snatched the book from my hands. "'The food of the spider monkey is mainly fruit and insects.'" Wishbone enunciated each word carefully. He winked at Gerald, then leaned toward me until his face was close enough to mine that I could feel his breath on my cheeks. "'In certain countries, their flesh is considered a delicacy.'" He closed the book and passed it to Gerald without taking his eyes from me. He rooted around under his smock, found what he was looking for and dangled it in front of me. "You know the routine," he said, an empty cigarette pack between two fingers.

● ● ●

I took my time doing Wishbone's errand. He hadn't given me a countdown, so I thought I'd at least make him wait awhile for his nicotine. The shipyard was on skeleton crew because we'd lost the Navy contract—four hundred people out of work at my uncle's company alone—and the *Kaga* was one of only three ships in for repairs, leaving seven dry docks empty, rising up along the waterfront like vacant stadiums. I wandered into the next yard over, Yard Five, thinking about Gerald's monkey. I wondered if Wishbone could actually get it for him or if that was just talk. I hoped he could, for Gerald's sake. Cruel to lead him on. I had this picture in my head of Gerald at home in an easy chair, the television on in front of him and this spider monkey next to him on the arm of the chair, curling its tail around his shoulders. It was a nice picture. They were sharing an orange, each of them slipping damp wedges of fruit into the other's mouth.

I could hear the lifting cranes churning behind me, men shouting, metal banging on metal. But Yard Five was still and quiet. Dust puffed up beneath my steps. The infrequent wind made me shiver. Two rails set wide apart, used for launching ships, ran down to the water's edge, and I balanced myself on one and teetered down the slope to the water. A barge lumbered along the river with seagulls turning circles above it.

When I was nine years old, my parents took me to the launching of a two-hundred-foot yacht, the *Marie Paul*, built here for a California millionaire. My family had been invited for the maiden voyage, and we mingled with the beautiful strangers under a striped party tent that sheltered a banquet of food and champagne and where a Dixieland band fizzed on an improvised stage in the corner. There were tuxedos and spangled cocktail dresses along with the canary-yellow hard hats that my uncle required. The women from California wore short dresses my mother never would have worn, exposing tan and slender legs that seemed to grow longer when they danced.

One of these women proclaimed me the cutest thing in my miniature tuxedo and hard hat. She hauled me away to dance, my mother shooing me politely along despite my protests. We did the stiff-legged fox-trot that Mother and I did at home, the only dance I knew. "Loosen up, baby," the woman said, stepping away from me after only a few turns. "Dance like you mean it." She shimmied around me, overwhelmed me, the rustle of her dress and swish of her hair, her hands slipping over my arms and shoulders, her perfume and warm champagne breath, her brown thighs gliding together, her exposed throat and collarbone. This woman did the christening, shattering a bottle of champagne on the prow. The *Marie Paul* was the most magnificent thing I'd ever seen, with a sleek stern and muscular bow like a tapered waist and broad chest. It was polished to incandescent white, with a swimming pool at the rear, a helicopter pad on the topmost deck and four Boston Whalers to serve as landing craft strapped to the foredeck and covered with a purple tarp. Workmen on overtime scurried in its shadow. My dance partner was tiny beneath the yacht's bulk.

Ships are launched sideways, set on giant rollers and drawn down the tracks with heavy cable. When that one hit the water and careened to starboard, sending up a tidal wave of spray, I thought she would go under, that she would keep rolling, slip beneath the slow, brown water and go bubbling to the bottom. I screamed in panic and shut my eyes. My mother pulled me against her leg and said, "It's all right, Ford, honey. Look, it won't sink. See, it's fine." The *Marie Paul* found her balance, came swaying slowly upright, thick waves rushing away from her on both sides, as if drawn by our cheering. Tugboats motored in, like royal attendants, to push her out to deeper water.

• • •

I met my uncle on my way back from the supply wagon. He was giving three Japanese men a tour of the yard, all of them in business suits and yellow hard hats. When he spotted me, he yelled my name and waved me over. I stashed Wishbone's cigarettes in my pocket.

"I'd like you gentlemen to meet my nephew," my uncle said, slapping my shoulder. "He's learning the business from the ground up."

I wiped my palms on my coveralls and shook the hands that were offered. Each of the men gave me a crisp bow. They wore black leather shoes filmed over with dust. Since last summer, I had grown three inches. I had my uncle's size now, and we towered over them.

"Hard work," the oldest man said. He made his voice stern and gravelly, to imply that physical labor was good for you.

"Yes, sir."

"You better believe it," my uncle said. "No cakewalk for this boy."

My uncle was grooming me. He had no children of his own. Moneywise, my old man did all right as well, exploring the wonders of gynecology. But as I had thus far displayed a distinct lack of biological acumen in school, my parents viewed the shipyard as the better course for my future. My father's routine sounded considerably more pleasant, but I didn't argue.

"Ford, these gentlemen own the *Kaga*." My uncle put his hands in his pockets and rocked back on his heels. "They're thinking about letting us build them another one. Wanted to see a work in progress."

"She's a fine ship," I said, and they bowed again.

"*Arigato.*"

Normally, there was a cluster of men dawdling at the supply wagon, but there were no customers now. No one wanted to be caught loafing. All around us, men were busy at their jobs—swarming on deck, unloading a hauling truck over by the warehouse. It was like a movie version of a bustling shipyard. The air had a faint tar smell and was full of wild echoes, the resolute clamor of progress, the necessary bang of making something from nothing. If you stepped back from it a second, weren't sweating in the guts of the thing, it was sort of heartening. You could almost see giant ships growing up out of the ground.

"Well," my uncle said. "Back to the grind, boy."

When I returned to the *Kaga* with Wishbone's cigarettes, I heard voices drifting up from the hold, and I knew that he and Gerald hadn't yet gone back to work. There was an unspoken understanding among the men, a costly one if my uncle got wind of it. The longer a ship stayed in dry dock, the longer you had a job. My first summer at the yard, I was an industrious dervish, eager to learn and make a good impression. It wasn't long before I figured out why no one wanted me on their crew. If I worked too hard, they kept up, afraid I might inform the higher powers. These men walked a fine line. The ships had to be repaired in reasonable time, of course, or there would be no business at all, but if they were finished too quickly, it might seem as if fewer men were needed, or the interval before the next ship arrived might be long enough that layoffs became necessary. The work had to be timed perfectly, not too slow or too fast, or the balance would be upset. It wasn't laziness that slowed the work, as my uncle complained, it was fear. Except for Wishbone. I don't know what slowed him down. Wishbone wasn't afraid of anything that I could tell.

I took off my hard hat, belly-crawled to the hatch and hung myself silently over to watch them. Gerald and Wishbone were on their backs with their feet propped against the far wall, passing a joint between them, its glowing tip visible in the semidarkness. They were giggling like stoned schoolboys.

"Whadju tell him?" Wishbone was talking now, holding the joint between two fingers, blowing lightly on the coal. He dragged and offered it to Gerald, but Gerald waved it away.

"I said, 'Yo' dumb ass standing on a trip wire and you want me to stay and *talk?*' Boy want somebody to keep him company while we wait for the EOC. Don't explode when you step on it, see. They blow when you step off, get the guy behind you, which in this case is me. I said, 'You crazy as you are dumb.'"

Gerald laughed a little, which got Wishbone started again. It took a minute for him to get back under control.

"You leave him?" he said, finally.

"Naw," Gerald said. "I stuck around awhile. Guess I'm dumb as he was."

"Shit, Gerald," Wishbone said. "The Nam."

"It wasn't all bad," Gerald said. "Saw my first monkey in Vietnam."

They stared quietly at the ceiling for a moment. The sun cast a spotlight beam that fell just short of where they lay, and I could see my shadow in the dusty light. I could feel the blood behind my eyes, could smell all the dead fish that had been there before us. I had been thinking about crashing angrily into the hold, doing an impersonation of my uncle, shouting, "Heads are gonna roll around here," and watching them scramble to their feet in panic. But I decided against it. I was already late with Wishbone's cigarettes. I stood and tiptoed away from the hatch. Then I approached again, saying, "I'm back, fellas. Sorry it took so long," unnecessarily loudly, making extra noise, the way you clomp around when coming home to a dark, empty house to give the burglars or ghosts or whatever time to clear out.

• • •

When I got home, finally, I walked around the side of the house to the pool, stripping as I went. My sister was stretched on a lounge chair in her American-flag bikini, one knee up. A boy her age was lying on his side on a second chair, watching her, two sweating glasses of Coke on the table between them. I must have been a strange sight in my boxer shorts, my body pale from hours below deck, forearms and face smeared with sweat and grime, like an actor in blackface only partly painted. They looked up when I passed, and Virginia started to say something, but I didn't give her a chance. I plunged into the clear water, cutting off the sound of her, and let myself glide, rubbing dirt from my arms and cheeks as I went, leaving a distinct, muddy trail in the water. I floated to the surface in the deep end and hovered there, belly down like a drowned man, until I had to take a breath. The water was pure, cold energy on my skin.

"Mom's gonna kill you for not washing first," Virginia said.

"Mom's not gonna find out, is she?" I paddled to the shallow end and stood looking her in the eyes. The pool was chest-deep at this end, and my body felt almost weightless in the water.

"She might."

"She won't," I said.

"I'm Art." The boy with my sister was as tan as she was, and his hair had been bleached almost white from days in the sun. "You must be the brother."

"You getting laid, Art?" I said without looking at him.

"There's an idea," he said. Virginia socked him in the arm and he winced. He was wearing floral-print trunks and a bulky diver's watch, one of those that's pressure-tested to something ridiculous like six thousand feet. Virginia said, "That's it. I'm getting Mom."

She stood and padded across the deck toward the sliding doors. I said, "That's a mistake, Virginia," but she kept walking, skipping a little over the hot pavement. She snapped her bikini bottom into place with two fingers as she went. "Bitch," I said. "Dyke, cunt, whore."

"Whoa now," Art said. "You shouldn't talk to your sister like that."

I climbed the four concrete steps from the pool. My body felt huge and slick and dangerous. It would do whatever I wanted. I walked over to Art, and he stood to meet me. We were almost the same height, and our bodies made a stark contrast, his browned and indolently soft, mine white like hard marble. I leaned into him, our faces inches apart, and gave him an evil wink. "Don't fuck with me, Art," I said. "Just don't." We looked at each other a moment longer before he sidestepped me and followed Virginia into the house.

• • •

My sister had a remarkable propensity for never appearing sleep-worn. I didn't know what went on in that bathroom of hers before the lights went out, but she woke each morning in mint condition, emerging from bed as fresh as she went in, no puffy eyes, no crust around the mouth, not a hair mashed out of place by the pillow. She said it was because she never dreamed. But one night, not long after my meeting with Art, I was startled from sleep by something and jerked awake, heart fluttering, thinking I'm late for work, the house is on fire, whatever, to find my sister standing at the window in my room looking out.

"Jesus Christ, Virginia, you scared me shitless," I said. I rolled over to look at the clock. Five-thirty. The night crew at the yard would be getting off any minute. "Get the fuck outta here. I've got an hour left to sleep."

Virginia didn't answer right away. She was wearing a white knee-length nightgown, and the light coming through the window made her shape a silhouette beneath the fabric. Her hair was smooth and perfect on her shoulders. My room faced the golf course and I could see morning mist just above the ground.

"What the fuck, Virginia?" I said.

She turned toward me and I knew that she was asleep. Her arms hung loosely at her sides, her fingers curled up a touch. Her eyes were open but as distant as the moon. The world was pulling itself together outside. Sprinklers ticked sleepily on the golf course, a garbage truck ground its way down the street. I pictured Wishbone and Gerald, right then, finishing the first leg of a double shift, coming up from below deck, oiled with sweat, blinking at the dim morning like coal miners.

"Eighty feet," Virginia said.

"What?"

"It has to be eighty feet." Her voice was hushed but firm.

"Okay, Vee, no problem. Eighty feet." I got out of bed and put my hands on her warm shoulders and piloted her back down the hall to her room. She didn't resist and climbed into her bed, a four-poster with an embroidered canopy, when I showed it to her. I couldn't fall back asleep after that. I wondered what my sister was building in her dreams.

• • •

Gerald's monkey was on its way. Wishbone had contacted the Jap, and the wheels of black-market commerce were turning as we spoke. I didn't know whether or not to believe him. It was true that the repairs on the *Kaga* were nearly finished and her crew was filtering back into town, so he could have been in touch with his connection. But I had trouble seeing how a drug dealer from Japan was going to get his hands on a monkey from Brazil. For Gerald's sake, I remained skeptical.

"Wishbone, where's your guy gonna come by this monkey?" I said.

We had finished welding two new plates into the deck and had one more to burn out and replace. The seams from the new plates ran along the deck like tiny, steel molehills. We were kneeling around three sides of a square, burning along white lines drawn in chalk, the heat between us enough to burn the hair from your arms without protection. I could feel the heat pressing against my clothes, could feel it on my tongue when I took a breath.

"What *is* that sound? It's almost like a woman," Wishbone said. "You hear something, Gerald?"

Gerald chuckled beneath his mask. Bootsteps echoed above us.

"All I'm saying is, according to Gerald's book, spider monkeys live in Central and South America." The metal beneath the tip of my flame bent and glowed molten orange. "Your guy's not going anywhere near South America."

Wishbone shut down his burner and waved at Gerald to do the same. Gerald and I screwed down the nozzles that controlled the gas, reducing the flames to tiny blue pinpoints. Wishbone lifted his mask and breathed in deeply through his nose.

"Listen here, little man, I don't ask questions." He narrowed his eyes at me. "I tell the Jap what I want, and he gets it. Simple as that. Like magic. That's why they call me Wishbone. You trying to discourage Gerald? Make him think his wish won't come true?"

At that, my skin prickled. I glanced at Gerald. His mask was still down, the bar of window over his eyes blurred by the heat, but I could tell that he was watching us. We were standing directly beneath the hatch and I could see a block of clear sky above the ship. "Of course not," I said. "I just don't want him to get his hopes up."

"So you think Gerald can't work it out for himself, that it?" Wishbone asked. "He's just some dumb nigger got to be looked after?"

"Fuck you, Wishbone."

Wishbone leaned back on his elbows, his temples and neck tracked with sweat. He smiled, then, all the anger in his face suddenly gone, his features smooth with pure delight. That smile was the most terrifying thing I'd ever seen.

"You hear that, Gerald?" he said. "Nephew's pissed."

"Leave the boy alone, Wishbone," Gerald said, snuffing the flame on his torch and raising his mask. He looked tired. "You know he don't mean no harm."

Wishbone cocked his head and examined me a moment longer, still smiling that amused, unnerving smile. "What Gerald wants, Gerald gets," he said. He fished in his pocket and brought out his cigarettes. He shook the last three from the pack, snapped two of them at the filter, crumbled the grains of tobacco between his fingers and situated the remaining cigarette between his lips. He said, "What do you think I want?"

For an instant, I thought about saying no, thought about telling Wishbone to go fuck himself. But I didn't. Something in me resisted the impulse. I don't know whether it was guilt over what Wishbone had said about Gerald or just plain fear or something else entirely, but I dropped my mask and shed my smock and gloves and made my deliberate way up the ladder and into the air.

Outside, the sun was shocking. That was the brightest sky I'd ever seen. A perfect day for sunbathing. I wondered if Virginia remembered her sleepwalking. I walked over to the supply wagon, waving occasionally at one man or another who acknowledged my passing. Everyone knew me. The boss's nephew. The guy who ran the supply wagon saw me coming and had a pack of Winston Reds waiting for me when I arrived.

He smiled and shook his head and said, "Wishbone's daily bread." I forked over the two bucks, thanked him and turned to retrace my steps across the yard. Right then, the ground rocked and I had to grab the counter for balance. The tremor didn't seem connected to anything, seemed to come from the earth itself, scattershot and violent, but I saw the source when I turned. For a second, less than a second, I could see the thing, a thick, twisting cord of flame growing up out of the *Kaga* like a vine.

Then it was gone, and I was running hard for the ship, dodging through the wedge of bodies that rushed down the gangplank and away from the explosion. I found Wishbone on deck, four men pinning his arms and legs, telling him, "Lie still, Bone. It's gonna be all right. Don't move." His eyes were squinched tight against the pain, his mouth wide open, his lips chapped-looking, but he wasn't screaming. He was naked, his clothes disintegrated by the fire, and his skin was raw and crinkly all over, like the edges of burned paper. Several men were jetting fire extinguishers into the hold, white vapor billowing back, but the fire was already out. That sort of flame is a supernova, gone in a flash.

I caught one of the men by his shirtsleeve. "Where's Gerald?" I said. "Let me down there. Gerald's down there. Shut that thing off so we can see him."

He dropped the extinguisher and grabbed my arms.

"You don't wanna see him, son. Believe me."

I let him lead me away from the crowd and sit me down on a spool of heavy cable. My uncle had arrived on the scene by then, and he came over to where I was sitting. "You okay, Ford?" he said. "What happened? Jesus Christ, your mother would've slit my throat if you'd been down there."

"Gerald wants a monkey," I said.

"Of course he does," my uncle said. "You bet, pal."

My uncle drove me home early from work and dropped me at the front steps. I don't think he was ready to face my mother. I didn't tell anyone at home what had happened, just blew right past them, headed down the hall to Virginia's bed. I climbed in, unwashed, and jerked the covers to my chin. I had this crazy idea that my dreams would be safer there. Virginia came in eventually and said, "What the fuck do you think you're doing?" Without opening my eyes, I slipped one hand free of the covers and gave her the finger, and for some reason, that was enough. I could feel her standing there quietly, watching me. After a while, she said, "You look like a little kid," then closed the door behind her and left me alone.

● ● ●

To hear Wishbone tell it, Gerald was the smoker. Pack a day at least, must've warned him a hundred times not to smoke around welding lines but he wouldn't listen. Gerald was an old-timer, set in his awful ways. I stood against the wall of my uncle's office a week or so after the accident and waited my turn to speak. My mother was beside me, her hand lightly at my elbow. To my surprise, I felt no anger at Wishbone's lying. The skin on his face was still whitish pink in places, and his sleeves were buttoned to the wrist, covering his scalded arms, and he wore a newborn's light blue knit cap to protect his tender skull. His hands trembled and his eyes were rheumy, his vision blurred, he said, since the accident. He looked weak, vulnerable, afraid, squinting across the conference table at my uncle and at the men from the insurance company. I wanted to know what made him think I wouldn't expose him. All the shit he gave me. Maybe he thought I was afraid because he was black or that I was ashamed of being white when he wasn't. Maybe he thought his cigarette run had saved my life and I ought to be grateful, despite everything. But what I wanted to know more than anything was how he survived and Gerald didn't, because for an instant, the amount of time it took to burn away the flammable air, that hold was pure, white conflagration, molten gas, like the center of the sun. Nothing could have lived in there. But here was Wishbone telling these lies right in front of me, burned but alive, breathing in and out like the rest of us when he should have been dead. After things had settled down on the deck that day, I walked over to the hatch and looked in. Two policemen and some emergency personnel were milling around a lumped sheet of blue tarp covering what must have been Gerald's body. It's funny, but the stink of all those rotting fish, that death smell, it was gone.

When my turn to speak came, I had to answer only one question: Ford, can you corroborate everything this man has just told us? After but a moment's hesitation, I lied. I'd planned on telling the truth, but in the space of that pause, I thought of Gerald wanting that monkey. He had died believing it would come, hoping for it, and that didn't sound so awful all of a sudden. And I thought of Wishbone, of what good it would do me to ruin his life, what sort of justice would be served. And, strangely, I thought of my sister, so far away from all this, troubled only by rare bad dreams.

"Yes, sir," I said. "He's telling the truth."

I looked at Wishbone, but he wouldn't meet my eyes. He was crying without making a sound. It turned out that he had been standing directly beneath the hatch when he struck the spark that brought the air to life. He had been lifted out by the force of the explosion, shot free of the hold like a cartoon spaceman. One minute he was standing in a perfect square of yellow light with his friend before him; the next, he was riding a grim column of fire.

The Kind of Luxuries We Felt We Deserved

by **JONATHAN BLUM**
1997

My stepbrother Donny's twelfth birthday was all boys and Melanie, my stepsister. I deejayed, but it was no use. Donny and his friends just grouped up in a half circle behind the turntable and kept requesting the same three Van Halen songs. From our spot near the sink, Melanie and I watched the boys bump shoulders while one of them tried jumping into a half-split in front of the refrigerator. After a while, Melanie got sick of the Van Halen and told Donny that his friends had no chance of ever getting girlfriends if this was the coolest they knew how to be. Finally, the boys got bored and began poking around the house for some action. A few of them ended up in the garage fooling around with my free weights and looking through Donny's new *Car and Driver*, and the rest took off behind the pool and started smoking a joint in the backyard.

Melanie wanted to dance now on the Chattahoochee stone floor of the screened back patio. She was looking tight and nasty, and she knew I'd want to see her shake that body. In the bathroom earlier I had stood aside while she whipped her hair around getting ready for the party. She'd asked me to smell the rose-citrus perfume on her collarbone and tell her whether I thought Bobby, her old boyfriend, would like it. I put my nose in her moussed hair on the way down. She knew I was in the bathroom to see what she had on. A black nylon shirt and a big yellow beach towel. We had bedrooms across the hall from each other.

When I wouldn't play the song she wanted, Melanie went to her room and called a guy. I could hear his truck gurgle up to the house a half hour later. She clapped her heels down the hallway tiles and called one of Donny's friends a starved little pervert on the way out. The boys who had been smoking came back inside and wanted to get into the liquor, but I wasn't about to let them do that.

"Stop giggling like it's your first time," I said, "and maybe I'll let you watch some cable."

Our parents came home before the good movies started. Liz brought a sheet cake from Publix for Donny, with a Matchbox car and the number 12 in blue plastic on the icing. For a present she had gotten him a pair of ten-pound dumbbells, the kind I had told him to ask her for. Donny's friends wanted to take their paper plates back outside to listen to more Van Halen on the patio. My dad asked where Melanie was.

"I have no idea," I said.

"What do you mean, no idea?" Liz said.

"She didn't tell me."

"So she just left?"

"I'm telling you, lady," my dad said. "Your daughter is out of control."

"Listen you, friend. I'll worry about my daughter. You just keep worrying about you and your son."

"Everybody's been partying just fine without her," I said.

"That's right," said the scrawny pervert kid who had been hooting at Melanie.

"Let's enjoy some birthday cake," Liz suggested to Donny and all his friends, "and then Larry and I are going to have to drive you little guys home."

● ● ●

Melanie got back about one thirty and cuh-clacked cuh-clacked down to her room. I could tell no one in the house was asleep when she threw her purse down on her bed. She went into the bathroom to take off her makeup, and Liz followed her. They were in there for a while. Melanie said "Good-night, Mom" real loud, and they went back to their rooms. I could hear Liz creak into bed on the other side of my wall. My dad wasn't snoring yet. The fan was on but not the air conditioner. I had just a sheet over me. I was hot.

Melanie waited about ten minutes before she came to my room. The way she would do it, she really didn't give a shit. Melanie in pink heels, heavy stepping on the carpet, the collarbone that I liked so much, baby bread-roll neck, acid-wash jeans with fringes along the seams, the blonde bangs curled with mousse and sprayed down to her eyebrows, fat, rolling, sexy, and I couldn't wait until she would kneel down in front of my pullout sleeper and put her elbows on my legs.

"You suck," she said.

"What are you talking about?"

"I'm just kidding."

"What did you do tonight?" I said.

"How much do you want to know?" she said.

She bit her lip and touched my chest. I flexed.

"Was it Bobby?"

"Bobby's an asshole."

"So where'd you go then?"

"Chris's boat."

"Chris the contractor?"

"He is so cool."

"I thought he lived in the Keys."

"I told my mom I went to the game. You better not say anything."

"Your mom's a bitch," I whispered.

"Oh yeah, and your dad."

We stopped talking and listened across the wall. Nothing but snoring and the cricking of bugs outside the window screen. It was dark in the room. I could not see Melanie's ears behind her hair. The hair was everywhere, over her shoulders and down to the tops of her breasts, with smoke, perfume, beer coming toward me, and the harbor I could imagine down off Old Cutler Road.

We didn't start talking again. Something felt different. Melanie's fingers moved down the sheet to what was waiting there between my legs. She held it there. I swallowed my breath. She was looking at me, the stupid look, when her eyes crossed and she looked like a retard. She had me. I was thinking of a twenty-six-foot boat and her sitting at the bow.

I kept holding still. She had the tip of her tongue between her lips. Then Melanie did something no girl did before. She brought that sheet down and she tied it around my ankles. I looked up over my head and saw a lamp.

Melanie said to me, "I can't help myself anymore."

"No problem," I said.

I wondered what she was thinking of mine, if it was ugly to her or if she thought that Chris the contractor's was nicer or more mature. Afterward, Melanie was biting her lip again, and her hair smelled a little like me now, too.

"I think I love you," she said.

"You can do that any time you want," I said.

• • •

The next day was Saturday, and when I walked into the kitchen for cereal, Liz was in her purple quilted robe and fuzzy slippers, picking at leftover birthday cake and browsing catalogs and junk mail. She was a board, no body, just long and bony like all the women my dad ever went out with. Donny sitting next to her with his new ten-pound iron dumbbells at his feet. I could hear my dad coming in through the garage from a run.

"Were there boys smoking marijuana cigarettes in this house last night?" Liz said to me.

"No," I said.

Donny sat sideways in his chair, facing the pool.

"Did you see any of the boys here last night smoking marijuana cigarettes?"

Donny curled a dumbbell with his right arm. I could tell she had already questioned him.

"I didn't see anybody doing anything."

"This is my house, Mr. Vince. And you're an influence on these children. What in the hell were you doing last night while we were gone? Dealing drugs at a birthday party?"

"What's your problem, Liz? You already know what I was doing last night. I was playing music, like Donny asked me to."

"And that's all you know about the drugs?"

"I don't know what you're talking about."

"Well, I think you're a liar."

"Well, I think you're a schnauzer."

My dad walked into the kitchen in his blue running shorts. His quads had some definition. Donny was still looking out at the pool. He knew if he turned around and looked at me, I might come over there and beat his face.

"Larry."

"That's me."

"Donny's friend Todd's mother called this morning. Todd told her some of the boys last night went out to the backyard and smoked marijuana cigarettes. While we were gone and your son was in charge."

My dad was breathing heavily. His running shoes had mud on the soles. Sweat was trickling into his headband and down the hair on his arms to his wristbands.

"You know about that, Donny?" he asked, holding up the side entrance to the kitchen with his hands.

"Donny wasn't involved. This wasn't all the boys, just some of them."

"Who started it?" my dad asked Donny.

"She's trying to tell me I gave them pot," I said.

"Who was in charge?" Liz said to my dad. "And watch your shoes, please, on the kitchen floor."

My dad jumped up and started curling himself on the lintel at the kitchen entrance. He did one pull-up, then two. He kept his legs straight. One of Liz' framed pictures, with oranges and grapefruits and a border of white blossoms, shook on the wall behind the table.

"If that breaks."

"You're hysterical," my dad said. "You know that?"

"Get out of my kitchen," Liz said. Then she hollered it. "Just get out of my sight, and take him with you. I don't want one more day of this."

• • •

My dad and I showered and went to the movies. After that we went looking for an apartment. We stuck to the area near Dixie above 136th, near where we lived. Every manager wanted to rent to my dad. He had a decent job, and he brought cash. But my dad couldn't settle on an apartment. Not even the one that had a sauna, a Jacuzzi, a pool, a basketball court, a shuffleboard court, a game room, a security guard and about twenty fine single women in bikinis lying out and sipping drinks from fluorescent plastic cups. He just kept saying to me, "One divorce is one thing, two divorces—it's humiliating."

• • •

The next week Liz stopped talking to me completely. Two words at a time, most. "*My* refrigerator!" "*My* house!" I could see that she and my dad were going to start losing it on each other soon, but I didn't give a shit. I was working light construction during the week, and I was getting big. My upper body was smoking. Weekends, I would bench rounds of 180 in the garage and polish it off with some lats. I kept wishing Liz would lay a finger on me the wrong way, so I could pick her up with one fist and crack her over my knee. Instead, she kept spazzing about little things. She would come out to the garage in the middle of my workout and stretch over me for a broom like my body was the biggest inconvenience to her. Or she would come up behind me in the pantry, wagging a finger, and I would flex my shoulders and pecs and just growl in her face—*ruff ruff ruff, grrrr*. Melanie asked me to be nicer to her mom. I said, "For you, Melanie," and I brought my hips up closer to her chest and slid a leg across her cushiony body.

Melanie liked to come in my room when our parents were making up. She would kneel in the dark in front of my pullout sleeper making sexy breath noises in my ear while her fingernails skated across the rips in my abs. We couldn't hear the words our parents were saying on the other side of the wall, but we knew from their voices what they meant. If the TV was on, that was a peace sign. It meant the grown-ups had gotten in a better mood, and they'd be fucking the creaks out of the bed frame soon. Their starting in was like the sound of rails splitting to me. Their voices hush, Liz's legs spreading, coochie-coo, and you could feel the jolting of the headboard. Melanie and I would stop what we were doing, sit up in the shadows of each other's bodies, me hating her mom, her hating my dad, and crack up to ourselves about the way grown-ups were until she was sucking on her lower lip and I was holding whatever parts of her were closest to my hands.

Melanie started spending less time at home. She was getting more involved with Chris the contractor, who was twenty-seven and had a mustache. She was skipping school and going sailing with him. She kept telling me how mature he was. She would tell me this like I should be jealous. Her mom didn't know about this guy. When she got D's in geometry and U.S. history, Liz asked her if she needed a tutor. Melanie told Liz her teachers hated her. Liz believed her. At dinner my dad told Melanie her problem was laziness. He asked her if she planned to graduate. Then Liz cleared her throat and made my dad look at me.

"Living at home, almost nineteen years old, flunks his first exam at community college and decides he's just going to drop out. I think before you criticize someone else's child, you ought to take a good look at the one who belongs to you. Speaking of laziness, not to mention a future."

"I'm saving for a car," I said. I wanted to call Liz a bitch. A nasty bitch with a slut daughter. "And a better set of speakers."

Liz wouldn't talk to me. She wouldn't look at me.

"You're not buying a car until we talk about it," my dad said.

He was trying anything he could think of to bond with Liz.

"I'm getting a Testarossa when I'm twenty-one," Donny said.

"And you're taking me to the beach," Melanie said.

"If I feel like it."

• • •

One night, Donny knocked on my door when Melanie was inside with her fingers on my balls. He said he had to use the dictionary for a school paper. The lights were off, and I was wearing just a pair of sweat-shorts. Melanie had on a plump white undershirt and dancing tights. I was warm and stiff and I dragged the sheet up over myself.

"I don't care," is what he said.

I turned on the lamp. Donny was a porky little brown-haired dude in an Italian-striped racing shirt and colored underwear.

"You don't care, what?" his sister said.

"Anything."

"Donny, are you just going to stand there half naked or are you going to get whatever you came in here for and leave?"

"I don't have to listen to your ass," Donny said.

I checked out Melanie's rolls in the light by the bookcase. I wondered what her and Donny's father looked like. Who'd mated with Liz and produced these two?

"Just wait till you need me," Melanie said.

"For what?" Donny said.

"Wait till you're trying to get a girlfriend. I could say whatever I want to them about you. Just remember that."

Donny made a pathetic muscle and showed it to me.

"When I do my curls, I keep my back straight," he said.

"You're getting there," I said. "Now you got to gradually increase your sets. And remember your breathing. But don't overdo it. You're just a kid."

"Why don't you go work some of that baby fat off right now, Donny? I don't think anyone invited you into Vince's room," Melanie said.

Donny looked at me.

"You heard her," I said.

Melanie sat back against the wall on my sleeper. My dad shouted out to us to get in our own beds. Melanie made a face. There were sea-grape leaves and hibiscus bushes outside shaking from the long, whis-tling gusts of wind.

• • •

That Saturday we were supposed to have brunch as a family at eleven o'clock. It was already storming when I woke up, the big raindrops pop-ping against the shutters and bushes. We waited at the table for Melanie, who I knew would be hungover. At three in the morning she had shown up in my room wasted, in heavy mascara and a pink net blouse, blubbering

"Chris is an asshole" onto my leg. She smelled like puke and rose citrus. I didn't want to see her cry. I lifted her into her own bed.

At eleven, Liz was walking through the kitchen in her quilted robe like she had something to say and she wasn't saying it. I was sitting at the table across from Donny. In a paper-thin jogging suit, my dad was flipping French toast and singing "Rain, rain, go away." He put out the napkins and the silverware. None of us could hear Melanie moving in the back of the house.

"I'm going to count to ten, and I promise I will not lose my patience," my dad said.

I turned around, and Liz took a hard look at me.

"Do you know what time she got in last night?"

"What are you asking me for? Didn't you sleep in this house last night?"

"Don't answer her like that, Vince," my dad said.

"I don't know when," I said to my dad. "Maybe Donny knows. Donny knows all."

Donny had wandered out onto the patio floor, which had puddles all around the edges of the pool. He was barefoot with his head down, punting up little splashes of water with his toes. He was moving away from us. The sliding glass door to the patio was open, and it was moist in the kitchen and loud from the rain.

"Do you know or don't you?" my dad said.

"I don't know," I said.

Liz walked to the back of the house. My dad put the oval serving plate of French toast in the middle of the table next to the syrup, the jam and the margarine. Everyone had a cut grapefruit on a plate.

"Now!" my dad called to Donny.

Then he lowered his voice and leaned down to me.

"I'm asking you not to push Liz."

We ate brunch without Melanie. Liz kept giving me looks in the silences. My dad finally asked about Melanie's status. Liz said she wasn't going to make it to the table, and my dad said that was obvious. He took Melanie's grapefruit and put it on his own plate. Then he realized he was about to start another fight, and he asked Liz if Melanie was feeling okay. Liz said she thought Melanie had a fever. My dad put his fist in his teeth and looked at his wife with puffy eyes.

After brunch Liz was going to take Donny to Cutler Ridge Mall, but Donny couldn't find his money. He whimpered about how he'd put a twenty right next to his bed yesterday. Liz said they'd find it later, she wanted to get out of the house now. My dad said, after they left, "Let's just take a drive."

We ran out to the driveway with our hoods over our heads. He turned the ignition, but he didn't shift into gear.

"Do you think we should just move out?" he said to me. He was staring at the flat-tile roof of the house.

"I didn't marry her," I said.

Above my dad's head I could see the patterns of rainwater beating down on the T-top. His gold chain was outside the zipper of his jacket, and he had deep lines across his forehead that looked like ripples of muscle to me.

"I won't get anything," my dad said. "I'll get half of nothing. It'll all be hers."

"It was all hers to begin with," I said.

"That's not what marriage is supposed to be," he said. "It's supposed to be half and half."

"It was never equal. Her last husband was loaded."

"But we've bought a lot of things together," my dad said with a crack in his voice.

"Well, we'll take them," I said.

"If we do leave," he said, "you have to treat Liz with dignity."

I looked at my father. I didn't know what he was talking about. I knew Liz had some kind of control over him, and once he told me he was in love with her. I felt sorry for him. I wondered what it was like to be forced to still care about someone like Liz six years later. I clicked the garage door closed and looked in one more time at my bench and free weights. I could picture Melanie lying on her back with stuffed animals and messed hair all around her, winding the curly phone cord across her bed, talking on the phone with some other guy.

• • •

The next day when my dad got back from a long run, he told me the plan for how we were going to move out. He sounded scared, but like he was going to do it. Tomorrow he would make a deposit on a two-bedroom apartment in the complex with the sauna and all the females. Since Liz worked three days as a hygienist, eight thirty to four thirty, my dad and I would both take a day off work one of those days, rent a van and move out as much stuff as we could while she was gone. We could probably make it with all our stuff in three trips.

My dad set the date for a week from Wednesday. It was in the middle of the work week, in the middle of the month, so Liz would never suspect.

"This is the best way," he said to me more than once, confidentially, that week. "Because I want to be fair, and at the same time I know that if I sat down with her and tried to reason out a separation, there'd be fireworks. You've seen how unreasonable she's been getting the past few months."

Now my dad was telling me every reason he had ever thought of why it was a good idea to move out of Liz's house. What a temper she had, how bossy she could be, how moody. He busted on Melanie. She was proof that Liz was a bad deal. Melanie was an overweight, out-of-control delinquent, and Donny a spoiled child. If Liz had ever really cared about their marriage, she'd have put him before them once in a while.

Alone in my room, I practiced how many clothes I could carry in my arms at one time. How many magazines, lamps and porcelain figurines of Liz's. The move on Wednesday was making me feel like I was leading a two-man adventure quest. I stood on the thin foam mattress of my pullout sleeper and struck Mr. Universe poses. "Can our hero safely liberate the palace treasure before the dragon witch returns and starts breathing down spears of fire?" I asked out loud.

I consoled Melanie about Chris. She told me her problems, and I listened to them. If she wanted to give me a blow job afterward, I let her. I rested my head back on my hands and let her get to work. I was out of there. I didn't give a shit.

• • •

The morning of the move, all of us wound up in the kitchen at the same time. Liz was wearing her all-whites, and she had her wiry hair up in barrettes the way she always wore it to the office. Melanie had on a large football jersey from our high school with a lineman's number on it. Tight-ass jeans and plenty of lip gloss. She was pouring two glasses of Five Alive by the sink for herself and Donny. My dad was next to the refrigerator, chugging coffee.

"I'm leaving," Liz said. "Be good."

"Love you, Mom," Melanie said. "We will."

"All right, Larry," Liz said.

"I'll see you," my dad said, like he was about to cry.

Liz kissed Donny on the forehead. Donny had pretty much stopped talking to me, too, lately. He picked up his things and walked to the bus stop.

In a few minutes Melanie went out the front door to wait for her ride. I went down the pathway after her. Her tight jeans were looking good.

"Is number 61 Hector Villanueva?" I said when our feet were on the edge of the street. I used to play some JV cornerback.

Melanie was looking up the block to see if anyone was turning our way.

"Uh-huh," she said.

"I know that guy."

"Yeah, he said he knew you."

"That guy can squat," I said. "Especially for a Cuban."

Melanie wasn't saying anything about him.

"How much is he squatting now?" I asked her.

"I only just started hanging out with him," she said. "I can just tell you he's built."

A car came up our street, but it wasn't Melanie's ride. Already the sky was blue like the middle of the day, with a sun you couldn't put your eyes near, and all the big white clouds were whizzing by over other people's houses.

"Are you into him?" I said.

I checked out Melanie from the side. She shrugged and pushed out her lips. "Doesn't he have a black Trans Am?" I said.

"Stick."

"I bet it's nice inside."

"Leather interiors."

"When were you guys hanging out?"

"Why are you asking me all this shit?"

"I don't know. I'm just trying to remember what the guy's like."

"He's hot," Melanie said. "He's fuckin' hot is all I can say."

Melanie had her fingers combing through the back of her hair and her curvy ass sticking out in my direction. She was wearing Wayfarers and looking upward slightly. I was standing there taking her in and not just her body. Her face. What it really looked like in the daylight, the shape of it around the sunglasses. The way her mouth would smile and perk up when she saw Villanueva in the parking lot before school.

"That guy's on 'roids, isn't he?"

"Excuse me?" she said.

"I knew it."

I wanted Melanie to look at me, at my arms, the color of my tan and the definition. Then I said to her, "'You're going to be late.' I said it twice.

"Could you write me a note, please? Daddy?"

"Funny," I said. "Nice mood today."

"I'm just kidding."

"That's cool," I said.

A bunch of girls pulled up in a white Rabbit on the other side of the street, and Melanie got in the far door with her books against Villanueva's jersey. I walked back into the house past the banyan tree with its long mossy branches set up along the gutters of the roof.

My dad started getting panicky in the garage, but I calmed him down. We got a van with a luggage rack on top.

"All right," he said in the driveway with the garage door open. "I just want you to get our stuff. I don't want you even touching anything that belongs to Melanie or Donny. You understand me? We're going to do this completely fair and square. You carry, I'll load. Then I'll go do a check inside and make sure we got everything."

My dad kept stopping and catching his breath.

"What about stuff that's both of yours?" I said. "Like the bedroom TV. And what about the gas grill? That stuff?"

"Anything we bought while we were married, we'll deal with that at the end. Just get all the stuff that's only ours first. That's going to take at least two trips by itself."

I had on my brace for lifting. The first thing I grabbed was my dad's exercise bike. Then all the other things of his that took two hands. Most of what was in my dad's bedroom belonged to Liz anyway—the bed, the artwork, the chest of drawers. I emptied his half of their walk-in closet and laughed at how lopsided it looked. I gathered big clumps, stretching my arms around them.

We took the first load over to the new apartment complex around eleven thirty. Our unit was on the second floor. We unloaded the van and stacked everything in a mixed-up pile right inside the front door. A shoe falling in a blender, a jump rope around a jockstrap. I was bolting up and down the stairs about three times as fast as my dad, leaping from a few steps up and landing on the run.

"You got to pick up the pace," I said. "Don't get beat by the heat."

We were both sweating like animals when we got back to the house. No shirts. My dad was bouncing on the tips of his shoes on the hot driveway, waiting while I cleared more stuff out of the house. He kept looking around the crazy trunk of the banyan tree to see if anyone was coming. He told me to go faster, just get the important stuff. He was starting to get worried that Liz would come home before we were finished, think that we were stripping the house and lose her mind.

The more worried my dad got, the rowdier it made me. I was starting to want to do everything he had instructed me not to. Just take random shit from everywhere and throw it in towels and load it up. I had the air conditioner down to a nice moving temperature. A rolled bandanna around my forehead, cut-off blue jeans, the leather brace and steel-toed work boots. I felt wild.

In front of Donny's room, I plotted what kind of damage I could do and how quickly. What could I take that would piss Liz off the most? I jumped up and slapped the hallway ceiling, straight vertical, ten times in a row. The idea that I was never going to have to look at Liz's face again was making me feel like anything was possible for me. I did twenty clap push-ups and ten more on fists.

With my chest out as far as it could go I flung open the door to my room. I didn't own much. What I had didn't even fill up the van. My dad said don't forget the rest of his kitchen stuff, and living room–stuff and patio stuff. While I was back inside, I started doing some rearranging. I tucked Liz's diaphragm under Donny's pillow. Then I dropped one of her silver rings in the toilet tank in the master bathroom. After that I turned over all the photographs of her and my dad together.

A few more trips, and I wasn't satisfied. So I began taking. I wanted Liz to know that she hadn't gotten away with the last six years. I took all the quarters out of her change tray in the pantry, dumped them in a pillowcase with some other things she would notice were missing, like her two-liter plastic bottles of Diet Coke, and carried the whole package out to my dad in a paper grocery bag. I took Donny's ten-pound dumbbells, wrapped in one of my sheets. I wanted more, so I went for Donny's baby teeth that Liz kept in a little lined box in her bathroom. I put the clasp box in my front pocket until I could decide if I really wanted to take it.

By three thirty, the second load was at the new apartment, and my shoulders were getting pooped. Now my dad had to make the big decisions. What to do about the three major items he and Liz had acquired as a couple: the Sony color television in the bedroom, which had remote and a better picture by far than the living room TV; the gas grill, which he had gotten the deal on from knowing the floor manager at Service Merchandise; and the Chinese screen that Liz had picked out at an art fair on Key Biscayne, and which my grandparents had bought for them as an anniversary gift.

My dad wanted to discuss these three items with me. He said, "Disregard all the money I've spent over the years on repairs and improvements to the house."

I said no question, the gas grill was ours. My dad did all the grilling, replaced the canister. Liz would not miss the grill. My dad agreed.

The other two items were a different story. Liz was attached to that television, and she had a possessiveness about the painted bamboo screen, too. We were going to have to pick one or the other.

I uncabled the TV and hoisted it with my elbows. My dad wanted to make a final sweep of the house while I packed up my weights and gear from the garage. We would roll out the gas grill together as the last thing, close up the house and stop for subs on the way over to the new apartment.

In the doorway leading out to the garage, with the sweaty TV almost slipping in my fingers, I practically knocked into Melanie and Donny. Melanie had a fat new hickey. Her breasts were shapes of hills coming up out of the 6 and 1 of Villanueva's shirt.

"You really think you're taking my mom's TV?" she said.

I was looking at her neck. I could feel the weariness in my arms.

"I know you didn't take anything out of my room," she said.

"I'm just doing what my dad told me to," I said.

The garage smelled like a swamp. I tried to let the two of them by, but they didn't want to move.

I kept waiting for Melanie to do something extreme. Grab the TV, beg me not to leave. Maybe wrestle me down and have Donny pile on.

"What, did you and Brainiac just skip work and try and get whatever you could out of the house when my mom wasn't looking?"

My dad came around the front of the garage, gesturing to me in confused hand signals. Melanie shot a repulsed look at him, and she and Donny took off past me for the back of the house. I felt a cool little rush of breeze from Melanie. I held the scent of it in my nose. I let it wash across my face.

"I think we probably ought to get going pretty quick," my dad said. His gold chain was swinging against his chest of hair. His work slacks looked tight around the middle.

"No shit," I said, walking the TV to the van.

I started hating the van. I started hating everything that was going on the whole day. The bags in the back, everything I'd switched around. I threw my brace into the van and shut the doors.

"What time is it?" my dad said. "I got to make sure that I get everything I need out."

"I'm not leaving without every single one of my weights."

"First you're helping me get the grill."

"I'm telling you, Donny is not going to get those weights."

"I'm telling *you*, she's not going to walk away with two out of three."

I followed my dad to the back patio, and we started rolling the gas grill across the Chattahoochee floor. The sound of the squeaking and rolling made me want to kick something hard. Donny opened a door from the bathroom and shut it right away. I could picture the expression on his pudgy white face when he realized his little curl bar was gone. His box of baby teeth kept rubbing against my thigh. I was walking backward. He saw my eyes.

My dad and I were pulling the grill across the grass to the driveway when Liz showed up. My dad's arms clenched. His mouth was a straight line.

He walked slowly toward the van, and I stayed put on the grass. Then I walked behind the van on the other side of it from my dad and her. I didn't know the plan. I stayed at the back of the driveway behind the van, almost on our next-door neighbors' lawn.

"You are shit," Liz said to my dad from in front of the garage. "You are so full of shit I can't believe it."

They were less than three yards from each other, and Liz was standing, guarding the inside of the garage. My weights were behind her. She had taken out her barrettes, and she looked as though she had a black-and-gray terrier lying across her head.

"Where are my children?" she said.

"They're in there," my dad said.

"So what are you going to do now? Pack up the grill, call it a day? Huh? That's not your grill, partner. *Not.*"

Liz waited. My dad didn't talk.

"God help you if you took one single thing out of this house that doesn't belong to you."

Liz waited again for my dad to say something.

"You just stay right where you are," she said.

"This is my home as well as your home," my dad said. "And I'm going to go in there and get the rest of what's mine."

"Don't threaten me, Lawrence. Bad idea."

Liz went inside. Her white hygienist outfit made everything feel more serious. My dad stepped back toward me, and I came up close to him.

"I'm not taking any chances with her," he whispered. "I want you to go call the police. I mean it. I'm not taking any chances. I'm going to try and settle this with her the peaceful way, but I want them here just in case. There are still things I need to get out of the bedroom—and we're taking that grill."

The way the sky was, and the sun, it felt like it had been the middle of the day all day.

• • •

I took my dad's car up to Old Cutler Road and called the police from a gas station. I said there was a domestic situation. The whole time the lady on the other end was talking to me, I was thinking of Melanie's bedroom. Me with my knees on her comforter and Melanie doing her nails over the carpet, telling me things in private.

I drove back to the house about ten miles an hour. I kept punching the buttons, looking for anything decent that wasn't love songs or talking. I parked a ways up from the driveway and walked very slowly across the front lawn toward the garage.

I didn't have to see her to know Liz was on the warpath. My dad had apparently done something to piss her off royally. And not just my dad. Vince is a lying thief, Vince is a bully, Vince thinks he can bluh bluh bluh bluh bluh bluh bluh. Talking about marijuana and a twenty-dollar bill and bullshit from five years ago that I didn't even know what she was talking about. I got up closer so I could see her. She was standing with her knees in position like an ogre in dentist-office clothes ready to defend its cave. She said if either one of us touched another thing that belonged to her, she was going to go into that kitchen, get her sashimi knife and cut him up.

Now I had my boot against the back fender of the van. All five of us again. The dumb faces of Melanie and Donny on the steps at the back of the garage. Our parents between us. My dad wanting to whisper something in my ear, but I wouldn't lean in to hear it.

"Well, I guess she told us," I said pretty loud. I was ready to go toe-to-toe with Liz. Once and for all. I was ready to pick her up by the hair, swing her around the garage a couple times over my head and whack her up against my bench set.

Melanie *pfffed* like she was so disgusted about something, she couldn't take it. I gave her a look. I let her know she wasn't all privileged and special now that she was letting some 'roid-freak lineman suck on her neck.

My dad told Liz he had only wanted to divide things up the fairest way. She didn't need to overreact like this. "The marriage has run its course," he said. "We can both agree on that."

He said to Liz, "I just want to get some papers from the bedroom. I'm not even going to discuss the grill right now, okay? We'll let the lawyers do that."

"Just get out!" she said. "Leave. And don't you dare stand there and tell me I'm overreacting. Goddamned coward. You and coward junior slinking around my house all day with a moving van while I'm at work. How the hell do I know what the two of you took?"

Liz was turning pink and red. I was just standing back, checking out my triceps, letting my dad do all the work.

Liz waved Melanie and Donny back inside the house. Donny looked at me the way I raised him to look at me, like he better respect me or keep his fucking head down. Melanie. I wondered what she might start saying about me now when I wasn't around.

I could see the green-and-white sheriff's car pull up in the front yard under the banyan tree while Liz was still screaming her lungs out about dignity-her-ass. One big old flappy-cheeked Dade County sheriff behind the wheel with a writing pad and a shotgun right there next to him.

Liz saw the car on the lawn and started patting herself all over, nervous. She put a barrette between her lips, then pinned back one side of her hair. I waited for her to pin back the other side, but she didn't, and by the time the sheriff was walking up to us, she looked even battier than she did before.

My dad didn't bother to put on a shirt. I didn't either.

"Folks," the cop said, pacing toward my dad. He was about my dad's age, nicely shaven, with a big, beige patrolman's hat on, and uniform pants tucked into knee-high black boots. "Came to check on a disturbance. This the proper residence?"

"Yes it is, sir," my dad said.

Three of Donny's friends came by on motocross bikes, saw us, checked out the sheriff's rifle and his V8 Caprice, and walked their bikes into the house through the front door. It was the first time all day I noticed anyone on the block even being around.

I had my eyes on the cop, his mirrored sunglasses hanging off his shirt pocket. He was nodding and sweeping his eyes around. Taking notes.

"I don't see any disturbance," the cop said.

"Actually, sir, my wife has stated that I am forbidden to enter my own house."

"You let your wife talk to you like that?" the cop said.

"Not usually," my dad said. "No. But she's been getting a little rough around the edges today. You know."

"This your residence?"

"It is my residence. My son and I live here, and we want to be able to go into the house peacefully and get the rest of what belongs to us."

We all looked at Liz. She had a face like she was choking on ideas.

"Officer, I can't believe what's going on here."

The sheriff stood there and gave Liz the once-over. Chewing on his ink pen, jotting down notes.

"Officer, that man and his son went into my house while I was at work today and put things in that van that do not belong to them. The definition is stealing. Stealing is what that is. That grill belongs on my patio, and that television belongs to me too. And my son is missing things. Valuable things. You can put that in your report. And there's going to be other things, except I haven't even looked around yet to see what else. You know, if the chicken liver wanted to move out so much, nobody was stopping him. Do you see me stopping him from moving out now? I'd prefer it if he left."

"Lady, let's get this straight. I am not the judge."

The cop paused to make sure we were all listening. His radio was steady, the static over the dispatcher's other calls.

"Festivities are over. End of round one. Going to be nothing else going, nothing else coming. I'm working on sixteen hours straight, and I've seen all the trouble I'm going to see for today."

My dad was starting to get mopey now—drooping his eyes, hanging his face, holding himself like you'd think someone was forcing him to stand up on his own two feet.

"And there's been plenty of it," the sheriff said. "First thing this morning took a dashboard out of a baby's sternum. Going to be half the right side of that kid's face. Bloodbath. Perfectly avoidable, too. Vehicle trying to pass on a two-lane across a double-yellow. So I spent all morning with the kid in emergency, spent the rest of the day helping out on a kook with a hostage, and my work isn't done yet. Got to stop at Eckerd's after this, pick up some vapor rub for the mother-in-law, or no one's letting me in the front door when I get home. See, it's trouble and a mess out there, but so easily avoided. You gentlemen have another place to sleep tonight?"

"Yes, sir," my dad said.

"Suggest you lay it down for today."

I'd never taken my eyes off the sheriff. His bulletproof upper body, the knife on his belt. He had a legitimate chest. I was judging from his upper arms.

"Excuse me," I said. "I just have one request."

I looked the sheriff in the eyes. I wanted him to know I was different from my dad and Liz.

"What if there's one thing of mine, right in the garage, that I could just load up in about five minutes? It's all it would take. Anybody can watch me."

"Son, how's your hearing?"

My dad muttered that we were on our way. He said we would get the court to give us the rest of what was ours.

Liz was still standing in front of the garage, waiting for us all to take off. I looked in behind her at my 180-pound bar on the bench stand. I could picture her throwing the iron wells one by one against the floor of the garage after I was gone, or clearing out everything that was mine in there and promising to buy Donny a whole new set of weights.

The sheriff nodded to us and got on his radio. Then we drove toward the new apartment complex in a kind of procession. First the sheriff, then me, then my dad in the rental van. When we got to Dixie, the sheriff turned left. I honked good-bye and waved out the T-top. The sheriff flashed his yellow roof lights, and I honked some more and blasted the speakers.

• • •

The rest of the week I called in sick. I kept going for swims and taking showers. I used Liz's quarters on video games. I set up my stereo, but that was it.

My dad kept bellyaching how much worse this was. He ate frozen enchiladas by himself on the carpet. He asked if I thought things were really over with Liz. I put on some trunks and went down to find the sauna.

I had never actually been in a sauna before. It was just a wood-slat stall with a wood-slat bench. I shut the door behind me and stripped naked in the room. I found the heat dial on the wall and turned it up to the max. I was thinking about that baby that lost half its face.

I tightened my abs and let them go. I pretended I lost half my own face. With my fingers like a cutting knife, I cut myself down the line of my nose and all the way down the middle of my skin. I kept one eye shut the whole time I was cutting. Then I cut the base of my belly in half. Then halfway diagonal across my chest. I cut an X where my sternum made the center. I made squiggle cuts all over my flesh.

Afterward I took a Jacuzzi and let the water swirl around in the net of my trunks. It was Saturday afternoon, and there were bodies galore. The whole scene outside the community building was blowing me away, the landscaping of the walking paths, the vanilla smell of lotion, the row of green coconut palms in the turf around the pool. The place was loaded. I approved. I could hear Jimmy Buffett playing on somebody's tape deck. Guys at the hibachi were getting high. There were girls with loose bikini strings getting rid of their tan lines, rubbing their shoulders down with cocoa butter and tropical oils.

I had my left arm at ease along the edge of the tub. Across from me, a couple of stewardesses were dipping their toes in the steaming water, talking about their hectic flying schedules. Now they were laughing about the bubbles and climbing in. They had one-piecers on but some action underneath.

As soon as they were sitting, one reached into her shoulder bag and pulled out a cold bottle of pink champagne. "We've got to celebrate, Julie," she said.

Behind me, in the rush of the water jets, I could feel Melanie's excited hams around my ass, the pulse from her body streaming under my legs. I felt the grip of thighs, the press of breasts to my back.

The stewardesses raised a toast. They clicked their cups as if they were about to sail off on a cruise.

Now I could feel Melanie beside me, and I tried to think of some way that all of us could get acquainted. We live in the Palm Springs apartments, too, I rehearsed in my head. Personally, I work construction, and Melanie here's still in school. We used to have a house together not far from here, but it didn't have the kind of luxuries we felt we deserved.

On the other side of the tub, Julie was pinching herself about her new promotion and tipping some champagne on the other one's hair. "Par-*ty*," they said together.

I still couldn't get over the landscaping job. I stretched an arm a little farther around Melanie's shoulder and asked her if she could believe all this was ours. I was pretty sure she was starting to feel more at home in the Jacuzzi. Just the way she was biting her lip and not saying anything, moving in closer like nobody was watching.

A Little Advance

by KARL IAGNEMMA
1998

I once dated a girl who took me home for Christmas. This was when my hair was in long dreadlocks and I was working nights at 7-Eleven. The job wasn't as bad as you might think. I read magazines all night, and everything was free. The surveillance cameras didn't work. My boss was too cheap to fix them.

I'd been living like that, in a holding pattern, for about two years. During the day I worked on my sculpture, which I'd long ago begun to hate. It was a collection of rusty car parts piled together in the shape of a cow. Once I'd had a concept of what it meant, but now it was just a shit-heap in the corner, a monument to failure. My apartment was a small, rancid studio behind Herefordshire Preparatory School, and some days I'd stand at the window and watch them, the boys and girls with so much love around them, and it would sicken me to tears. Self-pity, I'd found, was like whiskey: You need more and more and then eventually it does nothing for you. I tried to stay optimistic. I'd wave down at the little people, and once one of them waved back.

And then I met Carol. She was tall and pale, swan like, with a cloud of fine white hair. She smelled like lemon and soap and baby powder. It was what I imagined angels must smell like.

Carol had a white-knuckle appetite for sex. She loved to touch my dick. She was like a little girl with a pet hamster. I remember reading about people who fasted for weeks, then had shimmering, wondrous

197

visions. Sex with Carol was like that. It was like burrowing into the part of my brain that holds smells and colors. It was like jumping off a waterfall.

She asked me home for Christmas after we'd been dating for a month. "Question," she said. She placed a single finger on my chest. "What are you doing tomorrow?"

It was Christmas Eve and we were holed up in my dingy room, under the covers, naked. Carol's skin was smooth and slightly moist.

"Working."

"Call in sick. I told my mom I was bringing you home for Christmas. Switch with someone."

The year before, I had worked a double shift on Christmas day. I'd sat behind the counter with a stupid Santa hat on my head and read *Four Wheeler* magazine and once in a while sold a gallon of milk. At about midnight a young Chaldean kid walked up to the counter and said "Hey, Santa," and stuck a small pistol out through the fly of his baggy jeans. I couldn't move, and then I realized that the gun was plastic, a toy, and suddenly this joke was terrifically funny, until I saw that his friend had the real gun pointed at my head.

I asked her, "Are you serious? Because I'll come if you're serious."

She seemed to think about it for a second. "Yeah, I'm serious. But don't get your hopes up. You haven't met my family."

"Don't talk to me about families. I could tell you a few stories about families, believe me." Carol shook her head. "We're not dysfunctional or anything. That's the funny part: We're completely normal."

I climbed out of bed and pulled on a newish pair of jeans. "Let's go to the store. I'll talk to Rahman."

Rahman hated giving time off. When I came into the store he had the Slurpee machine pulled apart and was working on it with a Crescent wrench. After I told him my story he pulled a rag from his back pocket and wiped his hands carefully, and said, "No."

"My mom's cooking this goose," I explained. "I'll bring you some pumpkin pie. I promise."

He shook his head. "No. Okay? The answer to your question is no."

"Don't be such a fucking Grinch. Come on."

He crossed his arms over his chest and shook his head. "Rahman," I said, "it's Christmas." But Rahman was Muslim. He didn't care. He turned back to the Slurpee machine and gave it a long, stingy stare.

"All right, Rahman. You win. Merry Christmas." I put my name tag on the counter and kicked the door open and walked out into the frozen parking lot like a champion.

• • •

Carol picked me up at seven, and after we cleared the city limits she explained what she wanted me to do. "Just be yourself," she said. She was wearing a tight black T-shirt that said BITE ME. "These people are so uptight, it's like they're about to explode. You should hear the way my grandpa tells my mom he loves her. *I love you!* Like he's barking at her." Her lips curled into a tight grin. "And then there's my brother—I can't wait for him to see your hair. God! He's going to have a conniption."

"I don't know," I said. "I have this tendency to piss people off when I'm being myself. I can't help it."

"So what if you do? Don't worry about it. It'd be good for them."

I shook my head. "I just have bad luck with Christmas."

She glanced over at me. "Jesus Christ, Joel. Relax. Please?"

Carol talked tough even though she clearly wasn't. She had a certain frailness. With her leather Harley jacket and flannel shirt and lacy fuck-me-now lingerie, she wore a gold charm bracelet: little hearts and seahorses. She worried about lactose and saturated fat, and at night she ground her teeth; it sounded like she was chewing marbles.

But I didn't mind that. Carol had the kind of beauty that wasn't just in her face, but in her hands and shoulders and neck, her voice. She was just nineteen. I was twenty-four with no job, no car and a mouthful of smoky yellow teeth. It was hard to see why she was attracted to me at all. But she honestly believed I was an artist, and in artists a degree of ugliness can be considered sexy.

I'd known Carol only a month but already I'd begun to think about her at unexpected times. Staring at the toaster in the morning, or copping a smoke in the back room at work, I'd find myself thinking about her laugh or her graceful fingers or her shiny red fingernails. It was embarrassing how much I thought about her. I hadn't had a girlfriend in over a year and knew I was very lucky. Every time the phone rang I felt a tiny wrinkle of fear; I expected it to be Carol telling me how sorry she was, that things just weren't working out. *You're really a great guy, Joel.* I'd heard this several times before and it was basically the same every time. *I'm still going to call you, okay?* Some mornings she'd show up at my apartment at nine and hurry to class three hours later, and that evening, standing at the refrigerator in my underwear, I couldn't be sure if she'd really been there, or if I'd dreamed her.

• • •

Carol's house was enormous. It looked like a gigantic gingerbread house, with a layer of snow spread like frosting over the roof and shutters and chimney. There was a man standing on the roof when we arrived. He was holding a snow shovel and wearing a plaid woolly hat, the kind with earflaps. His breath puffed out in thin white clouds. As we drove up the long driveway, he waved at us.

"That's my brother, Ronald," Carol said, waving back. "I have no idea what the fuck he's doing up there."

"You've got to be kidding me," I said. "You're loaded."

"No." She killed the engine. "My dad was loaded, and now I guess my mom is, but I'm not. Don't give me shit about it, okay?"

"I just can't fucking believe it."

Inside, I stood in the middle of the family room and stared up at the cathedral ceiling. I'd never been in a place like this. I felt giddy. It was the kind of house I'd seen in *House Beautiful*. The paintings, the cut flowers, the softly ticking clock: The room had an understated grace, signaling the presence of serious money. Even the air seemed thicker and warmer, more nourishing.

"Cut it out," Carol said. "Haven't you ever seen a skylight before?"

"I love all this."

"What?"

I gestured broadly.

"Well, you get used to it. Believe me."

I gave her a dubious look. "It would take me a long time to get used to this."

After a minute she called to me from the kitchen. "Do you want some lunch? There's a ton of food here."

For the entire ride over, I had been starving. But I wasn't hungry anymore. I circled the room, running my fingers over the smooth, polished furniture. Warm sunlight trickled in through the high windows. I flopped down on the sofa and took off my jacket and put my feet up on the end table, and I closed my eyes. It felt so natural. I wanted the television, and the grandfather clock. I wanted the tall bookcases. I wanted everything.

• • •

Carol's brother looked like a shopping mall mannequin, with tiny rimless glasses and khaki pants and a plaid sweater, his hair swept back and shellacked in place. "You made it!" he said, slapping at his snowy pants legs. "I was starting to get worried."

We were in the kitchen eating lunch. There was prosciutto and melon and smoked salmon spread out on the counter. My plate was mounded over. Half a brioche was stuffed in my mouth. Carol's mother, Jeanne, had come downstairs soon after we'd arrived, and now she sat across the table sipping tonic water. She looked like a smaller version of Carol, but when she spoke her voice was breathy and slow, like a sigh; she seemed to recognize something fundamentally sad about the world. She was staring at my hair.

Ronald sat down at the table, plucked an olive off his sister's plate and examined it before popping it into his mouth. "You're probably wondering what I was doing on the roof."

Carol shrugged. "Not really."

"I was shoveling," he said. "I read this article yesterday that said a roof can collapse if there's more than eighteen inches of snow on it." He took another olive from Carol's plate and grinned goofily. "I was saving our roof."

He was so earnest, like a boy in a Norman Rockwell painting. I had an urge to tousle his hair or give him a noogie, or just slap him.

"There's like six inches out there," Carol said.

Jeanne touched Carol lightly on the forearm. "Did I tell you your grandfather is coming today? Your aunt says he's been difficult lately, so we'll have to . . . you know. Take it easy." She sipped her tonic water and smiled gently at her daughter, then at Ronald, then at me. I excused myself to get more soda.

In the kitchen, I pretended to rummage in the refrigerator, then I tiptoed into the dining room and then into what was probably the study. Someone had obviously been reading *Interior Design*. The Prairie School decor, with subtle Japanese accents, was exactly as I would have done it. Often as a kid, I had daydreamed about just such a house. I'd pictured myself tinkering with the movement of the grandfather clock, or sipping a mint julep on the patio, or tooling around on a John Deere riding mower on a hot August morning, bare chested, the front lawn a vast, open territory.

I snuck back into the kitchen. I felt wonderful. I'd always viewed my poverty as somewhat noble, but as I stood in front of Carol's packed refrigerator, I knew I'd been wrong. There is nothing noble about wanting. Nobility comes from having plenty but taking only what you need, and not overindulging. There is no virtue without temptation. Any idiot knows that.

I poured myself a glass of Coke, then on second thought cracked open a cold Heineken.

"You know," Ronald said when I returned, "being up on the roof reminded me of a story I heard about this fireman in Muskegon." He leaned over the table. "This fireman went out one cold night on a call to a trailer home. Apparently those houses are pretty flimsy, because the entire roof had collapsed, and all that was left was a shell, really, four walls. So the fireman went searching for the family, and he found them in their beat-up old pickup, trying to keep warm. A middle-aged man and his two young daughters. And you know what they were doing?"

Carol's arms were crossed over her BITE ME T-shirt. "Is this one of your little stories?" she asked. "Because we just got here, Ronald. We're really not in the mood right now."

Ronald smiled patiently at me. "You know what they were doing?"

Carol sighed loudly. "Playing three-handed bridge. Smoking crack. We don't care, Ronald."

"Please, Ronald, tell us what they were doing," Jeanne said. "I'd like to know."

"They were singing Christmas carols. They were sitting in the truck singing *Away in a Manger*. Isn't that something? It struck me as very hopeful. Beautiful, in a way." He took another olive and chewed it meditatively. "Just out of curiosity, Joel, are you at all religious?"

"Oh, God. For Christ's sake, Ronald." Carol closed her eyes and exhaled. "Please just ignore him, Joel. He gets a little overexcited about Christmas."

"I wish you could have a better attitude," Ronald said. "That's really all I'm asking."

"Ronald," Jeanne said. "Why don't we just leave it alone, okay?" Her smile faded into a tired grin, the memory of a smile. She was tapping her index finger against her empty glass.

"Give me a break, Ronald," Carol said. "You used to hate all this as much as I do." She turned to me. "Ronald used to make himself vomit so he wouldn't have to go to our Aunt Helen's house. He'd eat something disgusting, rotten hamburger or old yogurt or something, and then he'd do jumping jacks in his bedroom until he puked. Every time. Then he would climb into bed and whimper until my mom found him. He'd be like, *My tummy*——"

"Okay, Carol," Ronald said, reddening. "Okay. I admit that I used to dislike spending Christmas with them. But people change. They grow up, for one thing."

"Oh, fuck you," Carol said.

Ronald smiled and picked up the newspaper. He opened the business section with a righteous snap.

"Fuck you," Carol said again.

• • •

Carol refused to give me a tour of the house, and instead took me up to her bedroom. It was pink and yellow, with a border of dancing bears. It was the room of a twelve-year-old. "Do you have any of your little-girl clothes?" I asked her.

"You wish. God, I hate being home. I truly despise it." She rummaged in her bag for a joint, then lit it up and sucked the first quarter-inch off. She waited a second, then hit it again. She was something of a hog when it came to weed.

"Pass it," I said.

"I should have warned you about my brother. He's been 'saved.'"

"Isn't he kind of young for that?"

"It happened a couple of years ago, when he was a freshman. My mother's still a little freaked out. She's sort of happy about it and sort of not happy at all."

"My mom had a boyfriend like that. He talked Jesus to us all the time. Jesus, Jesus, Jesus. About everything." I shrugged. "She dumped him."

"It's annoying," Carol said, shaking her head. "He used to be this cool guy, and now he's just this . . . guy. And he's constantly *forgiving* me, even for things I don't think are wrong. It's his way of hurting me." She took the roach from me and smoked it down to nothing. "Do you have any brothers or sisters?"

"A sister, sort of. She moved to Alaska when I was six."

"Well, you're not missing a whole lot." She got up and closed her bedroom door. "What I love about coming home is that it makes me appreciate strangers more. You know? People you know absolutely nothing about?"

I turned to answer her, but she placed her index finger against her lips and said, "Shhh." She pulled off her T-shirt and jeans in two careless motions. She wasn't wearing anything else. Carol climbed onto the bed, looking straight at me. "I guess I'm in the Christmas spirit," she whispered. "The spirit of giving, and all that."

"What if someone comes in?"

But that didn't seem to bother her too much. She touched me with her beautiful fingers, and there was nothing I could do. In a few seconds we were underneath her Raggedy Ann comforter. She was smooth and strong, an eel, all muscle. The sweat rolled down my face and dripped from my chin into the hollow of her neck. "Come on," she whispered, yanking at my dreadlocks like they were reins. "Come on."

And then there was a knock on her bedroom door. *Rap rap rap.* Polite but insistent. I hovered above her, frozen.

Carol whispered, "Don't worry about it." She gripped my ass. "Keep yourself a little quieter, is what that means."

It took me a little while to get convinced, but when I did I gave her everything I had.

Later, while Carol was brushing her teeth, I started thinking about Christmas in my mother's house. The wreaths were always hung crooked and stank of mothballs. The bows were crumpled. And the Nativity scene was a cheap plastic set, a Kmart special. There were three sad sheep with their legs broken off, and the little Jesus had a cigarette burn on his belly. Only the wise men were unmolested. They stood together, gazing down in horror.

I hated Christmas morning. My mother wrapped everything, in a pathetic attempt to make the Christmas haul look bigger. It only made things worse. While I was tearing open sweatsocks and bottles of mouthwash, I knew that other boys were unwrapping the good toys, the ones that needed batteries. On Christmas night I'd lie awake, weepy and frustrated. I wanted to chisel every Atari cartridge and Can Am car and Lazer Tag pistol on the planet into thumbnail-sized pieces.

Carol's house was nothing like my mother's house. People would arrive soon from distant parts, and even if they hated one another they'd shake hands and swap presents and carry on like long-lost friends. They wouldn't get drunk on Night Train Express and climb onto the dinner table, shrieking for an ex-husband. No bathroom windows would end up broken. It was as if you could buy civility like you could buy cigarettes, or oatmeal.

I wanted to explain this to Carol, but when I turned to her she was sitting on the edge of the bed, worrying a cracked toenail. Her knees were pulled up against her chest and her entire body was tucked in, as though she were preparing to receive a great blow. A stray strand of hair had fallen loose and curled underneath her powdered chin. My God. She was nineteen years old, and beautiful. And rich.

After a while she noticed me staring and asked, "What?" and I reached over and brushed the hair back from her face.

"Nothing."

• • •

When we went downstairs Jeanne looked at Carol and arched her eyebrows and said, "Honey? They'll be here soon."

Carol picked up an envelope off the table and opened it. "Is this my Christmas present?"

Jeanne was wearing a velvety black dress and diamond earrings, and she smelled like wilted roses: a lonely, expensive smell. She smiled at me, then took her daughter's arm and whispered something in her ear. She was shorter than Carol and had to go up on tiptoe. It was an oddly touching sight. Carol said, "What?" Her mother smiled at me and said, "Excuse us for just a minute," and led Carol into the kitchen. After a little while Jeanne came out of the kitchen and headed upstairs, and Carol followed, rolling her eyes.

In the family room, the mantel was covered with pictures of Carol and Ronald: eating candy apples at some cider mill, making snow angels on the front lawn. One picture showed Carol and Ronald with a tall, bearded man who must have been their father. The children were sitting on a wooden porch swing and the bearded man was hugging them both from behind, and all of them were frozen in open-mouthed laughter. Then I saw Carol's Christmas envelope lying on the end table. I peeked inside: There was a card and a check for $2,000. A spasm shot through my bladder. I dropped the envelope, and then Ronald came in and plopped down on the sofa and gave me a queer, nervous smile. "Great tree," I said.

"It is, isn't it?"

"We used to have a fake one," I said. "Half the branches were missing. The thing looked like a cactus."

"We've always had real trees. My father used to cut them down a few miles from here, on a tree farm. Gorgeous full trees. Douglas firs and Scotch pines, mostly, but we'd get the occasional blue spruce."

"Well," I said. "Maybe I'll go see what Carol's up to." The sight of the $2,000 check was freaking me out.

"Hey, Joel," Ronald said, "I'd like to apologize for this morning. For asking you if you're religious, and everything. Sometimes I go a little too far."

"Don't worry about it."

"You sure?"

"Sure. No big deal."

"Okay. Good. Carol gets pretty annoyed when I talk about religion. She won't even listen to me, let alone come to church. You know what she calls me? A *Bible-banger.* I don't even know what that means." He sat forward on the sofa, staring into his hands. "I'm not trying to convert you, Joel. It's just something that's important to me."

"I can respect that," I said. "It's okay. Really."

There was something in me that felt sorry for Ronald. It was his face that did it, his milky, uncomplicated skin. It was a face that could never hide a lie, and this made me want to fuck with him just a little. "My problem was that I could never buy into that whole 'unconditional love' thing," I told him. "It always seemed kind of flaky."

Ronald looked at me. "Flaky?"

"Yeah. I mean, don't you ever feel guilty?"

"No. Well—about what?"

"Because He loves you and you didn't do anything for it."

Ronald's voice when he answered was slow and prissy. "It's unconditional, Joel. It means you don't have to do anything. It's like a gift."

"Yeah, but say I give you a gift for Christmas and tell you it's unconditional. I'm still expecting you to get me something. Of roughly equal value."

"Joel," he said, but stopped. He looked confused. "It's not like that. I could give you something, and I wouldn't expect anything at all in return."

"Really?"

"Of course."

"What would you give me?"

Ronald took a breath, then exhaled slowly. A pink flush spread from his ears to the side of his neck. "What would you want?"

I named a figure that didn't seem too unreasonable.

• • •

A white Cadillac pulled into the driveway at four, and Carol said, "Showtime." She'd brushed her hair out and changed into a black velvet dress, like her mother's. She wore a strand of pearls and matching earrings, and she looked wholesome and beautiful, and I could not stop looking at her.

"Don't give me crap about this," she told me. "Okay? I'm serious." She sniffed the shoulder of her dress. "Shit. I smell like weed."

Jeanne hurried into the room and turned the music louder and said, "They're here," and rushed to the front door. We heard the doorbell, then a collision of happy voices, feet stamping in the front hall, the closet door opening and closing. Carol was gnawing on her thumbnail. She went over to the stereo and turned the music even louder. "Ave Maria" was blasting. A car horn tooted, and another Cadillac turned into the driveway.

I said, "Your *whole family* is rich."

Her relatives began wandering into the family room. Her Uncle Joseph had a taut pink scar winding from his right earlobe down into his sweater, like a slash from a bottle fight, but everyone else looked tanned and vigorous. They looked like actors impersonating rich people. Carol hugged each of them, then slipped her arm around my waist. "Joel's an artist," she informed them. "He does abstract sculpture with old car parts." No one seemed to know what to do with that fact. One aunt laughed hysterically. She slapped Carol playfully on the elbow and said, "Really, Carol, my goodness," but when she saw that Carol wasn't laughing, she gave me a confused, terrified look.

Soon the family room was loud with laughter and clinking ice cubes and Karen Carpenter's bittersweet voice. I sat with Carol in the corner of the room, sipping champagne. Carol's aunts and uncles seemed to share the same laugh—a breezy, confident chuckle—and I admired and hated them for it. Jeanne was working the room with a platter of extra-large shrimp, and when she saw us she gave Carol a cartoon frown and whispered, "Come on, Carol. Introduce Joel to everybody. *Mingle.*"

Carol ignored her. "My mother is afraid my aunts will think I'm rude or something. It's her biggest fear. Once Ronald got caught smashing car windshields with a golf club, and she didn't even punish him. She just made him promise never to tell anyone about it." She sipped her champagne. "The funny thing was, he told everyone."

I took Carol's empty glass, and in the kitchen I refilled it with champagne, drained it and filled it again. When I came back into the family room Carol was gone. She wasn't on the sofa. A band of sweat burst onto my forehead. I went back into the kitchen and drank another glass of champagne, then worked my way through the study and living room and foyer. No Carol.

I stood in the kitchen, drinking champagne. I wanted to go into the family room, but for some reason I couldn't get up the nerve to move. There was something powerful I couldn't explain, like gravity, grabbing at me. A group of Carol's teenage cousins were slouched in the corner, bored. I wanted to be one of those kids. I wanted their parents to laugh at my jokes and ask me what I thought about the PLO or derivatives trading. All the hours at the 7-Eleven, all the magazines I'd read: I was prepared to talk about anything.

Finally Jeanne appeared next to me, holding two glasses of champagne. She offered one glass to me. "Have you met everyone? Carol's not the best for making introductions."

I nodded. "I think I freaked out your father. With my hair."

Jeanne smiled. "It would take more than that to scare my father. Trust me." She sipped her champagne. "Have you seen my daughter lately? I can't seem to find her anywhere. She was supposed to help with the hors d'oeuvres."

"She was here a few minutes ago," I said testily, "and then she left."

"She's probably upstairs hiding from me. She does that sometimes." Jeanne touched her forehead distractedly. She seemed mildly drunk, and even drunk she radiated an aura of melancholy. It occurred to me that some of her sadness was probably caused by Carol; this made me feel vaguely guilty. "You know, Carol hasn't brought anyone home since she was a freshman in high school. Isn't that strange? You're the first one of Carol's friends I've met in a long time."

Jeanne shook her head. "Anyway, I'm glad you could come, Joel."

"Me too."

She looked at me skeptically. "Are you having a good time?"

I nodded. "This is how I always pictured Christmas should be, when I was a kid. You know: the fireplace, the big tree. The music, even. This is basically it."

"Really?" Jeanne pursed her lips. "This is how our Christmas has always been, and it's starting to feel sort of hokey. I was thinking we'd try something new next year. A change."

"Don't change anything," I told her. "You shouldn't, I mean. This is perfect." Jeanne laughed. "I like you, Joel. You're the most optimistic person in this room. I appreciate that." She reached toward me, and for a second I thought she was going to pinch my cheek. Instead she took one of my dreadlocks and rolled it between her thumb and forefinger. She smiled. "I've always wanted to do that."

For a few long moments I felt completely at ease. I wanted to stand on the sofa and belt out a toast: to Jeanne and Carol and Ronald, to Christmas, to everything. The tree was lit up with hundreds of tiny white lights, like stars. Someone, one of the uncles, threw his head back and laughed. His laughter filled the room and floated up to the ceiling. One of the young cousins dashed into the room and clung to his mother's leg, and she bent down and scooped him into her arms. The safety of that room! Suddenly it was easy to understand that Christmas is a religious holiday.

I put my champagne glass down. My hands were trembling; I felt high, buzzed, even though I wasn't. I told Jeanne, "I quit my job yesterday."

"You did?"

I nodded. "To come here today. I quit."

Jeanne was cheerfully confused. "You quit to come here? Why?"

Then Carol grabbed me by the sleeve and said, "Come on." I followed her upstairs to her bedroom. "Now?" I asked. "Are you serious?" She grabbed her toothbrush from the bathroom and stuffed it into her overnight bag. Then she opened the closet and pulled out my jacket and shoved it at me.

"What?" I said. "What is this?"

"We're leaving."

"Why?"

"We're just leaving." She zipped her overnight bag, then opened the closet again and yanked her jacket off its hanger.

"Hey," I said. "Hello?"

"Okay. Fine. Ronald said you tried to extort money from him. He said you tricked him into promising you nine hundred dollars."

"What is this suppo——" I said, but then I remembered. "Oh, that. I was joking! I was just fucking around." I wanted to laugh, but Carol wasn't smiling.

"He told me about your little conversation." She went to her bed and jerked the comforter back. "It didn't sound to me like you were joking." She smoothed the tousled bedsheets. She punched both pillows. "Ronald's a dork, Joel, but he's not a liar. Okay? I mean, why would he lie about something like that?"

"I never said he was a liar. Maybe he just misunderstood me."

"Well, I understand you." She resettled the comforter and sat down on the edge of the bed. Her right hand trembled on the hem of her jacket. "And, you know, he was going to give it to you. He was actually going to give you the money, the big idiot. I'm not letting him."

"But I don't want the money."

"You're not getting it."

"I don't want it. I was joking. Really."

"Right, Joel. You don't want the money. How am I supposed to believe that?"

I touched her elbow, but she closed her eyes and twisted away. She wouldn't look at me. "I just want to go. Okay? I feel sick. I feel like I'm about to puke."

"You want to leave right now?" I asked.

She nodded violently. Small tears were starting at the corners of her eyes.

"You don't even want to stick around for dinner?"

Carol's Honda was blocked in, and it took twenty minutes to get people to move their cars. I waited in the garage, shivering. Each time the door opened a blast of sound and light would spill out into the cold, and my heart would squeeze. Finally the driveway was clear, and Carol came out of the house, trailed by good-byes. "Merry Christmas, Jonah!" I heard someone shout. As we drove away I looked back through the rear window and saw Ronald, standing on the driveway in the glare of a powerful floodlight, wearing his woolly hat. Snow swirled down around him. He was just standing there, watching us.

• • •

When we were still half a mile from my apartment I said, "Drop me off here."

"For Christ's sake. I'll take you all the way home. I'm not a sadist."

"No. Leave me here. There's something I need to do."

Carol gave me a look, then pulled over onto the snowy shoulder. Neither of us had spoken a word during the ride home. She shifted the car into park and said, "I don't think we should see each other any-more." She pronounced the words carefully, like she was translating a foreign language.

"I realize that."

She seemed surprised. "You're okay with that?"

"I think I'll survive, if that's what you mean."

"Joel, I'm sorry about this. Really. I'm just . . . sorry." She shook her head. "I shouldn't have brought you. I'm just such a moron some-times."

"It's okay. You brought me because you wanted to piss off your brother. Or maybe you felt sorry for me. It's Christmas. You were doing your good deed, right?"

"Wait. Joel——"

"Don't get me wrong, I'm glad I went. I just wish I'd gotten that money from your brother. He was *this* close to giving it to me."

Carol stared at me.

"You know what I told him?"

"No. I don't."

"I talked Bible to him. I used that line about the poor in spirit, which is me, inheriting the earth. I told him I needed a little advance."

Carol shook her head. "You have problems, Joel. You have some seri-ous problems."

"Well, I'll see you. Fuck you. Merry Christmas."

I climbed out of the car. The highway was empty, but Carol's Honda sat idling on the side of the road. I kicked her rear bumper. "Fucking *go!*" I shouted. Finally Carol dropped the car into gear. As she pulled away, I heard the soft click of the electric door locks.

The parking lot of the 7-Eleven was empty. It smelled like gasoline. Through the plateglass window I saw Rahman polishing the front counter with a rag. He scrubbed it methodically, then began buffing the glass cover of the hot dog rotisserie. I felt old, like I'd seen everything and would never again be surprised, and this scared me. I stood on the curb in the cold until my ears began to ache, then walked slowly across the parking lot.

I pulled open the Plexiglas front door, and a single bell jingled. Rahman looked up from the rotisserie. When he saw me he did the strangest thing: He smiled, like he was happy I'd come back.

My heart. For a moment, it ached with joy.

The Date

by **EDWARD LAZELLARI**
1999

She had two heads. That was my initial response after she opened
the door, but, as I soon discovered, they in fact shared one body.

"Clarise?" I asked, praying that the aberration before me was not
her. But even before she opened her mouth I knew this was my client.
There could be no other reason why the job was paying so much.

"That would be me," she said, smiling. "You're Norman from the
escort service, right?"

For the life of me I could not come up with a reason why I wasn't
me and at the same time explain why I knew her name. So I nodded
and walked into the apartment. I mean—yeah, she had two heads, but
that was no reason to hurt her feelings. Besides, the job paid more
than any other I'd ever had. I just wished my dispatcher had prepared
me before sending me out on this assignment. This was what I got for
being low man on the totem pole.

"Norman, this is my sister, Patsy," she said matter-of-factly and pointed
to the head on her right shoulder. "We're conjoined twins."

Well, of course you are, I thought. What the fuck else would you be?
"Hi, very nice to meet you," I said as normally as possible.

"Whatever," was Patsy's response. I got the distinct feeling that she
didn't really want to be there.

The apartment was nice. Huge windows showcased the western sky-
line across Central Park. The last remnants of dusk were beginning to

fade behind the buildings and lights were coming on everywhere. I was fairly sure none of the furniture came from Ikea. A glass spiral staircase with a gold banister led to the upper level of the duplex. Whatever these two did for a living paid extremely well.

Clarise had a strangely confident demeanor, one I would not have associated with a woman in her situation. It was businesslike; she somehow reminded me of an accountant. Patsy had shocking red hair. Clarise's was a natural auburn, and so, no doubt, was Patsy's under the dye. They wore a black evening dress, custom-made, I assumed. Clarise told me to make myself at home and asked me to name my poison. I had actually quit drinking the day before on the advice of my doctor.

"Scotch," I said. I was not going to make it through this night sober. In my head I was compiling a list of the darkest, most out-of-the-way places in Manhattan that I might take Clarise/Patsy to. The fewer people who saw me on this date, I thought, the better. She brought me my drink, which turned out to be a double. Good girl, I thought. Whatever her faults, at least she's grounded in reality.

I sat on the right end of the couch, which I discovered was the wrong end. Clarise explained that it would be rude to Patsy if we conversed with her in between us. I was to sit on the left end. Patsy's dates sat on the right end. "I don't understand," I said. "Am I not escorting both of you tonight?"

"Oh, no," Clarise said, as though this were some major faux pas on my part. "You're my date tonight." Heavy emphasis on my. "Patsy is just tagging along."

"I don't pay for men," Patsy interjected. I sat silently with my drink in hand, no doubt sporting a perplexed look, because she quickly added, "*I* have a boyfriend," stressing the word like a spoiled little girl.

"You don't say!" I said without thinking. From her expression I could tell she was annoyed by my astonishment.

"Is it so hard to believe someone could love me?" she said.

"Look—either be civil or hush up," Clarise told her sister. "He's my date. Keep your conversation to an absolute minimum or put up half the money for the service." Clarise's businesslike veneer was slipping.

Patsy turned her head the other way with contempt. I downed my scotch in one quick gulp and politely asked for another.

"Of course," Clarise said. "Patsy, Norman would like another drink."

"It's over there Norm—knock yourself out," Patsy responded.

"Patsy! Norman is our guest. Let's get up and fix him a drink."

"Norman is your employee. Do we fix drinks for the maid?" Patsy's refusal to get up put Clarise in an embarrassing situation. Apparently they each controlled one side of their body and had to work in unison in order to move about or even accomplish the most basic tasks. I offered to get the drink myself and to freshen hers while I was at it.

They sat glaring at each other while I took my time at the wet bar, glancing at the photos on the piano and the walls. They had had a surprisingly normal childhood, considering: graduations, proms, picnics, recitals, birthdays and even Little League baseball. Clarise/Patsy were apparently far more dexterous than I would have guessed. The photographs showed that they came from a family chock-full of one-headed people. I looked at the paintings hung around the room. One, or both, of them had taste. I brought back the drinks and sat at the correct end of the couch. I asked Patsy if she'd like a drink also.

"Only one of us drinks at a time," Clarise said. "Otherwise we tend to get drunk too quickly."

I nodded. I can only imagine what the expression on my face must have looked like. I was numb with amazement. Patsy had lit a cigarette, resulting in a strange smoky halo wafting behind Clarise's head like some kind of ethereal frame. It reminded me of Morticia Addams's idea of a smoke from the old TV series. "So you share everything," I asked, glancing at their torso.

"Oh, no," Clarise said, defensively. "Mostly the blood supply. We're parapagus twins."

"Oh, right," I said, feigning comprehension. Patsy rolled her eyes and blew air from her lips. She seemed to have a shrewder idea what others might really be thinking than Clarise did. "We share everything from the gut down," she said. "Our torso looks like one body, but we've got separate spinal columns down to the waist."

"I've got my own heart," Clarise said, like a child with an ice-cream cone.

I could see that telling their story was wearing thin with them. They looked to me to be in their late twenties. How many times must they have told their tale in the course of their lives? I decided to curb my heightened curiosity, both to be polite and to keep in line with the rules of the escort service. The client always sets the agenda.

"You know—it might be easier for us to converse if I sat there," I said, pointing to the chair placed facing the couch. Clarise didn't like that idea. She said I was fine where I was. The smoky halo behind Clarise was the only indication that there was any activity going on back there. It was clear that she wanted Patsy to stay out of the conversation as much as possible, and Patsy's head out of my line of sight.

"Are you a professional escort man?" she asked, changing the subject.

"Uh, no. I'm a law student at NYU. Escorting women is better than waiting tables," I said with a stab at humor. This was true on most days at least. "I've been told I have what it takes—that is, physically—so I figured, Why not? My tuition's extremely high and, as you know, the money's pretty good."

Clarise smiled and said, "Well, you certainly are handsome." Then she brushed my ankle with her foot. "Tell me," she asked, "do you ever sleep with your clients?" I downed my drink in one quick gulp. My face contorted and I felt flushed from the burning in my throat. It bought me a few extra moments before I had to give my response.

"Well, you're only my eighth client," I stammered. "My last one was old enough to be my mother, and, believe me, I didn't try."

Clarise could tell I was attempting to sidestep the question. She continued to smile as her foot found its way under my pants leg. I was beginning to feel warm as her toes rubbed up and down my calf, but I wasn't sure if this was from the scotch or from her advances. Regardless, I felt a bulge forming in my crotch. I considered it the ultimate act of betrayal by my body. She noticed it and smiled. The next thing I knew, she was rubbing my crotch with the ball of her foot.

"Did *she* try?" asked Clarise.

"Try what?" I asked anxiously.

"Did she make the moves on you, silly?"

"Well, yeah, actually she did."

"And?"

I was really in the shit at that point because, as it turned out, I did sleep with the client. I could tell Clarise suspected this by the way she smiled as my eyes shifted, trying to avoid her gaze. She found my discomfort amusing.

"He fucked her," Patsy chimed in. "He fucked her brains out."

Yeah, I did. The woman was in her late fifties, but she was attractive—and she had only one head. My hesitation gave me away. Clarise had gauged my scruples, and it would be that much harder coming up with an excuse to get out of this predicament. I mean, I couldn't tell her I didn't want to sleep with her because she was a freak. This was the best-paying job I'd ever had and I was on shaky ground here if I couldn't keep the client happy.

I jumped up under the premise that I was going to refresh my drink, and I offered to do the same for her. She just smiled at me in a naughty way. I felt both pairs of eyes follow me to the bar. I imagined them mentally stripping away my garments the way I'd done to women a hundred times. It made my hackles rise.

THE DATE

Any other date would have mentioned that I'd arrived only twenty minutes ago and was already on my third double scotch. Not her. She was in tune with reality. She *wanted* my inhibitions to relax. She smiled every time I headed for the alcohol. I decided to take it easy and mixed a single with some water added in, standing behind the wet bar as though it were some kind of shield—a little fort of glass and steel between me and her. From the other end of the room I asked her what she did for a living.

"I'm a stockbroker," she answered.

"Oh, really?" was all the response I could muster. She probably worked for Shearson-Ringling Brothers. I had to suppress a smile. Anyone who could overcome such a burden in life and still manage to make something of herself deserved a little respect. "So you earn enough to afford all this?" I asked, indicating the apartment.

"Well—yes and no . . ."

"Go ahead—tell him," Patsy interjected. Clarise threw her sister a glare. Patsy continued. "If you won't tell him I will."

"My date—my conversation," Clarise noted. She turned her attention back to me. "You ever see those Doublemint gum commercials—the ones with the twins?" I nodded. "Well, we filmed one of those when we were teenagers." Clarise began to contemplate her cuticles, leaving me to ponder this new information.

I tried to recall ever having seen this advertisement but drew a blank. Perhaps the sight had been so horrific, I had blocked the memory. "I don't remember seeing that ad," I said.

"Well, there's a reason for that." Clarise hesitated. Patsy looked ready to burst if her sister didn't finish the story. "You see, we were local celebrities in Chicago. One of the executives thought it would be a cute idea to use us in a commercial. But no one outside Illinois had ever heard of us, and the ads didn't test well in market research—they ran them for test audiences and got very low scores."

"One old lady threw up!" Patsy said gleefully.

"So they weren't going to run them. Our lawyer didn't like what they were offering as a kill fee. We stood to make quite a bundle on residuals, so we threatened to turn this into a civil rights case about discrimination against the handicapped."

"No way in hell you could have won that," I interjected, surprised into tactless sincerity.

"We knew that. They had every right to pull the ad," Clarise said. "But our feelings were really hurt and we wanted to get back at them. Wrigley's didn't want to chance the publicity, so we ended up settling for five times our original fee."

"Next thing you know, Clarise uses the money to buy Microsoft at twenty dollars a share. The rest is history."

"That's amazing," I said. I made a mental note to research the specifics of their case at the law library. Stuff like this was the reason I was going into law. "And Patsy—are you a broker too?"

"Well, Patsy never finished college," Clarise said in a disapproving, maternal manner.

"Oh, just drop it," Patsy said. "It's so old."

"All you had to do was try. I mean, it's not as though you weren't there in class anyway. You wasted all that time!"

"Hey, it was my time to waste. You just feel guilty because I never bitched about having to go when we both knew I wanted to be anyplace else. You just hate that you owe me."

"Owe you? Anything I owed you for letting me finish college I've paid back in spades."

Curiouser and curiouser, I thought, as they continued to bicker. I was running out of things to do behind the bar, so I meandered back to the center ring, where I made a startling observation as I resumed my seat next to Clarise: The more I drank the better she looked. By herself—that is, if I ignored the other head—she was actually an attractive person. The girls had distinct personalities. The physical manifestation of this was that they wore their hair differently, breaking the symmetry. Patsy's hair was in a punk crop, while Clarise wore hers long and free. It was pretty hair.

I realized that at some point, if I kept drinking, I'd have double vision. This notion was somewhat appealing until it occurred to me that double vision, not being selective, would lead to four heads on two bodies and only compound my predicament. Did I want to get to that point of inebriation, which seemed to be only about four drinks away—two if they were doubles?

The doorbell rang. All three of us looked at the front door in mesmerized unison, as though we were in a scene from *Children of the Damned*. I heard someone calling Patsy's name. Clarise appeared upset.

"I can't believe that you invited him over," she cried.

"I didn't invite anyone over. He's my fucking boyfriend and he's allowed to stop by any time he wants to."

"Well, I'm not getting up to let him in," Clarise said. "This is my night. We agreed on it."

"He's not going to go away," Patsy said, as she tried to drag her sister off the couch. Clarise wouldn't budge. "Why can't you just treat him right?"

THE DATE

The doorbell rang again. Clarise was more and more upset. "That scuzzball can just stay out there. After all I've done for you—putting up with him—you can't even let me have one night for myself?"

"Don't you pull this shit, Miss High Fucking Society," Patsy said angrily. "I'm always going to your boring cocktail parties so you can shmooze with investment bankers and high-finance gurus. God! When was the last time we got to hang out in Soho, or go to a gallery opening?"

"But he's such a scuzzball! He's going to give us herpes one day! Or worse!"

"*Herpes!* You're the one who hired a fucking gigolo. If anyone's going to give us herpes it's him!" Patsy retorted, pointing to me.

"You're an ungrateful waste of life," Clarise cried.

"Go fuck yourself," Patsy responded.

"Bitch!"

"Freak!"

"Ahem," I grunted.

Clarise reddened, Patsy paled. "I'll get it," I said. The incessant ringing was giving me a headache. When I opened the door I faced a small, grungy-looking man who came up to my chest. He had light brown skin, long woolly black hair, a black mustache, boots, ripped jeans and a leather motorcycle jacket with a Hell's Angels patch on the arm.

"Who the fuck are you?" he growled. The guy reeked of sweat and beer and garlic. I got the feeling I was living in interesting times, in the Chinese sense of the term. His attitude was confrontational, to say the least.

"Hi, I'm Normal—I mean, Norman," I said, trying to sound natural.

He strutted into the apartment and eyed me cautiously. He looked to the girls and then back to me. His eyes were slits and his mustache formed a thin black line. Everything was silent as time slowed to a crawl. He looked again toward the girls and rubbed his stubbled chin with his hand. Then he turned, shook his finger at me and asked, "Did you fuck Patsy?"

"Who, me? I never touched her!" Clearly, that was not what I would expect him to say.

"Don't play no fucking sematics game with me, motherfucker, or I'll cut ya," he snarled. His vocabulary told me this was someone who thought too highly of his intellectual capacity.

"I'm not playing with *semantics*," I said defensively. "I'm Clarise's date for the evening." The girls hurried to introduce me to Patsy's boyfriend, Ben. They had regained their composure. Watching the two of them move in unison was amazing. After all these years together they had managed to achieve some state of grace in their motion. "I'm strictly

Clarise's escort for the night," I added. This seemed to have the opposite effect from what I intended. His agitation only grew.

"What, you think I'm a fucking moron?" he snarled. "You take out
one, the other goes with you too. You ain't got no freakin' choice!"

"Look, man," I said, "you're going overboard here. No one's hitting
on Patsy. I've barely talked to her. Clarise is my client. If anything happens tonight, it's between me and her! It's nobody else's business. I'm
just trying to make a living here."

I couldn't believe I had actually said that. I was defending my stake
in a woman I wanted no part of. This was quickly becoming a testoster-
one-driven pissing match. Patsy looked frightened, no doubt because I
outweighed her boyfriend by a good thirty pounds. Clarise looked confused. She was unusually quiet. She had two men fighting over her—a
situation I figured she had never experienced before. I don't care what
feminists claim, women love this shit.

Ben looked about ready to take a shot at me. Patsy pleaded with him
to let it alone. He bit his lip and settled down. I felt as if I were trailing
in some kind of competition. I was trying to catch up with events. I'd
felt off-center since Clarise had answered the door. Between the sisters and the scotch, there always seemed to be information beyond my
reach. I was certainly missing something important at the moment.

Patsy murmured softly into Ben's ear, like a jockey whispering to a
racehorse before a match to calm it down. But Ben shook his head vehe-
mently. He was not keen on whatever she was telling him. I was getting
fed up with his attitude. It was obvious that Clarise had to endure this
hotheaded jerk every time Patsy went out with him. I wondered how
Patsy found a boyfriend when Clarise couldn't. Maybe it was the circles
she traveled in. Maybe Patsy was just that much more interesting. Who
knows? But I did get the feeling that Clarise was lonely. Perhaps I was
her fantasy date, her expensive way to experience a little romance on
her own terms. Maybe she just wanted to be the center of a man's attention—a man who wasn't Ben. For all Clarise's accomplishments—physical, educational and professional—maybe all this girl really wanted was
some loving to call her own. (I have always been surprised at how pro-
found good scotch whiskey tends to make me.)

"Don't you think you're being a little selfish?" I asked Ben. I wanted
to move the night along so that it could end and I could get paid. "After
all," I continued, "Clarise has a right to some attention too."

Ben looked at me with contempt. His hands were trembling, palms
up. He searched for the right words to express what he was feeling—
it seemed his only option other than throttling me. I stared at him.

"Don't you have eyes?" He pointed at the girls. Patsy seemed annoyed, Clarise mustered a weak smile. I looked at them: two arms, two legs, two breasts, four eyes, four ears, two mouths, two noses and a nice black evening dress. I looked back at Ben, confused.

"They only got one pussy!" he yelled in a rage. "You can't fuck Clarise without fucking Patsy too, you somabitch." The girls' eyes anchored the floor. It finally dawned on me. Throughout life they had to share every moment together, even the intimate ones we monoheaded folk take for granted.

Patsy spoke to Ben gently. "Be fair, Ben. Clarise and I have tried to arrange things to make our lives bearable," she explained to him. "Otherwise, how could we function? What everyone else in the world takes for granted are hurdles for us. Even something as simple as going to the corner to buy a quart of milk requires the other's permission. You knew that, Ben. She doesn't enjoy sex with you. She does it for my sake. I wish she could appreciate you for the brilliant artist that you are. Then maybe we could share your love. But we're different people and we like different things. She needs a chance to live her life too."

Ben took her words with a grain of salt. "But who ever heard of a time-share vagina?" he cried.

Time-share vaginas are said to be quite popular in France, but I kept this tidbit to myself. I didn't want to break the moment. Patsy seemed to be getting through to him. To my horror I realized it would now be much harder, if not impossible, to get out of sleeping with Clarise/Patsy. After this brouhaha and my history with the previous client, I'd have to be Truman Capote to come up with a story to get me out of this mess. I was not particularly thrilled about traveling somewhere Ben had been, either.

I excused myself to go to the bathroom. I hoped a few moments alone would produce some resolution to the situation. I put the seat down and sat on it with no particular purpose (or newspaper) in hand. The intermission lent itself to some esoteric reflections about the state of my life. As I sat there, staring at myself in the mirror, I came to the conclusion that as a person I was about as deep as a puddle of water. My ethics and scruples were in a constant state of flux and my morality was questionable. I was the prisoner of my greed, the victim of my desire to make an easy buck. Upon this revelation I smiled—I was going to make a terrific lawyer. Whatever nature excluded from my spirit I could subsidize with material wealth.

And then I heard the front door close

Clarise/Patsy were alone in the living room smoking a cigarette, drinking a scotch. Ben was gone.

"Is everything okay?" I asked.

"No," said Patsy. "But it'll do for now. Did everything come out all right?"

I had been in there for quite a while "I thought it'd be better if I weren't in the room."

"I'll bet."

"Should we sit down?" Clarise asked.

"Let's go out," I said. "Let's get the evening started."

"After all, he's on the clock, you know," Patsy muttered.

"Excuse me, but do you have a problem, Patsy?" I knew that if I didn't address Patsy's attitude now I would be the butt of her jibes all night.

"I do have a problem, Norman. What are your intentions?" Clarise got a worried look in her eye.

"My intentions? What do you mean?" I asked, as if I didn't know.

"Cut the bullshit, Norm."

"Patsy, please!" Clarise cried.

"Look, my sister's great at options and mergers, but she's a spaz when it comes to matters of the heart. You have probably spent half the evening trying to figure how to get out of this assignment." She paused as she blew smoke out of her nostrils, giving the impression of someone who was prepared to fight. "Well, the check won't bounce and she deserves to get her money's worth, so let's forget the crap about going out. She wants to fuck some *GQ*-looking stud. She wants someone who's not Ben. So what's it going to be, rent-a-stud? Isn't this what they teach you in law school? How to fuck your fellow man for profit?" Patsy took another drag on her cigarette and blew the smoke out meticulously. The moment dragged on as I tried to decide what I was going to do. "Do you play or do we demand a refund?" she added.

That was it in a nutshell. Normally, I didn't have to sleep with the client if I didn't want to, but these two could cause problems for the agency that might lead to my dismissal. They probably kept that lawyer from the chewing-gum case on retainer. As Patsy stared me down, I realized she had the qualities of a good lawyer herself, something that surprised me coming from an arty type.

"Fine," I said evenly. "It's been a while since I've been in a threesome. You understand we accept tips—in cash, of course. No reason to alert Uncle Sam about revenue that I need more than he does." The girls smiled.

"I'm a two-headed bitch, not a communist," Patsy confirmed. The girls went to their purse and pulled out five Ben Franklins. "Five now, five later if you actually manage to ring our bell. Consider it an incentive."

Generous, I thought. This would be the most I had ever made in a single night. And, despite Ben, I had the impression that Patsy didn't mind the situation as much as she pretended to. I chugged down the rest of my drink.

Their bedroom was huge. In the center was a king-size canopy bed made up in satin sheets. French doors led to a balcony overlooking the park. The moonlight coming through the glass made a checkered pattern of light on the bed. I took them by the hand and started to kiss Clarise. She had a pleasant minty taste. We were quickly out of our clothes and rolling around in the bed. I began to suckle her breast when I felt Clarise's hand on my cheek, trying to pull me away from it.

"No, sweetie—my breast, here." I realized that I had Patsy's breast. These girls were wired to separate sides of their body, whereas I instinctively go for the bigger one first. Patsy has a bigger tit than her sister, I thought to myself, remembering my own sisters' boob rivalries. As I swung to Clarise's side I caught Patsy's eye. She wore a sly smile.

I licked my way down to where only a single woman existed. With a thousand bucks on the line I was going to ring their bell, and to hell with where Ben had been already. As I touched their button with my tongue both girls groaned generously, knotting the bedsheets in their hands. I took my time and was rewarded with a heavily glazed chin for my efforts. Finally I plunged in, taking care to remember whose neck to nibble on as I thrust my way to a big payday. And yet the whole time something was bothering me. There I was, having sex, nibbling on her neck, trying to figure out why something felt wrong other than the fact that it was sex for money or that my partner had two heads.

They wrapped their legs around mine and stroked my back and neck as I thrust myself into them. Patsy stroked my head, running her long fingers through my hair. Clarise grabbed my right butt cheek and squeezed tight, pulling me into her. As I continued to pound my way to freedom and wealth I turned to the left to find myself locking stares with Patsy. And then it hit me like a revelation. Gazing into her eyes, seeing her grimace, watching her bite her lip with pleasure, I realized I liked Patsy. I mean, I liked Patsy a lot. Her attitude and her fire were much more appealing than Clarise's were. Patsy could take charge and stand up for herself. Her cynical nature, her biting wit—these were the things in a woman that turned me on. And wasn't she flirting with me—flirting silently with her eyes right there next to her sister? For a moment, I was sure she'd be willing to trade Ben in for another type of bad boy. The notion amused me, and I pondered it as I continued to fuck them. I wouldn't even have to worry about whether she'd put out or not—she already had. She was rich. If she had a taste for the unscrupulous type then maybe I could be her sinister half. I continued with Clarise, wishing I could kiss Patsy instead.

They came.

Hearing two women groan at the same moment from the same orgasm was surreal. I came soon after. As far as I was concerned I was out of there. As I started to get dressed I caught sight of them in the mirror. They lay in bed exhausted; Patsy and I gazed at each other through our reflections. She wore a devilish grin. They seemed satisfied. Maybe Ben wasn't ringing their bell. Maybe this was an ideal way for Patsy to keep Ben as a boyfriend and get some satisfaction on the side. College or not, Patsy had the better instincts and she wore the pants in this relationship. I had the feeling that manipulating Clarise had become Patsy's way of dealing with her resentment of her sister. They had an odd relationship. They never could be alone. Clarise stirred and Patsy shifted her gaze from me before her sister noticed.

"Patsy?"

"Hmm?"

"Where's the condom?"

"The condom?"

"You did give Norman a condom to put on."

"He's your fucking date. When Ben comes over, I provide the protection. When you have a date, you supply the rubber."

"When did I ever have a date? The condoms are in the drawer in the night table on your side of the bed."

"How could you be so fucking stupid!"

"I've never had a man over. Why don't you take an interest in what goes on with your own body?"

"Bitch!"

"Slut!"

I left the room. I found the purse and helped myself to the rest of my bonus. As I shut the door behind me they were still at it. Items were being flung about and shattering against the wall. What if I had knocked them up? It wasn't my problem. It wasn't as though they couldn't afford all the options.

As I entered the elevator I was greeted by an old lady taking her poodle out for a walk. I smiled in return, then noticed it was still fairly early. If I cabbed it to the Village, I could catch my fiancée coming off shift. As the elevator doors shut, I fingered the cash in my pocket, then I startled the old lady when I said, "Geez, what a way to make a living."

The Collection Treatment

by YAEL SCHONFELD

2000

The Aurora Hotel was a scab-colored building in a bad part of town. Its two front doors, the first made of latticed iron and the second of thick, heavy wood, were always closed and usually locked. The only way it could be identified as a hotel was by the hand-painted sign suspended from one of the first-floor windows. FULL BATH, the sign declared. COLOR TV. DAILY, WEEKLY AND MONTHLY RATES. SAFE! The last word, *safe*, and its accompanying exclamation point had actually made Audra laugh out loud when she saw them for the first time, and Audra did not laugh often.

She was not sure exactly what *full bath* meant. The *color TV* part of the sign was a blatant lie. There was no TV, color or otherwise, in Audra's room. There was a small sink in the corner, but the hot and cold water could not be turned on at the same time. Freezing cold or scalding hot— this was a choice Audra faced every time that she used the sink.

When she paid for her first month's stay at the Aurora, Audra was told by the manager, Sophia Croff, that a maid would be coming by every week to change her linen. This was also not true. There was no maid. Sometimes Sophia herself would stride around the hotel carrying sheets and pillowcases and handling her heavy key ring with a self-important jangle. Audra believed that she did this merely as an excuse to enter the tenants' rooms and poke into their possessions. This could be done satisfactorily only in their absence, and since Audra was usually present, her sheets had yet to be changed. She did not mind. She was not fond of changes, anyway. If the smell got to be a problem, Audra thought, she could turn the sheets over. That would suffice for a while.

Many of the rooms looked out only on the grim gray fire escape at the hollow center of the building, but Audra's room was privileged in this respect: It offered a view of the street. When she stood by the window, Audra could watch the cars going by on the road. She could see people settling into the plastic chairs of Eddie's Diner on the other side of the street. If she stood by her window at exactly seven thirty, as she did almost every morning, she could see Will Finn set out for his morning run.

Will's thick, fair hair was always shower-wet at seven thirty in the morning. He would pause just outside the latticed iron door, jogging in place for several minutes before he began the actual run. No matter how cold the day was, he would be wearing shorts and a white T-shirt. From her second-story window, in a dark, long-sleeved cotton shirt that had not been changed for days, Audra watched him with a pleasant sense of bafflement and wonder. His skin seemed to glimmer with an almost unnatural cleanliness. How could he achieve it here? They shared the same shower, at the end of sthe second-floor corridor. The hot and cold water in the shower could be turned on at the same time, but even the combined efforts never amounted to more than a pallid trickle. If she stood under it for hours, she would never be as clean as that.

And the thought of running for pleasure here, in this place, was equally alien. It was, Audra thought, almost as funny as SAFE! though it did not make her laugh. Standing by her window at various hours of the day, Audra had seen plenty of people running. But none of them, she was sure, thought of it as jogging. None of them did it for fun.

After jogging in place for several minutes, Will would turn right and start running down the street. Audra would watch him run past CHECKS CASHED 24 HOURS A DAY and Eternal Bliss Chinese Restaurant and another hotel, the St. Elliott. She watched until he was a distant blur of steady, pounding motion. She watched until he disappeared completely. After that, she shifted and stretched slowly. She shrugged her shoulders. She ran her hand through her dark, delicate hair, dull and brittle from lack of nourishment. This was usually the extent of her own daily exercise.

• • •

Audra knew Will Finn's name, as well as several other things about him, because she had talked to him. This was not a common practice among

Aurora's residents. Most of the residents were men, and most of the men were furtive. They scurried down corridors, hunted desperately for keys, avoided eye contact and mumbled indecipherable greetings when they happened to meet someone.

Audra, too, was furtive by nature, but the elusiveness of the men made her perversely bold. She stared straight at them without speaking when she saw them in the halls, as if she knew something awful about them. Sometimes she left the door to her room half open, and the men would turn their heads as they passed, despite themselves, and then look away sharply when they saw her, as if they had been slapped.

Will Finn was not furtive. His steps on the way to the shower down the hall (he took two showers a day, before and after his run) were purposeful, unhurried and somehow distracted, Audra thought. On the day she met him, on his way back to his room after the second shower, she gave him an ominous, lingering look. Will stopped and introduced himself. He even reached out to shake her hand, though most of what he shook was sleeve. Audra's black sleeves extended down to the base of her thumbs.

"So, have you been here long?" Will rubbed his wet hair with a towel as he asked her this. He was wearing more formal clothes now, a buttondown shirt and dark trousers.

"Almost a month. I was staying in another place before, but they had bugs in the bathroom at night."

Will nodded. "This isn't a bad place. I mean, it could be worse."

"It can always be worse," Audra said. She was following him back to his room but lingered in the doorway until he gestured her inside. "I like it when they just take your money and don't ask you any questions. Not like when you're trying to rent an apartment or something, you know?"

Will froze momentarily in the act of hanging up his towel. He turned back to look at her, then nodded again, slowly this time. "I know what you mean. That's one of the advantages, with hotels."

Audra was taking in the room curiously. Will did have a TV, though he would later tell her he had bought it himself, at a garage sale, for $32. He also had a small, old-fashioned tape deck, which stood on the single table, surrounded by piles of neatly labeled cassettes. His bed was made, the white edge of the sheet tucked precisely over the thin brown cover, the way things are arranged in real hotels. A black suitcase lay open in the far corner, full of folded clothes.

"I've seen you running," Audra said conversationally.

"You must be an early riser, then."

Audra shrugged. "Do you do it to lose weight?"

"What?" He tilted his head slightly, uncomprehending.

"Running. Because it's not very effective, you know. There are a lot of better ways. Although you don't look like you need to lose weight." Appearances could be misleading, Audra knew.

"I don't run to lose weight." Will looked baffled, as if running and losing weight were two unlinkable concepts.

"Then what for?"

"I——well, mainly because it makes me feel good. While I'm doing it, and after I'm done. And also because it's a habit, I guess. I've been doing it for . . . for a while. It connects me with myself. The way I am now with the way I used to be." He smiled, but the smile was surprisingly joyless. "I never thought about it like that. But I guess that's it."

"And that's a good thing? Being connected with the way you used to be?"

Once again, Will faltered. He looked up from tying his shoes as if he had suddenly forgotten what shoes were. "I guess it must be," he said softly. "I mean, I'm doing it, right?"

Since he seemed to be expecting an answer, Audra nodded. "Right. I've seen you do it."

"Anyway, it's probably a good idea." He ran his hand through his hair in a brisk, practical gesture. "With the job I have now, I don't get much exercise. I work in a store," he said, before she could ask. "Stereo equipment."

"What did you do before that?"

Will Finn shook his head as if he did not intend to answer, but then did. "Counselor. At a high school. I used to go out with the kids on field days sometimes. So I could count on some exercise every once in a while. What do you do?" he asked quickly.

"I don't work," Audra said.

"You're looking for a job?"

"Not really."

Three weeks after she had arrived in the city, Audra wrote to her parents, describing what she would be forced to do in order to support herself when she ran out of money. By then, she had seen enough to be quite detailed. The money—not a lot, but enough—had been arriving steadily ever since.

"You're an artist, then," Will said.

Audra considered this briefly. "Something like that, I guess."

Will nodded, satisfied. "Lots of artists here. Artists and crazy people."

"What's the difference?" Audra asked.

Will seemed to think she was joking. He smiled, but Audra did not smile back at him.

• • •

If she was an artist, her art was not very time-consuming. It left her with plenty of leisure and Audra took to spending part of it in the lobby of the Aurora Hotel. Surprisingly, the Aurora did have a lobby. Its windows were slightly below ground level, and consequently, it was in a constant state of dim, wintry light. The lobby included one frayed orange couch, three greenish armchairs, a coffee table, a large TV and a candy machine whose slot was jammed with some kind of metal chip someone had tried to pass off as a quarter.

Sophia Croff treated the lobby as her own private living room. At first, she had glared at Audra every time she found her settled into the armchair in the corner, watching whatever station the TV had been tuned to. But Audra merely stared back blankly, and after a while, Sophia took to ignoring her, and after that, she seemed to genuinely forget that Audra was there. Most of Sophia's guests followed her lead. It was not hard to ignore Audra. She did not fidget, she wore dark clothing and she usually did not interfere in other people's conversations.

All of Sophia's visitors were men, which made Audra remember something her mother had told her long ago: Never trust a woman with no female friends. The words had stuck in Audra's mind, though unreserved trust was not one of her problems.

Most of the men would visit the lobby either as a prelude or as an epilogue to their visits to Sophia's room on the fourth floor. The talk, in either case, was not very stimulating, as far as Audra was concerned. The preludes talked mainly in monosyllables. The epilogues mainly grunted. Sophia complained about the residents, her maintenance man, high expenses and low profits and the endless work of running a hotel. Audra had heard it all before.

The most interesting visitor was a man Sophia called Vic, with a sharp, raspy sound, like a match being lit. Vic reminded Audra of an evil cowboy, dyed, slicked and leathered in black. Audra had never seen him go up to Sophia's room. Although sex seemed to play some role in their relationship, the role was not obvious. Money also played some part in it, as did knowledge. The two of them often talked about what they knew.

"I know how you got that table," Vic said softly when Sophia told him to take his boots off it, not budging. "And the sofa. And the television.

And this place." He gestured inclusively with the red burning tip of the cigarette he held.

Sophia snorted. "You know. You know. And I knew how old they were, your little friends. But I gave you a room anyway."

Then they both laughed, Sophia loud, Vic smooth and stealthy.

Sometimes, when residents passed by on their way to the stairs, Sophia would give Vic a short summary of their essential traits and character flaws. "Gambler," she decreed in a low voice when she saw the man Audra knew as 221. Vic raised his eyebrows in interest, but Sophia shook her head. "Not cards. Games. Ball games on TV."

Another resident, a stooped balding man from the third floor, evoked a snort of derision from Sophia. "This one, he keeps pictures under the mattress. Naked pictures. Like he is twelve years old."

In her corner armchair, Audra nodded silently. The man, she knew, lived in the room directly above hers. She also knew at what time he liked to look at his pictures, and the exact pitch of the responses they evoked in him. This was the sort of intimacy that the acoustics of the Aurora created.

Occasionally, Sophia and Vic would lapse into a language that Audra did not understand. She did not think she was the reason for this. Sophia now seemed to regard her as one more inanimate feature of the lobby's decor, and Vic had rarely acknowledged her existence. It was something in the flow of the conversation that seemed to make them switch back to some older, shared dialect. English was comfortable enough, expressive enough, worn and thoughtless enough for most things. But not for everything.

Vic switched to this other tongue when he first saw Will Finn. Will was on his way back from work. His hair was wind-ruffled, his stride energetic and brisk. He waved a polite greeting to all of them as he walked toward the stairs. Vic raised a languorous hand in response, his eyes following Will up and then lingering on the place where he had been. The foreign tongue emerged briefly from his mouth to touch his upper lip, followed by a sly, low stream of incomprehensible words.

Sophia seemed amused at first. Her tone echoed his own; there was no need for Audra to understand her words in order to know the sort of thing she was saying. But then she grew serious. She shook her head fiercely, causing her thick black hair to fly around her, compressing her mouth into a starched little line. No, she said, several times, in her own language. She assailed Vic with something sharp and emphatic, an order or an admonition.

Vic asked a question, smiling, cool and knowing.

"Not yet," Sophia said. After a moment, she smiled, too. Her fingers, with their pointed, white-painted nails, gestured in the air as if marking a length of time, or stroking an invisible cat.

• • •

For lunch, Audra frequented Eternal Bliss, the Chinese restaurant she could see from her window. She would order one of the lunch specials, which consisted mostly of rice. Although Eternal Bliss provided its customers with plastic forks, Audra chose to eat her meal with chopsticks. She would hunt down the grains of rice one by one. For hours, she would manipulate them patiently, corner them into the appropriate position and deposit them carefully in her mouth. When she finished, her plate would appear almost untouched. The patterns of her rice picking had swept over it as ineffectually as a gentle breeze blowing through a field of wheat. And yet lunch had received an apt portion of the day. She had granted it a generous amount of time and effort. The question of food, always a loud and resonant one for Audra, had been addressed.

Will Finn also occasionally ate his lunch at Eternal Bliss. The first two times that his lunch break partially overlapped hers, he had not noticed her when he came in, and Audra, tucked dimly between the kitchen and the bathroom, had done nothing to attract his attention. She watched Will study the menu, converse briefly with the waitress, return the smile she offered. He had brought a newspaper with him, and he leafed through it while he waited for his food. When the meal arrived, he folded the paper and placed it on the chair opposite him. Like Audra, he chose the chopsticks over the plastic fork. But in his hands, they were not ingenious devices of procrastination. They darted over his plate with the grace and precision of two well-practiced dancers, adept at coordinating their steps. Audra watched the dance of the chopsticks like a burn victim watching a display of fireworks. Her lips parted slightly. The slow, antlike procession of grains of rice to her mouth stopped completely.

• • •

On the third time their visits to Eternal Bliss coincided, Will noticed Audra before she noticed him. She was sitting at one of the outside tables this time, taking in the sights and sounds of the world where she lived: a loud argument over a parking space, a street woman busily squirting her person and possessions with a large, silvery spray can, and a scruffy man dressed in layers of gray who was showering passersby with verbal abuse, with a consistency and dedication that Audra could not help admiring.

"Your boyfriend's cheating on you!" he was yelling at a girl in high heels, as Will Finn seated himself at Audra's table.

"You're taking a break, too?" he asked.

Audra made an ambiguous sound. She speared two grains of rice, squeezed them painfully between her chopsticks, and placed them on her tongue, where she let them linger for a while.

Will nodded. "I get half an hour for lunch. There are a couple of closer places, actually, but the food is terrible."

"And the food here?" Audra asked.

"Well, the rice is okay, and so are the vegetables. I'm a little wary about the meat, so I——" The waitress arrived and Will ordered. "So I usually go with something vegetarian," he concluded, once she had left.

Audra nodded. The meat that was part of her own lunch special was piled in a little fortress of tough-looking scraps at the side of her plate. She had fished them out with her chopsticks before she had even touched her rice.

"I probably should eat more meat, though," Will said. "And more vegetables. It's a problem when you eat out a lot." He looked at Audra's plate. "You probably should, too."

"I eat what I want to eat," Audra said.

Will did not seem taken aback. "Well, sure, you can eat anything you want, but if you're thinking about your health, and what's good for your——"

"That's why I came here. So I can eat whatever I want and sleep whenever I want and not talk to anyone I don't feel like talking to."

"You did it again today, right?" The scruffy man was now following two older women carrying plastic shopping bags, who did their best to steer away as quickly as possible without breaking into an actual run. "You left the gas on. You forgot to turn it off. Right? Right?"

"Right," Will said, as if softly answering him. "So you came to the right place. Everyone does their own thing, and nobody asks questions."

"They watch you, though," Audra said. "They're still watching you."

"I don't think they're watching." Will was shaking his head slowly. "Not really. And if they are, they've probably seen it before. They don't care that much." He looked at her, seeming almost to be imploring her for a confirmation. Audra shrugged.

The waitress arrived with Will's order, just as the scruffy man found another victim, a tall, stooped man shuffling by with an uneven gait.

"It's back," he called out to him with manic glee. "You're pretending it isn't, but it is. It's going to get you this time."

The tall man continued on his way with a blank expression.

"Hank," the waitress said, "if I give you an egg roll, will you take it over to Eddie's for a while?"

The scruffy man in gray turned toward her. "Billings," he said ominously. "That's where it happened. In Billings."

"Shut up about Billings. Now you're not getting anything." She turned and went back inside.

"Is that an artist or a crazy person?" Audra asked.

Will stared at her uncomprehendingly for a moment. Then he remembered. "I guess it's hard to tell sometimes," he said. "Maybe neither. Maybe both." His chopsticks performed their eloquent dance with the rice as Audra watched. "When I was training for my job—my old job—I learned a little about it. Mental illness. Going crazy. Whatever. And I thought I got it. I thought I understood. But I had a very abstract kind of attitude." He paused, looking down at his glass of water and then picking it up to sip absently. "I think I might have a better sense of it now," he said quietly. "I can imagine what it might feel like."

Audra nodded, saying nothing.

"Do you want my fortune cookie?" Will's plate was nearly empty. He was already turning over the white slip of paper that the waitress had placed by his plate on a little brown tray. The cookie lay beside it.

Audra shook her head. "I never open mine. I just throw it away. I don't like opening fortune cookies."

"Well, you can open this one. Because it won't be your fortune. It'll be mine."

"I don't care about the fortunes," Audra said. "I just don't like that sound they make when you break them open."

Will shrugged, a suit-yourself shrug. He placed money on the little tray, four dollars for the lunch special and a two-dollar tip. "I guess I'll see you back at the hotel, then." He smiled at her before he left, and Audra flashed something back, something that might have been a smile. She watched Will step out toward the road and pause at the stoplight. The man in gray was approaching him slowly. And then a small black van turned the corner and drove by, and Will Finn stepped back blindly, as if he were trying to retreat into the wall. He stumbled and almost fell, and this sudden awkwardness was so foreign that it had Audra craning forward in her seat, alert and coiled.

Will recovered his balance almost immediately. He turned back toward her with a shaky, apologetic smile. "I thought—I don't know what I thought."

His face had gone slightly whiter, all except for his lower lip, which looked unnaturally red, as if he had just bitten down on it, involuntarily and hard.

By then, the man in gray had reached him. He drew closer to Will than he had to any of the others, and Will did nothing to stop him. He seemed to be waiting for the man to reach him.

"They found you," the man said, almost kindly.

"No," said Will Finn.

The man the waitress had called Hank nodded emphatically. "They found you. They're not done with you yet."

Will Finn stepped out into the street. A passing car honked at him and screeched to an unnecessarily abrupt stop. Will gestured to the driver, apologizing or perhaps thanking her for not running him over, and hurried to cross to the other side.

Audra watched him until he was gone. This happened much more quickly than when she was looking down on him from her second-floor window. When she could no longer see him, she played with the rice on her plate for a while, but she had lost interest in the chopstick game.

After a moment, she picked up the fortune cookie. Holding it well away from her, as if defusing a bomb, she cracked it open with one determined motion of her thumbs, wincing as she did, wincing again at the dry, slithery worm whisper the tiny slip of paper inside the cookie emitted as she extracted it.

"Friends long absent are coming back to you" was what the fortune said. This message was typed between two small, blue, round faces, both smiling widely.

•   •   •

Audra was not expecting any visits from long-absent friends. She had never had many friends, anyway, though there had been some girls she had been friendly with. She had met most of these girls in hospitals and had become friendly with them because they had a lot in common. Together, they schemed and complained and compared notes and tactics. Silently, fiercely, they competed, using one another's fluctuations to assess their own progress, like balancing weights on an old-fashioned scale. Some of these girls were now dead, but Audra was not expecting any visits from the live ones either. These were not the sort of girls who tended to keep in touch.

In fact, except for the occasional check from her parents, there was not much to connect Audra to the place she had come from. She liked the idea of traveling light. Except for her basic wardrobe, all of which could be fitted into her one floppy blue denim bag, there were only a few prized possessions.

Audra unzipped her bag and took these out shortly after she returned from her long lunch at Eternal Bliss. Some of the prized possessions were mementos from home. They had heavy, ornamental handles decorated with small, dainty flowers, and smart, reliable blades. The others, in their little plastic bottles, were less impressive at first sight. But they made a friendly, welcoming rattling sound as Audra held them affectionately in her hands, eggs from which chicks might someday hatch, warm and comfortingly heavy with potential.

• • •

"I have a letter for you," Sophia Croff told Will Finn as he passed through the lobby on his way toward the stairs.

From her habitual chair in the corner, Audra had a good view of Will's face as he received the news. The familiar clearness of his features was unmarred as he shook his head.

"Must be a mistake. It's probably for the previous occupant."

"It has your name on it. Look." Sophia waited until Will stepped closer, closer still. Then she rose and languidly produced the letter from one of the deep pockets of the wine-colored wool cardigan she was wearing. Will held out his hand, but Sophia was not ready to relinquish the letter just yet. She extended a precise fingernail to underline the name of the addressee. "William Finn. That is you, right?"

Will nodded. "That's my name, but I didn't give this address to——" He grew abruptly silent, his forehead nearly touching Sophia's as they conferred over the letter. "Could I see that, please?"

"It is from——" Sophia tilted the letter with a leisurely gesture. "Professional Recovery Services. Do you know who that is?"

"Can I see the letter please, Sophia?"

To Audra, it appeared as if Will finally had to tug the letter forcefully out of Sophia's hand. He looked down at it and nodded once. "Thanks," he said, and turned back toward the stairs, holding the letter in his left hand.

"Aren't you going to open it?" Sophia asked innocently, still standing in the place where he had left her.

"Later," he said without turning back, his voice muffled, as if, by some typical trick of the Aurora's acoustics, it was arriving from another floor, somewhere far above or below them.

"Recovery." Sophia repeated the word to herself. "Do you think he is sick?"

It took Audra several moments to figure out that the question was directed at her. Sophia was not looking in her direction, but still facing the stairs, which were now empty. Will had that effect on people, Audra had noticed; something of him seemed to linger behind even after he was gone.

"He looks pretty healthy to me," she told Sophia.

"That's true, but you can't always tell, right?" Sophia's profile crinkled in perturbation or distaste. "Sometimes, they look all right on the outside, but on the inside——" she rolled her shoulders in an expressive gesture. "What can you do, then?"

"You can stay away from them," Audra said.

Sophia turned toward her. "*You* can, maybe," she said after a moment. Then she laughed, long and jagged, like feathers being ruffled the wrong way.

• • •

The next day was grim and windy, and Will Finn, in his T-shirt and shorts, looked newly vulnerable. He did not hunch his shoulders or put his arms around his body to protect himself from the cold, but Audra, vigilant at her second-story post, sensed a new acknowledgment of the weather in his stance. The winds could sway him more easily now, the rain could penetrate the veneer of his thin clothes, the frost could sink long, yellow, numbing teeth into the perfectly formed toes Audra imagined flexing in his white sneakers. He jogged in place for the customary five minutes, causing Audra to nod once in approval; she was fond of routines, particularly this routine. But then, instead of turning right, he paused suddenly on the sidewalk, his head jerking sharply to look up and down the street. Then, in a swift move marked by the inelegance of an abrupt decision, he turned left at the corner of Fairfax Street, causing Audra to lose sight of him almost immediately.

• • •

She was not surprised to discover that Sophia had chosen that particular day as appropriate for changing Will's sheets. Audra was alerted to her presence on the floor by the distinct jangle of keys, just beyond the bend in the corridor, shortly after nine in the morning. Audra gave her several minutes, then wandered outside her own room, not bothering to close the door after her.

Sophia had not bothered to close the door to Will's room, either. The pale green sheets and pillowcases that provided justification for her presence (although she clearly did not expect to have to justify her presence to anyone) were strewn in a careless pile on Will's neatly made bed. Sophia was standing by the window, squinting at Will's letter. She looked up in irritation at the faint squeal that the door emitted as Audra entered the room.

"What do you want?" She sounded weary more than angry, a woman used to negotiations and compromises.

Audra shrugged. "Thought I'd see if you needed any help here. With the sheets." Sophia did not deem this worthy of more than a brief snort. She stared down at the letter for a while longer. Then she thrust it brusquely at Audra. "I don't understand this. I don't speak this language."

Audra looked down at the printed page. The letters were slightly smudged, somehow unclean. Will's name and address, including his room number, were printed at the top. The letter opened abruptly, without even the most superficial display of cordiality. "Despite repeated demands on our part," it read, "you have yet to settle your outstanding debt to our client's satisfaction. Any additional delay in settling said debt will result in our proceeding with further collection treatment. Please contact our office within the next seven days in order to——"

Sophia snatched the letter from Audra's hand again. "It is about money, yes?" she said more than asked.

Audra shook her head slowly. "I don't speak this language, either."

"Money," Sophia said again, more confidently. She bent her head to study the letter again. Audra watched a dense smile bubble to the surface of her face. Sophia looked up, but Audra's gaze did not waver. After a moment, Sophia refolded the letter, returned it to its envelope and placed the envelope on the low, round table. She studied the envelope briefly, turned it over and nodded, satisfied. Then she turned toward Audra again and gestured with her chin toward Will Finn's bed.

"You wanted to help with the sheets? So help with the sheets."

For a long while after Sophia had left the room, Audra continued to stand in place, very still. When she moved, her joints shifted into gear with a creak of protest that seemed to echo momentously in Will's empty room. She knelt down next to the bed, sorting through the pale green linen with cautious, skeptical hands. It did not seem particularly dirty, nor particularly fresh. Attached to one of the sheets, she found a little tag that said "St. Mary's" in someone's neat cursive handwriting. Audra let the pale green sheet fall from her hands. She hoisted herself up to sit on the bed, and leaned over to take Will's pillow. The intimacy of slipping her hand between pillow and pillowcase filled her head with a momentary dizziness. She stripped the pillow slowly, gently, as if it were a fragile, bashful creature.

When Will Finn entered his room about two hours later, the bed was made. Audra was standing by the table, idly running her finger along the edge of the envelope from Professional Recovery Services, which had been opened in a precise, straight line, probably with a knife. Will Finn stared for a moment.

"I took half a day off from work," he said, as if it was his own presence, and not hers, that required an explanation. "I told them I thought I was coming down with something."

•   •   •

"It's a girl. A woman," he corrected himself. "She was more of a girl when I met her. And it's not about money. She thinks—she feels I made her a promise and broke it. She's saying I misled her."

"Did you?" Audra asked.

"Not intentionally." Will paused. "I never promised her anything explicitly. I never meant to. But I think I understand now how she could have interpreted it that way. Although I'm not sure what I could have done differently, without being cruel in another way. I apologized. More than once. But that's not enough. That's not what she wants."

"What does she want?"

Will Finn shook his head. "She hired this agency, and . . . they won't leave me alone. I had to leave my job. My friends, my apartment, the city where I was living. I thought they would be satisfied. But they're not. She's not." His eyes, which had been fixed on the envelope lying in his lap, turned to Audra briefly. "I can't give her what she wants. I can't." He looked down again, turning the envelope in his hands. "And . . . I've got nothing left now. Nothing."

Audra's eyes surveyed him starkly. "You don't know what nothing is."

"You're right," Will said immediately. "I shouldn't be talking like that. There are people living on the streets out there——"

Audra shook her head impatiently. "I'm not talking about that. I'm not talking about *things*."

"What, then?"

Audra shrugged. "About nothing," she said softly. "That's what I'm talking about. Nothing."

"I don't know what you mean," Will said, resigned.

Audra nodded. "Right."

A joyless half smile flicked across Will's face. He rose from the floor, where he had been sitting beside her, leaning against the bed, to survey the room. "I was going to just pack everything and get out of here," he told her. "That's why I left work early. I can be packed and gone in twenty minutes. It won't be a problem to find another hotel."

Go, said a silent voice in Audra's throat loudly. Leave. Run. It works, at least for a while.

Somewhere lower, blind and mindless, something clenched violently.

What she said, impassive, was, "What for? If they found you once, they'll find you again."

Will nodded, and the weight of the gesture seemed to move through him like a bolt of gravity, seating him heavily on the bed, bending his head, trimming away at his vitality like the shears of an efficient gardener.

● ● ●

When she did not close her door completely at night, the crack between the door and the frame let the light of the hall's nighttime illumination into Audra's room. On the evening of her conversation with Will Finn, shortly after ten o'clock, it also let in the sound of Sophia's return to the second floor. In her off-duty hours, Sophia wore clogs with wooden soles that made an emphatic sound against the thin carpet in the halls. Audra traced the advance of the clogs as they drew nearer and then passed her room without pausing. She noted the exact moment when the clogs turned the corner of the corridor.

"You are awake?" Sophia asked, somewhere beyond the corner, as she knocked loudly and turned the knob at the same time. The reply was muffled by the creak of the closing door.

In her own room, Audra was lying on her back, one wrist tucked under her head. This pose was beginning to affect her circulation. The blood hummed and tingled in protest as it tried to make its way to her hand and fingers. A similar, speedier effect could be achieved with a rubber band, or a clothespin.

Audra was thinking about Will Finn's bed. Although the bed was essentially no different from her own, Audra had had a sort of vision about it as she was changing Will's sheets earlier that day. She had seen herself lying in Will's bed, on her back, as she was lying now, her hair streaming out around her, sleeping in a way she could never remember actually sleeping. It was a Snow White sleep, placid and dreamless. It was the sort of sleep you sank into effortlessly, with no external aids or internal tactics. It was the sort of sleep you had to be shaken out of, and even that might not do the trick. It was so still, so sweet, you might never want to wake up again.

No sleep of any sort seemed to be awaiting her now. Restless, Audra rose and slipped out into the corridor. The perfunctory carpet rasped against her bare feet. The Aurora seemed to shimmer with a heavier, nocturnal breathing. Outside the door to Will Finn's room, the abandoned wooden clogs lay suspended in a small victory dance, one of them pointing straight ahead, the other tilted drunkenly on its side.

Audra raised the still-pulsing hand that had been trapped behind her head and brought it closer to her eyes. In the dim, bluish light, it was impossible to see if the hand showed any signs of the little adventure it had undergone. But the blood was keenly felt, rushing urgently to reassert itself, buzzing warmly like something live. So much blood, flooding the tips of her fingers. Despite her best efforts, still, so much flesh and blood.

● ● ●

The smell in the lobby almost drove Audra away as soon as she entered. A thick, red, meaty smell, made even more obscene by the thin, mocking camouflage of spices. Its source, she saw, drawing closer almost despite herself, were the plates that Sophia and Vic were holding in their laps. But in the static space of the insulated lobby, it was everywhere. The air itself seemed weighed down with near-visible particles of the plump pinkish slabs and the clotted brown sauce which coated them. Breathing through her mouth, as sparingly as if the air were being filtered through a thin tube inserted between her lips, Audra made her way to her usual armchair.

"I'm always hungry," Sophia was saying to Vic, dismissing some earlier comment of his with a wave of her hand and the fork it was holding.

"But more hungry today," he insisted, placid.

"No."

"Yes." Vic's teeth revealed themselves briefly underneath his black mustache, sharp, white and carnivorous. "You feast at night, you will be hungry in the daytime."

"You know me." Sophia's tongue flicked out to lash at a drop of brown sauce suspended at the corner of her lips. "I have feasts in the night, I have feasts in the day. . . ."

"But this is different. This is . . . young blood." With no warning, Vic turned toward Audra and smiled, as if something in this comment had suddenly incited him to notice her at last, perhaps even to invite her to partake in the conversation. She retreated into her chair as far as she could. In Vic's lap, the heavy meat sizzled silently with an obscene pink leer. "It gives you a good appetite, yes?"

Sophia laughed. "Why are you asking me? You know all about young blood. You are the expert."

Vic acknowledged this with a modest bow of his head. His darkly shining eyes had flicked back toward Audra again. "Do you have any food for your little guest?" he asked Sophia.

"What?" She stared at him blankly until he projected a lazy thumb toward Audra.

"I don't want any," Audra said, shaking her head emphatically. For a moment, she had forgotten to breathe through her mouth, and the smell assailed her again, making her head spin with a thrust of nausea as vivid as a stroke of lightning between her eyes.

"I don't feed the guests," Sophia said, sounding disgusted by the very idea. "The guests can feed themselves."

"You feed me."

"I give you——" Sophia groped for the word. "Leftovers." She nodded, pleased. "When I am done with it, you can have it."

"Really?" Vic smiled, leaning forward in his seat.

"Maybe." Sophia rolled her shoulders, suddenly petulant.

Audra could feel Vic's eyes following her as she rose to leave, taking care to maintain her distance from both of them, as if expecting a sudden jab from one of their forks.

"Do you starve all of them like that?" he asked as she was leaving the room.

Audra did not catch the low murmur of Sophia's answer.

"No," Vic said in reply. "It's good. I like it."

• • •

Will Finn was late the next morning, a fact which Audra took almost as a personal insult. She had, after all, been standing by her window and waiting for him for nearly half an hour. When he arrived, at last, at five to eight, the renewed familiarity of him was enough to soothe her for a while. She surveyed him closely as he stood jogging just outside the Aurora, the white T-shirt clinging damply to the small of his back, the gray-blue socks climbing smartly up his ankles, the fair hair framing his face with careless ease, ruffled occasionally by the wind. Everything seemed to be in place. If Audra did sense a brief, atypical jerkiness in his motions, it was gone by the time he set off for his run along the usual track. Her eyes followed him for as long as they could track him, past Eternal Bliss, the St. Elliott, the closed doors of a bar called Ken's Den. Will was running smoothly. He turned his head sharply toward the road once, twice at the most.

Audra herself was not quite back on track. The smells and echoes of yesterday lingered heavily somewhere in her sinus cavities. She did not go out for lunch. Instead, she plunged into her stash of prized possessions and picked out several pills with careful, loving care. Once the selection had been completed, she let them nestle in her hand for a while. The hand was cool and dry; the pills did not grow damp or sticky. One by one, she put them in her mouth and sucked on them slowly. The bitterness was good; it pervaded her gradually, like a stream of cold air filtering into a large space. Audra could feel it coating her body from the inside with a thin insulating layer of acrid frosting. Everything on the outside grew dimmer and less urgent. This was how she passed the next two days, in a dim, cool, bitter haze.

By the afternoon of the third day, she was ready to venture out to the lobby again. Sophia was there, alone, watching TV; the set was radiating a consistent soundtrack of self-indulgent laughter. Sophia was not laughing.

"Where I come from," she said, seeming to direct her comment toward a larger audience than just Audra, perched in her pale green armchair, "if you talk to your parents like that, they slap you. Like this." She thwacked the side of the couch expressively.

"I'm glad I don't live where you come from," Audra said.

Sophia made a sound, which seemed to convey something like "you should be." For a while, they watched the show in silence.

Will Finn came in as the titles were rolling. He wandered toward them, pausing uncertainly just outside the frayed carpet that marked the boundaries of the lobby. "It's raining," he said, and Audra noticed the wet lashes crisscrossing his buttondown shirt.

Sophia gestured him closer with an intimate flick of her wrist. "Next time, you tell me when you invite the phone company here, right?" she said, making the words sound flirtatious, like a secret lovers' code.

"What?" Will's forehead was briefly creased. His glance wandered to Audra, as if expecting an explanation.

"Those people from the phone company were here. To install your line."

"To install my line," Will repeated.

"Right." Sophia leaned forward in her seat. Her hand reached out to touch Will's jaw lingeringly. "It's all right," she said, soft and somehow lewdly maternal. "You can have a phone, if you are staying for a while. But you should let me know, yes?"

"Yes," Will said. Then he turned and went upstairs.

Audra waited through the commercials and the next show's theme song before following him. The door of his room was open, as if he were waiting for her, or someone else. Will was standing by the round table; his cassette cases were neatly arranged around the empty space where the tape deck used to stand.

"Look," he told Audra, handing her one of the cases.

Audra looked. The cassette was still in its box. She was momentarily distracted by the sight of Will's handwriting, detailing its content in clear, legible script. It took her a moment to notice that the actual magnetic tape had been meticulously removed from the cassette. It was now no more than a useless plastic shell.

"They're all like that?"

Will nodded. He wandered over to the other side of the room and knelt by the bed, lifting the edge of the cover up to look under it. "They took the books, too," he commented matter-of-factly. "And I had some letters, and a kind of journal here——" he kneeled lower, making sure. "They took those, too."

"They didn't take the TV," Audra observed. She turned it on, then immediately off again.

"Right," Will said with a smile Audra had no way of interpreting.

"They left you another letter," she told him. She had just noticed it, lying on top of the previous one.

Will walked over to the table, and with an understated, economic gesture, tore the unopened letter from Professional Recovery Services once, then twice, then three times.

"It doesn't matter anymore," he told Audra. "They can have whatever they want now. I don't care. I don't."

Audra nodded her acceptance of this.

Will smiled his indecipherable smile again. "Actually," he said softly, "I'd almost like to see them try. I'd almost like to see them try and take anything from me from now on."

• • •

Standing at her window, facing the bustling, empty street at seven thirty A.M., and then at seven forty-five, and then at eight, Audra resolved to start getting up later. This was not an effortless feat. Her body was accustomed to its own rhythms. At seven, invisible springs would snap her eyes open like a china doll's. A futile, relentless nervous energy would course through her with an almost audible humming, urging her up, out of bed, into coiled, alert verticality. But Audra was used to overruling her body's sporadic displays of willpower; this was, after all, only the last battle in a long, ongoing, bloody war which Audra was used to winning. She knew all the tricks. She played dirty. When necessary, she was more than prepared to use unconventional warfare, biological and chemical weapons of all kinds. Gradually, she extended the duration of her night into previously unknown realms: eight thirty, nine A.M. and beyond, into the dim sheltered brightness of winter noons, sun straining weakly against the clouds like something left waiting too long.

Perhaps, in his room beyond the corner, Will Finn was also adjusting his circadian rhythms. Brushing her hair by the window one morning, a short time after ten, Audra saw him returning from his run. Will paused before entering the Aurora, jogging in place, breathing heavily, squinting as if the light were hurting his eyes. Audra opened her door and ventured out to the corridor to wait for him.

Will seemed glad to see her. "Hi," he said. "I wasn't sure you were still here. I haven't seen you in a while."

Audra examined him briefly, noting no obvious physical changes. "Aren't you going to be late for work?" she asked. "I'm not working anymore," Will said. Audra nodded, casual. "What about money? The rent and stuff like that?"

"I'm not paying rent anymore, either," Will said, trying for matter-of-factness but falling short along the way. He looked at Audra, shrugged, looked down, smiled, touched her shoulder in a brief, friendly gesture of parting, then walked past her on his way to his own room.

Audra remained in the corridor for a moment longer, listening. She listened as if she could take in the whole of the Aurora with a single tilt of her head, determine exactly how many people were present at a given moment, identify which of them were in their rooms and which were not, pinpoint the location of any person she was looking for. In fact, it was a while before she managed to find Sophia. She had to traverse the whole second floor and part of the third before she found her in room 312, smoking one of the absent tenant's cigarettes.

"He leaves chocolate in his drawers," Sophia told her when she turned to see Audra standing in the doorway, as if continuing a conversation that had been briefly interrupted. "There will be ants everywhere. Look."

Audra looked. There was, indeed, a half-unwrapped bar of chocolate lying in one of the drawers, nestled between the man's yellowy-white undershirts. Sophia nodded once and blew an emphatic stream of smoke in the general direction of the window, as if she had just been vindicated.

"So what about those no-rent deals?" Audra said.

Sophia turned toward her, raising an eyebrow, waiting.

"You think I could get me one of those?" Audra asked. "Somewhere?"

Sophia's eyes mapped her slowly, from the dusky toes of her bare feet, to her brittle, breakable ankles, the thin hollow tubes of her legs, her bony torso, twiggy arms covered by ribbed black cloth, eyes staring too directly from a raw, stark face under dull, dark hair.

"You could try," Sophia said with a small shrug, managing to convey quite eloquently exactly what she thought Audra's chances of success were.

● ● ●

The last time Audra saw Will Finn was a grimy, hooded dawn. Something had sparked her awake, shooting forth from the rumbling core of hollow that she had been nurturing more intensely in the past few weeks, like a small flame feeding on the marrow of her bones. In the early light, she was suddenly buoyant and wide awake. The feverish haze of the last few days grew fiercely animating, like a new form of energy, propelling her out of bed and toward the window.

The mood of the street seemed as foreign as her own. The stores and restaurants were still closed, their iron shutters looking like heavy lids gummed shut by the thick, gray light. Two tall, dark men were conducting a negotiation of some sort outside Eddie's, seeming unnaturally placid and leisurely. In the recessed doorway of Ken's Den, a figure muffled by numerous layers of cloth lay sprawled on the ground like a giant cocoon. On the opposite sidewalk, Will Finn was walking toward the Aurora with slow, cautious steps. Audra watched him draw closer. Then, silent as a ghost in the oversize gray sweatshirt and white cotton shorts she slept in, she left her room and glided down the stairs.

Will's face was covered with a fine layer of sandy stubble. His white shirt was creased as if he had slept in it, but his eyes were shining with an almost painful wakefulness. His hair was springing stiffly from the back of his head, as if it had recently undergone some shock. His steps were tentative, as though, under his feet, the ground were performing a demanding, hungry dance. Examining him slowly, exhaustively, Audra experienced a brief spurt of perverse, malevolent hope, like a deep pinprick just below her collarbone. And because she knew it did not truly matter, because she had grown used to speaking her mind, she explained it to Will.

"You look like I feel," she told him.

"Right now?" Will asked, his eyes careening momentarily before they focused on her face.

"All the time," Audra said. "Like I feel all the time."

"Poor you," Will said, his voice tender, commiserating. Audra shrugged. "Do you mind if we sit down?" he asked. She shook her head. The concrete steps of the Aurora were comfortingly cold and hard beneath the thin fabric of her shorts. Beside her, Will was distantly, quietly warm. His arms were wrapped around his knees.

"I was at a party," he said after a while. "It was really . . . long. Really long." He rubbed his hand across his eyes. "Do you know that guy Vic? Sophia's friend?"

"I've met him a couple of times," Audra said. She waited, but Will said no more. Together, they watched the scruffy human cocoon on the other side of the road lumber to its feet with a single flap of dark wings and stalk heavily down the road.

"You know what?" Will said. "I never asked you what kind of artist you were."

Audra considered this for a moment. "I'm——I think it's called a body artist?" She had heard the phrase a while back and had liked it immediately, though, until hearing Will's question, she had never linked it to herself.

Will nodded, seeming satisfied. They were sitting in companionable silence when the black van pulled up next to them with a loud screech of its brakes. Neither of them moved as its two front doors opened simultaneously to discharge two triangular, bullet-headed men, whose lack of expression was so similar they could have been brothers.

Will rose slowly as one of the men strode toward him. The other lingered behind to open the back door of the van. As Audra watched, a woman emerged from the vehicle in a graceful sequence of black, heeled pumps. The sleek bob of her hair trembled prettily as she strode toward Will Finn, whose arm was now in the hold of one of the blank-faced men.

"Beat it, lady," the man said, turning back toward Audra, just as his associate said, "Scram, kid."

Audra did neither. Instead, she rose and followed Will and the first man as they commenced to meet the woman from the van halfway.

The woman stepped closer, closer still, until Audra could feel the heat of the woman's breath on Will's face. Berry-flesh lipstick and bruised eye shadow had been draped over the youthfulness of her face like a veil. Her eyes were bright as a broken bottle catching the sun. They flickered toward Audra, then, with thoughtless dismissal, turned back toward Will.

"You owe me," she said, her voice jagged and unappeasable. "You still owe me. You do." She stepped back, turning to the second man, who was still standing beside her. "Go on. Do it."

Audra approached Will as the two men flanked him. By now, it seemed, she truly had become invisible. Neither of the bullet-headed men uttered any objection. No reflection of her presence could be found in Will Finn's eyes.

The first man peered into Will's face, shaking him, almost experimentally. Will's expression was impassive, his body limp and unresisting. The man exchanged a brief glance with his partner, then turned toward the woman, whose stance was taut with hungry expectation.

"It's no good," he said flatly.

"What do you mean, it's no good?" She tossed her head wildly, impatiently.

"I mean, it's no use. There's no point doing it now. Someone's already collected here. There's nothing left."

The second man nodded in confirmation. He had already let go of Will and was wiping his hands clean in a weary, disgusted gesture. "He's right. Look for yourself if you don't believe us."

Her mouth pursed in a thin, crimson line of frustration, the woman drew closer, as the two men stepped out of her way. Audra, too, stepped forward, unhindered, unnoticed. She watched the woman station herself just opposite Will, her face hovering so close to his that, for a moment, it seemed as if she was going to kiss him. But she did not touch him. For a long, dead moment, her eyes bore into his. Then she nodded slowly.

"Okay," she said softly. "That's it, then. We're even now."

• • •

In the dusky comfort of her room, Audra unpacked her prized possessions and assembled them on the bed around her. The last few weeks had diminished their ranks considerably, and even the ones that remained were reduced in potency, birthday presents that had been unwrapped and displayed too often.

Audra picked up one of the little pill bottles, shook it softly, returned it to its place. She replaced it with one of the ornamental knives. Shifting up the thick gray sleeve of her sweatshirt, she applied the knife in a single, deft stroke. The resulting line blossomed like a new, tentative branch, sprouting, red and raw, from a gnarled old trunk. Its precise, elegant curve was as gentle as that of an embryo, or a question mark. Audra sat and stared at it for the longest time.

Fishboy

by MATT MCINTOSH

2001

Shortly before I turned eighteen, my dad drove me across the country to begin a college career in fisheries at a less-than-half-rate school in Nebraska, fisheries being a field that at the time I believed was the source of all true knowledge. No matter what the source was, or is, I wasn't having any luck getting into four-year schools, and, not too long before graduation, I received a letter in the mail offering me the opportunity to enroll. I didn't remember applying, actually. But things had not been going well for me at all, and when this school said they wanted me to come and, yes, they did offer classes in fisheries, I thought someone in this world of sorrow had finally been born with good sense and that I'd better go.

I hadn't seen the old man for a long time before our drive because there'd been a night when the girl he'd been sleeping with had showed up on our porch with a suitcase in her hand and nowhere to go. There was a big and very loud row, during which my mother—a woman who honestly hadn't been in her right mind for a long time—was, in spirit at least, wounded mortally. She was doped up on a mixture of Valium and alcohol and this probably should have served to deflect the brunt of the wound; but when she answered the door and that girl started talking, I think something inside her broke. Whatever that string is that holds a person together, it snapped. She came to life for a second and screamed her head off—she made a high-pitched shrieking sound I could hear from my younger brother's room—and then she stopped; she stopped yelling, then stopped talking and wouldn't start again. My dad left us that night and disappeared for a long time. She upped her intake, spending all her time in front of the television or shuffling around the house, holding on to pieces of furniture or my brother's head to keep herself steady. It was heartbreaking, really.

This wasn't the only reason I was troubled that year, or the reason I ended up where I did, but it did tend to complicate things. There were other significant components. I had developed an obsessive preoccupation with a girl at school two years younger than me named Emily Swanson. Also significant, I was suffering from an irrational but very real fear of paralysis. I was afraid I might cross the street one day and something crippling would happen—a car would come barreling around the corner, say, and send me into orbit. Maybe something would fall on me—a block of ice from the wing of a plane—and shatter my spine. Or I'd be forced into a situation where it would be the heroic thing to do to throw myself in front of a runaway train to save a girl, always a particular girl, from harm. The train would break from the tracks at a speed of more than one hundred miles an hour, and I, close by, would ponder: Should I throw myself in harm's way for her?—when in my imagination I would hold off the train, stopping it for a moment in its tracks to give me more time to decide (I could only hold it off for so long). Could I save her? Should I save her? When this situation would unfold in my mind, the girl was, ten times out of ten, Emily Swanson.

My dad and I drove straight through and arrived on a Monday. There wasn't much to the town, just a few stores down the main strip, a bank, a movie theater showing two films that had come and gone from my town months before. No one was around. There was a ghost-town feel to the place that unsettled me. My dad smiled and pointed. What he wouldn't give to live in a rustic place like this one. This is how life used to be, Will. You don't see this anymore.

We found my apartment a few blocks away. I'd taken it sight unseen— the basement of a run-down pre–industrial era house. We walked through piles of leaves, down the stairs at the side of the front porch and into what was going to be, from here on in, my new home. I took one look and my heart sank.

"What do you think?" my dad said.

It was essentially one large room with a kitchen against one wall to the right as you walked in, a row of windows facing the kitchen, and a couch and an alcove with a bed to the left. The paint on the walls was peeling and dingy, the tile floor had dips and little holes in it, the low ceiling was made worse by a network of forehead-level pipes, and the kitchen reminded me—down to the huge metal sinks—of the old moldy kitchens where I would wash dishes with the ladies at sixth-grade camp.

"It's crap," I said. "It's a piece-of-crap shithole." I ducked into the bathroom and locked the door behind me, staring at the red painted floor while my dad unloaded the car.

And my dad, who was a good guy, really—a good guy who had become fed up with his family, with his life, and had decided to make a break for it—spent the next five days fixing up the place. He cleaned and painted the walls and doors. He bought me blankets, tablecloths to cover what scant furniture there was, matching towels and dish sets, rugs to cover the floor, fans to combat the heat, a new bed; he filled the refrigerator with food, redid the wiring, bought three stand-up lamps and handed me two hundred bucks to start a bank account. He set up my fish tank, an old thirty-gallon number, on a small coffee table that he bought at a department store and used heavy-duty hooks and wires to position a mirror above my bed at an angle so that I could lie on my back and watch the reflection of the tank and close my eyes and fall asleep without moving a muscle.

After five days, he packed up his things into his duffel bag and sat down next to me on the bed. He put his hand on my shoulder and I knew he was about to get at something.

"I'm sorry, Will," he said. "I'm sorry about what happened. It wasn't fair on you boys. It's just—goddamn it," he said. "I'm really lonely, Will." And then he started to cry.

I sat and watched in amazement until, after about a minute, he blew his nose into his handkerchief, wiped his eyes and said, in a dejected tone, "Your mother's not well, Will. She's not."

This struck me as a departure. "She's all right," I said.

"No," he said. "She's not. I'm sorry but she's not. She needs help."

"She's fine," I said. "You're the one who's not fine, Dad."

The truth was my mother was far from fine and hadn't been fine for a long time. She had tried, when I was younger, to understand the circumstances of what she felt had always been wrong with her but could never quite put her finger on. She read books. She bought tapes. She sought professionals and listened to them. They took her back to the source. That is to say, she came to understand herself perfectly, and over the next few years she began to sink deeper into pills and alcohol as a means of coping with that understanding. By the time I left for Nebraska, she'd very nearly lost her mind.

"You're the one who needs help, Dad," I said. And then I told him some things I would regret. I told him I didn't care about anything, not about him, not about my mother, not what he did to my apartment or where he slept or how many girls he fucked. I said I didn't care that he had disappeared for so long. I didn't care that he hadn't called, or visited, or checked on us. I said I was glad I hadn't had to see his face. I told him that I really didn't give a crap about any of it and I'd had a shitty time driving to Nebraska with him and I wished he'd disappear again and leave me alone, let me get the hell on with my life. I could tell it hurt him tremendously. He told me he was very sorry I felt that way and then he picked up his bag and left.

When I heard his car drive away, I walked outside, up the stairs onto the front lawn. It was evening and the sun was gone and the stars were beginning to show up for the night. I watched the red taillights get smaller as he drove back down that road, back toward Washington and his apartment by the airport. I watched those lights for as long as I could, but then they went down something and disappeared. I poked at the enormous cold sore that had attached itself to my mouth as we'd driven into town. I cleared my throat a few times. I spit a big loogy onto the grass and walked back downstairs.

I picked up my notepad and wrote: *The O.M. started bawling. Drove away back home. Good riddance.* I lay on my bed and stared up at my fish tank. My angelfish hovered off to one side, staring out of the glass, making gasping motions with her mouth, and my four remaining goldfish swam awkwardly on the other side. Occasionally one would hover over the ceramic caste, or float near the bottom, a skin's width away from the rocks. This made me feel terrible for some reason. I went into the bathroom and put some Neosporin on the corner of my mouth. I put a large Band-Aid over the whole length of my mouth and looked at myself in the mirror. Then I lay down on my bed again and closed my eyes.

But as I was lying on my bed with the Band-Aid over my mouth, I heard something very real, something that had nothing to do with imagination. First leaves crackling. Then slow and heavy footsteps from the stairway outside my door. I turned my ear. My fish turned toward the door. The footsteps clopped their way down and stopped at the bottom. For a few moments nothing happened. I could hear myself breathing, the fish tank bubbling. We waited for what might happen next.

The door exploded. A white light filled the room, then a yellow light, then a red light, and a sonic boom, followed by a series of high-pitched screeching sounds. From the opening in the doorway, a long red flame burst in and split the room in half. A tall man walked in. Dressed in a black bodysuit and a gold fireman's mask. He held a shiny gold flamethrower.

He walked around my apartment and, slowly, methodically, began to light everything on fire. He opened the refrigerator and stepped back. He pulled the trigger and with a roar the inside went up in flames. He walked into the bathroom, there was a whooshing sound, I saw a glow. Then he came back in, walked across the carpet, and stood in front of me. He spoke words, deep and thunderous but unintelligible behind the fireman's mask. Then he turned back to the rest of the apartment and fired again. The drapes went up and the walls and then the floor, and the fire raged to the ceiling.

I was terrified—I was trembling with fear. When I made up my mind to move—and what I was going to do, I have no idea—flee, most probably—I'm sure if I could have I would have dashed through the flames, ducked beneath the burning doorframe and run off into the fields—when I made up my mind to move, I couldn't. It was as if someone had tied me to the bed, or given my entire body a case of lockjaw. I could only stare up at the mirror. I watched, petrified, as the man in black walked over to my fish tank and sprayed it with flame—*whoosh!*—the water boiled and my fish burst their seams. The water turned red. I closed my eyes. He came over to the bed and opened them. Shook an angry finger at me. I closed my eyes again, and when I opened them a few seconds later, his monstrous back was passing slowly through the doorway. The flames trailed him like the train of a robe.

The light on the other side of the door went out. The room became very quiet, slightly chilly—no trace of what had just happened, no fire, no smoke, only me on my bed staring up at my fish tank, scratching at my cold sore through the Band-Aid.

• • •

Emily Swanson. I had, by the time I left for Nebraska, whacked off for a significant part of the year exclusively to the one picture I had of her, which was on a flier for Ivar's Fish Bar, a reasonably priced fish joint across from the mall, where she worked as a waitress. I had been struck by the photograph and I took it into my room. I think I have it in a box somewhere. She was wearing a white blouse and showing two rows of perfectly straight white teeth. Her blonde hair was up on top of her head, a few strands dangling in front of her face. A dark space beneath her jawline may have been the result of a smudge on the camera lens, though I could never tell conclusively. *Welcome to Ivar's,* the caption says. *How can I help you?* I kept it beneath my bed and took it out whenever I felt it necessary.

It probably goes without saying that I wasn't a very popular kid. I'd had a difficult time making connections with people my age, but not from lack of trying. I liked people, or at least, the idea of people. At different times in my high school career I'd been involved with choir, band, weight training club, dance club, math club, Young Republicans, Young Democrats, Students for Kind Relations with Russia, Students Against Exploitation, the American Morality Preservation Society, drama club and others that I can't remember. I spent a lot of time in meetings, and formed the Decatur High School Fisheries Council my senior year, of which I was the only member.

And then my dad broke our hearts and left, and I spent a long time unable to see the good in anything. The world became a place filled with blatant sorrow. I stopped attending meetings. I spent a lot of time in my room with my fish, or in my brother's room, watching him play, or on the couch, watching television with my mother. But one day toward the end of that final school year I was walking down the hall after science class when I saw the girl from the Fish Bar flier leaning against the wall, her backpack slung over her left shoulder, waiting to go into history. I recognized her immediately and my heart jumped into my throat. I mean it. My heart leaped into my throat.

I bribed a kid who worked in the office to tell me what her name was, what her story was—she'd been kicked out of St. Mark's for questionable behavior—what classes she had, her hall locker. I changed my routes through campus. I made sure to pass by her locker as often as I could. I spied on her in her classes through the thin strip of window built into the doors, and she always seemed bored. I found that she lived just a few blocks away from me on a cul-de-sac that, in twelve years of living in the same house, I'd never been down. And, after a few days of careful observation, I discovered that she walked home from school.

On a Tuesday, I managed to catch her at a DON'T WALK sign and I offered her a ride home. She looked around and got in. I said hello, and offered her my hand, which she shook. Her hand was very small. I told her a few rudimentary things about my life, true and otherwise, and soon we were outside of her house where, as well as I was able to, I asked her out on a date that she, and I've never understood why, accepted.

I skipped school the next day and drove into Seattle to find a suitable restaurant. I toured eight in the downtown area and finally reserved a table next to a window at a pricey seafood place overlooking the Sound. I washed my mother's car and had it detailed to the bone. I went into what had been my dad's closet and took out one of the suits he had left behind. I had it pressed. I made my brother and my mother dinner, fixed her a drink and on my way out, I straightened the pillow beneath her head and turned up the volume on the television. "Wish me luck!" I said, and I was off.

Emily walked out before I could get to the door. She was wearing jeans and a gray sweatshirt, her hair was held back in a ponytail. She stopped in the driveway, looking concerned.

"I thought we were going roller-skating," she said.

I was a bit overcome, and because of this, I couldn't do anything but stare.

"Will?" she said.

"I figured we might go into the city for dinner."

"I said I go roller-skating on Thursdays," she said. "Are you wearing a suit?"

"What?" I said.

"I told you we were going to meet some people," she said. "Why are you wearing that suit?"

"I already made reservations," I said. "I'll be out fifty bucks if we don't show up."

She made a face, squinting her eyes a little in what was probably confusion. "I guess I should go change," she said, and she turned around and walked back toward the front door. "I really wish you didn't do that."

"Sounds like a plan," I said.

We drove to the restaurant, a few miles an hour under the limit and in the slow lane for safety purposes, and everything went extraordinarily well. We ate and talked about school and the world. I told her my dad was a somewhat godlike patent attorney—whatever that was—and my mother was a freelance marine biologist. I created a world for myself that was more hopeful than the one that was currently developing. I told her I was considering Harvard and Yale but that I hadn't made up my mind yet. While I was talking, I pictured the two of us falling madly in love with each other and raising a litter of happy little kids. They'd have my blue eyes and her pink complexion and absolutely no resemblance to my parents.

Eventually, because there was no way around it, I had to take her home. She thanked me and I burst from the car and walked her up the driveway, and when we were at the door she turned around and—possibly feeling obliged to—patted my shoulder softly with her hand. And then I made a grab for her breast and tried to plant one on her neck, an act that served to fundamentally change our relationship forever.

I went home and slammed the from door loudly. I trudged upstairs and wrote in my notepad, *Dinner—exquisite. Grabbed Emily's tit. Blew it.*

We dig our own holes, I wrote, and attributed the quote to *Anonymous.* I don't think I knew what it meant, I thought she might eventually come around, but she never did. I though I could convince her to like me again, but I never did. That night I lay on my bed for a long time staring up at my fish tank, and then I drove around looking for my old man's car.

• • •

I was coming up with a grand philosophy that I normally believed wholeheartedly, and on my best days, at least halfheartedly. It was that *We live in a world built on sorrow.* That was the gist of it—it's written that way in my notebook—and I'm not sure exactly how I clarified it, even internally, but I think the whole thing had a lot to do with the way my mother had been deteriorating in the past few years. It made sense to me that she had tapped into something sorrowful and dangerous about the world and wasn't finding her way out of it. I was convinced that I was slowly tapping into it myself.

When Emily wouldn't talk to me, I resorted to strange manifestations of my sorrow. I began calling her at odd hours and asking her questions about sorrow and ache. I'd ask her if one could be sure of anything, really, in the world. Sometimes I would call and not say anything

She had my number blocked and I started slipping poems into her locker, poems filled with the most obvious and clichéd love imagery, rhymes with word like parlance and substance, and at the end (after what could be ten or twelve hand-size notebook pages), the last stanza would inevitably grow darker, the flower would die, the bird would mysteriously fall from the sky or get sucked into a jet engine, the beautiful fish would flop around without oxygen and die in the throes of melancholy.

A few times I showed up at Ivar's Fish Bar and ordered nothing but water. I'd say that I wished to be served by the young blonde gal from the flier. She would come out and pour my water silently, without looking at me. The third time I did this, I directed some loud and obnoxious comments toward the rest of the restaurant and I was banned for life.

I spent a lot of time sitting with my mother watching television or lying in my room. And then one night, after I'd tucked my brother in, I lay in bed and listened with my hands over my ears to my mother throwing up in the bathroom. I got up, went down into the garage and got my dad's ladder and I carried it three blocks to Emily's cul-de-sac and into the backyard of the house facing hers. I set my ladder up on the back patio and looked through the sliding glass doors where a man and a woman were sitting on their couch with the lights on, watching television. I climbed the ladder, slowly and very softly, and I crawled up the slope of the roof to the top of the V, and then I scooted down the other slope on my backside, inches at a time, until I was at the edge, facing the empty street and Emily's house, and then, carefully, I put my toes against the gutter and stood up. I yelled Emily's name until her light went on. She opened the window and put her head out. "I'm going to jump!" I said. "I mean it!"

"Don't!" she said. "Don't!" and she left the window. More lights turned on inside. I opened and closed my hands. I cleared my throat and waited. It was an overcast night and I was sweating. In the time between coming up with the idea in my room and actually climbing onto the roof, I'd become very frightened. My legs were shaking—they'd been shaking for a long time. I had a strange feeling in my stomach that was beyond simple fear, something more solid, and I was afraid it would make a sudden lunge and carry me over the edge with it.

People were beginning to come out of their houses and gather in the street. Emily ran out in a pink bathrobe with her parents close behind. I came close to falling off the roof right there.

"What the hell are you doing?" she said. There was something fearful in her voice.

"Nothing," I said. My own voice was shaking like crazy. "You look nice."

"Don't move!" her mother said. "Don't move! Someone's coming to get you down," Emily's mother said. "Just stay where you are."

"I didn't know it was this high," I said.

I stayed exactly where I was. I waited, and shortly the police came and a fireman climbed up after me and backed me down. It took a long time.

The cops had me sit in their squad car while they talked to Emily and her parents, and then they got in and drove me toward home. I turned around and looked through the rear window as we pulled away and I saw Emily and her parents walk back toward their house, her dad's hand on her back, and then Emily, before going in herself, turned for a second and watched us drive down the street. There was something touching and romantic about that. I put my hand up to the glass, like I'd seen in a movie. It was a movie where a fugitive had been caught after a chase that had lasted thousands of miles, across every ocean in the world, and his girl tore her clothes and wept and fell to the ground as they were driving him away. I turned around in my seat and listened.

The cops warned me to stay away from Emily. They said her parents were going a little bit crazy with all of this, her dad especially, and it was time I stopped what I was doing, for everyone's sake.

I warned them about my mother before we got to the door. I said she'd been suffering from a bout of tinnitus and wasn't feeling herself. She probably wouldn't say anything, I said, and she didn't. She sat on the couch while they explained everything, her neck craned back against the cushion, and she stared at the quiet television, sipping from a glass. I sat in a chair and looked from the cops to my mother and back again. I nodded my head to seem agreeable. After they finished, they thanked her for listening, and then they took me outside to the front porch and told me they were going to send someone from an agency to come and see us, but I assured them that everything was fine. "She's not always like this," I said. "She's just not feeling well tonight." And besides, I told them, my dad would be home any minute.

When the cops drove away I went inside and stared at the television. A strange-looking man ran into an enormous church. Suddenly a brilliant light poured through the stained-glass windows and flooded the church. The man's face was filled with the light. It seemed like an odd idea for a movie. I checked to see if my mother was watching but she wasn't. Her eyes were closed and her head was tilted back against the cushion.

"This is a weird movie," I said.

I began fooling around with a glass bird that had been on the lamp table for as long as I could remember. I stuck it to my forehead and moved it around my face. "I don't know who those guys were," I said. "I think they were Jehovah's Witnesses."

She didn't laugh so I kept talking. "I wasn't trying to kill myself," I said. I felt the bottoms of my shoes with my hand. The man on the screen ran to the pulpit. He looked like he was shouting. Something bright flew in through one of the windows. "I don't know what I was trying to do," I said. "I thought it would just be me and her."

I went upstairs and lay on my bed. I watched my fish swim around above me. I felt very lonely. I kept picturing Emily looking back at me from her doorway as the police car pulled away. There were tears in her eyes. I sat down at my desk and wrote a thirteen-page poem about a man in a wheelchair who falls for a young blonde maiden, only to be hit by a semi as he rolls across the street toward her house. This one I seemed to mean more than the others. I put it in an envelope, wrote Emily's name on it, and delivered it to her mailbox before school the next day.

• • •

A few days later, Emily's mother called and invited my parents and myself over to their house. That afternoon I'd received the letter from the school in Nebraska asking me to come. I was flattered that they wanted me and felt a little bad that I'd have to reject their offer. But for this reason, and Emily's mother's invitation, I was in a definite whistling mood. I put on my dad's suit and slicked my hair back, then walked over.

I explained, when I got to the house, that my parents had been unexpectedly called away on business but that they sent their regards, and Emily's mother led me to a chair in their large living room. She stood leaning against one wall and I sat on the chair facing Emily's dad, running my finger over my eyebrows nervously. The house was a palace, high ceilings and paintings of little kids on the walls.

"Well?" he said.

"It's nice to be here, sir," I said, looking around. "So this is what it looks like from the inside."

"Why don't you tell me why you won't leave my daughter alone," he said.

"Excuse me?" I said.

"You heard me."

"I do leave her alone."

"I'm afraid you've got that wrong there, pal," he said. He seemed much larger than he had two nights before. He was losing his hair in the front and it made him look mean. I noticed his hands were clenched like he had bottle caps in them and was trying to imbed them in his palms. I did that quite a bit, myself.

"I'm afraid I don't understand," I said.

"I don't know where your parents are, but let me tell you something," he said. "I want to make it clear to you that this is your last warning. If you come within ten feet of her, I'll call the police. Quit calling, stop writing her letters and stop all your little fucking pranks. You're going to get yourself killed," he said. "Take that however you want."

I thought this one over while I rubbed my eyebrow. I was confused about the direction the conversation had taken. I wondered if Emily was upstairs. Her mother came and sat down next to her husband and leaned toward me. Her arms were crossed in front of her stomach and they pushed up her breasts. She had the same green eyes as Emily, the same color cheeks.

"Will," she said. "You're not acting normal."

"I *am* acting normal," I said.

"No," she said. "You're not."

"I am," I said.

"No. You're not."

"This is just a bit offputting, Mrs. Swanson," I said. "I have to admit, I thought we were going to talk about something different."

"Will," she said. "Listen. You have to stop harassing Emily."

I looked at Emily's dad. He was leaning back stiffly into the couch. "I'll certainly give it some thought," I said.

"You're a sick little fuck," he said.

"Frank," his wife said.

"You don't have to insult me, Frank," I said.

But Frank was riled up. He opened his hands wide. He leaned forward and pointed a finger at me. "Look, you little faggot," he said, but he didn't finish. He got up suddenly and went into the other room. He walked over to the bar against one wall, and began pouring himself a drink.

I looked at Emily's mother for a second. She was looking into the other room, where her husband was. She seemed concerned about him for some reason. I looked at him, too.

"She's sleeping with Jim Pierce, you know," I said. "They do all sorts of sick things together. I'm just telling you."

The glass dropped. Her dad came running at me. I saw it coming too late and by the time I did see it, I tried to brace myself against the couch cushion. I tried to turn away from it, but by then he had reeled back and knocked me across the side of my face. There was a pop and the world went blue. I rolled off the couch and onto the floor. I held my jaw in my hand. There was a loud, high-pitched ringing sound, and I blinked my eyes to keep from losing consciousness. I may have, actually, for a second or two. Then I was on my back, looking up at the ceiling. My soul was about to leave my body; I could taste it in my mouth. I put my finger to my lips and it came back red. Two people were yelling at each other. I made a noise in my chest and in my throat, the sound of confusion.

Emily's mother was kneeling over me.

"God, he's bleeding," she said. "Get a towel!"

"What?"

"Frank! Get him a towel! *For Christ's sake!*"

"I'm leaving," he said. And he left.

Something strange was happening and I began to panic. My muscles contracted, my body stiffened, my arms stuck to my sides. "I can't move," I said "I can't move!" I coughed into the carpet, rocking back and forth on my side. Things felt like they were tearing. I couldn't move and I kept yelling that I couldn't and Emily's mother kept yelling at me that I was fine.

"You can move!" she said.

"I can't!" I said.

"Yes, you can!"

"I *can't*." And I couldn't.

Of course, after a few seconds, I could. She gave me a bag of frozen peas to put on my face. I kept saying that I didn't know what had gotten into Frank. I stressed that I had just been sitting there peacefully, minding my own business. I wondered what my own dad was doing. I hadn't seen him in a long time. I wondered if Emily had heard all the commotion. Her mother helped me to her car, I put an arm over her thin shoulder for balance, and she drove toward my house.

Now the world was veiled in blue and it was blurry. The lights in the house seemed to pulsate rapidly. I could hear them moving, a high-pitched whir, and I wondered if the crack in the jaw Frank had given me had somehow scrambled my frequencies. Some of these lights emitted a faint but constant beeping sound that I could hear from the passenger seat.

"Can you hear that?" I asked.

"I should probably talk to your mother," Emily's mother said.

I didn't think this sounded like a good idea.

"She's asleep," I said. "I'll tell her about it tomorrow. We probably won't sue."

We didn't have peas, so I took a bag of corn from our freezer and iced my jaw on the bed. My angelfish floated quietly in her corner of the tank. The feeder fish swam around and bumped into each other. The bruise on my chin had turned into an almost breathtakingly beautiful swirl of blue and gray, but it was killing me. I closed my eyes.

The dream was based on an actual event that took place when I was six years old and my parents and I were having a picnic one evening on Dash Point Beach, a small state park on Puget Sound. While we were there, a boy tried to swim out to a buoy. He didn't make it. He drowned. We heard his mother standing far away on the edge of the water—the tide was out—she was crying out, *My baby! My baby!* over and over again. Her voice was sorrow and it filled the sky. We packed our things and left, drove home.

This is what happened, as well as I can remember it. But in the dream I had that night, I wasn't six, I was almost eighteen, and sitting alone on the beach except for the woman, the boy's mother, who was on her knees in the distance, at the waterline, crying out desperately, and two dark figures, who had come to stand on each side of her. They were stooped and whispering in her ears.

Then from far out, a mile maybe, under a red, sunless sky, the drowning boy's hands shot up above the water. I saw this from my place on the beach. I stood and attempted to shout toward the woman and the two figures with her. I jumped up and down and waved my arms. I tried to let them know that he was still out there, that he needed help, but no noise came from my mouth, and the louder I tried to shout, the more silent I seemed to become—or, the more silent I seemed to *feel*. I picked up a rock from the sand and threw it. Then I was an arm's distance away from him, hovering over the water. The boy was writhing around in it, gasping for breath. He pulled his shoulders up and pressed his hands down against the surface, trying to lift his body over the waves. The woman was shouting *My baby!* and I could tell that in the midst of everything that was happening, in the midst of his trauma, in the midst of everything, the boy was hearing it. I could tell he was hearing it because the more the woman shouted, the more frantically he tried to stay above the surface. Then there was another sound, a loud and violent creaking, and the sky was coming off its hinges—that's the only way to describe it—swinging back and forth, about to give way. The woman had now collapsed on the sand and the two dark figures looked out over the Sound at me, at the boy—the boy's shoulders sank—I was pulled away—and then the sky crashed down over everything.

Noise from the street woke me up, glass breaking and a series of thuds. I lay still for a second and then I got up and ran to the window. A man jumped into a big white car in the middle of the street and quickly drove away. I stuck my head out and tried to see the license plate, but he was driving too fast. He went around the corner and was gone.

I grabbed my notebook, put on my jacket and went downstairs. The television was on with the volume turned up loud. My mother was passed out on the couch. Her mouth was open and she was snoring. She looked uncomfortable. I put my hand up to my jaw. It ached.

My little brother put his head over the railing and looked down onto the living room.

"What is it?" he asked.

I looked up. "Nothing bad happened," I said. "Go back to bed."

"I heard something."

"It was just the wind. Go get in bed."

"Is Mom all right?"

"She's fine," I said.

I turned the volume down and went outside and walked out to the car. I looked at my house and at the houses down the block. Most of them were dark at this time of night. I looked at the sky, at the grass. I looked everywhere except in the direction of my mother's car. I didn't want to look at it until the last possible moment, but pretty soon I had my hands against it and was forced to.

There were shards of glass and red plastic on the ground. Both rear lights had been knocked out. I wrote this in my notepad: *Both rear lights out. Have been shattered.* I went around to the front, running my hand over the top. *Top damaged,* I wrote. *Looks as if someone took heavy object and swung with grt. force. Paint and frame damage. Headlights out. Windshld and other mnr. structure damage.*

After I had made my assessment, I walked back into the house and then straight into the garage, where I picked up the first blunt instrument I could find, which was a shovel. I walked outside to the car, to the passenger door, and I swung the shovel as hard as I could. A terrible metallic sound fled down the street, through the rows of houses, and when I looked, the door was dented so totally I'd never again get it open.

I went inside and put a blanket over my mother and took her glass and put it in the dishwasher. I turned off the television and all the lights downstairs. I listened to her sleep for a while. Then I went up into my room and on a piece of notebook paper I wrote a letter to the school in Nebraska, asking if they offered classes in fisheries. I told them I sincerely hoped that they did and that I would be waiting eagerly, on the edge of my seat, for their reply.

• • •

A few weeks later I graduated. I spent the summer mowing lawns around the neighborhood. My dad called one night and apologized for not making it to my ceremony. I hadn't gone myself, but I didn't tell him that. He said he was proud I'd been accepted into the school in Nebraska and that he'd be honored to drive me there. Since I hadn't yet figured how I was going to get there, I told him I could cancel my plans and go with him instead, under the condition that he'd make sure my mother and my brother were taken care of and given regular meals.

One of the original five goldfish in my tank died around this time. There'd been no warning signs. They had all seemed to be living normal and satisfactory lives. I found him dried out and bug-eyed on the carpet below the tank—for some reason he'd jumped ship. I put him in a plastic film container and my brother and I held a service in the backyard. I said a few words and then we buried him about six inches beneath the beauty bark.

After a week of steady icing, my bruise had gone away, but I had continued cold compresses for a few more days in case of long-term damage beneath the surface. I kept my mother's car parked on the side of the house and rarely drove it. Still, I washed it every Tuesday. I made sure the house was always clean and in good shape in case—although I never for a second believed it might happen—Emily might stop by one of these nights.

But she didn't and pretty soon it was time to go. The morning of our departure, I walked my brother to Winchell's and bought him breakfast. I told him everything I'd learned about the world, which wasn't much. People might let you down, I said, but don't let it worry you. You're not crazy, I told him. You're not even close to crazy.

I put my hand on his shoulder and told him he was the man of the house now, which meant he was going to have to take care of the old lady. He accepted this task with as much solemnity and tact as could be expected from an eight-year-old. He nodded his little head and took smaller bites from his doughnut.

My dad showed up at the house in the afternoon, and he and my brother loaded the car. I wandered around the living room picking up various things from various tables and inspecting them, and then I sat down across from my mother.

"I guess this is it," I said. I stood and stretched my arms above my head, then sat down again. "I don't have to go."

Then my mother did something uncustomary. She made a gesture that I would think about a lot from then on. She closed her lips tight and tilted her head. She ran her hand to the top of her head and took a handful of hair between her fingers and squeezed hard. She looked at me then, and there was something sorrowful, heartbroken and searching in her expression. That is to say, she was asking me—she wasn't saying anything—but she was asking me how things could have turned out the way they had, how what should have been a pleasant life could have taken so many unfortunate turns, and it's occurring to me now—I almost shouldn't say it—that it has been difficult for me to love anyone more than I loved her right then.

• • •

I stopped going to class after the second day. Fisheries 101, I found, was not the true source of all knowledge. The professor was interested in discussing ecosystems, water resources and pollution, river management, molecular genetics, marine environment, stock separation techniques and so forth. He was not interested, as far as I could tell, in answering the essential questions: why fish swim in schools, for example, or how they swim or breathe at all.

This was terribly disappointing. I stayed in bed the entire third day and didn't leave the basement. I started spending my time in the student center drinking Cokes and playing pinball and video games, watching people bowl on the three-lane alley. One night I fell in with a group of cowboys who had come from an even smaller Nebraska town to take jobs in the school cafeteria, which was located in the same building. They needed an extra man for bowling and one of them asked me if I wanted to play. I said I did. I sat at the scorer's table and every time my partner would even glance a pin, I would congratulate him on a masterful throw and try to give him high fives. Afterward they all got in a car and left me in the parking lot to walk home in the dark.

Later, I was sitting at my kitchen table drinking a pop. People were yelling and laughing in the street outside. I went out, walked up the steps and over to the front porch and sat down. I put my head on my arms. I felt, I might have said, bound by sorrow. I missed my mother and my brother and my old man. I missed Emily. I went back down inside and took the Fish Bar flier out from under the bed and then I took my notepad and decided to call her. I would ask her to come to Nebraska and live with me. I would beg her to come. I would apologize for the terrible things I'd done. I would tell her I was in love with her. I would tell her my heart was breaking. I would get on my knees and tell her I was falling apart. I would say I couldn't live without her and she would tell me—I hoped she would tell me—that she'd been waiting for a long time to hear me say it like that, that she would be on the first plane in the morning.

She answered after the first ring. The television was going in the background. A crowd was laughing about something.

"Please don't hang up," I said.

"Not this again," she said.

"No," I said. "I'm not going to do anything."

"I'm getting my dad," she said.

"I'm not gonna do anything!"

"Please just leave me alone."

"Your dad punched me in the face," I said. I don't know why I mentioned this, other than she wasn't reacting to my call in the way that I'd expected.

"I'm hanging up," she said.

"Let me ask you a question!"

"I'm hanging up. Good-bye."

"That's funny," I said. "That's a joke, right?"

"You need help," she said, and then she hung up.

"I do need help," I said. "I know it."

I put on my shoes and splashed my face with water. I put a fresh Band-Aid on my cold sore. Then I walked out into the darkness. I wandered toward the fields outside of town and down a series of narrow roads. I didn't know where I was going, but I thought for some reason that what I needed to do was walk, or maybe that I needed to *start* walking.

I whistled, but just listening hurt my heart. I kept walking, and in rural towns, those roads can turn around on you and you find yourself devoid of direction, and if you have never been good with direction in the first place, you can find yourself in a lot of trouble, which, after the third hour of wandering, I was ready to admit.

Clouds had come and covered the stars; they had, it seemed, removed the sky. I'd walked out into the darkness and gotten lost in it. I was alone in Nebraska. I wasn't studying fish. I wasn't going to class. I had no one who knew me by name.

The road forked and I stopped. The hills rolled away from the fences on either side. Two rows of radio towers stood off in the distance on the horizon, red lights blinking in separate rhythms. The Milky Way stretched behind them like a thin, tired cloud, like the rim of a great big bowl. It was an enormous universe. The wind was picking up. I was tired. My feet hurt. My shirt was wet. My jaw ached. I stared at the towers, at the lights. I watched them blink. And then I had a vision.

In the vision, I looked down on myself as if a camera were suspended above my head. It started with a shot of the inside of my ear and then it slowly pulled back and I saw my cheek and the side of my face and my closed eyes and my hair and my neck, and soon I could see most of my body, myself, curled up on the side of a road with my head resting on my hands like someone either dead or asleep. My jeans were rolled up past my knees and my legs were bare. And as the camera pulled back farther, higher, I saw a car—a mid-Eighties sedan, I think—idling quietly on the road beside me with its headlights on. Then the vision was over and I was left with the lights on the tower blinking in rhythm again.

I didn't see any other option than to lie down. I curled up on my side in a patch of cool grass next to the road and put my head on my hands. I stayed there, eyes closed, listening, and waited.

Soon I heard a car approach and stop next to me. I felt two people come and stand next to me, one on each side. One of them bent down and said something in my ear that I didn't understand, and then softly, gently, removed my arm; and my nose. The other pulled off my ears, then unzipped my pants and pulled off my dick. They bent down on either side of me and spoke into my ears, or what had been my ears—the holes that were there. They each said something that I didn't understand with voices I didn't understand, and my eyes filled and I started crying, because I knew something, or my heart knew something—the *answer* to something, and when you know the answer, it hurts terribly.

They got back in the car and another door opened and someone got out. He walked over. He crouched down next to me. I kept crying and didn't think to stop. He spoke words, and pulled my legs off.

I could feel my skin harden and emit a mucous membrane that covered up every hole; where my nostrils had been, the holes that were my ears, every opening but my mouth. My lungs tightened in my chest and shriveled up. I started gagging, my throat constricted and coughed my lungs up out of my mouth. I flopped in the grass, slowly at first, not breathing, and then, with every second, more and more furiously, more violently and painfully, the sky and what was in it a blurry mess above my head, and I knew, I absolutely knew, that unless someone came and got me to water soon—within seconds—I would die.

A door closed and the car drove away. Soon I lay still. The ground was hard underneath me. Something wet fell on my face. The sky opened, spread rain all over the ground.

Maybe not. But I remember clearly that it took a little while to recognize that I was there, somewhere, in between.

Que-Linda Takes the Rite Aid

by MORGAN AKINS

2002

Que-Linda sells cosmetics to housewives and teenagers at the Rite Aid. She wears a stiff blue apron over her pretty clothes and smiles a lot and hands out perfume samples and baby-size tubes of lip gloss. She makes the best of things. She does what she can.

Naturally, her name tag says only LINDA. Mr. Jennings doesn't have a sense of humor, and it's amazing that he hired her at all, seeing as she used to be (or, if you want to get technical, still is) a man.

• • •

Mr. Jennings slithers by the cosmetics counter on his hourly patrol, watching Que-Linda over the rims of his plastic bifocals, pursing his lips like he's tasting something sour. He makes marks on his clipboard and pretends to be surveying the stock. Maybelline, Cover Girl, Revlon. Then, just like that, he's gone, off scrutinizing Javier the stock boy, who is *Mexican*, or checking up on Benny, who is a *Jap*. There are mirrors around the ceiling of the store, tilted at an angle so that Mr. Jennings can sit in his office when his rounds fatigue him. He can sit in that cubicle and look up through the tinted glass at his mirrors. He sees *what's going on. He ain't no fool.*

According to him, there has been theft, increasing numbers of *troublemakers* and *hooligans* who come into the Rite Aid, *just waltz right in like they own the place*, snatching batteries and Kodak film, soda pop, sacks of candy.

And while someone dials the cops, Mr. Jennings stands outside the automatic exit, shaking his fist as they run away, their baggy pants and windbreakers billowing as their legs pump down the sidewalk. *Degenerates!* He screams. *You've got some nerve.* Then to whoever is listening, *No wonder this fine country is going down the shitter!*

Que-Linda watches, unemotional, from the cosmetics counter. She doesn't think thefts are really increasing. Theft seems to be a natural, if not daily, occurrence at the Rite Aid. And she ought to know, she's been there for seven years. And she doesn't think the U.S. of A. is going down the shitter. It seems to her it's been there all along.

• • •

Mr. Jennings rounds the corner by the shower caps. Que-Linda doesn't have to wear a watch to know that yet another mindless, pathetic hour of her life has been squandered. She puts down the nail file and *Teen Beat*.

Mr. Jennings *mmm-hmm*s when he sees the magazine, the front pages curled back and bent out of shape. It is no longer fit for sale. He eyes his clipboard and makes a mark on a form titled INFRACTIONS.

Then he tries to snatch the magazine away from her. But Que-Linda is quick; she flattens her hand on it, pressing it hard into the countertop, her fingertips turning white.

And just like that, as if he cannot control himself, Mr. Jennings slaps her hand. Hard.

In her shock, she relinquishes it and for a second they just stare at each other and neither of them says a word. She looks at his face. His mouth is one tight, pinched line.

After he leaves, the skin on her hand still smarts and it blushes pink as she tries to rub his slap away.

• • •

"Mr. Jennings was married, you know," she says.

"No shit." Benny is eating potato salad out of a deli container. He picks around the bits of green onion.

The three of them, Que-Linda, Benny and Javier, are huddled behind the dairy case, in the walk-in refrigerator, crouching on empty milk crates. They have on their coats. This is where they hide out to hold their meetings; this is where they work on their plan to destroy Mr. Jennings and his Rite Aid.

"Once upon a time——" she begins.

"If you're gonna tell it, tell it." Javier has heard this story a thousand times already. Benny hasn't done as much time.

"Her name was Rachael, but everyone pretty much referred to her as Poor-Rachael. As in, 'Poor-Rachael ran out of food stamps at the grocery store' or 'Did you hear what that bastard did now? *Poor-Rachael!*'"

Que-Linda pauses for a moment. She is a master storyteller.

"And Poor-Rachael was good people. Everybody liked her. They couldn't figure out how the hell a woman like her could get all wrapped up with a loser like him. I mean, we all fall in love with the wrong people. We've all been there at one time or another, right? You don't have to tell me about that."

Que-Linda smiles knowingly as Javier feels a pang for Tabitha, a pathological liar with double-D breasts, and as Benny conjures up an image of Mrs. Smith, the local librarian in her straight tweed skirts.

"The people in town felt for her, they really did. But they had lost patience with Mr. Jennings altogether. They saw him on the streets and they looked at him like he . . . like he was . . . well, a lying, thieving scumbag. And what can I say? They were right.

"So, one day, Mr. Jennings comes home to Poor-Rachael and their kids: Timmy and Tommy, the twins, and Rhiannon, for the song. The electricity had been shut off—the bastard refused to pay his bills—and the kids were playing checkers by candlelight, poor babies. Mr. Jennings waltzes in wearing a brand-new velour jogging suit and a hat, one of those soft, white fedora things. With a *bright red band.*

"Poor-Rachael takes one look at that hat, feeling her insides heat up. Feeling the rage start to boil, deep within her soul. And while Mr. Jennings is in the shower, rinsing off cheap perfume and God-only-knows what else, Poor-Rachael lights the place on *fucking fire,* using kitchen matches and a bottle of gin she had been saving for a special occasion."

"No!"

"Yep. And—get this—she flies into some sort of rage herself and just takes off, right then, dragging Timmy, Tommy and Rhiannon along with her.

"So, Mr. Jennings is in that shower a *long fuckin' time,* and when the big, strong beefcake firemen finally wrestle down the blaze, the paramedics standing by, Mr. Jennings is pruned all over and shivering, crying for his mother like a little bitch."

Benny blinks a few times before going hysterical.

"I love that story," says Javier. "Tell it again."

• • •

Que-Linda leans back against the rows of chilled milk and wonders if time does heal all. That Mr. Jennings and Poor-Rachael business was a long time ago, and now he says he doesn't touch the stuff anymore. Whatever that means.

She knows for a fact that he doesn't go to AA or NA because she does and he isn't ever there. She doesn't go to these meetings to solve her own problems, to collect little medallions applauding her hard-won sobriety. She goes there to pick up men.

Some very attractive individuals collect at those venues. Clubs, their attendees call them, in hopes of making them seem more social, more palatable, more . . . optional. And these individuals are irresistible to her. She finds their pathetic determination simply adorable.

Talk about falling in love with the wrong people. Que-Linda first laid eyes on Ricky Famone at a club meeting, an Italian stallion who, in retrospect, was *sooo* emotionally unavailable. He didn't know what the hell he wanted out of life. Dick or pussy, dick or pussy: It's not really that hard to make a decision. He could have just said both!

• • •

Incidentally, Mr. Jennings never did hear from Poor-Rachael again. Or the kids.

• • •

Friday morning Que-Linda tosses about restlessly in her Egyptian cotton sateen sheets, toying with the idea of calling in sick. She stayed late at the Gold Diggers' Club last night and her nerves are still rattling and rolling beneath her skin, and the bass is still knocking around inside her skull.

She almost calls Mr. Jennings. Almost. But thinking of Javier and Benny, she peels off her eyeshades and hauls herself out of bed.

First, she wrestles what she has come to refer to as her "dinosaur" (for it is her last surviving male part) into Lycra tap pants. Then she slithers into fishnet hosiery and a pair of kitten-heeled suede pumps. Finally, she buttons a scarlet silk blouse over her leopard-print brassiere. She bends in half and adjusts her silicone breasts, watching her reflection in the full-length mirror. (As her great-aunt Mimi used to say, cleavage is always in style.)

In the bathroom, guided by a surge of creativity, Que-Linda tosses her auburn tresses into a daring, impromptu flip. She clips on dangling rhinestone earrings that nearly sweep the tops of her shoulders.

● ● ●

When Que-Linda arrives at the Rite Aid, she parks in Mr. Jennings's spot, as she sometimes does when she's feeling naughty. Benny and Javier are outside by the Crystal Fresh water-dispensing machine, devouring jelly doughnuts and drinking watered-down hot chocolates. They greet her with co-conspiratorial grins and compliment her choice of footwear. Then all three of them go inside to feel the vibe.

Feeling the vibe has to do with sensing the atmosphere. The atmosphere is due largely to the unpredictable mood swings of Mr. Jennings. Some days he's riotously, inexplicably angry, and others there's a false calm over the place, a deceptive quiet that means Mr. Jennings is feeling crafty and can be found crouching in the aisles, spying on customers, nosing around employee lockers. And then there are the days when he is buddy-buddy with everyone, trying to weasel out information on other employees, bribing them with discounts, plying them with free merchandise.

All of these moods, his employees agree, are dangerous.

Today there is no vibe at all because Mr. Jennings is out sick, reportedly with some type of *potentially contagious infection.*

Trinket Rosetti is the assistant manager, it says so on his name tag, and he is behind the one-hour-photo-drop desk, reveling in the responsibility of being in command. All of his chins quiver with excitement.

Benny and Javier and Que-Linda grumble to one another. Being subjected to Trinket Rosetti is almost worse than a day of cat and mouse with Mr. Jennings. Que-Linda gives Trinket a daggered glance as she moves down the Eyes and Feet aisle, then she turns and blows him a kiss.

Que-Linda was there the day Trinket was hired, straight out of the can. Some petty crime got him time inside, but he didn't have the attitude for prison. He wasn't a tough guy or a criminal mastermind. Rumor has it that he was some big man's trinket in the joint and the name just stuck. You'd think he'd want to ditch a name like that.

On his first day at the Rite Aid, Trinket's parole officer accompanied him to meet Mr. Jennings and go over the particulars, like a parent dragging his kid in by the ear to discuss matters with the school principal. Trinket just stared like he was used to being humiliated. Like it was okay with him.

• • •

Throughout the day, Trinket tries to uphold the Jennings standard by creeping around the store, keeping an eye on everybody. It's laughable.

• • •

A little later, Que-Linda sneaks a peek around a rack of romance novels. Trinket is on the phone at the photo-drop desk, winding and rewinding the cord around his finger. He has been talking for forty minutes, painstakingly describing to his mother the details of Que-Linda's general bad manners. "Nobody respects me," he whines into the phone, stamping his foot. "Nobody!"

That said, Que-Linda takes the opportunity to lift a bottle of cheap champagne from the Liquor aisle, tucking it into her armpit, making her way to the black plastic double doors that lead to the dairy case. It is almost lunchtime and she suspects Javier and Benny are already waiting for her.

Then out of nowhere, Trinket is blocking her path.

"Oh, fuck. What do you want now?"

"Mr. Jennings is at home and needs you to come by."

"*Ex*-cuse me?"

"He forgot some papers in his office and would like someone to drop them off."

"What do I look like, your errand girl? Why can't you do it?"

"I'm in charge here, *Linda*. I can't abandon my post."

• • •

Que-Linda sips champagne through a tall plastic straw as she drives to Mr. Jennings's house. The directions are written in Trinket's knowing hand on a piece of crisp, white paper. In a way she's happy for the errand because even though it is a semi-nice day, it's still cool enough for her faux ermine Eisenhower. If she didn't look so fabulous, she might be in a bad mood.

Mr. Jennings's street is a suburban cul-de-sac, and at the end, where the road rounds, there are small children on Big Wheels, supervised by two overweight mothers wearing stained sweat suits. The mothers watch Que-Linda as she pulls up in front of Mr. Jennings's house; their stares are cold as she gets out of the car, hooking her purse over her wrist.

A shoulder-high black iron fence edges what appears to be Mr. Jennings's property. On the gate hang two different signs, fastened to the iron rungs by wires: KEEP OUT! says the first one and the next: BEWARE OF THE DOG. The latter features a menacing, apparently rabid German shepherd, saliva dripping from its exaggerated fangs.

Que-Linda is surprised to find the gate unlocked. She stands in the yard, expecting to be mauled, but there is no dog. She waits a little longer, but the dog does not come.

She turns back to find that the mothers and the children have vanished. One of the Big Wheels has been overturned and the pedals are still spinning.

• • •

The front room is small and dark and obnoxiously tidy. There are family pictures on the walls and knickknacks on the side tables—things normal people would have lying around. Que-Linda can't believe she's here. She can't even believe that Mr. Jennings has a house. Before now he just seemed like a ghost, like a bad dream, an evil spirit that lived at the Rite Aid.

Mr. Jennings is in bed, holding the covers up to his chest like a teenage prude. He's pale and looks different without his glasses.

"No dog?" she says.

"Dead."

Que-Linda flings the manila file folder onto the foot of the bed and turns to go.

"Linda——"

"What?"

"You look nice today."

She fingers her flip. Straightens her blouse. "I know."

"Do you want to stay for a bit?"

He pats the space on the bed next to him. His face is changed. He looks almost——

"I have cancer," he says suddenly, his eyes becoming moist.

She swallows and shifts her weight.

"And there's nobody for me to tell, if you can believe that. There's nobody left to talk to. Could you?"

Mr. Jennings pats the bed again and for a second she thinks, *I have turned hard inside*. So she sits. And crosses her legs. Tries to find a place for her hands.

"I'm so—lonely." He sounds almost relieved to admit this. In fact, he smiles a little at this confession.

"Everybody's lonely." She can't think of anything else to say.

There is a black-and-white photo hanging over the bureau, a young, dark-haired woman wearing a pale dress. Mr. Jennings nods, swinging his head sadly. His eyes, however, are still flat and focused.

• • •

On her way back to the Rite Aid, Que-Linda is so angry her mascara smears. Her temperature is above boiling. She feels like her face is going to melt right off her head.

Javier and Benny are waiting for her, playing jacks on the floor of the Children's Interests and Games aisle, ironically the only aisle that cannot be completely surveyed by the slanted ceiling mirrors. They stand up as she approaches, like soldiers greeting their general.

"What was it like?"

"What happened?"

Que-Linda isn't sure which part to tell first. She could begin with the striped bed sheets, the missing glasses, the cup of cold herbal tea on the bedside. Or maybe she should just get right to the part when Mr. Jennings put his hand on her thigh, *Are you lonely, too? Is that it?* How he slowly, calmly ran his hand up her leg to her crotch. *Well now, what do we have here?*

"He's worse than we thought," she says instead. "He's the worst."

Benny looks at Javier.

"What did he do?" Javier is obviously worried.

Que-Linda stands up straighter.

Who do you think you're foolin'? You aren't a woman at all. His hand was on her wrist, his knuckles turning white. She tried to shoot up and get away, but his grip held her. He pulled her closer so she could smell his breath. *You're nothing but a joke, a freak——*

"We have to get him," she says. "Today's the day."

They have been planning this over countless lunches huddled in the dairy case, and now they are ready.

• • •

After Javier and Benny help Que-Linda reapply her makeup in the bathroom, they show the rest of the employees and the pharmacists to the door. Everyone gathers their things, leaving without question, not wanting to spoil this rarity. Under Mr. Jennings's regime, they never get afternoons off. Then Que-Linda, Benny and Javier go after Trinket. He is easy to subdue, and once he's scared enough, he's relatively quiet and obedient.

In no time they are into the safe that Jennings keeps in the office.

There are things in the safe that can and will get Mr. Jennings into trouble. Surprising things. And there is money, too. The armored bank truck comes at four every Friday, so at three thirty that afternoon there is more money in the safe than there has been all week. No outrageous fortune, by any means. But it'll do.

They pack the money into a plastic bag and Trinket says, "You won't get away with this," like he's starring in a *Batman* episode. Que-Linda can almost see the lit-up *Bang! Pow!* and *Wham!* overhead as Benny and Javier lay into him.

By three forty-five, they have what they want.

A ravenous fire is burning in the front of the store.

Now the overhead sprinkler system has been triggered and everything from beach balls to toilet paper is getting sooty and soggy. Everything is on its way to being ruined.

Hooligans and degenerates have come out of the woodwork, seeming to sense the Rite Aid's imminent demise. They are streaming through the automatic doors. They fill knapsacks and pockets and shopping carts with the things they have always dreamed of stealing. Everywhere it is pandemonium and Mr. Jennings's Rite Aid is a sinking ship.

● ● ●

Que-Linda is behind the wheel with Benny and Javier next to her. Trinket is hog-tied in the trunk, right where he belongs. They can hear him thump against the spare tire as Que-Linda burns rubber out of the parking lot, mercilessly whipping around the corner at top speed.

If this life were a musical, the three heroes would break into glorious song.

1%

by **HARDIN YOUNG**
2003

The war started when a few members of the Order macheted our sergeant at arms, Ray Ray Alvarez, at a bar and grill in San Jose. They told him to take off his colors. Our colors were the same as our allies', the Soldiers of Mars: red on white, a top and bottom rocker, and a sidepiece—your standard three-piece patch for outlaw motorcycle clubs. They were also the same colors as the Order's, practically an invitation for someone to go alpha male on someone. Another problem was the 1% patch Ray Ray was sporting on his leather. They said he was no one-percenter and it was an insult to the guys who were. Now, Ray Ray was a big boy, and he told the Order guys there was only one way to find out if he was a one-percenter, so they ratpacked him: whacked him with machetes and kicked the guacamole out of him. Ray Ray lived but he was a quart low on the red stuff and being held together with stitches and surgical tubing, shit shoved up his nose and dick. Luger and I went and saw him at the hospital. "Hey, Ray Ray, don't you worry, bro. We're gonna kick mud holes in those chumps."

Ray Ray made a beeping sound in between the Darth Vader breathing, but I saw it in the way his eyes stared up at the ceiling: He wanted us to kick mud holes in those chumps.

I also told him I'd just have his old lady pay the hundred dollars he owed me, if that was okay.

That night in bed I told Nona about it. "I don't understand. I thought they were fighting the Soldiers of Mars," she said.

"We're allies." My club was the Freak Patrol.

She sat up on her side. Nona had dark skin and long black hair and the best rack money could buy. There is nothing like a two-year-old pair of tits on a thirty-year-old body, like adding a whole new wing on the house. She had a scorpion tattoo on her right boob and a Little Devil on the inside of her thigh. She claimed she was mostly Indian, Paiute or Lummi or some other tribe long demapped, but nowadays everybody claims to have some Indian, like if they got a skin in the bloodline that somehow excuses their other land-swiping ancestors. Whatever helps them sleep at night. At the rate we're going, someday we'll all claim we're spades. Me, I don't sweat the past. The skins got the shaft? Call it God's will. My people put your people in chains? Your people should have had their shit together.

"What does that mean? You get all the Soldiers' problems but none of the rewards of their business?"

"It means we hang out. We ride together."

"So you could be killed? Or go back to prison?"

"I'm not going back to the joint."

Nona was a stripper at the Silicon Palace. You know that stuff you see in the movies about the kindhearted stripper who just does it to pay for college or to support her daughter? Total horseshit. Most of them are geeked on gak or shooting dope, one step away from prostitution, basket cases whose daddies were never around. Or were around a little too much. We'd talked about making an amateur porno movie to sell on the Internet—what can I say? chicks dig me—but hadn't got around to it. Nona snuggled up closer.

"I'll hide drugs in my pussy and mule them into the prison for you. I'll write petitions. If you die, I'll get a tattoo on my back of you with a big mustache and a headband."

"Right on."

"Just be careful. Don't act without thinking, like you did with Charlie."

Her boss, Charlie, fired her from the Pink Poodle because I kicked in his car door after he asked her to be in a threesome. I'd been trying to get Nona to do that for months, and this cocksucker wants to chisel in and turn it into something sleazy?

"This is so exciting," she said, climbing on top of me. "You could be maimed. Or crippled. You might have to eat through a straw."

We fucked till the pictures fell off the wall, then I made her make me a sandwich.

• • •

I first got the bug when I was a kid. My father and I were on a road trip out West, South Dakota, Wyoming, somewhere. We stopped for lunch, and bikes suddenly filled the whole street, a wall of chrome and thunder. There must have been a hundred of them, long-haired Vikings in leather, gunning engines and sneering at the hicks in their feed-store caps. Four guys gassed ahead to block the next intersection, a bike blocking each lane of traffic on each side of the street so the pack could roll past. It was fucking beautiful.

I went to my first Bike Blessing two years ago, when I was twenty-eight. You could feel it a mile off: the rumble of Thunderheader pipes, twin cam engines, speakers blasting Monster Magnet's "Space Lord." Incoming clubs converged on the road: the Henchmen, the Alky-Haulers, the Ghost Mountain Riders. Guys in spiked helmets with their honeys hanging on tight. Gunned-up peckerwoods sleeved with cheap prison ink. Missing links with their guts slung over their belts, riding big baggers with windshields. In the lot in front of the club were Twisted Souls on Knucklehead choppers and Mad Hatters on rat bikes, Hell's Angels on Sportsters and Galloping Gooses on Dyna Glides. Bikes were electric blue and blood red and tricked out with drag pipes and monkey bars and beautiful leather saddlebags you could smell from twenty feet away. A bail bondsman's promotional van handed out T-shirts. Broads in leather tops shimmied past with their poopers hanging out of their chaps, and there were old-timers with gray beards down to their belts and 1% tattoos on their arms—"1 percent" signifying the extra chromosome, the superpredator, the one percent of all humans who would survive a nuclear war with the cockroaches.

And me, Wade Parker.

They raffled off a Shovelhead and had a bike judging, then the priest blessed bikes with holy water from the back of a pickup. I was there with a partner from the joint, Ted Manley. While I'm mentioning Ted, I should come clean about something. Now, I'm not proud about it, but I'm not sorry. Things just get twisted up in the joint. When Ted and I were cellies, we had a third cellie, a junkie named George. Ted and I are big guys, both over six foot, and we were hulked up at the time, so we figured if we didn't do it, someone else would. George kept a clean house and made us coffee, and I trained him to crawl beneath my bunk in the morning and gently shake me, whispering, "King Wade, it's time to get up. Coffee is ready, your highness." It was all in good fun, and

Ted and I laughed about it many nights while liquored up on pruno. When we got short, we figured we needed to get our heads screwed on right before we hit the bricks, so we traded George for a carton of squares. I guess you oughtta file that away for later.

Ted and I ran into a guy from the Harley shop where I'd started working. They called this guy Luger because he had a tattoo of a gun on his stomach and it looked like he had a Luger shoved down his pants. He was with the Freak Patrol and asked if we'd seen anyone with Order patches. There was a rumor they were crashing the blessing.

"If you need help, I'll nut up," I said.

"Save it," Luger suggested. "It's club business."

"Fuck that, man," I said. "I'll throw down for the fun of it."

"I appreciate that, Wade," Luger said. "Hang on a second."

Ted looked at me: "What are you doing?" He was an ugly redhead with a crew cut and freckles and arms loaded with bushy hair. He had a fucked-up upper grille and squinty eyes, and it looked like you could hit him with a two-by-four straight between the peepers and it wouldn't bother him none. In the joint, he used to stir his cotton with his needle and could never figure out why his rigs were dull.

"I hear these guys ride hard," I said. "Maybe this will help get me in."

"You can ride with me," he said.

"You're fucking married, man." To a real hog too, the sort of broad that would slap down twelve bucks for a margarita and a box of squares but bitch about a three-dollar gallon of milk. She had a little Dirty Sanchez mustache and a crappy little bike and always wanted to ride with us.

Luger came back with the sergeant at arms from the Soldiers of Mars, a huge fucker named San Jose Scott. He had bushy pork chop whiskers, his arms black with ink. He was holding a bunch of red bandannas.

"Luger says you're in," he said.

"Fuckin' A."

Scott tied a red bandanna around my arm. This way if two clubs were fighting we wouldn't get confused.

"You're all right, bro," Scott said, thumping me hard on the chest. Luger also invited me to come to church, their weekly club meeting, on Thursday. Ever though the Order didn't show, I had the Freak Patrol's respect before I even attended a meeting.

• • •

The Order was the fastest-growing motorcycle club in America. They'd cracked the old top five—the Vagos, the Outlaws, the Mongols, the Soldiers of Mars, the Sons of Silence—and knocked the Mongols out of southern California, looking to run the state. We'd heard rumors: They were started by Vietnam vets after the war and were into the occult and satanism, and their initiations involved torture and branding. They were into strip clubs, prostitution, meth, the usual shit. It was a turf war, about money, prestige and power. During a recent rally, the cops had pulled over two vans filled with automatic weapons, only a block away. Right before the attack on Ray Ray, the Order had been seen around town in packs of sixty, wearing scabbards.

It was time to draw a line in the sand.

The Milpitas chapter of the Soldiers of Mars, enforcers of the red and white, got on the horn. They were going to make a show of force, and that meant allies—like the Freak Patrol—needed to man up. In this neck of the woods you don't charter a club without letting the Soldiers know, and you sure don't fly their colors without clearance. We were a local club—one charter out of Holy City, about thirty guys—while the Soldiers were national. If they really needed some muscle, though, they could call in a Nomad chapter to break some asses off. Nomad chapters rode thirty thousand to forty thousand miles a year, hitting every major rally, going anywhere there was trouble—the last true one-percenters.

At night, riding Nona, I close my eyes and imagine riding as a Nomad. Nothing but fists and asphalt forever.

"Hey!" she'd say, hitting me. "Hey! It's me under here! Me!"

• • •

What did I do to get thrown in the joint? It's not complicated: I tried to rob a store with a broadsword. I was chasing the bag bad back then, shooting coke to even out the dope. I don't even remember going in the place. They showed pictures from the security cameras at my trial: me banging on the store doors after I got locked in with an emergency button; me standing in about a half foot of chips and cookie packages as I tried to chop up the Plexiglas security cage around the counter, where the little slope who'd locked me in cringed; me stabbing the frosty machine; me lying on the ground holding my bloody leg while the slope stood over me waving a piece.

I got five years, did forty-two months. I tried to rap with the Aryans—I dug the white power thing and all—but when they started saying I had to stick to white pussy, man, I had to shine those yahoos. The bikers you could reason with: All that shit about wind in your hair and the open road and a nice-looking broad hanging on, it was the only thing keeping me from going crazy when I racked in for the night. I'd never felt like a part of nothing, but I fit right in with those guys. A few bikers even helped me out when a wetback broke off a shank in my side. The doctor said I might have died otherwise, but then, he didn't know I was a one-percenter.

• • •

One night the Order rolled past our road captain's house, twenty of them going slow, eye fucking him, letting him know they knew where he lived. He stood on his porch with a hand behind his back, pretending he had a piece. We put together a list of names and addresses using Luger at the Harley shop, where I'd been fired after the service manager caught me banging his girlfriend in the bathroom. If a guy with an Order patch got work done, Luger lifted his name and address from the work order. Then Nona got harassed, so four of us met at the Iron Monger.

"Yeah, man," I told them, "they yelled at her, spit on her car, blocked her. She couldn't figure out what was up. She freaked out." I took a drag off my cigarette. "When she got back we figured out she had a club sticker on her bumper."

After she'd calmed down, she said it was sexy "getting jammed." She thought she might have run one over when she tried to ditch them. There was a long silver scratch and blood on the side of her Camaro. She'd spent so many years fighting off her stepdad, those chumps didn't stand a chance.

I added, "So you better warn your people if they got a sticker, they might want to scratch it off."

"When we're riding alone, maybe we shouldn't wear our colors. You know, for safety," Boston Bob, the club president said. He looked like Ron Jeremy but without the big cock thing going for him.

"Safety?" I said. "These colors cost me three hundred dollars. I had to kiss your asses for six months. I had to run bags of blow up to the Soldiers in Frisco in the middle of the night. I worked my ass off. My colors ain't coming off."

I noticed then that it had gotten quiet. A bunch of guys had entered the place. They dressed like bikers, lots of prison tans, and their arms had big raised scars. Then I saw the scabbards. The shit hit when a few Soldiers stopped them halfway across the room.

Since you're expected to take one for the team, I always take two. Before Boston Bob and the others were even standing, I was on the other side of the room with my chair, going alpha male on their asses. I knocked one peckerwood out cold and broke two legs off the chair on another guy's mouth. I kicked a third guy in the stones, then wrestled another to the ground and chewed his nose off. I made animal sounds. I'll do that. I was getting ready to chew an ear off when I saw Luger getting choked by a stringy-looking guy. I grabbed a pool stick and broke it on the dude's head. Then I realized Boston Bob was getting his ass kicked by two guys. I lumped one good on the jaw before I got lumped on the melon from behind. I crashed to my knees, hearing bells, everything suddenly black. I was out only a second or two, but when I got back to my feet, the Order was already gone. The bells were police sirens. I stumbled over a broken TV, which I realized was what hit me. Blood dripped from the caved-in screen.

Luger caught my arm. His face was bloodied, an eye already closing. "Come on, man." Our rides were out back.

I glanced around: The place was a shambles, broken pitchers and tables everywhere, guys crawling in puddles of beer and blood with their faces leaking, hysterical broads streaming out of the bathroom where they'd been hiding. My head was wet, bits of glass embedded in it. Blood was all over my mouth.

"Jesus Christ, Parker," Luger said, "I thought I was hearing a dog."

• • •

A few nights later, coming home from the bar, I noticed a guy on a bike. I pulled up slow so I could get a good look at the patch: some kind of Hitler guy waving his fist, a 1% patch. The Order. I took my Mace out and came real close to him: "Hey, bro, you got a taillight out." When he flipped his visor up to look at it, I sprayed him. He wasn't worth getting off my bike, and I didn't want to open my stitches. I told Luger about it, but he got all bent out of shape, said I shouldn't be doing anything without club-member backing.

I said, "Hey, man, calm down. Does your pussy hurt?"

He said he had to talk to Boston Bob and hung up.

This got me thinking. It bugged me the way the guys folded the other night, a lot. Now Luger acts like the voice of reason. Maybe the Freak Patrol wasn't such a good match for me. Maybe I had a little more go in me than the rest. The Soldiers of Mars had an open-door policy on Freak Patrol members. We could patch out in a few months rather than the usual year or so. But I'd gotten a big-ass Freak Patrol tat on my forearm—Dizzy, our mascot, a broken-down clown holding a whiskey bottle and a gun. I've run into guys who had huge parts of their arms blacked out because they quit their club and the club wouldn't let them walk around with its tats on them. So there was that to consider.

I went to see Ray Ray at the hospital because I was supposed to meet him that night he got whacked to get my money but I spaced it. He looked like the fucking mummy, all wrapped in gauze. Since Ray Ray was half Mexican he was related to most of southern California, and they were packed in there too, all sweating and praying. There was even a priest, since Ray Ray had stopped breathing earlier that day. His old lady, Esperanza, kept kneading his chest and bawling, *"¡No te mueras! ¡No te mueras, mi amor!"*

It looked like a bad time to mention the money to her.

I could see the priest was getting nowhere with the confession, so I said I had some information that might be helpful. I'd heard with Catholics, if you just get it all on the table right before you die, you can still go to heaven, which is great: Fuck up your whole life, sneak a sorry in under the wire. The priest, Padre Ramirez, thanked me but said it didn't work like that. He took me aside and asked if I was prepared to meet my maker. I asked him if that was a threat. He apologized, said Ray Ray might have to meet his maker with his soul still stained with sin. He asked if I ever felt something was missing from my life, if a great weight I could not name pressed down on me. I admitted that while I was in prison I kind of took advantage of a guy and that sometimes I dreamed about him screaming. I even had nightmares about getting shanked by him. He gave me his card, said I should stop by. Yeah, fat chance, I said.

I felt rotten and needed a drink, so I gave Ted Manley a call and we put some booze away. He's quiet when he's sober, but as he gets liquored up, he scoots closer and closer until he's two inches away, yelling in your ear.

"That ain't right, man, that ain't right! Letting a partner just die like that!" he shouted. "Sitting around waiting! Are you not men?"

I remembered I had a list of names and addresses of guys in the Order. We came up with a plan.

We picked up more liquor, then stopped by Nona's to borrow her car. She'd gone out with a friend. We set out for the closest house on my list, some lump named Van Clausen who lived off McLaughlin in a crappy little duplex. I banged on the door. I guess I thought lights would come on or he'd call out or something, because the door opened a lot faster than I expected. A short, hard-looking guy with a pussy tickler corked me right in the nose while I was trying to remember what the plan was. It involved duct tape, because I was holding a roll of it.

While Ted whomped a mud hole in Clausen's face, I shut the door and made sure no one was in the back room. It was filthy. The guy didn't have a garage, so he'd been rolling his bike inside, the carpet black with grease. I went to make sure my nose wasn't broken.

"How about some of that duct tape, Wade?" Ted called.

We taped Clausen up pretty good. Ted suggested we really humiliate him, do a Georgie on him, but I felt that as a representative of the club I couldn't be doing that shit. That patch made me answer to something higher.

• • •

The next thing I knew, someone was pounding on me. I kept a Desert Eagle under my pillow, and it was in my hand before my eyes opened. I put the gun to their head before I realized it was Nona.

"Are you fucking totally insane? There is a man in my trunk! You fucking kidnapped someone!"

I decided not to shoot her and sat up for a moment. Apparently Ted and I had dropped off the car last night, clean forgetting about the dude in the trunk.

"I went to the fucking grocery store this morning, and what do I find in the trunk? A fucking body!"

"He's alive, right?"

"He shit himself!" she sobbed. She was a wreck. I could tell she'd been doing coke all night.

"Come on, take some Vicodin. This is not a problem," I said. "We're just getting even for Ray Ray. Don't worry, baby. I'll get rid of him lickety-split."

She sniffed and nodded, gathering herself. A dark hush came over her: "Are you going to kill him?"

I put my arm around her. "Nah, we'll probably just hurt him real bad."

"Can I help?" she whispered.

Nona wasn't thinking right, so I fed her Vicodins and put her to bed. We had a church meeting that night, and Ted was helping me take Clausen there. The meeting was at our treasurer's house. Sonny was a manager at an automotive store, so he knew how to keep the books. He lived in a nice suburb, Morgan Hill, no Mexicans or anything.

It was dark when Ted and I pulled in, all the bikes out front. We came late so we'd miss the first half of the meeting, when guests and prospects could attend. The second part of the meeting was called Heavy Duty—

patch holders only. I popped the trunk. Right off Clausen starts struggling and yelling something even though his mouth's taped. He smelled
nasty. I whacked him with the tire iron, then we took him inside.

"Christ, Wade," Sonny said, throwing the door closed. "What are you
doing?"

"I got one."

"Mother of God, why'd you bring him to my house? I have children!"

"That's your problem. We're having church, right? I thought we
could vote on how we get even for Ray Ray."

"Hey," Ted said, "he's coming to. He'll start getting squirmy."

We ignored Sonny and took Clausen downstairs. Everyone was sitting on folding chairs, drinking coffee out of Styrofoam cups. It looked
like an AA meeting. We dumped Clausen on the floor and explained
the deal. No one wanted anything to do with my plan. They were all
tough talk and brotherhood until the opportunity to prove it presented
itself.

"You have got to get rid of him," Boston Bob said. "Self-defense is
one thing, but this is kidnapping. You're talking about torture."

"I can't believe this," I said. "Ray Ray, our brother, is dying in the hospital. And what are you doing about it? Nothing. You're all gutless punks
trying to mad-dog your way out of it, but not one of you has the sack to
stick your neck out for a brother. You make me ashamed—ashamed!—to
wear these colors." I took my vest off and flung it on the floor. "I thought
we stood for something! I thought this meant something!" I noticed Dizzy
on my arm. "And this fucking tattoo!" I stormed into Sonny's garage,
found a big-ass wood file. I returned and began filing the tattoo off my
arm. I didn't get far before six of them wrestled the file away, but my arm
was all fucked up and I got blood all over the carpet.

Point made.

So Ted and I ended up dumping Clausen off on his porch. We figured since we didn't squeal when they jammed Ray Ray, they wouldn't
squeal either. We still parted his bike, though.

• • •

"I heard what happened," San Jose Scott said a few days later on the
phone. "We appreciate your commitment."

"Fuckin' A."

"And we'd be happy to let you prospect, but you know we can't have
any of the loose-cannon shit. We all need to be on the same page."

"Sure, Scott, as long we ride hard and kick ass."

"You know the Laughlin ride's coming up next week?"

"Yeah."

"We got a Nomad chapter coming in from up north. We're all going to ride down together, in case shit happens."

"Sounds great."

"So you really kidnapped that guy?"

"Fuckin' A."

• • •

Ray Ray died ten days before we all met up at the Soldiers' chapter house in Milpitas to make the Laughlin River Run. They'd planted him at noon the previous weekend, but I was too hung over to make it. Instead, I got a small cross on my back with R.R. in the middle. When I called Esperanza about the $100, she freaked out, said his hospital bill cost thousands. I figured I'd let it slide for a while, but I wasn't going to let her buddy-hustle me just because Ray Ray went over the wall. Hey, I got bills too.

The Soldiers were swilling beers on the front lawn as local guys rolled in. The Nomads showed up about forty minutes later. They rumbled in and parked and climbed off their bikes and slapped shoulders and joked with their brothers, but since I was a new prospect I just stood around slugging whiskey. I noticed one of them was kind of a pretty boy, long dirty-blond hair and scraggly beard, trying to look hard, but you could tell he wasn't. Then I realized: George! I stumbled over.

"Hey, Georgie!"

His eyes got wide for a second, but he didn't let on. "Do I know you?"

"Yeah, it's me, Wade. You know, King Wade?"

"I don't know you."

He turned to say hello to someone. I grabbed him. "Hey, little princess, why's it gotta be all that? Why don't we bury——?"

He spun around and slammed my chest. "I said I don't fucking know you!"

About forty guys stood around listening, and I realized I better ease off. "Sure, sure, okay. No problem."

San Jose Scott grabbed me: "Is everything okay?"

I told him it was. I could see George muttering to a couple friends. Scott introduced me to some of the Nomads, told them I was the crazy motherfucker that kidnapped Clausen.

We could have made the ride to Laughlin in one day, but we took our time, stopping off at watering holes. We camped outside of Bakersfield, where San Jose Scott was from, and got loaded and told tales of glory. George avoided me all night. I tried to take him aside and tell him I was sorry, that I wouldn't bring it up again. He got mad and walked off, said he didn't know what the fuck I was talking about. Some people, they can't let go of the past.

The next day we hit Laughlin, a little Las Vegas about one hundred miles south of Sin City, along the Colorado River, overrun with eighty thousand bikers. We hit the main strip in early evening, on the lookout for the Order. A lot of the guys had pieces, but I couldn't risk a weapons charge if a cop stopped me. You could feel the tension as everyone parked their bikes at Harrah's, looking around, not saying much. We saw the Apostates, the Sons of Vulcan, the Hatchetmen, lots of West Coast clubs but no Order. We checked in, and a guy from the Ghost Mountain Riders said he'd seen them earlier, but he didn't know where they were staying.

Scott brought a bunch of blow, so we did a few rails and went to the casino downstairs. We threw our money around like a bunch of drunk Arabs. I hung with the guys from the Milpitas chapter, but there were Nomads around too. I got stupid drunk, started razzing George, calling him little princess.

"Hey, maybe if I pulled out my cock you might remember me then?" I said to him once, when everyone was out of earshot. "You got a good look at it, right?" His face turned so red I thought he was having a heart attack. The guys kept asking me what was up, and I'd say, "Aww, George can tell you." George just got redder and redder, then stalked off. Some people say I overdo things.

I say the rest of the world is half-assing it.

Things get fuzzy after that. I started winning big at the 21 table, laying down $100 and $200 bets, doubling down and winning. Some of the guys wanted to go to a different place, and a big group took off. A little after that, I started losing and yelling at the dealer, slapping waitresses on the ass. The pit boss ejected me from the casino. I wandered upstairs and finally ran into a guy named Roach from the Nomads chapter. He said San Jose Scott wanted me. They'd gone back to do a few more rails.

There were six guys in the room, Scott and several Nomads. And George, holding a broomstick. They didn't look like they were having a good time.

"What are we doing?" I asked.

Scott shrugged, sighed. "George here's been telling us you were a booty bandit back in the joint."

"You gotta be fucking kidding me!"

A Nomad blindsided me with a haymaker, slamming me into the wall.

"It's a yes or no question," Scott said, getting off the bed.

"What about dick-sucking Geor——?"

Another fist hit my jaw.

"It's too bad," Scott sighed. "I like you, Wade. I hoped this was going to work."

They rat-packed me.

• • •

The next day, I read about the war in the paper. I was at the county hospital recovering from internal injuries. At 3:36 A.M.—right after they'd thrown me down the stairwell—six Soldiers of Mars were walking through the casino when they ran into twenty members of the Order. It was a bloodbath. Guns blasting, machetes flying. Nine died—five Soldiers, four Order. Thirteen wounded, some bystanders. Every member of each club was immediately detained; dozens more were arrested on warrants, drug possession and weapons violations. Since the Soldiers pulled my vest, I was left alone. I couldn't believe my luck. Five of those six guys were dead, and I could easily have been one of them.

Probably I should have thanked George—he was the only one who lived—but since he was on the floor above me in critical condition, I decided to sneak up there at midnight and turn off his breathing equipment instead. I felt strange afterward, wondering how I survived it all. Nona came down, said she was so proud of me. I even gave Padre Ramirez a call. He hauled his ass down there lickety-split, about the time they were zipping George into a body bag, and he gave me the dope on eternal salvation. Maybe getting cornholed with a broomstick changes a man, but all that shit he was talking about—Pasqualie's wager, Paul going to Damascus to whomp on Christians and suddenly getting the Word—it made sense. I thought about the guys I rode with, one-percenters supposedly, how so many were dead and how I always just dust myself off and get back up. Maybe there's a reason a guy can survive anything, a higher purpose, and as I saw myself reflected in the padre's sunglasses, I just knew, man. I knew God had a plan for me. Me. Wade Parker. Christ's wingman.

I couldn't wait to get started.

Aqua Velva Smitty

by **SARA JOAN BERNIKER**
2004

E ven with my back turned, I could feel Aqua Velva's eyeball staring me down.

Okay, so maybe I'm not such a nice guy. But it wasn't supposed to be like this, I swear. But that don't change what it is: Ushie dead on the kitchen floor with her mouth open, like she's trying to finish the argument that ended when her head hit the corner of the table.

I got to get her out of here before she starts to stink. It's ninety fucking degrees outside, and the air conditioner's busted. There's Delores to think of too. She's not due back till midnight, but the way my luck's running she'll come home early.

Aqua Velva's staring through the hole he punched in the wall separating our apartments. The old fuck wants something. Turning away from Ushie, I step into the kitchen doorway and flip him the bird. "Get lost, Aqua Velva!"

"Don't call me that, Joe Carmine. How many times I gotta tell you?

"Fuck off, Aqua Velva!"

Aqua Velva's been living next door since before the flood. Longer than me and Delores, and we've been here twenty years. In a building like this, it pays to mind your business—that's something he'll never learn. I don't say shit to the dopers who set up shop by the mailboxes, and I don't call the cops when the welfare cases upstairs celebrate their monthly checks by punching out their kids. Someone could get cut to pieces right outside my door and I wouldn't say shit. But not old Aqua Velva. No, sir. He shuffles around the building like the goddamn welcome wagon. Delores says he's lonely. Buy a dog, I say.

Christ, even from the kitchen I can smell him—a funky reek of dirty skin and stale Kools marinated in Aqua Velva aftershave. How did you think he got the nickname? I gave it to him and he hates it. His real name is Smithsonian James, and everyone calls him Smitty. Everyone but me.

Fucking dumbass Ushie! Why'd she have to come over? I just wanted to sit in front of the tube and watch the Yankees kick the shit out of Boston. I told her a million times she wasn't allowed here. Our dates are strictly at my shop, though sometimes I drive her out to the Sound as a special treat. I can't believe she's dead.

Half an hour ago she was jabbering at me like a yappy pooch in a fat lady's handbag. Then I hit her and she fell down and—thump-thump-thump. I thought it was my heart busting out of my chest, but then plaster fell onto the living room floor and I saw Aqua Velva's big brown eye through a fist-size hole he'd hammered through the wall, right above the sofa. Through it he can see Ushie on the kitchen floor with blood in her hair and me standing over her.

"Oh, Joe," he said. "Whydja hafta go and do that?" Like I'd disappointed him somehow. Like he was my pop.

Fuck him! I should take one of those fondue sticks we got for our wedding and jab it right through his eye. What does he want? He's canny—knows how to play the angles so he gets what he wants. Until today I would've thought his wants were few: some company, a six-pack of Schlitz in the fridge and bebop blasting from that nice Bose radio his nephew sent him a few Christmases back.

But now I think he wants me crazy.

I might not be the brightest guy in town, but I got survival instincts. I'll figure a way outta this. No way I'm spending twenty years at Rikers holding my breath every time I drop the soap. I don't want to be nobody's bitch, just like I don't want to be Aqua Velva's friend. Maybe that was a mistake. If I'd stayed on the old man's good side, this wouldn't have happened. But I don't got time for regrets. I got shit to do.

Even dead, Ushie's still beautiful. I crouch down and kiss the side of her neck, right beside the little mole shaped like Texas, half expecting her eyes to open like in a fairy tale. Nothing happens except that my stomach rolls over. Ushie don't taste quite right. She always tastes soapy and sweet, like Kool-Aid in a badly rinsed glass, but now she's just dead and getting cold.

Maybe she had it coming, but that don't make me feel better. I really liked Ushie. We had a good thing going. Why'd she have to fuck it up?

"You promised me, Joey," Ushie had said in the kitchen. "You're supposed to marry me. That's what people in love do."

Ushie knew I was already married, but she didn't care. To her, Delores didn't exist.

Why the hell am I thinking about this shit? My life used to be pretty good. Money in my pocket, a cute wife who liked to shake her ass on Saturday night. Gone now. The money and the Delores I married. She got mean, and she got fat. She's a pig. I wouldn't fuck her now if you paid me.

Not like my Ushie.

• • •

When we were first married, me and Delores used to laugh at Aqua Velva, who was ancient even then. We'd run into him in the hall, and he'd stare at us from behind big scratched sunglasses like the cop in *Cool Hand Luke* wore. It was hard to look at him with a straight face. About five feet tall with mud-colored skin and a cockscomb of Brillo-pad hair like Don King's on top of his little peanut head. It's streaked with gray now, but back then it was so black that Delores used to joke that he used shoe polish instead of pomade.

We joked a lot back then, me and my Delores.

In a voice that creaked like a rusty screen door, Aqua Velva would say, "Gonna be a hard day out today, folks. Feel it in m'bones. Somethin's gonna happen that ain't gonna be good. Somethin' bad. You watch yourselves out there."

He made these predictions all the time, but nothing ever happened, not to us anyway. It's a safe bet that something happened to someone—every day's a bad day for some poor slob. We'd smile, all friendly-like, and he'd shuffle past, thighs squeaking on account of his leather pants. A biker. Probably the only black geriatric biker in Pelham, probably in all of Westchester County. Still rides a stripped-down piece-of-shit Harley that he fixed up himself with seashells and toy cars glued all over it. Whenever he rides down Christie Street, the bike spits a plume of black smoke you can see all the way from Manhattan.

It was hard not to laugh at Aqua Velva, but we tried our best. Back then I liked him, so me and Delores would wait till he was out of earshot before we'd set our giggles free. We'd laugh, she'd touch me, and if we weren't late for work or due at her loudmouthed mother's for dinner we'd go back to our apartment, throw the dead bolt and laugh a little more, this time on the floor with our clothes off.

Me and Delores had our moments. We weren't always brawling. But we haven't slept in the same bed in two, three years now, not since she found out she would never have kids. Not since she started spending time with Aqua Velva for sympathy.

I didn't used to hate Aqua Velva, either, didn't used to be scared of him, either. I guess it began four or five months ago when I started fucking around with Ursula Rosenthal.

• • •

My shop—Carmine Brothers Auto Glass—is right across the street from my apartment building; it's pretty convenient. Me and my little brother Jerry ran it together till he took off last year. His wife wanted a divorce, and Jerry got scared. He's got five kids and didn't like the idea of paying child support for ten or twenty years. So he loaded up his truck and drove away. Didn't even leave a note. The last I heard, Teresa and the kids were living with her parents in Jersey. No one's heard from Jerry.

At first I was pissed, but when I met Ushie I was glad Jerry was gone; he would've been on her like Delores on pie. When we were teenagers, he'd steal my girlfriends all the time. Would've stolen Delores, too, except I met her the summer he was planting trees in Oregon, pretending to be a hippie on account of all the free dope and pussy.

"Hey, Joe," Aqua Velva says from his side of the wall. "Yo, Joe! I got somethin' to say to you."

Fucking Aqua Velva!

"Be right back, Ushie," I say to my gal on the floor. I hover in the living room doorway and peer at the hole through half-closed eyes. "What you want, Aqua Velva?"

"C'mon, Joe," he says. "Don't be a pussy. Come wheres I can see you."

"Fuck you. If you can see the kitchen, you can see me right here." The hole is three or four feet off the floor, next to a big photograph of Delores wearing too much makeup and showing all her teeth.

"Whatchew gonna do, Joe Carmine?" Aqua Velva asks. His soft, creaky voice reminds me of why I used to think he wasn't such a bad guy. He is, after all, the only one in this fucking dump who gives two shits. He gets groceries for the crippled broad up on seven. He keeps an eye on the little kids when they fool around in the hall, and he plays cards with the lonely old Spanish guys who don't speak English. At Christmas Aqua Velva decorates the lobby and goes caroling on every floor.

"You got yourself in some mess, boy."

"I don't know what the hell you're talking about."

"What's Ursula doin' on your floor, then?" He chuckles. "The day's flowin' away, Joe. 'Fore you know it, Delores gonna be walkin' up dem stairs."

"What the fuck do you want?"

Aqua Velva laughs. Whatever his angle, it's gonna be bad. His eyeball glares at me, the iris as tired and brown as the corduroy pants I had as a kid. They'd been my cousin Sal's, and by the time I got them the crotch had worn thin and the color had faded to baby shit. I hated those fucking pants.

"Get away from that hole," I say. "Come on over here and we'll talk it out like men."

"You ain't no man, Joe. Ain't even a boy. Whatchew think Ursula's daddy gonna do when he finds out she dead? He won't bother widda cops, thas for sure."

Fuck this shit! Enough!

"Where you going, Joe?" Aqua Velva asks as I stumble down the hall. "You'd best not try to run away———"

Even with the bathroom door closed and the tap on full blast I can hear him. "Can't 'spect to get away wid dis———"

I'm fucked.

•   •   •

Aqua Velva's right. Ushie's daddy wouldn't bother with the cops. Reuben Rosenthal, in his sixties, is not a man to fuck with. He's one of those religious Jews but no pussy. He's more like those crazy Israelis you see kicking the shit out of the Arabs on TV. He has six other kids, but Ushie's the youngest and the only one who lives at home. He loves her like crazy. Everything would've turned out different if he'd left her at home where she belonged instead of bringing her to my shop.

It was on a Tuesday morning, and I was playing solitaire when this big, old, battered-to-hell Jew-canoe Lincoln rolled into my bay. An ugly spiderweb crack covered the driver's side of the windshield, and the rusty bumper was plastered with blue-and-white stickers with squiggly foreign letters. A bunch of laminated pictures hung from the rearview mirror; I found out later they were all of Ushie.

I was happy to get a little trade. Business had been shit lately, and the bills were piling up. The shop used to do pretty good, but that was a long time ago—back when I still had all my hair and Delores's ass could still fit through the door frontward.

A wrinkly, wiry, mean-looking old man wearing a wide-brimmed black hat and a black suit got out of the Lincoln. He limped like he'd been walking on a broken ankle for forty years and was just starting to get used to it.

"Windshield's busted," he said, slapping his hand on my desk.

"Didn't think you came in here for no ice cream sandwich," I said.

"How long to fix it?"

I was about to tell him three, four hours tops—I had time on my hands since Discount Glass up the thruway started undercutting me—and then I saw Ushie. She stood beside the car wearing a baggy blue dress that couldn't hide her curvy body. Little, like her old man, but with blonde hair, wide-spaced brown eyes and a pouty mouth. She reminded me of a Barbie doll. Even in that old-lady dress, she was the sexiest thing I'd seen in years.

"How long?" the old man asked again, staring at the price list over my desk. He hadn't noticed me eyeballing the girl, and that's the way I wanted to keep it. Limp or not, he looked tough.

"Four hours maybe. You want to wait around, have a seat?" I jerked my thumb at the crappy plastic chairs against the wall, but he shook his head. Worried that he might get back in the car and drive away, I said, "Three then, and it'll be cheap. Cheap and fast, sir."

From the start, Ushie had me doing stupid things.

The old man nodded and limped out to the street with his daughter. "I got errands to run," he said. "Take good care of my car, boy."

Boy, for God's sake, like I was some punk kid who would steal his tires as soon as he turned around.

Twenty minutes later the girl came back alone. She strutted into the bay and stood so close I could smell her cherry bubble gum. Curling her hair around her finger like a pinup from the 1940s, she said, in a whispery kitten voice that made me want to bend her over the hood of her father's Lincoln, "Daddy's busy with his friends, and I'm bored."

She looked over her shoulder to the street like a little kid watching out for teacher and lifted her skirt above her waist.

It wasn't till later, much later, that we actually had a conversation. She told me about going to school in a little yellow bus and how she helped her mother make dinner every night and about her dolls and her friends and her dog, Jacob.

If I'd known before I fucked her, I never . . .

Shit, who knows? All I'm sure of is that my gut started to burn as soon as Ushie opened her mouth. She looked twenty-five but had all the smarts of a six-year-old.

• • •

Not knowing what Aqua Velva is up to makes me nervous, so I edge out of the bathroom and down the hall. The apartment smells meaty. Probably from the asshole hippies upstairs; they're always cooking something stinky. It can't be Ushie, not yet. When she fell, her skirt had rucked up over her ass, showing off pink panties and the backs of her pale thighs. My first instinct—before checking her pulse or asking, "Ushie, you okay?"—was to kneel on the floor, spread her legs and take her from behind.

But I didn't—that's something, right? So I'm a bastard and a pervert and a killer, but I didn't fuck her after she was dead.

"I wouldn'ta started up with her if I'd known," I say out loud.

"Sure you woulda," Aqua Velva's voice says, louder. The eye is gone, leaving only the dark hole and the old man's creaky voice. "If you really gave a shit about her, you woulda stopped after that first time, Joe. Ain't no nice guy takes advantage of a retarded girl."

Well, sure, Ushie was a dummy, but smart in her own way. She managed to sneak away from her retard school once or twice a week to visit me, didn't she?

"I know why you killed her, Joe Carmine."

"The fuck you do!" And I could hear my voice tremble.

In a singsong squeak unlike his usual old man's baritone, Aqua Velva says, "I heard you! Kissy-kissy-love-ya-honey. Then she talked-talked-talked and out came the fists. Boom-boom-boom and baby fall down. Didn't like the good news, didja, Joe?"

"It was an accident!"

"You didn't plan it," he said, "but that don't change what you done."

Through the wall I hear a snuffling, coughing sound: The old man is crying. Not boo-hoo wails like Ushie when she thinks I'm mad or the way Delores leaks when she's pissed—like each tear is a dollar she don't want to spend—but a low weeping that reminds me of my father.

Jesus Christ, I don't need this shit. I haven't thought of Pop in years, and I don't want to start now. My old man was never good for anything but horses and women, and even then he was a loser. But Aqua Velva is crying like Pop did when he found my sister Judy dead in her crib. She hadn't been sick; she just died. It happens sometimes. The house was so quiet. Ma was still in bed and Jerry wouldn't be born for another three years. I didn't say a word, just stood in the doorway and watched Pop cradle her against his chest. If he'd seen me standing there, he would've knocked me into next week. Pop was a private man. He didn't like other people—even family—knowing his business.

On the other side of the wall, Aqua Velva weeps like my father. "Ushie, poor Ushie——"

It pisses me off. He's not allowed to call her that.

Real sly, like a jungle cat, I creep up to the hole from the other side of the room with my back pressed against the wall—it's his blind spot.

"You didn't deserve this, girl——"

I slam my fist into the wall and the picture of Delores falls behind the sofa and smashes. Leaning in close, I say, "You don't talk about her, understand. She's not your business, and neither am I."

Like Pop, I don't like no one prying.

"She was a nice girl, Joe," Aqua Velva says. "She didn't hurt no one. She was like a little kid. Whydja hafta kill her?"

That word—*kill*—sucks the strength from my legs. I sink down to the floor and wrap my arms around my knees. I wonder if Aqua Velva is sitting the same way, with just the wall between us. Like this is a confessional and he's the priest. Up till now I've been thinking of it as the Accident, or maybe the Big Fuckup. But this is the Murder . . . I am the Killer.

"Useta see you two acrosst the street," Aqua Velva says, his voice smooth and controlled. If I hadn't just heard him crying, I would've never believed it. "I'd wonder how you could go around with a girl like that, knowing what you did. Might as well've gone over to Lincoln Elementary and found yourself a kindergarten kid to fuck.

"Useta hope Delores'd find out or that Ushie's daddy would drive up the street in his big ol' Lincoln and shoot your ass dead. Almost called him myself—I know Reuben since he was a kid stealin' newspapers offa delivery trucks."

"So why didn't you?" I'm trying to sound pissed off, but my voice sounds scared and sad, like a little kid who wished someone would've taken away his baseball before he busted the window. "You coulda stopped me, Smitty." His right name slips out, but he doesn't notice.

"What are you, some fuckin' kid?" Smitty asks. "Wasn't my job to stop you." His voice gets soft. "Besides, Ushie looked happy. Nice girl like her deserves a little happiness. If I'd known what you were gonna do, if I coulda saved her, I woulda. But by the time I made m'hole, she was on the floor and you was starin' at her like she was a whore spread acrosst a bed."

Not much I could say to that.

"You're a grown man, Joe. Bad deeds'll catch up with you fast enough without my help."

"Can the fortune-cookie bullshit," I say, getting up from the floor. It occurs to me that I'm a moron. Not for killing Ushie, which was an accident, or for being a bad husband, which is hard to avoid, but for sticking around this hot apartment. In the kitchen a fly crawls across Ushie's neck, right near her mole. It seems like a sign. Like God wants me to leave before it's too late.

I know I'll burn for it in hell and maybe fry for it up here if they catch me, but I'm kind of glad she's dead. Someone that stupid shouldn't be allowed to play at being a grown-up. It's like false advertising, that great body hiding such a tiny little brain. She wanted me to marry her, for Christ's sake!

Better she's dead.

The baby, too.

I don't like to think about that. Ushie was a retard, but she did something in two months that Delores couldn't do in our whole marriage. Poor retard baby. Poor retard Ushie.

I've got to pack a bag and get out. Like Jerry. Like Pop, too. He's been dead for years, but he didn't do his dying around here. Pop took off to California when Jerry was still a baby. Sometimes he'd send postcards of women in bikinis on sandy beaches. California seems as good a place to go as any.

"You still there, Joe Carmine?"

"I'm gone," I say to the old black biker who doesn't know that the whole neighborhood busts a gut every time he walks down the street. "Nice shootin' the shit with you, but I'm outta here. Don't try to stop me."

"Wouldn't dream of it, boy. Nothin' I can do if you've set your mind to leave."

"Damn straight, Smitty."

"'Bout time you called me by my rightful name," he says, finally noticing. "Think of the trouble you would have saved yourself if you'd never gone with that nickname."

The old fuck was probably right. But he had it coming. I'd been down in the basement doing my own laundry because Delores had been spending so much time away, mainly with him. It made me mad, and when he came up to me near the dryers and put a hand on my shoulder I shouted, "Get away from me, you old fuck. You stink."

I pushed him down and laughed when he started to shake. "Gonna cry, Aqua Velva? That's your name from now on. Aqua Velva!"

Making an old man cry isn't the worst shit I ever done, not by far, but everything that came after seems to hinge on it. Maybe Smitty would've been a friend to me. A pal, the kind who tells you it's not smart to step out with a stacked retard who gets knocked up 'cause she don't understand birth control. Or maybe is dumb enough to believe a baby would make me leave Delores. Maybe if I'd let Smitty talk to me.

Don't matter. It's done, can't be undone.

Out in the street, a car door slams and garbled voices float up through the open window.

"See ya round, Smitty," I say.

The old man laughs. Through the hole I see his shiny, white teeth and dark, flexing lips.

Shit! I run across the room and peer down at the street. A familiar black car is parked up on the sidewalk, hubcaps twinkling in the sunshine. Three men—two big and young, one little and old—in black hats and black suits disappear beneath my building's awning.

I got to get out of here——

"Thas right, you run," Smitty shouts, still laughing. "Run, Joe Carmine!"

I hear footsteps in the hall, too light to belong to a man. These are feminine footsteps I've been hearing for years. A key turns in the lock as I remember the old-fashioned rotary-dial telephone on Smitty's counter. Jesus Christ, I spent too long in the bathroom.

"Joe, you home?" Delores calls from the front hall. "What's going on? Smitty——"

The men crowd in after her. "Who the fuck are you?" she cries. "Joe? What's going——"

Delores rushes into the living room, takes one look at my face, stares into the kitchen. Her scream is loud enough to draw Reuben Rosenthal and his sons in after her but not so loud that I can't hear Smitty's cawing, croaking old-man laughter.

Statehood

by **KEVIN A. GONZÁLEZ**
2005

It's your twelfth birthday and you're halfway through your fifth
O'Doul's. You're keeping score, kneeling on the stool beneath the
blackboard, ready to dodge any dart that bounces off the wire. At
Duffy's, the bar is also the front desk. Your father sits there, telling stories. He's the only local in a crowd of expats, and they all listen to him.
"Washington," he says. "Supreme Court. The World Series of lawyers. I
kicked ass." "Cassius Clay," he says. "KO'd Coopman in five. I was there
ringside." "Raúl Julia," he says. "We sang at the Chicken Inn. The two
of us. Calypso. Before he was famous. And then he died." He always
bows his head after Raúl Julia. He stretches his thumb and index finger
and cups his forehead. His hand shields his face like a visor. He points
at a soggy *San Juan Star* headline. Any headline. "This," he says, "is why
Puerto Rico should be a state." He's got a winner on the dartboard, but
if no one tells him he's up, he'll keep talking all night. You know he'll
keep talking all night.

You imitate the shooters when the bar is empty. You know everybody's style. Warren Z. holds the dart up to his forehead like he's a
sailor on the lookout post. He's got a wooden leg. Nobody knew about
it until a dart bounced off the bull's-eye rim and stuck to him, through
his jeans. He just kept walking, dart stuck to his leg, feeling no pain.
Pete Gibbons does a double take: He touches the dart to his cheek and
opens his mouth. From a side angle he looks like a video-game ninja

that throws up darts. His wife, June, never hits the dartboard. Instead, she hits the wall. The Camel poster. The blackboard. The scorekeeper's stool. Once, she punctured the red part of the neon Budweiser sign and made it bleed. You don't keep score when she plays. No one does: It's too dangerous. Jimmy Joe Baker stands on one leg and trembles. Dirty Dave clacks his tongue three times before each shot and his bad breath sprays out. Oscar Beefeater holds his gin and tonic in one hand for balance. Norm, the bartender, lets the darts explode out of his wrist. "Wrist," he says, trying to teach you. "Wrist, wrist, wrist." He grabs your wrist in his hands and moves it back and forth like a fulcrum. "Wrist!" he says. "See? Wrist." He's one of the worst shooters. Your father brings his dart back over his shoulder like he's throwing a football. He owns Hammer Heads. You own Hammer Heads. Everyone owns Hammer Heads. Warren Z. sells them. He's also a bookie and the darts league president and a real estate agent. He looks like a weasel.

The shooters take turns buying you O'Doul's as a reward for keeping score. Pretty Pat, one of your father's girls, gives you a twenty for your birthday. She tells you to bet it on the illegal video slot machine. If you win, you keep half. If you lose, you lose nothing.

Your father has four girlfriends. You keep their names straight. You never let on that you know what you know. "So discreet," your father tells his friends. "This kid, he'll juggle six skirts someday." In English class the nun asked everyone to describe themselves using one adjective. "Pretty," Nicole said. "Fast," Edgardo said. "Smart," Julio said. "Discreet," you said. "Discreet?" the nun said. You winked. "You know," you said, "discreet." She sent a letter home to your mother, and that's when you forged your first signature. Your mother keeps busy bending and rebending clothes hangers, trying to record the perfect answering-machine greeting, flicking all the light switches on and off twenty-two times after putting her mama's-boy new husband to bed.

Pretty Pat tells you which buttons to push and how many times. You hit all fruits. You hit three triple bars across the middle and play the bonus round. You keep trying to hit the cherries, the ones that pay the best. You play till after the croupiers file in from the hotel casinos, which close at three. You lose everything. Duffy's never closes.

On the way to Pretty Pat's she stops to pee in the Banco Santander parking lot. There's a soft couch at her place. You've slept on it before. Your father tosses you a pillow. "No sweat, Tito," he says. "You'll pop those cherries someday." He steps into the bedroom and shuts the door. Laughter leaks through the door frame. The next morning your father asks if you saw Pretty Pat peeing by the bank. If you saw her. The glowing relief. The almost pleasure. You nod. "How her eyebrows," your father says, "unraveled." You keep nodding.

• • •

You're spending December with your father while your mother's on her honeymoon. You haven't seen him since the divorce. Fourteen months, and he shows up in a Bronco with a glove box full of country music. Boxcar Willie. Moonshine Willy. Willie Nelson. He sings their songs out loud, badly. "Why," you ask, "are they all named Willie?" His building is beside Andy's Café, where they sell drugs instead of coffee. It's across the street from Duffy's and Burger King and the TraveLodge. He's got a caved-in double bed, no sheets, no visitors. Many sirens pour through the windows at night, compliments of Andy. Sometimes you visit your grandfather in his mansion. Your father brings him chocolates from Domenico's and waits for him to die. You go to Duffy's every day. Your father always takes the Bronco, because after midnight the Burger King is open only for drive-through. Duffy's has an early-bird breakfast at six, and the late-shift hotel workers come in. Sometimes you're still there. Sometimes your father rear-ends Mitsubishis at the drive-through. "Whiskey River," Willie sings, "take my mind."

Happy hour is from four to six, both A.M. and P.M. Matilde, the owner, won't give you your O'Doul's at two-for-one because they're nonalcoholic. She busts your father for legal advice and gives him a drink as a consultation fee. She refuses to give refunds for the pinball machine. A full rack has only eight ribs on Tuesday, Rib Night. On Wednesday five mixed drinks get you a half-priced appetizer. On Thursday the San Juan oldies station broadcasts live from the dart room. They have a twenty-song lineup and Duffy's is always tuned in. At any time of day there's a 10 percent chance they're playing "My Girl" by the Temptations or Del Shannon's "Runaway." You hate Thursdays. Monday is darts league night, new to Duffy's. Your father was a Reef Crabber until your mother had him arrested at the Reef Bar & Grill for refusing to pay child support, and he was too embarrassed to ever go back. He was a Dunbar's Viking until Phil Hunt pointed at you and said, "Who's this little prick and what's he doing here on league night?" and your father hit him with a bar stool and got eighty-sixed from Dunbar's. Norm, the bartender, started the Duffy's Devils, and he keeps telling his teammates that the secret's in the wrist. They're in last place. The other teams call them the Wristies. "Tito!" your father jokes, "Wrist! Wrist!" He makes a masturbating motion with his hand. He's a Devil.

Frankie bartends on weekday afternoons and league nights. She's got fake tits. "Go," your father tells you. "Give her a hug. Feel them." She's another of his girlfriends, but she's not like the others. She's your friend. She knows what's going on. She lives in one of Duffy's guest rooms with Linda, a waitress. Sometimes you take naps on her bed. Sometimes she looks after you while your father is out with Sherry, girl- friend number three. Sherry is married to Counterfeit Bill. Counterfeit Bill says he was asked by Reagan to run for governor of California, but he was too busy inventing a kind of packaging foam. In her room Frankie teaches you five-card draw. Seven-card stud. Six Back to Five. Pregnant Threes. She teaches you Free Enterprise. Take It or Leave It. Guts. Murder. She hands you a bottle of strawberry Boone's Farm. "Don't tell," she says. "I always wanted a kid." There are two beds and HBO and a stained hair drier screwed into the wall. "Ante in," you say. It's your pinball allowance against her tips. You never take anything if you win. "Ask me anything you want," she says. "Anything."

You're the official Devils scorekeeper because your math is better than everyone else's. You solve arguments. "Tito!" they say. "Two triple eighteens and a twenty?" "One-twenty-eight," you say. "Tito!" they call again. "Five seventeens and a bull's-eye?" "Wrist!" you say, and they all laugh. "One-ten," you say. "One-ten."

After the Devils get skunked, you shoot by yourself while your father fucks Frankie in her room. Late into the night you walk back and forth, from line to board, shooting, retrieving. If halogen lights could tan, you'd be blistered. Your Hammer Head flights flash by like hubcaps. You develop your own style. It's not all about the wrist. It's elbow. Stance. Finger placement. Follow-through. It's practice. It's vision.

• • •

On Christmas Eve your father takes you to Plaza Las Américas shop- ping center. He makes you stand in front of the giant imported pine tree in front of Woolworth's. The stifling scent floods the mall's ducts. The red letters of Woolworth's shine into the fountain, and it looks as if they've sunk to the bottom. "Look at the tree," your father says. "And close your eyes." You do everything he says. "Tomorrow," he says, "we'll be right here again. In front of this tree. Tomorrow." You open your eyes. He tells you not to ask any questions. On the way to Duffy's you tell him how much you hate all the Willies.

Your mother's mama's-boy husband's son is obsessed with Super Nintendo. After school starts up, he comes over every weekend. "Be nice to him," your mother tells you. "His mother is a lesbian." They've put bunk beds in your room. You have to eat pork chops every Friday because it's the kid's favorite. You're watching the Cubs on WGN Chicago: tie game, bottom of the ninth, Sandberg at the plate. "There's a drive!" the announcer yells. "It might be! It could be! It—" Your mother's mama's-boy husband's son turns on *Zelda*. You scream. He screams. You hit him. He hits you back. You pull *Zelda* out of the Super Nintendo and toss it over the balcony, eleven flights. Everyone agrees it's a good idea you start spending weekends with your father.

On Saturday mornings you play football on the beach. Your father has a good arm but no depth perception. He lost an eye in high school. The glass from his glasses splashed into the pool of his retina. It was a drinking accident, a brawl. "The background is always flat," he says. "I don't know what a sunset looks like." In the afternoons you watch college football and eat french fries at Duffy's. Norm lets you control the remote. At night you shoot with the shooters. No one calls you "that little prick."

At four A.M. you tell your father you're tired and he tells you that you have a brother. He's a day older than you. His name is Pepito. He's half Japanese. He has a black belt in karate. Also, he's a better dart shooter than you. Also, he can throw the football farther. Also, he's invisible. "Invisible?" you say. "Or imaginary?" "How dare you," your father says. "How dare you say that about your brother when he's sitting right there." He gestures toward an empty stool. He waves at the empty stool. Then he speaks to it. "Don't worry, Pepito," he says. "Tito doesn't mean it." "Tell him," you say, "that I say he's an asshole." Your father turns toward the empty stool. He waits five seconds. He starts laughing. "Oh, Pepito," he says. "Pepito, I can't tell Tito you just said that about him. He's my son too, remember? And yes, you may be right, but I just can't repeat what you just said. It's just too hurtful." Your father turns back to you, grinning. "Tell him," you say, "to go fuck his father."

• • •

In school you get all A's. This is never a problem. "Your English," the nun from English class says, "is remarkable." During class you practice your dart-shooting style with a pencil and she thinks you've raised your hand. She happily calls on you. You tell her it's all one big mistake. "What's the mistake?" she says. "Everything, Sister," you say. "Everything's a mistake." Some girls suddenly have breasts and older boyfriends. You start buying condoms at Duffy's men's room for a dollar and selling them at school for two. Everybody wants one, especially the older boyfriends. You make friends with the eighth-grade class. You make the basketball team. You forge everybody's parents' signatures when they get in trouble. Your mother quizzes you the day before tests. She throws the notebook at you if you don't know the answers. There are many sponges in her sink. One for spoons. One for forks. One for knives. One for pans. One for plates. One for spatulas. One for the other sponges. They are color-coded. "Goddamn you," she says, "if you mix them up."

You gamble the condom profit against Frankie. She serves you Boone's Farm with ice when she's working and you're discreet about it, acting like it's Hawaiian Punch. Frankie doesn't live at Duffy's anymore. Her roommate, Linda, left Puerto Rico. Everyone *wa-wa-wa-wa*-wonders why she went away, but you know why it was. You were at your father's the Sunday morning he got the call. No one knew Linda was pregnant: not your father, not even Frankie. She needed someone who spoke Spanish to deal with the adoption. Your father rushed her to the hospital, Johnny Cash on the tape deck. "I fell in," he sang, "to a burning ring of fire." You were there when the nurse brought the baby by mistake and Linda put her hands over her eyes. "Take it away," she cried. "I don't want to fucking see it!" A local celebrity couple with connections got the baby. "Blond, blue eyes," the doctor told your father in Spanish, smiling. "You sure you don't want it? Those are very, very hard to come by."

Frankie now lives in her boyfriend's trawler at San Juan Marina. His name is Troy, and they've been together for twelve years. She tells everyone they have an "open relationship." You don't know if there's such a thing as a closed one. Your father sits with Troy at the bar, telling stories. "The eye," your father says, "I lost in Nam." Troy asks him where he was stationed. "I," your father sips his drink, "don't like to talk about that."

Frankie keeps feeding you Boone's Farm on the rocks. You finger your Hammer Heads' points inside their case, in your pocket. You can't shoot till the league game ends. You can't be in the league till you're eighteen: There was a motion to make an exception. The team captains were on your side. Your father convinced the bar owners, all but the Reef and Dunbar's, and they've started letting you play in their weekend tournaments. Warren Z.—bookie, dart salesman, real estate agent, league president—made the case against you. "No exception for Tito," he said. "Then we'd have to let in every underage kid who wants to play." He said it as if there actually were other underage kids who wanted to play. Your father started calling him Weasel, and it's caught on. "Hey, Weasel," people say, "you got this week's lines?" You pull your darts out of the case. Frankie is serving Weasel a vodka tonic. She shoots you a wink. You wink back. Weasel is wearing beige Dockers over his wooden leg. You can't remember which leg it is. Eenie, meenie, minie, moe: You think this will be funny. You shoot a Hammer Head at his left leg. Before it lands, you shoot another. He screams. He screams again. Everyone looks at you and you can see yourself, reflected off a rusted mirror that has a beer bottle drawn inside it, and you know exactly what everyone is thinking. Who the fuck do you think you are, laughing at jokes you don't get! Who the fuck do you think you are, you little prick?

• • •

Matilde has removed the dartboard and put a bumper-pool table in the space. Everyone refuses to play bumper pool. Your father hates Matilde more than ever. June Gibbons was killed by a drunk driver in front of Duffy's. The drunk driver was a rich eighteen-year-old girl with a father in the Senate. She got off scot-free. The *San Juan Star* staff writers can't let it go. THE FIRST MURDER, the "Viewpoint" headline says, IS ON THE HOUSE. Your father holds up the paper. "This," he says, "is why Puerto Rico should be a state." Pete Gibbons sits on the corner stool beneath the TV, saying nothing. Your father is helping with the civil suit. In the old dart room the scorekeeping blackboard now says RULES FOR BUMPER POOL at the top. Matilde filled the whole thing out in laborious cursive. It took her an entire afternoon. One night you erased everything but the title. Beneath RULES FOR BUMPER POOL you wrote BUMP. BUMP. BUMP. BUMPETTY BUMP. THEN BUMP AGAIN. Matilde is still searching for the culprit. She can't find a good bartender from two A.M. till ten. Outside there's a drought and it's the hottest summer anyone remembers. The ceiling fans do lazy laps. Matilde is a sweaty trigger.

Your father's foot slips on the gas and his Bronco wrecks another Mitsubishi at the Burger King drive-through. He signs over another check to some teenager happy to trade a taillight for a few hundred: no questions asked, no numbers exchanged. The drive-through workers call this "the Bronco lottery." Drawings are at least once a month. Afterward you and your father sit on the caved-in bed, munching Whoppers. "Why," you say, "do these gringos come here? Why Puerto Rico? What do they want?" Your father finishes chewing and swallows.

"Nothing," he says. "And that's why." He says Norm was a big shot at Microsoft until his son OD'd. He says Linda got pregnant by a married man in Texas and couldn't bring herself to abort. He says Pretty Pat's husband left her for a Prettier Pat. He takes another bite "Who are these people?" you want to know. Your father shrugs his shoulders "What about Frankie?" you say. "That," your father says, a bite of Whopper tumbling in his mouth, "I don't know." He swallows and sips his Coke. "But there's always something."

In nine months you've won more than five hundred dollars in darts tournaments. Your father says Pepito has won more than ten thousand, but he competes internationally, he's in a whole different league altogether. The trophies all say your name, the date, the bar and the sponsor, usually a beer brand. You're a better shooter than your father, but you can't beat him one-on-one. Your father says Pepito always kicks his ass. You bring home a new trophy almost every other Sunday. Your mother arranges them by date. By height. By beer sponsor. Domestic and imported. Before she goes to bed she opens and closes all the cupboards, cabinets, closets. "What are you looking for?" you ask. "Nothing," she says. "Go to sleep."

You don't like Captain Liz, girlfriend number four. When your father goes home with her, you ask to stay with Frankie. After her shift you walk to San Juan Marina and she holds your hand. Troy is asleep in the V-berth of the trawler. You sit in the flybridge, drinking Boone's Farm. You start playing with the steering wheel. "Your father," Frankie says, "I thought he might have been someone for a second." You push the depth-finder button on the console. It lights up: nine feet. *Mira!* she says. "I'll be right back." She climbs down the ladder and into the boat. *Mira* is the only Spanish word she knows. The tone in which she says it sounds like scolding. She returns with a small jewelry box. She pulls out a joint. She lights it. You take a swig from the bottle. "Here," she says. "It's the best shit they've got at Andy's." You take a drag. This is the one thing your father told you not to do.

"I feel," Frankie says, "like I could tell you anything." You look up at the sky. You cough. There are never any stars in San Juan. "Do you think I'm pretty?' Frankie says. "Yes," you say. "I used to be," she says. "Why," you ask, "are you here?" You hand her the joint. She takes a long, slow drag. "I don't think," she says, "you want to know." She gives the joint back to you. The bottom of the sea is nine feet below you, but you're much more than nine feet above it. She tells you she was raped in the Everglades. She tells you Troy tracked down the rapist. She tells you they dumped the body somewhere between Fort Lauderdale and Bimini. You don't say anything. Her eyes blaze, dry, through the smoke. She says she's happy she got it off her chest. Then she asks if you'd like to see it. "What?" you say. "See what?" "Oh," she says, "my chest."

On Christmas Eve you return to Plaza Las Américas. Woolworth's has become Macy's and the fountain beneath the Christmas tree is not wide enough to reflect the entire blue M. "Close your eyes," your father says. "Remember how just yesterday I told you we'd be standing here again today? That was just yesterday. And tomorrow we'll be back again. In front of this tree. This same tree." The year is a cascade of instants you suddenly can't recall. On the way home you look out the car window and try to freeze the moment. A torrent of streetlamps. A billboard for Tele-Once's evening news. Merle Haggard on the stereo, "Going Where the Lonely Go." Your father's hands gripping the wheel. His wrinkled knuckles. You vow to remember it forever.

$$\bullet \quad \bullet \quad \bullet$$

At thirteen you become a nationalist. You start reading political philosophy. Your mother arranges the books alphabetically. Bastiat. Berríos. Bolívar. Burke. You buy T-shirts with portraits of patriots and poets on the front. Albizu Campos. Martí. Fidel Castro. Corretjer. You start using the phrase *Yankee imperialists*. "What have I done," your father says, "to deserve this?" You don't let each other finish sentences. You are both unyielding and blind. "Why," your father says "can't you be more like Pepito?" "You mean you don't want me to exist?" you say. "Well," he says, "if that's what it takes to get you to stop wearing Che Guevara on your chest, then yes, I don't want you to exist." Then he says, "But don't think for a second that Pepito isn't real."

Your father has moved in with Captain Liz. There are two bedrooms and one is sometimes yours. Your rich grandfather isn't dead yet, and your father is running out of cash. He gives consultations for free drinks. His specialty, once civil rights, becomes DUI law. Captain Liz's husband is in jail. Together they smuggled dope from South America in a twenty-four-foot Pearson, but she was never charged. The dope paid for the apartment. She wants everyone to know she really is a licensed captain.

You still get all A's in school, but your mother lets you study by yourself. You start dating a girl a year older than you. You skip a few darts tournaments to take her to dances. Movies. Minigolf. Sometimes, on the weekends, you stay with Frankie in the trawler and get high and mess around. Sometimes you don't think anything is real, that there's a camera in every corner of your room, where the ceiling meets the wall, filming your every move. Your mother skips around the house so as not to step on the cracks of the tiles. She no longer cooks pork chops on Fridays: The husband has moved back in with his mama.

Norm calls your father at Captain Liz's and says it's an emergency. You drive with him to the station, Billy Ray Cyrus on the tape deck. Matilde is under arrest for having an illegal video slot machine at Duffy's. She grips the bars of the holding cell. "A cigarette," she says. "I need a cigarette." There are lines running through her face and bags under her eyes. "So," your father says, "you want a cigarette?"

He pulls out a pack of Marlboro Lights. "How bad do you want it?" He slides a cigarette out of the pack and holds it up. "What do you want from me?" she says. He clutches the cigarette between his thumb and index finger and dangles it just outside her reach. "I want you," he says, "to get rid of bumper pool."

You've won eight straight games of Called Cricket against your father when Counterfeit Bill, your father's girlfriend's husband, walks in. "Is Matilde here?" he says sneakily, and she's not. He asks your father if he can have a moment. They sit at the bar. Bo Diddley leaks out of the oldies station. "I need some legal advice," Bill says. Your father lights a cigarette. He orders a fresh drink. "I love the fried shrimp here," Bill says. "You ever had it?" Your father shakes his head. "Last night," Bill says, "I asked Matilde if she would give me some of her batter, the kind she uses for her shrimp, so I can make it at home for me and Sherry, and she said yes, to just ask the bartender for it when I left. And then when I left, around three, I asked the bartender for my batter, and the bartender told me to go fuck myself. So I told him to go fuck himself. Then he kicked me out, pushed me out the gates. This was all in front of people, you know. All those guys from the casinos were here. My wife was here. It was fucking humiliating." He looks as if he's just about to cry. "Bill," your father says, "the bartender's new. He probably had no idea what the hell you were talking about. Matilde probably forgot to tell him, that's all." "I don't care," Bill say. "I want to sue. I want you to take my case." Your father looks at you and rolls his eyes. "Sue on what grounds, Bill? Tell me, what's your case?" Bill's hands snake through the air. "I was humiliated," he says. "I want punitive damages. Don't you think I deserve something? I mean what do you think?" Norm looks at you from behind the bar and shrugs his shoulders. Your father takes a sip of his drink. "I think you batter grin," he says "and bear it." Norm bursts out laughing. Bill stands up and kicks his stool. He calls your father an ambulance-chasing asshole. A shameless motherfucker. Your father says nothing. You can hear the Bo Diddley lines falling from the ceiling between Bill's curses: Got a tombstone head and a graveyard mind / "Dirty cocksucking spic." / I lived long enough and I ain't scared of dying / "Son of a spic whore." Your father doesn't move, his arms perched on the bar like surrendered weapons. Bill kicks his stool again and it falls apart. Then he leaves, sobbing. Hey, hey—who do you love?

The next day, when you walk into Duffy's, Matilde is pacing back and forth, talking to the cops. There is a pool of blood on the men's room floor. The steel towel rack has been ripped off the wall, and it is bent and bloodstained, jutting out of the trash can. The two A.M. bartender is nowhere to be found. A policeman soaks up a sample of blood. "Counterfeit Bill?" you say. "Maybe," Matilde says. "Norm said he made some scene the other night." She hires someone to clean the mess and calls the *San Juan Star* to place another ad for a bartender-receptionist. "I," she says, "have just about had it with this shit."

•   •   •

Your basketball team makes it to the finals of the McDonald's Tournament. You're down by two with three seconds left. Your father and your girlfriend are there. You introduced them before the game. Somehow the ball ends up in your hands, and you miss at the buzzer. "Pepito," your father says, "would've hit that shot. Then the team would've won." You look away. "Well," you say, "it's a shame he's not real." Later that night you ask him what he thought of your girl. "You're wasting your time," he says. "Pepito already fucked her." On your next date you threaten to leave her if she won't have sex with you. When she bleeds, Pepito dies. You try to forget her name, but it follows you down every hallway.

When you walk into Duffy's, Matilde is singing along to the radio. She is tending bar and gives you and your father drinks on the house. There are no bags under her eyes and no lines running through her face. "What," your father says, "are you so fucking happy about?"

"I sold," she says. "I sold this shithole to the TraveLodge." Your father looks as lost as a child. You look around. On the walls are rusted mirrors with the names of beers written inside them. There is a dartboard whose black numbers have turned white and a pinball machine that tilts if you look at it and always a 10 percent chance of the Temptations or Bo Diddley or Del Shannon singing in the background, and sixteen rooms with HBO and stained hair driers screwed into the wall. There are coasters that look like giant hosts, chipped and stacked by the lemon bowl. WELCOME TO PARADISE, says a sign behind the bar. NO BULLSHIT, says another. UNATTENDED CHILDREN, says the last, WILL BE SOLD. You look at your father. You smile. You're trying to remember how long it's been since you were a child.

Ozark Lake

by NICK CONNELL
2006

The girl was fifteen. It was summer, and she lived with her family in their summer home, in a patch of woods on a lake. Because she found nothing much to do at home, and because she did not have a car, she became used to walking a two-mile road to her best friend's house. It was a gravel road, winding and forested. On rare occasions, the girl's mother offered to drive—when she had planned a trip into town already for groceries or book club. She never offered otherwise.

"What has she got to do that's so important?" the girl always complained to anyone who'd listen.

The mother spent most of her time on the phone or in town, with other mothers. When the mother spoke the girl rolled her eyes. She was a gossip, and it made the girl mad. The mother complained all the time. The girl had a nice life. She lived in a beautiful house. All she did was mope. She had nice clothes. The mother had had crummy clothes when she was a girl. What was she so depressed about?

The girl's best friend was Connie, and she lived in a house just like the girl's at the north tip of the woods. When the girl asked to walk there the mother would put down the polish for her nails and raise her eyebrows. She spoke of trucks filled with farm boys and highwaymen. It annoyed the girl, and she paid little attention. "Don't be dramatic," she would say, drawing out the words. She would tell her mother to stop being clever. She knew if she pleaded enough, she would be allowed to leave, so long as she came back before dark.

For the girl, life in summertime was mere existence. Her younger brother had been sent away to camp. She knew a few girls from school, but they lived on the other side of the lake, so she really only spent time with Connie. At times she thought she should get a job as a waitress because it would be something to do, but the nearest restaurant was ten miles—too far to ride her bike. She watched television late into the night. In the morning she slept until her room was too hot for sleeping. She ate oranges or toast for breakfast and drank milk when she was thirsty. Most days she lay in a hammock her father had strung up for her, hoping to catch a spot of sunlight, and if it was the right time of day, she could. Her skin browned easily, and she was careful to avoid browning too much. Her mother had warned her against it.

The girl and her family lived in a large, square, blue-and-white bungalow, built into the side of a wooded mountain, by the shore of a lake. The mountain was small, like a bluff; a round top rolling out of the side of a slightly larger jagged mountain to the east. The mountains did not have names, at least not that the girl was aware of, but the lake at their base was called the Little Niangua, a branch of the larger, more crowded Lake of the Ozarks. The lakes had originally been a system of rivers and creeks that were dammed long ago, creating a series of connected waterways, deep enough and wide enough for motorboats. From above, the Little Niangua was shaped like a feather—the girl had seen it on maps—a narrow streak of dark water edged by wisps of cove that reached into the cracks between mountains. From the ground it was winding and unpredictable, surrounded by steep slopes of wooded land. Boaters flew through the channels and tipped to their sides around sharp bends, skimming the surface and leaving giant wakes that pleased swimming children near the shore and angered fishermen. The girl had never heard of two boats crashing, but she waited to hear of it.

On the weekends teenagers piled into boats and drove to a cove they all knew of, where they anchored and tethered together. There were at least one hundred of them. They blasted the music on their radios and climbed into one another's boats. Occasionally the girl was invited to go with her friends from the other side of the lake. It made her angry to have to say no. She had been allowed to go once, and she remembered it to be sublime. The boys had been familiar. They were older but not much older—seventeen and eighteen. They offered to take the girls for rides on their Jet Skis, but the girls never went. Connie said they were dangerous, and the girl listened because she trusted her. Connie would shake her head and mention a name, like Allison Webster or Marybeth Peters, at which all the girls would scowl, checking one another's faces to make sure they all felt the same way. "I *know,*" Connie would say. One had let her boyfriend pee in her mouth, and the other had been with two boys in a pool at the same time.

"She got infected," Connie said. "They had to pump the water out of *her.*"

• • •

The girl hated her father, a lawyer who worked in a town an hour's drive from the lake, but he was rarely around. She figured he didn't notice when she took $20s from his wallet or when she wore tight skirts. But she had overheard him ask her mother if he should take the girl shopping for new clothes. Once he had left a note on her bed, a promise to build her a hammock, and it had made her sad. But then he had.

The hammock hung from a pair of oaks, a mess of twisted limbs covered in vines. The vines caused rashes if they were touched. He chopped them down and they grew back, so the girl learned to avoid them. She bought a radio. It was decent, but the hammock was in a low part of the woods, and the radio only picked up nearby signals, so she listened to news programs mostly. In June a local girl went missing. She had been a rich girl, apparently, pretty and smart. It was a tragedy. Her name had been Sharon O'Hara. The police never found her, and listeners called in to the radio station to help out. Some said she was in the lake. Others said they spotted her alive in a truck, looking scared and beaten. Nothing came through. Another girl went missing. The announcer on the radio urged vacationers to be vigilant. Young girls should stay at home and, when they had to be in public, not wear makeup or skimpy clothes. The girl thought it was silly, but she also wished she had been the girl to go missing. The mother didn't listen to the radio, and the girl kept the stories to herself, but it wasn't long before the mother heard of them from another mother at the supermarket. She told the girl to forget about walking to Connie's.

"They could be anywhere," she said. "It could be anyone."

• • •

It was July—in the morning. The girl was lounging, and then she remembered the lakeshore foot trail she had used as a child. It ran through the woods to a hidden cove, then along a rock wall that at its peak fell twenty feet, straight down, to the water below. She found the trail, a line of worn, packed earth, a few branches and things stuck in the path. On the way she stumbled over roots and scraped her legs on thorns. Gnats swarmed in black clouds at her face. Her shirt tore, and she stripped to her bathing suit. Before long she was halfway to Connie's.

At a ledge of rock she stopped to look and to rest. A boy drove past in a red motorboat, hollering and leaving behind a frothy wake. It was hot, and the trees did nothing to block out the sun. She figured he meant to annoy her, because he circled and boated back. She wanted to hold up her middle finger, and in the moment, the sun beating down, she felt a sudden pang of sick excitement, as if she had been dared, and her heart began to pound.

The boy slowed the boat and waved. He called out. She started walking but turned her head, looking with contempt. She made sure to toss her hair over her shoulder and crane her neck. He looked older than the boys she knew, wearing sunglasses and a white polo, which he wore unbuttoned and probably untucked—she couldn't see his bottom half. His hair was messy but shiny and cool, like guys she saw in the magazines, not dirty and unkempt like the local boys'. In the sunlight she saw the grooved muscles of his forearms and that his cheeks were flush.

"Whatcha doing?" he asked, cupping his hands around his mouth. His voice held a self-assured, conceited quality, high-pitched and loud. She didn't answer. He asked where she was going and she said, as if it was his business, she was going nowhere. He laughed.

"It's too hot to be out here for no reason."

"Sure," she said. She said it slowly.

"Sure."

He smiled, wiped his brow with the back of his hand and then covered his eyes, squinting. His lips curled back, and he put a hand to his hip. He looked expectant. "Why don't you get in?" he asked. She shrugged her shoulders. She thought he was pretty. Her mother always said she could tell a person by his looks.

"Where would you take me?" she asked.

"Nowhere," he said.

"Nowhere?"

"That's where you're going, right?"

"You're a smartass."

"Come on. I'll surprise you."

"Do you think I'm stupid?"

"I think you want to have fun."

"I don't even know your name."

All she wanted was to get in the boat and go. It didn't matter where. If her mother found her missing, she would be upset. She would call Connie, sure. Everyone would know she was gone. It made her feel cruel, to think of her mother worried. She was surprised to feel that way. Worse, her father would punish her.

"Come on," the boy said. She couldn't tell if he was grinning or annoyed.

"How do you expect me to get in the boat?"

The trail was ten feet above the water. She had gone diving from the rocks years before, with Connie, until their parents discovered them and told them to stop. They had obeyed at the time.

She disappeared behind the edge of the cliff, and he called out. It was quiet. Water lapped at the boat. A blackbird drifted overhead. Suddenly the girl appeared over the cliff, darting into the sky. She dove into the water with a muted splash. The boy whooped, punching his fist into the air. Seconds later she broke above the surface, smoothing the hair from her face. He threw out an inner tube on a rope.

"I don't even know your name," she said.

"I don't know yours," he said.

He offered a hand.

"I need a towel."

He opened a compartment and pulled out a blue towel. She climbed in, and he wrapped it around her shoulders, placing a hand on her back. She shivered. He said she was pretty, and her cheeks warmed. She stepped forward, out of his reach, crossing her arms in front of her chest.

She pointed to the dashboard. "How fast can this thing go?"

"You wanna see?"

"Yeah. Show me."

"You better sit down. Sit here."

He motioned to a seat beside him. She moved to the front, stripping off the towel to her bathing suit. She laid the towel across a bench and spread herself upon it, laying down, gripping the metal railing. "You'd better hang on," the boy said, and then he laughed and revved the motor, cruising out of the cove into open water. He was a smooth driver, she thought. The air blew over in bursts, then in a steady, heavy flow. She couldn't see land drifting away, but she saw the blue of the sky open above and heard the water rushing by, and when he tipped the boat to turn she reached her hand into the water. He asked her if she liked it, and she told him she did.

She asked where they were going. There was an ice cream shop she liked. It floated on the water. Did he know it? They should go there. She thought her friends might be there. It was a nice feeling to imagine them seeing her with him.

"I'm thirsty," she said. "I want a malt."

"I know another place," he said.

"Do they have malts?"

"Yeah. I think so."

They drove further, past beaches and shops and marinas. White sails drifted on the water like clouds. A red parachute soared overhead like a hawk. The lake forked, and they turned into a narrow arm. A two-story building stood at the shore; with a sloped roof and wood slats for sides. Three stacked decks wrapped around the outside. At the third tier were picnic tables, circles topped by yellow umbrellas.

He parked the boat and took her to the top. They sat in a corner, in the shade. A waitress in a bikini walked by, smiling at the boy as if she knew him.

"Hideous," he said when the waitress had gone. "Isn't she?"

The waitress came back with a pad and pencil. The girl opened her mouth to order.

"Can I get a malt? Strawberry?"

"We don't have malts."

"What do you have?"

The waitress sounded annoyed. "We've got sodas. Lemonade."

The boy spoke, a drink the girl didn't know, and the waitress nodded. The girl told him it sounded delicious. The waitress brought a large round misted-over glass of red slush. Two straws. They both leaned in to drink, their faces nearly touching. She noticed lines in the corners of his eyes. She coughed.

"You like it?"

She had never tasted alcohol.

"Yeah. It's good."

She had liked the smell, ripe and sharp, but was relieved when it was gone. She had only pretended to slurp through the straw, sucking but never into her mouth. He didn't seem to notice; he drank it all. They talked about music and films. At one point the girl noticed the dark-red hair of a girl she recognized, an older girl from school. She was gorgeous and popular and hung out with older boys. It was rumored she was pregnant. She wore a bikini top and tight jean shorts. A guy with a receding hairline was with her. She had looked in the girl's direction once, and the girl felt nervous, like she might throw up. But the red-haired girl didn't recognize her, and she was disappointed.

"How old are you?" he asked at one point.

"Seventeen," she said.

He smiled. She asked.

"Twenty-eight."

Something turned in her stomach.

She felt as if he had pulled something over her. But she hadn't asked him before, and he had had no reason to tell. She didn't know what someone his age should look like. He looked young.

"That's old," she said.

"Not old enough to be your dad," he said. His head bobbed and his lips parted, as if he were laughing. Grunting *uh-uh-uh* sounds came out of his throat.

He left money for the waitress, and they walked down the stairs, to the dock. The boy's steps were steady, assured, and he took the girl's hand. People watched and she liked it. At the foot of the stairs she saw a woman, wrinkled and smoking, staring, not like the others, but with her lips closed, hard with contempt. The girl thought of her mother.

He told her he would take her for a ride. She thought she should go home, but it was pleasing to be on the lake, in the boat, feeling the breeze and the sun. She lay down on the bench at the front, on her back, but pushed herself up to her elbows as they left to see where they were and recognized the homes. There were large cabins, white- and green- and brown-sided with tiny red-roofed docks. Of course they all looked similar from the back, heavily windowed and square-framed, but she was familiar with them and could tell them apart. She asked the boy where he lived.

"You wouldn't know the name of it," he said. "It's far."

"Where?" she asked. She said it casually.

He named something she had never heard of. She was unfamiliar with most of the lake. She could only ever tell if she was at home, or Connie's. Everywhere else was foreign because she never paid attention to where she was going.

He asked for her name. It made her uneasy. She pretended not to hear. He asked again, louder.

"My name is Sharon," she said.

"That's pretty."

He said his name was Kurt, and she said it was a cute name. He laughed, jerking his head backward. Brown curls fell over his eyes. She lay back down on the bench, feeling the hot sun. They cruised the lake at low speed, over the water. It relaxed her, and she nearly fell asleep. When she came to, the boy was still behind the wheel, driving. She could feel the wind rushing by, more intense than before, and she sat up. She didn't recognize the homes now. He was driving fast. It was late afternoon. There were people tubing and skiing. The boy saw she was awake. He was smirking, confident, like he'd remembered some secret joke. He winked at her, and she looked away.

"You bored?" he asked.

She yawned and stretched her arms above her head, shaking her hair loose to dry. Before she could speak, he knocked the lever forward, and they sped through a narrow channel filled with boats. He snaked through, nearly skimming pontoons and rafts and people. They honked their horns and the girl screamed.

"What the hell are you doing?" she asked.

She got up and moved to the driver's seat. She reached for the lever and pulled it back. The boat slowed. She was afraid he was upset, but when he spoke he sounded amused, only slightly disappointed. He asked her what the big idea was.

She thought of something to say. Other boats drifted by. Some were anchored. They were near a beach. Young people listened to radios in their boats, dancing and drinking from glass bottles. A group of girls drove by. They looked like her friends, but she could tell they weren't. They lowered their sunglasses and stared at her, then at Kurt. She scoffed.

"I want to learn," she told him. "Teach me how to drive."

He pursed his lips, and the red parts of his cheeks firmed. His eyes squinted as if smirking.

"This is great," he said.

"Show me."

He told her to stand in front of him, and he said he would put her hands where they needed to go. She did so and he did so. Bumps broke across her skin. He pressed himself tight against her. She thought she heard him mutter something like "Oh God," and she felt the short blast of breath on her neck.

"Simple," he said.

She took hold of the wheel and turned the ignition. There was a clock in glowing green figures. It was five P.M. Had they been out that long? She cursed under her breath.

"Which way back to my place?" she asked, taking the boat into gear.

"What?"

"I need to get home soon," she said. "Or my mother will know I've been gone."

"Let's go get some food."

"I'm not hungry."

"I'll buy you another drink."

"I'm not thirsty."

He laughed. It sounded forced. He pulled a beer from a cooler under the passenger seat and twisted the cap off, throwing it into the water. His lips met the bottle with a loud smack. He tilted his neck back when he drank. She watched the muscle where it moved, swallowing, and she wanted to touch it, or maybe put her lips to it. He offered the bottle to her. When she pretended not to notice, he held it in front of her face.

"Taste it," he said, and she shook her head. He shrugged his shoulders.

"Which way takes me home?" she asked.

"Where do you live?" he asked.

"Little Niangua."

"I don't know where that is."

"What do you mean you don't know where it is?"

"I just know Ozark Lake."

She couldn't see his face; it was turned away. He was spread across a seat, his feet propped on the dashboard, head tilted backward. He took another drink. She asked him how the hell he had gotten there in the first place, to her house. Her voice was shaky. She tried to sound confident. She didn't know if she was angry or scared or both. Everything was mixed up. It wasn't even called Ozark Lake. What the hell had she been doing? Her head was filled, warm with blood. Her skin was hot when she touched it. She felt sick.

"I was just screwing around," he said. "I just drove there."

"You don't remember how you got there?"

"No."

A family in a boat—father, mother and two girls—drove by. She thought of talking to them, to ask directions. They were eating sandwiches. The mother wore a broad-rimmed hat with feathers, as if she didn't know this was a lake and she was in a boat. The girls scowled, hunched over in their seats. When they passed they glanced at the girl, and she noticed them. They stared at Kurt, their mouths open. They looked stupid, and jealous.

"We're lost," the girl told him.

"You're kidding," he said.

"I'm not."

"That's fucking crazy." He sounded amused.

"What are we going to do?"

"We need gas. It's low." He pointed to the gauge. She hadn't noticed the gauge before. It made her feel worse.

"Do you know where there's a station?"

"Yeah. I know one."

He told her where to go. She drove at top speed, following the setting sun, because that was where he had said she should go, and that was all she knew of her home, that Little Niangua was in the west. She'd heard her mother say it once. They were on a remote section of the lake. Houses were tiny and few, gold specks hidden in thick, blackening forests.

He said she was going fast. Even he wouldn't take the boat that fast. Officials might pull him over. She acted as if she were listening. He kept talking. The high parts of his cheeks were red, and his lips seemed fuller. He was licking them. She didn't know how many beers he had drunk, because he threw the bottles into the water when they were empty. Once, he asked her if she had a boyfriend. She said no. He'd made a face like he was incredulous.

"You ever fallen for anyone?" he asked.

"I don't fall for people," she said.

"Well I have."

"How'd it turn out?"

"Not so hot, but I got a feeling things are changing. Things are turning in my favor."

She said nothing.

"You got a crush on anyone?" he asked.

"No."

"I do," and he paused for what seemed like a long moment. "She's gorgeous."

She tucked a strand of hair behind her ear and opened her mouth as if to speak and closed it back.

"Thinks she's smart, too."

"Who is she?"

She held the hair off her face. The sun made her skin freckle across her nose. For the first time she realized how he was looking at her, how he had looked at her all day, not like other boys, who were grinning and rowdy—pleading at best. His eyes were dark, shadowed beneath his brow. The red lips were pressed together, turned at the corners. He looked hungry. She told him she didn't know any girls around here.

"You just know Connie?" he asked.

She felt her heart pounding. She could hear it in her ears, too, thumping like the music on the radios. Had she mentioned Connie?

"You know Connie?" she asked.

"Yeah," he said.

"How?"

"Just do," he said. "We have fun together, me and Connie."

She had questions. She could have asked him where he had met her, when and what they had done or if they were friends. Did he even know her? Or just *of* her? Connie didn't keep secrets; she would have told her of him. Why hadn't she?

"Then it's her," she said. "I really only know Connie, and if it isn't her, I don't know."

"I'm pretty sure you know," he said.

She didn't want to say anything. She felt if she could only keep quiet, then he would be quiet. Lines were drawn in her mind. He could be the one; he could hurt her. The day seemed planned. Everything she had felt was something else entirely. When he touched her it had been possessive—he had grabbed her hand hard or planted his fingers into the skin on her back. In the moment she hadn't noticed; it felt protective, maybe, but they were around other people. The things she'd done weren't spontaneous; she'd done them to make her feel interesting, like she had felt when she jumped off the cliff, or at the restaurant, or even on the boat, at first. Now she wondered what had made her do it. She wanted to blame her mother. She thought of her searching, upset. It felt good to do so, but she also knew it was unfair.

For a while she drove. As long as she could do that she thought, Okay, I can handle this. He said nothing. She thought he was asleep but didn't turn to check. Her eyes were fixed away. The mountains, at first blue, turned to black in the darkening light. They were alone on the water, the lake left still and shimmering. They came upon a beach of rocks, and the water shallowed. Thin flags of smoke wafted from the shores. Three fires blazed like stars. Someone was burning leaves, or trash. The red flames spat upward, squelched at the tips in the black night air. The girl knew they were illegal, and she felt comforted that they had been placed there. She didn't know why.

Her heart quickened when she saw a red sign appear above the line of trees on the right-hand shore. She heard him move. He was awake. The sign read GAS and listed prices. He pointed. Below the prices were other signs, nailed crookedly down a rusted post. They read things like BAIT, BEER and CIGS. She told him she wanted cigarettes.

"And I have to pee," she said.

She pulled the boat into a stall, alongside a gas pump.

"You gonna help me tie it off?" he asked, grabbing the wheel, but she pretended not to hear, stepping out of the boat, onto the dock and inside a wooden shack, through a door where a neon OPEN sign hung.

Inside the shack it smelled of rotten dead fish and gasoline. The girl asked a balding, greasy man behind the counter for a phone.

"What you need it for," he said.

"I need to make a call."

"You one of Rob's girls?"

"You got a phone or what?"

"I don't got a phone."

"You got a map?"

He gave her a creased brochure from a broken display case. "Two-fifty," he said. She didn't have $2.50. She spotted a set of knives behind the counter and asked if she could see one.

"Which one."

"The big one."

He laid it on the counter. She grabbed it by the handle and told him the boy coming in to pay for gas would cover it and the map. She tried to walk out casual, but her legs felt wobbly and she thought the man might stop her. He said something behind her and she kept going. A door on the side of the store pointed to restrooms. She followed it outside. The boy wasn't by the boat, filling the tank. She peered around the edge of the shack and saw him enter. When he went inside she got into the boat. She cut through the ropes with the knife and pushed from the dock. The boat floated backward into the water. She turned on the engine, crashing into a buoy. She didn't even see the boy running out of the shack, onto the dock, but she heard him shouting. When she reached the middle of the lake, she turned and saw his figure on the edge of the dock, a thrashing shadow.

She opened the map. It confirmed she should go west, but she was at least twenty miles from home, and the tank was still low. She felt as though her heart had stopped. Never had she been so desperate. Her eyes were stinging. The wind had run her hair ragged. The air was getting cold, and she wished she had clothes to wear. She had no idea what she would tell her mother.

• • •

The boat ran despite the needle hovering below the empty line. Black mounds of land rolled past. Dark flecks of fish broke the surface as if breaching. A single white crane swooped downward to the waves. The girl feared getting stuck in a cove, or on a sandbar. Snakes hid in the weeds, and mosquitoes hovered like a fog. When the engine spluttered and the boat stopped, floating at a standstill, the girl waited. The lights of houses were on, a few hundred feet from shore. She was unsure where exactly she was trapped, but she guessed from the map and the way in which the lake split into three channels that she was floating near home.

The lake was deserted. Nobody was outside. She checked for paddles in a side compartment, to row ashore, but there were none. She spotted a crumbling concrete stairway and thought of swimming to it, but the water was dark and still and deep. She could yell for help, but who would hear her?

When she heard the distant sound of water crashing on the surface and spotted the speck of a Jet Ski in the distance, she didn't know how to react. It would be another stranger. Someone worse. Or a policeman. But there was no flashing light or horn. At one point she thought she should duck and hide, but she thought of her mother and felt determined. Hoping someone would see, she waved her hands in the air, despite the fact that the boat was cast in shadow; it had floated to the southwest shore. She yelled.

The Jet Ski moved closer. A thin streak of silver shone on the dash. The girl realized the knife was still out. She moved to hide it. The glove compartment was locked. She picked it. The door popped. Something glinted inside. An object was half hidden beneath a green notepad: a shiny metal gun. The girl stared, her breath drained, choking. She lunged over the side of the boat and vomited into the water, the yellow foam glazing the surface, then drifting.

She felt weak and her limbs were shaky. Looking up, she could make out the form of the stranger on the Jet Ski, the boy or man who apparently had pursued her to this point—because that was what it had become, a pursuit. It made her feel smart to have made it that way, and the sudden feeling made her stronger.

"What are you trying to do?" he asked.

She didn't answer. He gripped the handlebar and stood up. The Jet Ski made a rattled sound. He looked taller.

"God. I didn't think I'd find you." He said it half smiling, head tilted back.

"You don't know what I had to do to get this," he said.

She moved to the glove compartment and slid her hand inside. Her palm met the hard rubber grip of the handle. She had never used a gun, and she didn't think she could use one now. She didn't want to. It could be a toy, a water gun. She couldn't see enough to tell. But it didn't feel like plastic. If it were real, she thought, it might not be loaded. She breathed in. It didn't matter.

"I don't think I want to know," she said.

"Don't you?" he asked.

For a moment he was silent, moving carefully closer.

"I thought we were having fun," he said. "I thought you were having fun."

And then his arms were open, as if to show her he held nothing, like he couldn't possibly hurt her—and why would he want to? She was sure this was false.

"That's all I meant to do," he said. "Have a good time with a pretty girl. Now what am I supposed to do?"

He floated, feet away from the boat. The girl moved to the back, near the motor. She pointed the gun toward him. The barrel shook.

At first he looked surprised. His arms were back up in the air, and his face lost the hard look it had had before. His mouth hung open.

"What're you going to do with that?" he asked.

He laughed. It sounded forced.

"That's not even loaded," he said.

"Like I'd believe that," she said.

It didn't come out right, and she thought she sounded stupid. She tried to calm the shaking through her arm. It shook worse.

"That's a flare gun," he said. "Can't you even tell that?"

He'd seemed to slow, and that was all she wanted. More time. Time to think. She didn't believe him, but she also didn't want to hold the gun, or whatever it was, anymore. She set it down, softly, on the floor. When she looked up he was inches from the boat.

"What should I do?" he asked.

The voice was ragged, despairing, like he hadn't swallowed. She noticed the pathetic quality. He hadn't planned it this way, she thought. She thought, I've got the upper hand. Of all the girls he'd been with, none had given him this trouble. Or had they? Had there even been any? She was sorry for him but didn't know why. He grabbed the edge of the boat with both hands, as if to launch himself inside.

"This could have been fun," he said.

He lumbered. His hands grasped the smooth white of the boat. She knew the moment was important. But all she could think of was the lake. She was soothed, stupefied. Water rippled, seamless, behind a dark silhouette of the boy as he swung a leg over the edge. Houses on the southern shore were lit, window lights flickering like fire on the waves. Families were sitting down to dinner. Boats were raised on stilts, or tethered to the docks.

She thought of the people who didn't live near the lake and how they spoke of the beauty of it. She disagreed with them. The water was green and stank, and there were bugs, but she hadn't ever cared enough to tell them so. She had never cared about much. She didn't tell them what she thought, and how she knew, because she lived there, that the water was only beautiful from a distance, when a low rising or setting sun cast the deep middle of the lake in a rich blue. It looked different now. All this land, rising, these mountains, and the rippling water; she had never noticed before.

Her hands were behind her, holding to the slick edge of the boat. For a moment she felt relief. Her breath softened. A breeze blew across the water, lifting the hair from her face. It felt weird to notice it. He looked at her. His eyes flicked upward, then downward, like water gliders.

It happened suddenly and silently. Like a fish she allowed herself to slip backward, into the water. It hadn't called for force. The movement was smooth and easy as a dream. Water filled her nostrils. A swell of warmth spread from her chest, like fear. She fell deeply. Her body rolled, and then she reached her arms to the surface. When her head broke above the water she didn't look backward.

The boy, or man, called out. The girl kicked her legs. Her mouth opened for air and she tasted sweet mud and fish. A loud pop sounded, like snapping tinder from a fire. All she felt was the chill of the water, moving to the edges of a black, rippling plane, and all she saw was the black expanse of land before her, and above her, and then there was what she could not see, but what she knew was there. And she thought, at long last, that she was prepared, and she swam to it.

Contributors

SARA BERNIKER
Winning the *Playboy* contest was fantastic and surreal. I got an e-mail telling me I'd won a few days after April Fool's Day and was at first certain it was a prank. I think my favorite part of it all was seeing the artwork that accompanied the piece, the illustration winner along with the runners-up. There were so many different visual interpretations of my story and it was a real treat to see.

By and large, I'd say winning the contest was a definite plus for my writing career, such as it is. It's a fantastic credit to have on my bio, no question, and I've had the opportunity to come in contact with several agents and publishers as a direct result of that sale. Personal circumstances have forced me to turn my focus slightly away from writing over the last little while, but as I get back into it, I'm glad to have the *Playboy* credit to my name. I worry sometimes that the early success was my high point, my flash in the pan, but that's just typical writer neuroses, I think. All I can do is continue to write and continue to submit and look at even the rejections as steps in the right direction. And actually, I have *Playboy* to thank for my positive outlook on rejects, too. I've recently gotten a couple of very encouraging personal rejections from Literary Editor Amy Loyd that I've stuck up on my wall as inspiration.

NICK CONNELL
Winning the competition was wonderful. Not just an honor, but also a learning experience. I now have a good grasp of what goes on in the editing process and, in turn, have learned more about my own craft as a writer. Despite my age, my opinions were valued. As a result, my confidence is greater. I also allow myself to have more fun; I no longer worry about the likeability of what I'm writing, mostly. Getting published in *Playboy* served as that stamp of approval, sort of—that I got the okay as a writer, that what I was doing was worthwhile. This is probably an unhealthy way to operate, especially as an artist, but we have to strike that balance of censoring and editing ourselves and giving something unique and new. That's where art

succeeds best, I think. So, having my first published story in *Playboy* was the first hurdle I needed to jump as a writer, in order to feel like I could make a go of this. Often as writers we are told that our writing should be for ourselves, first, but I have always had a desire to be liked. Because of the contest I now have an agent with ICM. I look forward to publishing a short story collection and a novel someday.

RYAN HARTY

Ryan Harty is the author of the story collection *Bring Me Your Saddest Arizona,* which won the 2003 John Simmons Award for Short Fiction. His stories have appeared in *Best American Short Stories 2003, The Pushcart Prize XXVII, Playboy, Tin House,* and many other publications. He has received fellowships from the Corporation of Yaddo and the MacDowell Colony. At Stanford University he was a Stegner Fellow and Jones Lecturer; he received his MFA from the University of Iowa, where he was a Teaching-Writing Fellow. He is currently the Helen Hertzog Zell Visiting Professor at the University of Michigan.

• • •

I was in the writing program at the University of Iowa at the time of the contest, and it seemed that nearly every writer in the program had submitted a story. Because a number of past winners had been Iowa students, there was a lot of anticipation and excitement. Rumors were always swirling around Iowa (as they do at every writing program, I'm sure), and one day, while a few of us were having a late breakfast at a café, word went around that someone else had won the contest. It was over; the thing we'd all hoped for wasn't going to happen to us. We made a few jokes about it and tried to put it behind us.

When I got home that day, I found two letters in the mailbox. One turned out to be a rejection letter from another magazine. The other, I could see from the return address, was my rejection letter from the *Playboy* College Fiction Contest. Except that it wasn't. My girlfriend and I had to read it several times before we could believe what it said: I had actually won the contest!

The whole thing was very exciting: seeing my story on the pages of *Playboy,* a publication I'd long associated not only with beautiful naked women (though of course I associated it with that, too) but with a history of publishing accomplished, important fiction. The accompanying artwork by a student from New York's School of Visual Arts was fantastic. All of my friends and family were thrilled. I became a very minor local celebrity for a while, and afterward, when I submitted work anywhere, it was always taken much more seriously.

KARL IAGNEMMA

Winning the college fiction contest was a huge thrill. I remember staring at the notification letter from Alice Turner with a mixture of shock and disbelief—and then proceeding to run around my apartment, laughing hysterically, for the next twenty minutes. It was my first major publication, and led to an arrangement with an agent . . . all the things that made me feel that I'd finally become a real writer. To this day I have a framed copy of the title page of that story hanging in my office.

Since publishing "A Little Advance," I've published a book of short stories entitled *On the Nature of Human Romantic Interaction* and recently finished a novel entitled *Godspeed* that will be published in late 2007. My stories have received several awards including the *Paris Review*'s Plimpton Prize, and grants from the National Endowment for the Arts and Massachusetts Cultural Council. My writing has appeared in *Tin House, SEED, One Story* and *Zoetrope,* and been anthologized in the *Best American Short Stories, Best American Erotica* and *Pushcart Prize* anthologies.

ROLAND KELTS

You need to write, and so you write, but you have no control over whether anyone will want to read what you write. Alice K. Turner and her staff conferred upon me a great gift. Winning the *Playboy* contest in my early twenties made the young me shiver with dumb possibility: Perhaps, I thought, however naively, someone will want to read my writing. Right away, I received several offers from New York–based glossy magazines to write zeitgeist-oriented articles for decent money. The exposure toughened me, and the money was sorely needed. Publishers began taking me seriously as a marketable and not merely academic writer. On a broader canvas: the approbation from serious editors like Alice and her staff gave me the courage to explore the greater world. I have since become ensconced in Japan, my mother's homeland, and one of the more stimulating cultures on the planet in the twenty-first century. I published *Japanamerica* this year, and my first novel, *Access,* will appear soon. I pray it contains the very energy, light and life that Alice first recognized in me when she gave me the nod.

MICHAEL KNIGHT

Michael Knight is the author of a novel, *Divining Rod,* and two collections of short fiction, *Dogfight & Other Stories* and *Goodnight, Nobody.* A collection of novellas, *The Holiday Season,* is forthcoming fall 2007 from Atlantic Monthly Press. His stories have also appeared in *Esquire, The*

New Yorker, Paris Review and *Southern Review* and have been anthologized in *Best American Mystery Stories, Best of the South* and *New Stories from the South: The Year's Best.* He lives with his wife and two daughters in Knoxville, where he directs the Creative Writing Program at the University of Tennessee.

• • •

So I know the bio's pretty standard but it sums up nicely what I've been doing: writing, teaching, fathering, husbanding. As far as winning the contest goes . . . it changed everything, I'd say. *Playboy* gave my first collection a kind of patina it wouldn't otherwise have had, made "Gerald's Monkey" a kind of breakout story, lots of exposure and, all of a sudden here's a collection that looks interesting to editors and publishers and so forth. Honestly, I'd like nothing more than to win it all over again.

Edward Lazellari

Winning *Playboy*'s fiction contest was fantastic. Seeing my story in print in a magazine known for its writing (among other things) was a thrilling experience. Nothing boosts a budding writer's confidence more, and I remember thinking at the time, "I can do this." In addition, all aspects of my interaction with *Playboy* and its employees were pleasurable. Alice Turner, *Playboy*'s fiction editor at the time, treated me very well and we developed a friendship since that time. The session on the roof of the Crown building in New York City for the *Playboy* photo was also a blast.

I've been an editor at Standard & Poor's since 2002. Before that I was a managing editor at Golden Books, where I managed their mass-market color and activity books division.

In 2002, I had a one-act play called *Rubber Ducky* produced off-off Broadway in an anthology series created by Seth Kramer, called *Swim Shorts.* The series was reviewed in the Leisure & Arts Section of the *Wall Street Journal.* The following year, I helped associate produce *Swim Shorts II*, and we made it into the *New York Times* arts section. I've also written a fantasy novel, the first in a trilogy, and it has been shopped around by Phyllis Wender of Rosenstone/Wender. Also, I co-wrote a spec script for *Enterprise*, which, though the executive producer liked, he did not purchase. I began work on a second spec, but the series was canceled shortly thereafter. Today I am working on my second novel and co-developing a sci-fi television series that my writing partner and I hope to pitch to a network soon.

MATTHEW MCINTOSH

After publication in *Playboy*, *Fishboy* went on to appear as a chapter in the bestselling novel *Well*, which examines modern American life and its psychological and spiritual effects on the individual and society. Originally published in the US by Grove Press in 2003, *Well* has been translated into six languages, receiving critical acclaim and international recognition for its originality and the truth of its vision. (For more information please visit wellbook. com.) McIntosh lives in the West with his wife, writing full time.

DANIEL MUELLER

Daniel Mueller's collection of stories, *How Animals Mate*, won the Sewanee Fiction Prize and was published by Overlook Press in 1999. His fiction has also appeared in *Story, Story Quarterly, Mississippi Review, Prairie Schooner, Another Chicago Magazine, Crescent Review* and other journals and anthologies. He is the recipient of fellowships from the National Endowment for the Arts, Massachusetts Cultural Council, Fine Arts Work Center in Provincetown, Henfield Foundation, University of Virginia and Iowa Writers' Workshop. He teaches on the permanent creative writing faculties of University of New Mexico and Low-Residency MFA Program at Queens University of Charlotte.

• • •

I'm delighted that *Playboy* will be publishing an anthology of college contest-winning stories and, of course, honored to be included. "The Night My Brother Worked the Header" was the first story I completed in graduate school and the first story of mine to be published in a magazine or journal. I grew up in Minnesota, and when I learned that my story had won, my parents just happened to be visiting me in Charlottesville, Virginia. My father, a doctor, had thought my going to graduate school to practice writing fiction the epitome of idiocy, but that night at dinner when I showed him the notification I had received with PLAYBOY MAGAZINE embossed across the letterhead, he whistled over his tumbler of vodka on the rocks and said, "You don't say." A writer's first publication is his sweetest, and while I had by then made a decision to devote my life to writing fiction, the *Playboy* College Fiction Contest prize affirmed my choice, and in sixteen years I haven't once looked back. Whether they know it or not, Alice K. Turner and Chris Napolitano—with whom I was in frequent contact in the weeks and months prior to my story's appearance in *Playboy*—taught me a tremendous amount about how stories work, the effort required to bring a story to its ultimate, polished form, and the importance of a writer's being able to hear and respond to criticism. In the original draft I submitted to the contest, the story ended in gratuitous bloodshed and death. It had never occurred to me to question the ending, because it was the ending I had written the entire story for. But neither Alice nor Chris thought it successful in the least and asked me to revise it. To make a long story short, I wrote at least seven different endings in roughly a month and a half, and when I finally wrote an ending in which nobody died, Alice phoned me to say, "Yeah! You've written an ending that almost works!" Then she asked me to retrieve drafts of all the endings I had written and over the phone we pieced together an ending composed of sentences taken from each. It was not an ending I could have written on my own, though every word of it was mine. Since then, I've told this story to countless students when they've been too close to one of their own stories to see it clearly. And many times when I've encountered problems in my own work, I've asked myself, well, what would Alice do?

In addition to the prize that set me on a trajectory I'm still following, I'm grateful to *Playboy* for providing one of the most formative experiences in my writing life.

YAEL SCHONFELD

I still have a vivid recollection of receiving the letter that announced I had won the *Playboy* College Fiction Contest in 2000. It was evening, and I had just come back from having dinner with friends. I put my hand into the big wooden mailbox that was attached to the side door of the house where I was living. I fished out the slim envelope, and looked at the bunny logo embossed on it. I remembered quite clearly that, atypically, I had not sent an SASE along with my *Playboy* entry, and therefore, the fact that a response had arrived was significant. This was not just another rejection letter. I remember holding the letter in my hand, still unopened, and thinking: something good is about to happen to me. Winning the College Fiction Contest was definitely a good thing. There were many thrilling aspects to the experience: seeing my work in print in a major, nationally distributed publication for the first time; enjoying the visions of the student artists who had illustrated my story in the magazine; hearing the tales of my friends, not all of whom are regular *Playboy* readers, about their adventures in finding and purchasing "my" issue; and, of course, relishing the testimony of my mother (also not a regular *Playboy* reader) about proudly keeping the issue on her nightstand, even many months after its publication. Professionally, I feel like I should have made better use of the exposure and momentum I received from my story's appearance in *Playboy*. I did find an agent as a result, but that relationship didn't prove to be a mutually beneficial one. I have a short story collection (named *The Collection Treatment*, after this story) and a novel, *But I Know It's Mine*, which are looking for good homes. These days, I live in Portland, Oregon, with my husband and our two cats. I'm still working on finding that magical balance between writing, relationships and making a living, which I believe to be an aspect of many writers' lives. I recently quit my day job and am now trying to support myself as a freelance editor and translator; I'm hoping this is a step in the right direction, as far as my writing is concerned. Every time I open my mailbox, some tenacious, hopeful part of me is still expecting to see another bunny that will change my life.

PHILIP SIMMONS died in 2002.

ELLEN UMANSKY
I remember being disappointed when I first saw the envelope in the mail from *Playboy*. It was a thin letter, and thin, in my experience, generally augured disappointing news. I'm not sure I can describe the pure elation I felt when I realized I won. Something I had always secretly dreamed of—*maybe someday I would become a published writer*—had suddenly, astoundingly, come true.

After graduating from the University of Pennsylvania, I went on to attend Columbia's MFA program in fiction and began working as a journalist. In the intervening years, my fiction and nonfiction has appeared in publications such as *The New York Times*, the *New York Sun, Salon*, the *Forward* and *Jane*, and the anthologies *The Lost Tribe* and *Sleepaway*. I'm currently completing a novel, *The Art of Losing*, and live with my husband and daughter in Brooklyn.

VALERIE VOGRIN
Winning the contest was definitely life altering. *Carolina Quarterly* had accepted my first short story for publication just a month before, so it felt like something of an embarrassment of riches. The other students in my graduate program at the University of Alabama feted me—I barely recall a hectic night of celebrating at the local bowling alley—with me *not* bowling because the day I got word of winning the contest I severely sprained my ankle. So I was like a little writing princess propped up at the end of a lane, surrounded by admirers. Tony Earley brought me a dozen roses. This attention felt a bit awkward—I was surrounded by very fine writers, but they hadn't entered the contest. The contest

was a financial boon, too, of course. I traveled in Europe for six weeks that summer on the winnings. And I got the distinct pleasure of picturing my ninety-year-old grandmother walking down the hill to her local drugstore in Kiel, Wisconsin to pick up the extra copies of *Playboy* she'd special ordered. A bit of a letdown inevitably ensued, once the issue came out and the festivities passed.

Being a *Playboy* College Fiction contest winner has always brought me positive attention, though it took me a rather long time to capitalize on it. There wasn't a lot of need for editors and agents as I took eight-plus years to write my first novel (which in actuality was more like writing three different first novels). Set in Tuscaloosa, *Shebang* was published by University Press of Mississippi in 2004. I have continued to write and publish short fiction in journals such as *Black Warrior Review, Chattahoochee Review* and *New Orleans Review*. I have a story in the upcoming issue of *The Florida Review*. I taught creative writing in New York City and online for Gotham Writers' Workshop (and contributed a chapter on point of view to their fiction-writing handbook, *Gotham Writers' Workshop Guide to Writing Fiction*). I'm currently Assistant Professor of English at Southern Illinois University at Edwardsville.

HARDIN YOUNG

Actually winning the award was wonderful. I went out and celebrated with a bunch of friends and colleagues at a now-defunct bar, and it was probably the most fun I had in Fayetteville. Everyone was great. After the bar closed, we all stood arm in arm in a circle singing until the cops broke us up. I can't remember another night quite like it. Sometimes writing programs can be riven with petty jealousies, but everyone seemed genuinely happy for me, and I was deeply gratified by the display of support. In general, it was a good year for our program, as some other writers had similar successes.

My writing career hasn't exactly taken off. I really haven't written any short stories since "1%." I spent several years working on a novel the world decided it really didn't need. I threw another one away when I realized it wasn't going to be good enough. I'm working on one now, and am hopeful. I'm currently working as a speechwriter and ESL teacher at the University of Arkansas. I wish I could add more to *Playboy*'s greater glory, but I'm working on it.

Playboy attempted to contact every winner for this collection; we received no reply from Morgan Akins, Jonathan Blum, Kevin González, Daniel Lyons, Steven Ploetz, Brady Udall, or A.M. Wellman.

Also available from Playboy Press

Dear Playboy Advisor
Questions from Men and Women
to the Advice Column of *Playboy* Magazine
Chip Rowe

"It was here, in the Advisor, where *Playboy* willfully undercut the silken ease and bachelor suavity it projected elsewhere in the magazine. It was here where bodily matters went unairbrushed, where seduction proved beyond one's skillful way with imported vodka, where men would not infrequently be scolded for treating their girlfriends or wives shabbily. . . . A collection of zesty give-and-take from the column's past ten years."
— *The Atlantic Monthly*

Paperback • **ISBN 978-1-58642-130-4** • 368 pages
$16.95 ($22.95 Canadian)

The New Bedside Playboy
A Half Century of Amusement, Diversion, and Entertainment
Edited by Hugh M. Hefner

Playboy Magazine has published the works of some of the world's greatest writers, from Beat poets to Nobel laureates. Featuring fiction from the likes of Woody Allen, Gabriel Garcia Márquez, Jay McInerney, Michael Chabon, Joyce Carol Oates and Jane Smiley and an amazingly diverse selection of journalism, humor and cartoons, this anthology serves as a perfect bedside companion.

Paperback • **ISBN 978-1-58642-119-9** • 512 pages
$19.95 ($26.95 Canadian)

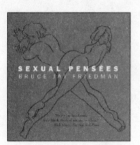

Sexual Pensées
Bruce Jay Friedman

"Friedman does the essential task of rescuing sex from the three P's — porno, prurience, and pomposity. . . . These are funny tales of people at their most naked, letting it all hang out, even if they happen to be fully clothed. We're never more ourselves than when we're doing the sexual dance."
— *Culture Catch*

Hardcover • **ISBN 978-1-58642-120-5** • 120 pages
$13.95 ($18.95 Canadian)

The Playboy Book of True Crime
The Editors of Playboy Magazine

The *Playboy Book of True Crime* includes twenty-one seminal works from the pages of *Playboy* that capture some of the most notorious crimes, criminals, organizations and investigations of the past several decades. This engrossing collection includes stories by leading print journalists and chroniclers of Mafia life, famous interviews, and accounts of some of the most fascinating and sometimes bizarre American murder mysteries in recent memory.

Paperback • **ISBN 978-1-58642-127-4** • 376 pages • $16.95 ($21.95 Canadian)